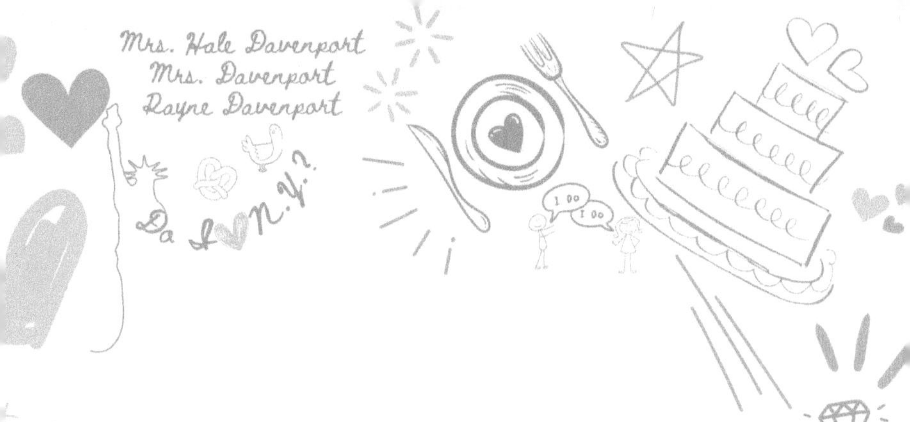

Calamity Rayne Gets Hitched

CALAMITY RAYNE
BOOK THREE

LYDIA MICHAELS

Calamity Rayne Gets Hitched
The Calamity Rayne Series
©2024 by Lydia Michaels Books
Romantic Comedy
BAILEY BROWN PUBLISHING
Horny Unicorn Press

Reading Order

Calamity Rayne Gets a Life (1)

Calamity Rayne Back Again (2)

Calamity Rayne Gets Hitched (3)

Calamity Rayne Veiled & Railed (3.5)

Calamity Rayne Over The Moon (4)

Visit www.LydiaMichaelsBooks.com for your
FREE eBook of Calamity Rayne Veiled & Railed

Dedication

For Amber Vasquez, my #1 stalker extraordinaire.
Thank you for raving about my stories with the relentless
affection and obsession of a true hero.
This one's for you.
—Lydia

Listen to the Soundtrack on Spotify!

Best of My Love by The Emotions
Newsies King of NY from Newsies Original
Motion Picture
No sleep til Brooklyn by Beastie Boys
Theme from New York by Frank Sinatra
Shoop by Salt N Pepa
Rapper's Delight by Sugar Hill Gang
Benny and the Jets by Elton John
You Don't Bring Me Flowers by Barbara Streisand
and Neil Diamond
Welcome to New York by Taylor Swift
Can't Stop by Red Hot Chili Peppers
It's All Coming Back to Me Now by Celine Dion
Chapel of Love by The Dixie Cups
Never Let Me Go by Florence + the Machine
I love it by Icona Pop
Time After Time by Cyndi Lauper
Someone Like You by Van Morrison
You Make My Dreams (Come True) by Daryl
Hall & John

**Listen to the Calamity Rayne Series
Soundtrack on Spotify!**

No Tiger in the Bathroom

SO I'VE GOT THAT GOING FOR ME...

No Clue Where I Am...
48 Hours Pre Wedding-gate

BED SHEETS TWISTED about my body like a straitjacket. I shivered, skin clammy and damp with chilled sweat. Despite the cool air I was roasting. Was I sick?

I tried to kick my foot free of the covers. Hale grunted when I accidentally nailed him in the shin with my heel. It was hotter than Satan's taint in this bed and I was having a Hades-grade-hot-flash.

Frustrated, I tussled through a middle-aged cage fight with the blankets and winced when pain lanced into my skull. Then my stomach sloshed and I stilled, covering my mouth and unsure what my body planned to do next.

Something wasn't right, so I sagged back in defeat. *Ugh.*

Blankets one, Calamity zero.

My brain buffered until I realized what this was. The world's most unpleasant surprise…a hangover. Right.

Hangovers were sneaky little fuckers. Souvenirs acquired through intoxicated decision-making, therefore always showing up unexpectedly. But if you want the truth, life's basically one long line of surprises, and in my thirty years I've never been prepared for a single one. So why start now?

Hello, I'm Calamity Rayne—fiancée of very grownup and powerful billionaire smoke-show, Hale Davenport. No clue how I got here or how I somehow managed to out-Darwin the bazillion other women who dreamt of waking up in my circumstances. I can only blame sheer luck, vagina magic, and the sporadic twist of fate.

My stomach gurgled and I groaned. Moaning hurt, and based on the throbbing in my skull, today would be another day passed on the struggle bus.

I was afraid to open my eyes. Was it normal for a bride to feel like a washed-up hooker days before her wedding? My fermented organs pumped through whatever sludge poisoned my insides as I tried to think of anything that might help.

God, thinking fucking hurt.

Arm partially numb, I blindly dragged a hand over my face. Long gone were the ideals of waking up like the polished, slightly tussled, beauties shown in the movies. That shit was pure fiction.

The reality was terrifying. Sweat-kinked hair, morning breath rank enough to make roadkill run again, an empty belly packed with toxic gas, and the gunked-up remnants of yesterday's makeup caked in the corners of my Venus flytrap eyes. This nightmare wasn't even neighboring the zip code of slightly attractive. I needed to get out of this raging inferno of a bed and wash the sweaty stink off me.

"Hale…" I groaned, nudging the scalding body beside mine and grimacing at the flammable scent of my breath.

How Prince Charming inexplicably wanted me above every other fair maiden in all the land was beyond me. It wasn't like I ever pretended to be more than the hot mess that I was. If there was such a thing as fixer-upper kink, Hale would be president of the club because, bless his overbearing, bossy heart, the man loved my catastrophic soul to a fault.

Long gone were the expectations of perfection. *Poof. Vamoose.* Hale knew exactly what he was marrying the moment he slipped that Victorian doorknob of a diamond over my unmanicured ring finger. He not only accepted the real me, he adored her—stubbled legs, unfiltered, profane blatherings, raging insecurities, and all.

Why? Because we were in love. L-O-V-E, love. I'm talking Jane Austen-grade desire with a dash of obsession and a heavy-handed dose of power. I could wake up looking and smelling like death because Hale could handle it.

Our bond ran deeper than some namby-pamby sort of lusty newlywed champagne. We were a potent, Russian-grade, punch-you-in-the-face-good-morning kind of love vodka. Tough. Resilient. The real deal.

Which was why I had no problem elbowing his scalding body off of me.

"Oomph," he grunted as my arm shoved

against the unmovable slab of muscle suffocating me.

Unlike normal mortals, Hale didn't stink like roadkill or regret in the morning. No. He smelled of fantasies and authority, sort of like the cool air of a bank that pumped James Bond-level pheromones through the ductwork.

Hale was a God. A walking aphrodisiac. A painfully beautiful masterpiece of perfection the paparazzi adored and gold-digging whores slobbered over on the regular.

The competition was fierce, and I should be forever grateful he even looked twice at a girl like me, which I was—trust me, I was—but at the moment I needed oxygen more than gratitude. I shoved him again, disentangling his roped limbs from my overheated body, and his grip tightened.

"Hale, I can't breathe." He clung to me like an octopus trying to crack open a clam. "You're a thousand degrees."

I needed water. Preferably a hose.

The lashes of my eyes seemed glued shut with some sort of expired horse paste. He cinched our bodies tighter, the length of Prince Everhard—a.k.a. his porn-tastic dick—wedged against the crevice of my ass cheeks. Morning sex was fun and all, but my head throbbed with what could only be the post-effects of a lobotomy gone wrong, so there would be no bumping stinkies this morning.

I mentally and physically prepared to shove his deadweight off me.

One… This was going to hurt.

Two… Just do it. Water would make everything better.

Three—

I flung Hale and the covers off and gasped for air. The revolting stench akin to post-Mardi Gras dumpster juice wafted in the air and I gagged. Dear God, was that me?

This was bad.

Prying apart my abused eyelashes, I blinked as the bleached sky blared through the large hotel window and blinded me. Glimpses of furniture filled my blurred vision as stark silhouettes came into view.

I stilled. Not my window. Not my hotel room.

"The fuck…?" Jackknifing upright, I immediately winced and fought the urge to hurl. Too fast. *Way* too fast.

My brain shook like a rattle and worked to retrace my steps, but I had no memory of coming here. Palming my face helped stave off the urge to hurl.

"Hale…?" I blindly nudged the lump of blankets to my left. Talking hurt.

What the hell did we do last night? I massaged my forehead, trying to dislodge what could only be the dull blade of a rusted hacksaw wedged between my eyes.

The slightest movement reverberated like a gong in my skull. Was I in a car accident? Maybe a bulldozer ran me over six or seven times. Every vertebra of my spine twitched as shards of pain raced down my legs into the soles of my feet.

Right on cue, my mouth began to water. I pressed the back of my fist to my lips and moaned. "Hale—" I hiccupped, my shoulders locking.

Any lesser woman would be rushing to the toilet but I was too off balance to walk.

"Hale." I shook the hard lump of blankets, desperately needing assistance—and probably a new liver.

My knight in shining armor typically took care of me whenever I got banged up. And I was currently dealing with an unparalleled hangover, so why wasn't he jumping into action? Where was my glass of water and magical hangover pills?

A wave of vom-chills hit. I heaved vocally, shivering as a cool sweat beaded across my skin. I was burning cold, visually impaired, and dealing with some sort of full-body brain injury that started in my toes.

"Babe?"

My comatose fiancé didn't respond like his usual, plucky, early bird gets the billion-dollar deal, Prince Charming self.

This had to be alcohol poisoning.

Everything felt…puffy and sore. My bones had a literal heartbeat. Even my fingernails were throbbing. I gave up my fight against gravity and collapsed back onto the bed.

So much for my anti-inflammatory, anti-alcohol, anti-everything diet before the wedding. This level of hangover was definitely going to show up on my face. Not good for my bride-to-be skincare regimen.

Those rules were unrealistic anyway. Just a few more days and everyone would stop obsessing about what I ate, drank, put on my skin, did to my hair, or wore on my body. I never realized how magnified a bride's life became once she accepted the ring, especially the ring from one of the world's most desirable billionaire bachelors.

The worst part about my elevated exposure in the public eye was how isolated and alone the attention actually made me feel. Even the ordinary people I once considered my closest friends started to treat me differently.

A year ago I was nobody. A waitress with two friends, living with her mom, and working in a corner pub situated on a forgettable street in Oregon. Today, I was someone I didn't recognize. But I was still me. Only now I was with Hale.

I loved Hale and had no regrets about agreeing to marry him but, truth be told, I was still processing my shock that he asked. I was also still learning what being married to a man of his stature would truly entail.

As it turned out, the role of billionaire bride-to-be was a rather singular, lonely position targeted by envy-induced criticism, painful comparisons, and endless disapproval from all angles. Hale was the silver lining, the end all be all of this shit show of a publicity smear.

He was worth the pain and tears.

He was worth anything because he was my entire world.

Not loving Hale would be as impossible as trying to stop a wave. So I pretended the public criticism didn't hurt and went with the flow, surrendering to the currents that beat me into the banks of this overwhelmingly opulent, superficial, super-critical billionaire world. Because that was the world Hale lived in and I only wanted to be by his side.

I massaged my face and groaned, waiting for this horrible zombie malaise to wear off. I could only imagine what I looked like. I should probably shower before he saw—or smelled—me.

I couldn't recall ever feeling this shitty before.

I tried to get up again and failed. It was going to take a crane to conquer gravity this morning. Fuck, even my skin hurt.

Slathering my tongue around my dry lips with the grace of a cow, I sighed. "Babe?" I nudge him. "D'you have water?" *Ack*, my mouth tasted like a bum's pocket.

The fact that Hale wasn't springing out of bed told me he felt shitty too. And *he* was the responsible one.

Flopping my weak arm over his back, I limply smacked him. "Hey, what'd we do last night?"

The agony in my head radiated to my teeth. If I learned anything from my time with the Davenports, it was that rich people had weird cures for everything. There must be an IV treatment to fix this. Some kind of mineral, or electrolyte cocktail that would make me feel human again. Either that, or I'd be lurching down the aisle like a leftover from Michael Jackson's *Thriller.*

Ugh. I cringed. All of high society would witness my shame and Hale would probably look perfect, as usual. The paparazzi would have a field day with that. We literally had to contact air traffic control to ensure no unlicensed drones would be flying overhead the moment we said our I-dos.

How the hell did this become my life? No way did Cinderella have to deal with this shit. Definitely needed some electrolytes. And coffee. And a few ice packs.

For the last few months, I lived in a petri dish of scrutiny as the world judged me through the lens of the most unflattering microscope. The paparazzi picked apart each pore and poked every tender insecurity I couldn't hide. I had no choice but to stomach their confusion over Hale's love for me like a full-body bruise that never healed.

Photographers and reporters flocked to my future husband like a herd of screaming goats gleefully prancing into the Alps. They reveled in his attention and would go to any lengths to be near him.

I was now a part of his world. A big part. So of course they watched me too. But I didn't wear publicity nearly as well as my flawless fiancé.

Hale adorned the papers like a Park Avenue cover model while I became meme fodder for the next generation. They admired, praised, and celebrated him. As Hale's pedestal got higher it cast a longer shadow, which gave me, his "overly ordinary", "slightly tubby", "bridge troll" of a fiancée a place to hide.

Yes, they actually printed those things about me in ink.

The public couldn't rationalize our relationship and I developed a masochistic curiosity about what horrible thing they might say next. I became the ultimate head-scratcher of high society. I'd love to say I was a big enough person not to care, but the volume of bad pictures and cruel headlines was too much for even the strongest person to survive unfazed.

I needed to know. I hated to know. I vowed to never read another tabloid again. I broke those promises. Then I secretly cried and repeated the process all over again—with much ice cream therapy of course.

Of course, the paparazzi idolized Hale. Who wouldn't? They thought I wasn't good enough for him. Deep down, I believed that, too, so they found my Achilles heel. But whenever I second-guessed our situation or feared Hale might come to his senses and leave me, he used his sexiness like a weapon of mass persuasion to calm my nerves and convince me I was exactly where I was meant to be.

The man had the compelling power of a sex sorcerer. Seriously, I craved his physical touch more than dairy, and that was saying a lot, especially since I never even liked sex before Hale. But right now, there was absolutely nothing sexy about me.

I felt around the cluttered nightstand for the phone. What felt like a glass bottle clattered and rolled, falling to the carpet with a soft thud. I gave up.

Obviously, I'd been slipped a CIA-grade numbing agent.

Tranquilized, yet somehow still aware of the pain spiking up my legs.

Did I walk on a bed of fiery coals last night? A sheet of nails or broken glass?

I needed aspirin.

Dragging my leg to the edge of the bed, I dropped my aching foot to the rug and my body started to slide.

"It's happening… Uh-oh—*oomph.*" I landed in a tangle of twisted limbs.

A wave of nausea swept over me. Pinching my nose and breathing deliberately, I waited for the woozy sensation to pass.

With the dexterity and grace of a newborn calf, I tried to push myself up. Gravity was a mother fucker. Face-planting seemed the best option, so I collapsed into a broken downward-facing dog with my cheek on the carpet and my ass in the air.

"Why is this happening to me?"

"Shut. Up."

My breathing stilled. Something wasn't right. That was not the deep baritone or sensitive language of my beautifully indulgent fiancée.

I peeled my plastered eyelashes apart and braved the blinding sun. "Ow, ow, ow, ow…" Blinking away the tears, I caught my breath. "Hale?"

When he didn't answer, I shifted my weight onto my knees and peeked over the edge of the mattress. One bony, masculine foot poked out of the cotton mountain, hanging slightly off the bed. *Was* that Hale's foot?

I poked it and he kicked. "Fuck off."

Uh-oh.

I ducked, back pressed to the bed, panic racing through my veins. My chest chilled as if I smoked a pack of menthols. My ears were just playing tricks on me. "Um, babe?"

"If you don't shut the fuck up and quit poking me I'm going to throw you out that window, Meyers."

Oh, God. Not good. Hale would never call me Meyers. But I knew who would.

I scrubbed my eye sockets with the heels of my palms as if that might clear up my memories.

It had to be Hale.

Had to be.

Or…

No, it abso-fucking-lutely could *only* be Hale.

Right?

Oh, God.

I faced the bed again, still kneeling on the floor, and fisted the covers. Slowly, I pulled the blankets. "Please be Hale. Please be Hale. Please be Hale. Please be Hale."

A glimpse of sun-bleached hair brought swift relief. Then it capsized as Barrett's face came into view. "Barrett!" I screamed. "What are you doing in my bed?"

Hale's brother catapulted upright. *"What the fuck?"*

My arms worked like windmills as I slipped on an empty beer bottle. "Shit! Why are you in my room?" Mayday! This was a major fucking mayday!

"Stop screaming, you lunatic!"

I slapped a hand over my mouth, eyes wide as I stared at acres upon acres of chiseled man-chest. *"Where are your clothes?"* My panicked words muffled against my hand.

"Jesus, Meyers! You don't wake a guy up like that." Barrett barked in an abused voice full of gravel, vinegar, and vitriol. "You've got the lungs of a harpy." He groaned and gripped his head, looking as rough as I felt.

I staggered, either still drunk or dealing with a massive case of vertigo. "*Gah*, my fucking head."

"What the hell did we do last night?"

My foot landed on something sharp and I tripped over a dingy high heel. My eyes widened. *Nooooo!* My poor rehearsal shoes. They were no longer white. Blotched and deformed, they lay discarded like biohazards on the wet floor.

"Why is the carpet wet? Where are we? And where's your shirt?" Questions downloaded like data into my pickled brain.

Barrett peeked under the covers. "It's probably with my pants."

"You're naked under there?"

"That's how I sleep. You have to stop shouting."

"Why are you in my bed?"

"This isn't your room." He glanced about the room, his face scrunched in confusion. "Technically, I think it's my bed."

Was it? We both looked unsure. But this definitely wasn't the penthouse I'd been occupying, so that sounded right. But why was I here? And why was the room trashed?

Pizza boxes and beer bottles littered the burgundy carpet. I squinted and cocked my head. Was that a fuchsia wig? Spotting my crumpled rehearsal dinner dress on the floor, I sucked in a sharp breath!

My gaze shot to my chest. Thank fuck it was covered in a T-shirt.

I frowned, stretching the material wide so I could read the upside-down print. *Word to your Muggle?* "What the…? Did I rob Dumbledore?"

Barrett massaged his temples. "If you don't stop talking in that shrill voice, I'm going to suffocate you."

Shrill? I scoffed. I was not shrill. Panicked, yes. But shrill?

Focus Rayne!

I rubbed my head. "I have to think. Do you remember anything from last night?"

"I—"

I held up a hand. *"Shh, shh, shh!"* The canned harmony of the Dixie Cups' broke the silence as my phone vibrated from somewhere in the abyss of discarded clothes and garbage.

I followed the tune as they sang about going to the chapel, stubbing my battered toes on bottles and slipping into a partial split when I stepped on a half-eaten slice of pizza.

Because that was a normal thing to find on the floor…

The chorus of *Chapel of Love* muffled from deep within the mess and Barrett growled, covering his ears. "Make it stop!"

"I'm trying! I can't find my phone."

"Damn it, Meyers!" Barrett flung the covers off his body.

"Mother of penis!" I covered my eyes, blindly following the music. "Put some clothes on!"

"Answer the fucking phone!"

I shook out the material of the dress and my phone sailed through the air as the ringtone silenced. Time slowed.

"Noooooooooo…" Barrett's grey eyes widened, but it was too late. My phone nailed him right in the cash and prizes and he dropped like a sack of meat.

"Sorry, sorry, sorry, sorry!" What did he expect walking around with something that big exposed to the elements?

He cupped himself, a quiet whimper simpering from his quivering lips as his eye twitched. His nostrils flared as he inhaled what would likely be a deafening roar sharp enough to puncture my skull.

I slammed my hand over his mouth as my phone rang again. "Be quiet! It's Hale!" I answered the call, smothering Barrett's injured cry. "H—Hale?"

Barrett squeaked.

"Rayne, thank God." Hale sounded immensely relieved. "I've been going crazy trying to find you."

Barrett glared over my fingers, his eyes bulging as he seethed with untethered rage and what I suspected was some pretty intense junk pain. I muffled the phone and gave him a death stare, warning him to stay silent.

"Baby, are you there?"

I covered the phone and pressed a finger to my lips. "Shut up and swallow your pain like a fucking girl," I hissed, rushing over to the window.

"Rayne? Where are you?"

"Yeah, I'm here." I stared into the blinding sun. Where the hell were we? "I'm, um, in the city. We—*I*—got a room."

"Is Elle with you?"

"Elle?" My mind recoiled as I went into avoidance mode. "No… Uh…" The thought of my best friend slash maid of honor brought about too many icky emotions to handle at that moment. "I wanted to be…" I glanced back at Barrett as he quietly whimpered and cupped his balls in the fetal position. "…alone." I bit my lip, fully aware that I was the world's worst liar.

"We need to talk about last night, Rayne."

Last night? My shoddy memories pieced together like an old flag rotting in a time-capsule, disintegrating through my fingertips as I tried to grasp reality. There was the rehearsal dinner, then the fight between Barrett and Hale, then… Oh, God…

"I'm pulling up your location now."

Technology would inform him of my location faster than my mushy brain could puzzle together the surroundings. Buildings cluttered the horizon, but none were the familiar skyscrapers I'd come to recognize from the Fifth Avenue view of the penthouse.

My jaw dropped when I spotted the East River. I was on the wrong side of the Manhattan skyline! Was that the fucking Brooklyn Bridge? *How the hell did I get here?*

"It says you're in Brooklyn Heights. Is that right? What are you doing all the way over there?"

If only I knew. "Um, you know. I took a cab."

Kind of true. I vaguely recalled being in a car. I remembered a lot of red.

"You took a cab to Brooklyn? Why?"

Yeah, there was no viable explanation to justify how or why I ended up in this direction. "I, uh, just needed time to think, so I got a room."

As I lied to my future husband, I rushed around the suite launching personal belongings onto the bed, ignoring Barrett's crippled form as he nursed his balls.

"Rayne, if you're having second thoughts,

don't. Everything's going to be fine. We're ready for this."

"Yup. Ready." Any attempt at a *put-me-in-coach* tone failed miserably.

"No more distance."

"Uh-huh." I couldn't find my purse and every step felt like the soles of my feet were on fire.

"We have some heavy, time-sensitive things to discuss today, and I need you to keep an open mind."

"Yep. Open as a quickie-mart."

He sighed. "Are you okay? You're safe?"

"What? Oh. Yeah. Let's talk about it when you get here. How far are you?" Every word out of my mouth reverberated through my skull like a cast iron frying pan falling down a flight of stairs.

"I'm about ten minutes away."

Ten minutes? "Perfect," I lied through clenched teeth. "I'll see you in ten." My thumb ended the call and I flung the phone onto the bed. "*What are we going to do?* Hale's going to be here any minute!"

A bellow spilled from Barrett's pained face.

"We don't have time for that!" I yanked the covers. "Get up! You have to get out of here."

"You nearly castrated me!"

"Put your pants on! Where's your other shoe?"

"Why do *I* have to leave? This is my room."

"Hello? Have you met your brother? If he catches you in here with me—*naked,* which I still don't understand—he'll lose his shit. I can't be the center of another peanut *brother* and *jealousy* sandwich. For God's sake, cover yourself!"

He shoved a hotel pillow over his junk. "I'm

probably incapable of fathering children now, thanks to you.”

“Stop being a baby. You’re holding that thing like you’re afraid it’s gonna run away. It can’t be that bad.”

“You hit me in the nuts with a cell phone! It hurts!”

I threw Barrett’s pants at his chest. “This is threat level midnight! Get dressed.”

Shoving the clothes aside, he yanked the covers over him. “I’m going back to sleep.”

“The hell you are!” I snatched the blanket, triggering an intense game of tug of war.

“Seriously?” He threatened to let go of the sheet. “Do you really want to pull that?”

I released the blankets. That thing was literally the size of the Death Star. And Chew-*cock*-a had enough screen time today.

“*Please* get up and get dressed. Hale’s probably halfway here.”

He groaned and shoved the pillow against his head. “Your voice is sharper than a dog whistle. Fuck off.”

“You’re acting like a man-shaped bag of crap right now! Barrett, you need to get out of here! Your brother will be here in—” I tapped my phone screen to see the time. “Oh my, God. Enough nursing your coin purse. Get up!”

I snatched the sheet, but rather than respond with the modesty of a normal human being, he posed like a cocky nude model of a Roman orgy painting.

I shielded my eyes. “Gah, you’re so gross!”

“You know, most women love looking at me.”

I scowled over my shoulder. "I'm not most women."

"There's no shame in admitting you like the view. I know the gods spanked me with the hand-some stick."

"I think you were spanked in the head. Stop being an egotistical dick face and get—*ugh.*" I shoved my fist into my side, fighting back another wave of nausea.

"Meyers?"

I swallowed but my mouth watered like a broken faucet. "I feel…" Oh, it was bad. "Shiny."

"Yeah, well, you don't look shiny. You look a little tarnished and green. Sort of like the washed-up corpse of Chester Copperpot."

I hunched forward and grasped the dresser. I could hardly move without feeling sick. "What the hell did we drink last night?"

"I think this is more than booze."

"What? You mean… d—drugs?"

"Maybe."

I didn't do drugs. I didn't know how to get them or prepare them. Hopefully, this wasn't any-thing worse than giggle dirt. Hale was *not* into the drug scene.

I looked at Barrett. "You think we were slipped the ganja?"

"Possibly. Or something worse."

"Worse? What's worse? *Huhp*—" I dry heaved and belched, breaking into a full-body sweat. My body felt like a duck trying to escape the inside of a beaver.

He cupped his head. "Maybe someone slipped us something. Acid or molly or coke." He groaned.

"But I don't think the devil's dandruff lingers like this."

"What year are you in? No one does coke anymore! I don't even know what Molly is. And where the hell would we get acid? It was my rehearsal dinner not a Woodstock concert."

"Drugs are everywhere, Meyers—"

"Gah, shut up." I covered my mouth and groaned, fighting wave after wave of nausea. "We did not do drugs. I graduated from *DARE*. I know how to make safe and responsible choices."

He snorted. "Then why don't you?"

I squeezed my eyes shut and pinched my nose. "Please stop talking."

He shifted on the bed. "Oh, fuck, are you gonna hurl?"

I went into Lamaze breathing and rapidly fanned my face. "Don't talk about it." My brow pinched.

"Do *not* exercise that demon, Meyers!"

"Gah! Go fuck a bag of glass, Barrett! Your commentary is only making matters worse."

"You puke on me and I'm done. I'll fucking lose it."

I dropped into a crouch and breathed out a hard exhalation.

This was my *Karmageddon,* my punishment for a lifetime of foolish choices, set to destroy whatever happiness I'd accidentally found.

A sneeze built in my sinuses the longer I fanned my face, but it was the only thing helping. The tickle traveled through my nose and throat. There was a fifty-fifty shot I would either sneeze away the nasties or hurl. I braced for complete annihilation. "Oh, God."

"Don't puke! Fight it!" Barrett scrambled to the farthest end of the bed.

I breathed faster, fanning my face and—*"Ah chh!"* I pinched my nose, which caused a full-body backup, sort of like a keg of dynamite exploding underwater. The rest of the sneeze needed to evacuate and escaped in a simultaneous fart.

"Dude…" Barrett blinked at me in a mixture of horror and awe. "I think your body just took a screenshot."

I garbled out a moan and rolled onto my side. Whatever that was, it hurt. "My body is rejecting me. I think I'm dying."

"I gotta say, I've never witnessed a woman do anything like that. It looked like a reverse orgasm. Did it hurt?"

"Yes, it fucking hurt." I groaned and flung a pillow at his face. "We don't have time for this! Pack up your broken balls and get out!" I needed to clean myself up. Hale would be there any second.

"Face it Meyers, he's gonna hear about this."

"You know how insanely territorial your brother gets. Please."

"Checkout's not for—Oh, shit, it's later than I thought."

"Damn it, Barrett! I need you to work with me here!" I was on the struggle bus, next stop Cry Town. My panic bubbled up in the form of tears as I tried to collect myself. "I just… You can't… There's…pizza sauce in my toes… My head… The wedding…I want…"

"All right, all right." He held up his hands in fearful surrender as my jaw wildly trembled. "Don't you dare cry, Meyers."

For months, I feared this moment would come. The moment I fucked up my entire future to the point of no return. I didn't know how or when it would inevitably happen, but I always sensed a disastrous end looming.

Waking up next to my fiancé's naked brother in a hotel room two days before our wedding seemed the kill shot that would put my happiness out to pasture once and for all.

"Relax. We'll just tell Hale nothing happened. He'll have his usual hissy fit, and then everything will—"

"Get off the bed!" Losing my patience, I shoved him off the mattress. "I'm not ruining my future over one blackout night of whatever the hell this was!"

He clambered to the floor in a heap of muscle and flesh, landing like a pile of broken mannequin parts. "*What the hell*, Meyers? When did you get so freakishly strong?"

Probably about the same time my future husband warned me of his impending arrival. Barrett shoved to his feet.

I tossed the balled-up sheet at him. "Cover yourself!"

"Stop throwing stuff at me!" He turned toward the bathroom, exposing his bare ass.

I squinted and scrunched my nose in confusion. "Um, Barrett…"

He disappeared into the bathroom. "What?"

The loud echo of him relieving himself broke

the silence. I scratched my head, truly confused by what I thought I just saw. "Were we playing with markers last night?"

"Huh?" The toilet flushed.

"Markers?"

"What the hell are you talking about?"

I searched the disaster area of the floor for clues. Any evidence of the last twelve hours would be helpful at this point. "There's, um, something on your back."

"Wha—" He went silent and I imagined him twisting to see the reflection of his back in the mirror. "No, no, no, no, no, no, no…" Barreling out of the bathroom, face furious, flaccid dick swinging like Gonzo's nose, he charged toward me. *"What the fuck is on my back, Rayne?"*

My gaze bolted to the ceiling. "For the love of God, my eyes!"

He circled like a dog chasing its tail. "Is it a fucking *tattoo*? I need you to look."

"No!" His voice stabbed into my brain like a rogue javelin. "It has to come off."

"Please."

Unable to refuse his worried plea, I lowered my gaze. "For the last time, cover yourself! It's like being in a room with a baby elephant!"

"I need you to look!"

"Then turn around and stop showing me your dick!"

He snickered. "Are you honestly this prude or are you afraid you're marrying the wrong Davenport?"

"Yeah, I really want the one with a tramp stamp."

His face paled and he turned, walking backward as he pointed his bare ass at me. "Fuck. Tell me it's not real."

"*Ew!* Stay back!"

"I need you to look closer."

I instinctively scurried away, pulling the hotel chair between us. "Stop pointing private parts at me!"

"For fuck sake!" He snatched my dress off the bed and shoved it over his crotch.

"Not my dress!"

"I need you to look at my fucking ass!" He shoved the chair away and pointed his butt at me. That was not the work of markers.

"Oh, Barrett."

"What? What is it?" Now, his voice was the shrill one. "Is it bad?"

The raised, red skin surrounding the inked image looked fresh and irritated. "I think I'm starting to remember." Yup. It was coming back to me.

"What is it, Meyers?" He twisted trying to see the mark through his blind panic. "I cannot have a fucking tramp stamp! My body is my livelihood!"

I nodded, my brow knit with empathetic regret but my instinct was to laugh so I pressed my lips tight. "I… I think… I think you wanted it."

"I'm a fucking model! My flawless figure is my instrument!"

At that, I lost it. Laughter punched out of me no matter how hard I tried to hold it in.

"Stop cackling!"

"I think you got it because you thought it would be really funny."

"Do I look like I'm fucking laughing?"

I didn't know what to tell him. It wasn't going to wash off. "I'm guessing you don't know what it says."

"How good are you at reading *your* ass? What does it say?"

The words weren't the problem. Not really. "Well, it's a portrait."

He growled, "A portrait of *what*? Take a picture with your phone so I can see it."

Yeah, like having pictures of Hale's brother's naked ass on my phone would make this situation any better.

"It's not that bad." It was horrible. "The work's decent and everything's spelled correctly."

He growled through gritted teeth. "What the fuck is it, Meyers?"

"I don't want to tell you."

"*Meyers!*"

"Fine! It's…um…Britney."

"What?" He bolted into the bathroom and several things clattered to the floor. *"Fuck!"*

"It's not that bad, Barrett. Maybe you can cover it up with something less…Y2K."

"It's a fucking tramp stamp!" He stumbled out of the bathroom, a look of sheer horror on his face. It would be a long time before he saw the humor of the situation. "My career's over."

"No, it's not. Models have tattoos. That's what airbrushing is for."

"I have the words *hit me, baby, one more time* permanently inked above my asshole!"

I smothered my laughter out of respect. There was definitely a prison joke in this mess, but the murderous look in his eye warned me to save it for later.

"This is all your fault!"

"My fault?" My memories were still too fuzzy to know if that was true. I might have encouraged him, but a tattoo would have ultimately been *his* choice. "You can't blame this on me!"

He gripped his head. "What the hell were we drinking last night?"

"I'm guessing turpentine."

"We have to retrace our steps." He *finally* stepped into his rumpled pants but winced when the leather of his belt bumped Britney's chin. "Ouch. Damn it. Were we around birds?"

"Birds?"

"I don't know. I remember…birds."

This was categorically the worst hangover in the history of humankind.

"Look, I'd love to Scooby-Doo our way through this mystery with you, but Hale is probably passing his keys off to the valet at this very moment. I don't have the strength—or the answers—to explain any of this right now. My head's killing me. My feet feel like someone tried to burn me at the stake. And my future's in massive danger if I don't get you out of here before your brother arrives. Do you want to start World War III with this degree of a hangover?"

A jagged breath skipped past his lips as he massaged his face. "It feels like my ears are literally bleeding."

The sense of uncertainty was making me physically ill. "Barrett, nothing happened last night, right?"

He scowled at me. "Like you even have to ask. He's my brother, Rayne."

"I know! I know. And I'd never cheat on him, but… How do we explain this?" I waved a hand at the rumpled bed and destroyed hotel room. Hale could not find us like this.

It didn't matter that Barrett was his brother. Remington was his father, and he'd slept with Hale's last girlfriend right under his nose. It was no wonder Hale had trust issues.

Barrett waved away my concern. "You need to have more faith in him. Hale's a big boy—" He froze. "Meyers…don't move."

I stilled. "What's wrong?"

Speaking slowly and quietly, he splayed his fingers and held up his hands in a calming gesture that only terrified me. "There's a *huge* fucking spider on your neck."

I screamed and went into a full-scale, spastic attack to remove any trespassing creatures from my body. My hands scoured my throat, swiping the small, furry fucker away.

It clung to my finger, so I rapidly ran in place, flinging my hands hysterically while squealing nonsense words. "Get it off! Get it off! Get it off!"

It landed on the bed and I shuddered, caterwauling as if I'd just been molested by a ghost.

"Oh." Barrett leaned forward and lifted the spider. "It's just a fake eyelash."

Depleted, I collapsed into the chair and caught my breath. "How is this my life?"

"Oh, please." He shoved his arms into a T-shirt that was several sizes too small. "At least you don't have permanent scarring. You're a few aspirins and a sports drink away from returning to your normal self. I, on the other hand, have been branded for fucking life."

I groaned, pressing my face into my palms. My skull had a literal heartbeat that throbbed like the impending theme of Jaws.

Barrett blew out a breath and leaned into the wall. "My bones feel like they're trying to escape."

I peeked through my fingers. "What the hell are you wearing?"

He pressed his chin to his chest and frowned. The shirt, clearly a girl's medium, had a flamboyant baby unicorn dancing in a tutu across a rainbow. Overhead, it read, *I'm Fucking Fabulous!*

"What the fucking fuck?"

"Can I please have that when you find your real clothes?"

He jerked the sheets off the bed and searched the room. "Where the hell's *my* shirt?"

"I dunno. Wanna wear this one?" His was way better.

He glanced at my muggle shirt and growled. Then he dropped to the edge of the bed. "My head is killing me."

"Mine too." I massaged my temples.

His fingers forked through his hair and stilled. "No." His hand cupped the back of his head, traveling up and down, pulling his messy hair. "No." He growled, "What the fuck did you do?"

My head shook. His hair appeared several inches shorter than it had been last night. "I didn't—"

"*Where's my fucking hair, Rayne?*" He sprang to his feet and started ransacking the suite.

"Maybe this is a new look for you—" I shut my mouth the moment he came storming toward me, his detached hair now in his fist and his eyes burning with flames of fury.

"You. Cut. My. Fucking. Hair."

I held up my hands in a gesture of peace. "Memories are a little sketchy, but I'm pretty sure you were on board with it."

"I'm going to fucking murder you!"

"Barrett—"

We silenced as there was a knock on the door.

Heart plummeting to the pit of my stomach, I looked at the entrance in horror. We were screwed. "That's Hale. You have to hide."

His nostrils flared. "No."

"Barrett, please." After everything else, I wasn't sure Hale and I could survive one more calamity. "If he finds you here—"

"Let him."

"I know you want to punish me right now, but in my defense, I don't remember anything from last night." Shit. What if we actually did more than cut his hair? "Your brother gets really jealous, and everything's supposed to be perfect for the wedding. Please don't mess this up any more than it already is. If not for me, for Hale."

"Rayne?" Hale knocked again and the tension in my chest tightened as I held my breath waiting for Barrett to give in.

"Please. I'll do anything. A permanent favor for the rest of your life."

He growled and shoved away. "Fine. I'll hide in the shower. You have thirty seconds to get out of here."

As soon as he disappeared into the bathroom, I grabbed my dress, shaking off any dick cooties that might have contaminated the fabric, and quickly slid it up my legs.

Hale knocked again. "Rayne?"

"One sec!"

I was operating with a blood-alcohol level well over the legal limit and my motor skills were massively off balance. Tossing the *Word To Your Muggle* shirt into the corner, I grabbed my ruined shoes.

"Ah, ah, ah…" I whimpered, failing to force my swollen feet into the now deformed fit.

I should have talked him into eloping. Then none of this would have happened. Having a big, traditional wedding was way above my grade level. I only agreed because I wanted to make Hale happy and prove I could play the role of the re-fined bride, suitable for a flawless, dreamboat of a groom.

Boy was that a mistake. Hale was perfect in every way and I was a walking disaster. The GOAT of hot fucking messes.

"Rayne, open the door."

I should have never let him convince me that I could handle this much pressure. This wedding was going to be our undoing.

Shoving my panic down, I leaned into the bathroom and hissed at the closed shower curtain that hid Barrett, "If you find any of my stuff, bring it back to The Plaza. Don't make a sound until we're gone." I pulled the bathroom door shut be-fore he could answer.

Forcing a smile big enough to cinch my skull

around my throbbing brain, I opened the door. "Hale. What took you so long?"

His grin dropped to a frown and his gaze darted over my shoulder.

I quickly stepped into the hall and pulled the door shut, my shoes clutched to my chest.

His hand shot out, catching the door before it could lock. "Hold on."

"Um, I'm really hungry…"

He pushed into the hotel room and scowled at the disaster. Bottles littered the floor and a pizza box hung open on the dresser, nothing but a cemetery of half-gnawed crust and bottle caps scattered inside. It was a lot of mess for one woman to make.

He glanced at the unmade bed and bent down to retrieve one very large male shoe. "And this belongs to…?"

I deflated. There was no use. "Please don't be mad."

"Why would I be mad, Rayne?" At first, I thought he might actually stay calm. Then I registered his loosely masked fury. "I find my fiancée in a hotel room on the other end of New York, a bed that stinks of God knows what, sheets a mess, your hair looking as though you've been fucked hard, and a *dead man's* shoe on the floor."

"It's not what you think."

"No? Then explain it to me."

I wished I could.

He stood, eerily calm, waiting for an explanation.

I broke into a full-body sweat. "I…" Swallowing, I tried to figure out where to begin but I was missing ninety percent of my short-term memory. "Let's just get out of here and get some coffee. Once I have food in my stomach—"

"Whose shoe is this, Rayne?"

Before I could answer, something clattered to the shower floor. Hale's gunmetal eyes shot to the bathroom door and he dropped the shoe, his hands balling into fists as he barreled forward.

"Hale wait!"

He shoved open the bathroom door and flung back the shower curtain.

Barrett froze like a deer in the headlights.

Hale's rage shifted to shock and he staggered back. We were fucked.

If at First You Don't Succeed

SKYDIVING ISN'T FOR YOU

THREE MONTHS Earlier

"TRADE," I said, dropping the enormous wedding planner binder Seraphina had gifted us for Christmas into Hale's lap and scooping up Elara from his side.

He lurched forward under the weight of the intimidating book. "What the hell's in this thing?"

"Our to-do list. Did you know that there are roughly six phases to an engagement? If your sister's plan was not to overwhelm me, she failed miserably."

I snatched a diaper out of the basket under the coffee table and laid Elara on the floor. She instantly rolled to her stomach and tried to escape, but I caught her ankle and dragged her back.

Hale opened the cover of the mammoth book and read the personalization Phina had professionally inscribed with our names and photos. "That's why I hired you a wedding planner."

"*Us.* You hired *us* a wedding planner." Bundling up the soiled diaper I hurled it toward the kitchen. It landed on the tile floor with a heavy splat.

Hale sighed, already getting up from the couch to move the dirty diaper into the trash can. He was always cleaning up my messes—and Elara's. "Don't let that book intimidate you. It's just a suggestion."

My head perked up. "Do you really mean that?" Dreams of a small, intimate ceremony came to mind. It could be on an exclusive beach with only our best friends and immediate family present. I envisioned our casual wedding clothes luffing in the wind against a cerulean coast and pink sandy beaches as the scent of coconut danced in the air. "I thought you wanted to do the whole New York thing."

"I do."

A tsunami appeared in my fantasy, wiping out the entire peaceful picture. I didn't tell my future husband that the thought of a big wedding made me physically queasy, because I didn't want to disappoint him.

This was Hale's wedding as much as mine. Plus, he was perfect in every pleasing but irritating way. He earned the perfect wedding. I wanted to give him everything he deserved, a sort of pre-marriage gift for the smoke-show groom before it sank in that he wasn't getting anything close to a perfect bride.

In my head, if I could pull off Hale's version

of the perfect Hale wedding, then I could fool all of high society into believing he wasn't marrying a woman way below his station. Who even said words like station and high society nowadays? Davenports did. That's who. They and the rest of the elite upper class lived their day-to-day lives like American royalty, whereas I lived my pre-Hale days like a person who took no issue with shopping in pajamas or using a marker to fix a scuff in a pleather shoe.

I lifted Elara by the waist of her candy cane pajama pants and let gravity do the rest as she sank back into her clothes—fresh diaper in place.

"So we're back to phase one—operation New York skyline." Otherwise known as wedding-gate and the greatest threat to my worried intestines of late.

Hale pressed a kiss to my head and took Elara. "You'll love it. Once we find the perfect venue, everything will fall into place." He shoved the enormous wedding planner aside as if it wasn't a book full of expectations and impossible standards.

To think, I once feared handling Hale's daughter as if she were a grenade with a loose pin, but now I'd take a hundred Elaras to just one of those books. My greatest fear was letting Hale down. No. Scratch that. I would most definitely let him down before we said *I do.* My greatest fear was disappointing him so much that he called the wedding off.

"You're sure you don't want to do a private ceremony like your dad and Jasmine did?"

He glared at me like he always did whenever I mentioned his father's latest marriage. Ignoring my comment, he pointed the remote at the television and put on the game. "Most women spend their entire lives dreaming of a big wedding."

I grimaced, collecting toys from the carpet and chucking them into the bin. I wasn't like most women. Not only did I lack the gene that made me good at girlie things, I absolutely sucked at planning.

Hale had such grandiose ideas. He not only wanted a New York wedding, he wanted a rooftop ceremony overlooking the entire metropolis. His expectations were what any ordinary person would call out of reach, and he used the word perfect way too often when setting standards.

When we started scouting locations, he had told me, *"I want a venue with a view of the gods."*

"What gods?" I had asked, Disney's King Titan and Hercules floating through my head.

"The gods hidden throughout the most influential streets and structures of the world. New York is modern man's Mount Olympus."

Sure, I thought, secretly believing his expectations might be a smidge high. He wanted a venue he could transform with a panoramic view overlooking all of Manhattan.

Rich people hired literal construction crews to throw parties. Pre-Hale, at the last wedding I attended in Oregon, I thought the chocolate-covered almonds were *fancy*. Davenports redefined the word.

Elara reached for *Meep Meep*, her stuffed sheep, and I handed her a bottle. She rolled to her side and happily cuddled the sheep. That girl had the life.

"What are you worried about, Rayne? I told you I'll pay for everything."

"Well, duh." I would have a hard time affording the flight from Florida to New York. The traditional idea of the bride's family paying for the wedding went out the window the moment Hale mentioned ice sculptures.

My family did not come from money. We were the basic, lower-middle-class people who had one very basic bathroom, an old television too big to mount on a wall with basic cable, no dining room and no need for formal dining, and basic cars with limited liability insurance that had all been pre-owned by other basic people before us.

The Davenports, on the other hand, had so much money they smelled like it. Hell if I could figure out what a man like Hale saw in a simple chick like me.

It wasn't my bed skills or beauty, I knew that much. And while most people laughed at my jokes, Hale was more reserved than most. But he did find me funny. Thank God for that.

"Try to enjoy the process, babe. Think of it this way, the sky's the limit and you can have whatever you want. Make it fun."

Fun was a tall order. I was so awkward even the title of bride-to-be intimidated me. But I did like the ring.

Holding out my hand, I smiled as the diamond caught the fading sun. My gaze drifted past my fingers as I looked longingly at the infinity pool. It would be a few months before we could swim again. January in the Keys was beautiful. Nothing like the wet, slush everyone was dealing with back in Oregon right now, but still too chilly to swim. Once the weather broke I planned on using the pool as a source of working out. Iron out some of this new baby weight before the big day.

Not that I had carried a baby per se. But I took care of Elara as if she were my own, and being that she was a kid with no access to her money or massive trust funds yet, I often compensated my efforts and worries with added calories.

Motherhood was stressful. Not that I was her mom. I knew my rank. But I loved that pudgy little peanut as if she were my own, and loving anything that much was terrifying. I was suddenly responsible for another human life. Me. A person who could barely take care of herself.

So, yeah, I ate my feelings. There was no law saying I wasn't allowed to eat a cookie from time to time if it helped me shoulder such massive responsibilities. And Hale liked my fluffy parts so we were both fine with my rounding waistline and softer thighs.

Speaking of, I searched the accent tables for the plate of snickerdoodles Marta had made. "What did you do with the rest of the Christmas cookies?"

"I ate them."

"All of them?" I could feel the outrage distorting my face.

"Sorry. There might be some pizzelles left."

My lip hooked upward in disgust. "Those aren't cookies. They're flat, flavorless pancakes people make so they have an excuse to buy weird ingredients in the baking aisle, like anise."

He pulled his eyes from the game and looked at me in confusion. "Huh?"

"Nothing." I went to the kitchen and came back with three pizzelles. One bite and the whole thing crumbled, making a mess. I discretely dusted off my shirt while Hale's focus was on the television.

"Can I have one?"

I looked at him for a long moment. It was among the shittier cookies, but I was a known hoarder of baked goods. In the end, I gave him one because I could deny the man nothing.

He ate it without dropping a single crumb.

I continued to stress over the upcoming wedding plans as Elara passed out in a drunken milk stupor on the floor, using *Meep Meep* as a pillow while a trickle of white drool dribbled from her pink lips. *Gah*, she was beautiful.

Moments like this, just the three of us, were my happy place.

The following day the Christmas tree came down and all of the new ornaments we bought were neatly wrapped and placed safely in storage bins for next year. This wasn't like the post-holiday shit show my family threw down every January when we wrapped dollar store decorations in crumpled newspaper and stuffed them into cardboard boxes. No sir. Davenports closed up Santa's shop in style.

All the bins were made of the finest red plastic and each ornament went into a uniquely designated cubby. Some decorations even came in individual velvet-lined boxes. Bubble wrap protected every fragile ball and some of the gold—yes, actual gold—ornaments returned to custom-fitted satin-lined jewelry boxes complete with latching hardware. The Davenport's Christmas packaging alone was of higher quality than my family's entire holiday display.

When I was a kid we just wrapped the ornaments and hoped for the best. Whenever we pulled the boxes down from the attic, everything reeked of wax and dust. I loved that musky, nostalgic smell and it made me a little sad that Elara might never associate that scent with the holidays.

The Davenport ornaments would smell of cedar because they weren't going into the attic. No way, no how. These bougie bangles were getting stored in one of many cedar closets throughout the house.

Hale had a crew for most things, so wrapping up the holiday was as simple as turning a page. One moment it was Christmas then it was not. Was that how our wedding would be, here one day then gone the next?

I sort of wished I could have helped with the undecorating. It would have distracted me from obsessing over our meeting next Saturday with Quinn Carter, the wedding planner Hale hired.

When Saturday arrived, I dressed myself and Elara for the meeting, then went to find Hale. He was in his office, phone to his ear, several hours into his day, and his serious enema-scowl in place.

"No, that's not going to work," he said in a voice he reserved for business. "Tell them to do it again and this time exactly how I instructed."

A shiver raced up my spine. He could be so intimidating when he wanted to be in-that custom tailored suit, platinum cufflinks, and designer leather belt. I wanted to drop to my knees, call him sir, and fulfill his every command, but we had wedding-gate to deal with.

"Dah dah dah dah," Elara said as soon as she spotted her father.

He grinned and reached for her little hand, while listening to the person on the other line. His scowl returned. "I'm done wasting time on this. Notify me as soon as the drawings are ready for my review." He ended the call and his business façade shifted flawlessly into doting father and handsome soon-to-be husband. "You ready for our meeting?"

"I think." I was dressed, teeth brushed, and face washed. That was about as prepared as I would get.

He pulled a jacket off the back of his chair and I frowned, wondering if my sundress and cardigan were too casual. Elara wore one of her dresses from Santa, which probably cost more than my entire wardrobe.

"Should I change?"

He glanced over his shoulder at me. "What do you mean? You look great."

Great was an overstatement. I got this dress at a tourist shop and I was pretty sure it was a coverup, not a dress. The sweater was from my college days.

I looked down at my toes. At least they were painted. I should probably put on shoes. "Can you take Elara?"

After handing off the baby I went to find my flip-flops. The moment I had them on my feet the doorbell rang.

Quinn was a middle-aged woman with mild plastic surgery and blonde hair that didn't match her dark brows. But she smiled the moment she saw Elara, so I immediately categorized her as friendly.

"Your home's beautiful," She complimented as we invited her inside. "I love what you've done with the landscape out front."

Hale's home was posh and masculine with enough sophisticated technology to make me regret never taking STEM courses in high school. Everything was digital and coded to the point that I struggled to operate the microwave.

He claimed having a smart home made life easier, but for an old-fashioned girl like me, it often led to a great deal of frustration, like when I can't get the damn buttonless dishwasher to work. But if I bitched, Hale's solution was to leave the dishes for the cleaning service, which seemed somehow worse in my mind.

We led Quinn to the dining room where the enormous wedding planner binder waited. I'd started nosing through it and filling out some of the pages, but my handwriting only seemed to muck-up the perfect book so I stopped.

Quinn, too, had a wedding binder of sorts. On the front, it said *Davenport Wedding*. I silently wondered if I should feel slighted that it didn't read *Meyers Davenport Wedding*.

Quinn opened her binder. "I always like to use this first meeting to get a feel for what the bride and groom envision as their perfect day." She paused and I realized she was finished speaking so I looked at Hale.

"Our vision's pretty simple," Hale said as his phone buzzed. His attention turned to whoever was texting him.

Quinn looked at me expectantly and I wondered why Hale kept mis-categorizing his vision with words like *simple.*

"I'm sorry. I have to take this," Hale said, rising from the table and drawing his phone to his ear before I could stop him.

I looked back at Quinn in clueless panic. "Um." I blinked, feeling like a kid accidentally seated at the grown-up table because someone mis-calculated the seats.

What did I know about weddings? I knew they said brides were supposed to pick a dress first. *They* being the wedding etiquette authorities, a group as elusive and influential as the Illuminati in my mind. I was already failing.

"I haven't picked out a dress yet," I blurted shamefully.

"That's okay. The bride's gown comes after the venue is booked. That way we make sure everything is on the same level of formality." She smiled and her sincerity instantly put me at ease as she withdrew a paper that said *Wedding Party.* "We'll give him a minute while we work out minor details and logistics. Why don't you tell me about your bridesmaids?"

"Bridesmaid. Just one. Elle. She's my maid of honor actually."

"So a small wedding party. Lovely. What's her name?"

"Elle Tuttle." I watched as she wrote down Elle's name with perfect penmanship.

"And has Hale selected his best man?"

I nodded. "His brother, Barrett."

"Davenport, right?"

"Yes."

I chewed my lower lip. "Is it wrong of me not to have Hale's sister as a bridesmaid?" I hated the thought of Seraphina feeling left out in any way.

"That's totally up to you and Hale. She's the only other sibling?"

"Yes." I could hear Hale's voice carrying down the hall. It didn't sound like he was hanging up any time soon. "I also have a guy friend, Tyler, I wanted to include."

"As a groomsman?"

"No, he and Hale have only met a couple of times. They're not close. Can he be a ring bearer or something?"

She looked up from the paper and her laughter silenced when she realized I was serious. "Well, if that's what you want, but typically ring bearers are young boys. If not a groomsman, how about an usher or a reader?"

"That would probably work." My stomach started to cramp. I wanted Hale's input on these decisions. "Maybe just write that in with a pencil for now."

She laughed. "These are only preliminary forms. Nothing is written in stone."

But she was using a very permanent gel pen.

"Sorry about that," Hale said as he returned to the dining room.

Instant relief unraveled the tension in my shoulders. "Do you want Phina in the wedding?"

He cocked his head and grinned. "I think that would be nice."

Good thing, because Quinn had already written down her name on the list in what might as well be a permanent marker.

"Rayne told me your brother, Barrett, will be your best man. Is there another friend or relative you'd like to have as a groomsman to escort your sister?"

It occurred to me that Barrett and Elle would be paired together and I smiled. They were already dating so that worked out perfectly.

Hale dragged a hand over the golden stubble lining the hard edge of his jaw. "I guess that would be my college roommate, Noah Wolfe."

Noah? Noah who? This was the first time I had heard mention of a Noah. "I've never heard you mention him."

"Sure you have. He lives in Philadelphia, about an hour away from New York. He was recently married. Remember, I went to their wedding just before you and I started dating?"

"Before we met? Sure. I remember it like yesterday."

Hale chuckled at my sarcasm and turned his attention back to Quinn. "I'll want to make sure his wife, Avery, is included in any plans as well."

Now we were adding an Avery? "You mean as a bridesmaid?" I asked, both reluctant and confused. I really didn't want a big wedding party.

"No, just as Noah's plus one so she doesn't have to sit by herself. It's perfectly fine to add her onto the head table, right, Quinn?"

"Absolutely."

"Oh." How did he know what was right and what wasn't when this was his first wedding too? Maybe this was the kind of propriety stuff wealthy guys learned while escorting debutants about the town during their adolescence.

Elara began to fuss, so I preoccupied myself with finding her a binkie while Hale went over some other details with Quinn.

"Do you have a date selected for the engagement party?"

My attention returned to wedding-gate. "We're having an engagement party?"

"It's pretty standard for a wedding of this size, especially with so many people traveling from around the country. An engagement party establishes the tone of the event and allows guests plenty of time to plan. Plus, you, the bride and groom, get one more reason to celebrate this momentous milestone."

I felt my mouth form a smile but it didn't reach my eyes. "Great. Are we inviting all the wedding guests, or is this just a small, family affair?" *Please say family only…*

"Oh, no, you'll want to invite everyone who you plan to include in your big day. And, just an FYI, etiquette states that you should never invite someone to the engagement party who isn't also invited to the wedding, but you can always add last-minute guests as the wedding gets closer.

Great, so we could add guests but not subtract. This party was turning into one of those creatures in Greek mythology that grew three heads every time it lost one.

I looked at Hale who seemed completely at

ease with all of these compiling plans. "Um, we haven't really talked about a guest list yet."

Hale squeezed my hand lovingly. "Miles emailed my dad's list this morning and I'm waiting on my mom's but she promises to have it to me by the end of the week."

Wasn't he just the star student of the class?

I had yet to ask my mom for a list, but I was pretty sure it would include her, myself, and my Uncle Rob. Then there was Tyler and Elle, a few past co-workers and that was a wrap.

"We should probably ask Phina to make a list, too, just to make sure no one is left out."

"Wouldn't want that to happen," I mumbled and Hale gave me a sidelong glance that turned into a reassuring smile.

"Rayne will also have a list of family and friends."

Yes, my three people would require the best seating and views of all the ice sculptures and gods.

"Great," Quinn said, making more notes. "Since you're planning a destination wedding, we'll want to start vetting vendors now. It's wise to lock in any photographers, bands, videographers, special entertainment, etcetera, as soon as you settle on a date."

My palms started to sweat and my stomach cramped. I reached for my coffee only to realize I'd left it in the other room. "Can I get anyone something to drink?"

"Water would be great. Thank you."

Hale watched me as I escaped what felt like an interrogation holding. Just as I refilled my coffee cup his hands landed on my shoulders, startling me.

"Hey, are you okay?"

"Me? I'm fine. Everything seems to be coming together perfectly."

"Rayne, look at me." He turned my body until I faced him, his towering form trapping me against the counter. Lifting my chin with a gentle finger, he forced me to meet his gaze. "This is still what you want, right?"

There was no doubt in my mind I wanted to marry Hale, but this wedding was growing more overwhelming by the minute. Looking up into those familiar silver eyes, the storm of panic in my stomach calmed and the tension in my back unraveled. This was Hale. My safe person. My anchor in a choppy sea. My everything. My partner. As long as he was by my side, anything was possible.

"I'm okay," I whispered. "Just overwhelmed."

"That's why we have Quinn. She's going to take care of everything."

I didn't need everything. "As long as I get us, I've got everything I need."

He smiled. "You're sure?"

I nodded, certain I wanted forever with this man more than my next breath.

His hand slipped beneath my hair, gently holding the back of my neck as my face angled upward. "Because if you're having second thoughts, now's the time to speak up."

New worry spiked in the pit of my stomach. "Are *you* having second thoughts?"

"Not even a little. I'd marry you tomorrow if it gave us enough time to plan everything. I'm all in."

His words reassured me and my panic subsided. "I love you."

Closing the distance, he nuzzled the edge of my nose with his then placed a delicate kiss on my lips. "I know this is a lot for you, but I'm here. We're in this together. And Quinn will be at your beck and call."

I was beginning to understand that a wedding was something completely different from a marriage. "I look forward to the moment we say I do."

"Me too, baby." He pressed a kiss to my lips and chuckled. "Then you'll truly be mine."

I was still processing the permanence of such a concept. Forever was a big promise. I wasn't worried about marrying Hale. But I was terrified he'd grow bored or get annoyed with me.

Too many times in life, people had politely asked me to be less—less hyper, less messy, less neurotic. I'd been programmed by experience to shrink myself down before others got tired of me or they inevitably rejected me.

Lower your voice, Rayne.

Sit up straight, Rayne.

Don't snort when you laugh, Rayne.

Your hips are too wide, Rayne.

You shouldn't swear so much, Rayne.

Suck it in, Rayne.

If you dressed differently, people would treat you differently, Rayne.

But Hale didn't like when I kept things inside. He wanted to know what I was thinking. He demanded I show him my authentic self. He said he liked the real me. All of me.

I should be flattered, which I was, but I was also scared because I was a lot.

Hale was my world now. I couldn't imagine a life without him, so I constantly found myself trying to temper my weirdness so he didn't change his mind and leave me.

"Rayne?" His thumb glided along my jaw as he looked at me in that way that told me I could never convincingly lie to him.

I really believed he could read my mind at times and see all the crazy neurosis I hoped to hide.

When I met his stare, he said, "You're who I want."

He sounded sincere, but…

I let out a breath and pressed my forehead against his shoulder. "I warned you."

When we started dating, I told him I wasn't good with commitment. Depending on me for anything more than a piece of gum in a pinch was a lot to ask.

"And *I* warned *you*, didn't I?" His body pressed against mine like a thunder blanket, calming and warming, exactly what I needed to feel grounded again. "I told you I wasn't letting you go, so stop eyeing the exits whenever you feel overwhelmed and start looking to your partner. This is about both of us. You can't get married alone."

With a sigh, I nodded. "I know." But deep down I also knew how busy Hale was.

The kind of wedding he wanted and the expectations he had implied that the next year would be full of planning. Literally months and months of planning. Maybe I just had to pace myself and take things one day at a time. We had plenty of time and even though Hale would undoubtedly get pulled away, we would always reconvene before any major decisions were made.

"Baby, you have to learn to count on me."

"I know. I'm just used to only counting on myself. Whenever I rely too much on people, they tend to get…" *Tired? Annoyed? Irritated? All of the above?* "You have a lot on your plate."

"I'm not people. I'm going to be your husband. You're my number one priority. You and Elara."

I sighed. He was saying all the right things, but my trust issues were deep seated and tied up with the first man I loved who inevitably abandoned me when I was only a kid. "I'm sorry I get so overwhelmed so easily. I'm working on it."

Hale was literally one of the most responsible men I'd ever met. Hell, he even adopted a child that wasn't his just to make sure that she had a good dad, and he was an incredible father to Elara. One would never know she wasn't his biological daughter.

He kissed the tip of my nose. "Lucky for you, I find your frazzled side very sexy."

I bashfully hid a smirk against the hard wall of his chest. "Remember the night on the yacht, when that hurricane was coming and I was freaking out?"

A low chuckle rumbled against my ear. "How could I forget?"

"You distracted me real nice that night."

His hands lowered to my ass and squeezed. "I'll always distract you when you need distracting."

At the end of the day, I didn't give a furry rat's ass about the actual wedding. But I wanted Hale. And I wanted to make Hale proud. If a big New York wedding would make him happy, I would do whatever was necessary to make that happen. Then, as planned, Hale would be irrevocably mine. This was basically a capture mission.

I looked up at him—my beautiful fiancé—and I smiled, certain he was more than I deserved and positive I would never let him go either. We were the oddest couple in this history of human mating, but for some reason, we worked. "In the eternal words of Luke Danes, I'm all in."

"Good, because I sort of have my heart set on spending the rest of my life with you." He kissed me and I softened, my nerves settling back into the manageable ball of chaos I was used to. "Now, who is this Luke Danes and do I need to kill him?"

"He's just a guy who owns a diner."

"Fictitious?"

"Yes."

"Then I'll let it slide." His hands rubbed soothingly down my back. "We better get back to our meeting. I left Quinn with Elara."

"Oh, boy." I grabbed my coffee and a bottle of water then Hale's phone rang.

He cursed under his breath as he looked at the screen. "I'm sorry…"

I sighed. "Try not to take too long."

"I'll do my best."

On my own again, I returned to the dining room and traded the bottle of water for Elara. "Hale's on another call. He said to continue without him."

"Your future husband's a busy man."

I nodded, accepting that Hale would always be busier than most. Inheriting one third of the Davenport legacy wasn't enough for him. He wanted to make his own wealth, not simply live off trusts earned from his father's success.

Beyond capitalizing in property management across the country, he'd spent years investing in hydropower and developing plans for water turbines off the coast of California. His plans were finally taking shape in actual infrastructure around the world. Getting his monstrous enterprise up and running required a lot from him. His presence was in high demand but at the end of the day, he always made me feel like his number one.

"Since it's just us ladies," Quinn said, flipping to a different section of the binder. "Let's talk themes. I usually recommend staying close to your natural style. That way you achieve something flattering and organic."

My natural aesthetic could be loosely defined with a lump of wool. But I didn't think *anxious ball of yarn* qualified as a wedding theme.

The wedding wasn't about me anyway. It was for Hale and he had a very specific vision in his head.

"I think Hale likes sophistication and luxury." Those words pretty much defined the groom's family, especially Hale who was the most cultured and refined Davenport of the bunch in my opinion.

She made a note. " Classic. Good. What about colors? Have you created a mood board?"

What the hell was a mood board? At the moment, my mood was teetering between hangry-lemur and skittish-bunny. "I don't know what a mood board is."

"Do you use Pinterest?"

"For recipes on occasion. But we mostly eat out."

"Well, there's a whole wedding world to be discovered on the internet. Once you create your wedding's mood board, you can add anything you like to it with the click of a button."

This sounded like homework. "What kind of stuff would I add?"

"Anything. Don't take it too literally. If you see a pillow that inspires you, add it. We don't necessarily need to find that exact pillow, but we can use it for design inspiration."

Inspiring pillow. Check. "What else?"

"Anything. You can add images of fine art, travel destinations you've visited with Hale, moody images that make you pause, clips from cinema—get creative with it."

My ears tuned into the hall as new pressure anchored me to my chair. Hale better wrap up that call shortly or we were going to wind up with a beer and tequila mood board because that was the only thing that struck me as inspiring at the moment. Then I wondered if I could somehow use this mood board project to get out of other wedding-gate work.

"You'll also need to create a registry before the engagement party. You can always add more as the wedding gets closer, but it's nice for guests to have a place to start. This is where your mood board will come into play. Guests will understand the theme and tone of your wedding at a glance when they see the sort of gifts you've selected for the registry."

The thought of people buying presents made me uncomfortable. The Davenports had more money than most. We should be the ones giving out gifts. Well, Hale should. I could afford to give out hugs.

The engagement party sounded like a scrimmage wedding before the real thing. Was such an event really necessary? Wouldn't an invitation be enough to let the guests know a wedding was coming? If I found a get-out-of-jail-free card on any side parties I was cashing it in. One big wedding was more than enough for my social awkwardness.

Quinn closed the binder and flattened her palms on the table. "I assume we've lost him for the rest of the meeting?"

I glanced at the hall. It sounded like he'd returned to his office which meant the call was important and required his full attention. I sighed. "Probably. But I'll catch him up on everything."

Maybe Hale would have some input about the moody pillows. If anything, he could probably relieve this crippling fear that I might choose the wrong thing and humiliate the Davenports in front of all their bajillionaire friends.

Quinn gave an apologetic smile. "I should have brought this up at the beginning of the meeting when we were all present, but I wanted to get to know both of you, first, so I had a better idea of what you envisioned."

She sounded ominous, like she was about to share something Hale should be present to hear.

"Is something wrong?" Was she breaking up with us so soon?

"It's a complication, not a deal breaker."

Oh crap. I drew in a big breath. Maybe it was better Hale wasn't here. "Give it to me straight."

"I'm aware that you want a venue with a panoramic view of Manhattan."

I nodded. That was Hale's thing, but I wanted it for him. "Yes."

"I found a venue. It's perfect really. A two-story open space on the fortieth floor, vacant, and already gutted leaving an open area of thirty-thousand square feet."

My eyes widened. Hale would love that.

"We could transform the entire place to fit your vision. There's room for ceiling installations and draping, we'd have a blank palette for breakout lounge furniture, stage rentals, acoustics, whatever you envision we could achieve in a space like this."

It sounded too good to be true. "You said there was a complication."

Her lips pressed tight and she dropped her gaze. "It's only available for the spring."

I hadn't thought about seasons yet. "Spring weddings are nice—"

"*This* spring, as in April."

My face slowly went slack. "Wait, you mean *this* April, as in three months from now?"

"I'm afraid so."

That was impossible. Maybe not for other brides. But for me, that was too fast. My stomach instantly growled as a cramp formed low in my belly. The stress made my scalp sweat.

"It would require some big bride energy," Quinn said with an encouraging smile, trying to make light of the atomic bomb she'd just dropped.

I didn't have big bride energy. At the moment, I only had big cramp energy. My insides felt as explosive as the first ten minutes of *Saving Private Ryan*. This was a big decision, and big decisions often lead to the shittipoos.

"I'll need to talk to Hale."

"Of course."

But I already knew what he'd say. He'd see it as a no-brainer. He wouldn't worry about the additional pressure because Hale could handle anything. That wasn't big groom energy, that was just him.

Quinn packed up her papers. "You don't have to make a decision today, but we do need to decide soon. The way I see it, you have three options."

"Three?" The cramps were getting worse.

"You could postpone the wedding."

I frowned, immediately disliking that idea. I wanted to lock Hale down. "How long?"

"Twenty-four months would give us plenty of time to find other venue options. We might not be able to find one as perfect as this, I mean, it has everything you listed in your original intake form—panoramic views overlooking the city, space for a guest list upward of three hundred people directly located in the heart of Manhattan."

Gah! It was perfect. We'd never find something that fit Hale's vision so precisely. "What are the other options?"

"Downsize the guest list. With a smaller headcount, we could probably find a location similar in your requested timeframe."

I loved that idea. If it were up to me, we would only have family and best friends at the wedding. But Hale wanted a big, traditional show and I wanted to give him that.

I frowned regretfully. "That won't be possible."

"You're sure?"

Not only did the Davenports know everyone and their mother, they had political ties, business ties, and even ties with their enemies. The social logistics of blowing smoke up one's ass was taken very seriously in wealthy circles. Removing one guest was like dislodging a wire from an active bomb. The whole plan could blow to shit.

"I'm sure. Hale has his heart set on a big wedding and the Davenports have a lot of close friends. What's the third option?"

She looked at me as if I already knew. "You two get married in April."

"Oh." I was so fucked.

Ich Leide an Kummerspeck

TRANSLATION—I SUFFER FROM GRIEF BACON!

HALE WAS STILL on the phone when Andrew arrived for his afternoon playdate at the park with Elara, so I texted Elle *911* and demanded she meet me for coffee.

"Ray, I don't understand what the big deal is," Elle said calmly as she sipped whatever green nightmare was blended in her cup today.

I stirred an extra packet of sugar into my double caramel iced macchiato, and she judgingly watched every granule fall.

"The big deal is that Hale is Mr. Sophisticated, and I'm a hot fucking mess. I can barely pull off proper dinner attire with a week's notice. How the hell am I going to be a bride in three months?"

"You just make it happen. There are checklists for this sort of stuff. And it's not like you're working with a budget."

I scratched at what looked like a hive forming on my wrist and scoffed. "Uh, yeah. I know all about the lists. You should see the size of the freaking wedding book Seraphina bought me for Christmas. It weighs more than Elara."

"You know, all that caffeine and sugar are probably adding to your stress."

I glared at her. "Don't start."

Elle hadn't fully recovered from the accident, but this seemed to be her new normal. Gone were the days of her long, luxurious hairdresser hair and obsession with high heels. Now, she wore her blonde waves clipped in an adorable pixie cut and mostly wore athleisure-wear. She juiced her veggies and lived at the gym. When she wasn't working out, she was training someone else.

Her body was in the best shape of her life, but it got annoying at times. Some days I missed my friend who would kill a log of raw cookie dough with me simply because it was period week. Now, she wouldn't even touch that *processed shit* and our cycles weren't synching anymore.

"I'm just saying, adding a little more activity to your day would bring down your cortisol levels. Going to the gym could help you unwind so you aren't constantly rushing to the bathroom whenever there's a big decision to be made."

I leveled her with a hard stare. "You're kidding, right?"

"I'm dead serious."

I looked over her shoulder at the display of pastries and counted to ten. "Exercising is your journey, not mine, Elle. I'm never going to be a gym person."

The old Elle would remember that. Hell, she'd even be on my side. But this new Elle-two-point-oh was training to be a physical therapist and interested in things we never cared about before.

"Ray, you're going to have to wear a wedding gown eventually."

My macchiato turned to sludge on my tongue. She did not just insinuate that I had to lose wedding weight. I had two choices. I could either vomit from the added pressure my maid of honor just threw on me, or… I stood. "I'm going to get a cupcake."

I left her in the booth with her lame, green protein shake that probably tasted like grass and bird shit.

By the time I returned with my cupcake, I had calmed down. Sometimes I needed to remind myself that Elle had literal brain damage and was missing a lot of our childhood memories. Her recovery had been a lonely journey for me, but I did my best to support her in any way I could. Like now, as I shoved a cupcake in my mouth so not to tell her what I really thought about her hurtful comment.

I slid her the other half. I knew she wouldn't touch it, but it was a piece offering all the same.

"No thanks. If you knew what was in there—"

"Sometimes you eat muffins."

"That's not the same."

"Yes, it is. A cupcake's just a flamboyant muffin. It won't kill you to have a bite."

"No thanks. If I'm going to have carbs, I'm going to get them from a real bakery, not a commercial coffee shop. Have you seen the bread they're serving? It looks harder than my childhood."

I snorted at her joke, glad she at least recovered those memories. "Facts."

Elle's childhood had been normal until her parents died. Then her brother became a junkie and a thief. If not for Hale, Chris would still be squatting in Elle's house. Lucky for her, Hale knew how to handle sticky situations.

He bought Chris out and made sure he evacuated the premises before the check cleared. Then he sent a construction crew to Elle's and completely flipped the house. By the time he was finished with the remodel, it was unrecognizable. All new appliances, beautiful hardwood floors, and fancy fixtures. He sold it for four times what he paid Chris and cut Elle a hefty sum in the end.

That was Hale, always the hero in a pinch.

Suffice it to say that after that Elle was Team Hale. She was also Team Barrett. She'd been banging Hale's brother since we all moved to Florida long-term. It was safe to say she liked the Davenports, which was good because I loved them.

"How's the bungalow coming along?" Elle had used some of the money Hale made her to buy a small house.

"It's great. I bought some new furniture but I haven't put it together yet." She grimaced. "The directions are complicated."

Since the accident, anything that required written instructions confused Elle. "Why don't you ask Barrett to do it?"

She shrugged. "I'll figure it out."

Her stubborn independence struck me as odd. She never used to hesitate when it came to asking Barrett for help. "You guys okay?"

"Yup."

Her answer seemed too quick and short. "Are you mad that I won't go to the gym? Please don't take it personally, Elle. I tried. Remember when I took that Yoga class?"

I had thought it would be cool to get my feet behind my ears for Hale, but it turned out I wasn't that bendy. I'd accidentally shown up at an advanced flow class instead of a beginners' level. Everyone looked like they were doing a high-speed escape through a room with invisible laser beams using only moves from the Matrix. I tried to keep up and was sore for days. Never again.

"I'm not mad."

"Good. Because I'll probably always be a gristle girl. Hale likes my body."

She rolled her eyes. "I wasn't trying to fat shame you, Ray. Your weight is fine. But physical activity can have a lot of therapeutic benefits, especially where stress is involved. I was only making a suggestion."

"I know." After the accident physical therapy really helped Elle, which was why she turned that passion into a career path. "I could probably walk more."

"That would be an improvement."

It bothered me that she didn't comprehend how physically exhausting it was to take care of a baby. Plus, Remington kept me busy most days, which was why Elara also had a nanny.

Elle finished her green drink and set it aside. "So, what's really got you stressed? I only have fifteen minutes. Let's hear it."

It also bugged me that our time was now rationed. I sighed and reached into my bag, withdrawing the latest tabloid I snagged at the market. "Have you seen this?"

Elle pulled the magazine in front of her and I pointed to the headline that read *Is America's Most Eligible Bachelor Settling Down or Just Settling For Less?*

"Page eight."

She opened the cover and flipped through the glossy gossip. "They're going to cover the wedding, Ray. Davenports are high-profile people."

"I know. I just wish they would give us more input. There should be laws against publishing pictures of people without their permission. That doesn't even look like me."

"Yikes." She found the photo that had me stressing. "Well, Hale looks great."

"Of course, he looks great. That's not the issue. I look like Sam the fucking hobbit."

"Who?"

"Frodo's friend. You know, the *Goonie*? He played Rudy? The guy the demi-dogs ate in *Stranger Things*."

She blinked at me, confused.

"It's irrelevant. I'm Hale's chubby sidekick. Every single picture they take of me I look like I'm at the *chew* part of a sneeze."

Elle laughed. "You're always talking."

"Yes, because Hale's pretty, and I'm chatty. But they don't write that. They just post these awful pictures and the world sits around wondering what the hell a man like that is doing with a woman like me."

"No one is wondering that, Ray."

"Of course they are. Why else would they print

the same story over and over again? It's just a matter of time before they haul out photos of all his anorexic exes and line us up in a comparison article that rips my self-esteem to shreds."

Elle cocked her head and slid the other half of the cupcake back to me. "Here, I think you need this more than me."

I ate it because big, ugly emotions should be consumed before they grow. "Did you know the Germans have a literal word for eating feelings," I said over a mouth full of frosted cake. "*Kummer-speck.*" Crumbs sputtered past my lips. I took a sip of my iced macchiato and wiped my mouth. "It translates to *grief bacon.*"

She shook her head. "Where do you read this stuff?"

"I spend a lot of time in the bathroom."

"*This…*" She took the magazine and held it like a rag. "Is trash. Stop reading it."

"But what if they're right? What if we're too different to make this work?"

"Ray, you *are* making it work. Hale loves you. Elara loves you. Fuck everyone else."

I let my arms flop onto the table and shook my head. "But what about the wedding? Hale has such a specific vision and I want to give it to him, but what if I can't pull this off? I mean, even normal women would struggle with planning a wedding this size in that short of time, right?"

"Hey," she snapped. "You're Rayne Freaking Meyers. You can do anything you set your mind to."

"You mean Calamity Rayne."

She waved away my words. "You haven't been

a Calamity since you started working for Remington, Rayne. Look at where you are, what you're doing with your life, where you're living, and who you're marrying. That stuff doesn't come from screwing up."

Okay, half of that was right. Yes, I worked for Hale's dad, one of the wealthiest men in the world, and yes, I was marrying his son, another one-percenter. But getting a job for the Davenports was a total fluke. Remington had been on pain meds and probably not thinking clearly when he hired me. There were way more qualified people for the job. And Hale had been stranded on a yacht with us, coming off a terrible rebound, and angry with his father. He probably slept with me that first time just to piss off his dad.

"Knock it off," Elle snapped again. "I can tell you're mentally dismantling your success when you should be celebrating it. For once in your life, Ray, just be present and enjoy what you have."

"I am present, but I'm also a realist."

"You're an over-thinker."

"Yes, about real-life problems."

She waved her fingers in a come hither motion. "All right then. Let's hear it. Give me some of these real-life problems you're stressing about."

She wanted a peek into my head? Fine, I'd give her the keys to the crazy farm.

"Okay, for starters, I have no social graces. Hale's attended galas since he was a kid and knows everything there is to know about etiquette. I'm completely awkward in normal social settings. Hell, I even speak louder at blind people no matter how much I know that doesn't help them see me. I use the F-word too much and I never know where to put my hands. Forks confuse me. Hale's an actual adult. My version of adulting is Googling stuff, and even then I don't follow through. I cut corners. Do you know how many candles I bought for gifts and kept? The guilt is killing me! But my house smells like a majestic bakery, so am I really sorry? The other day I couldn't find the dustpan, so I sneakily swept a pile of crumbs under the carpet. I swore I'd clean it up as soon as I found the dustpan. But I didn't. It's still there! And every time Hale walks over it I sweat a little. And let's say we do postpone the wedding—"

"Is that an option?"

"Yes, but we would probably have to wait two years to find a place this perfect again. *Two years,* Elle! Think of everything that could go wrong in two years. We're still dealing with a pandemic. Weird diseases like rickets and polio are coming back. Putin's a wild card. The government keeps talking about aliens."

"You did not literally just reference Putin in regard to your wedding plans."

"I'm just saying it's obviously unsafe to postpone when tomorrow is this unpredictable. But most of all, what if two years is too long and Hale realizes he's made a huge mistake?"

The moment the words actually left my mouth I admitted that was my biggest worry. I glanced at the picture of him in the magazine and felt how off-balance we were. Every day new reminders pointed out our differences.

"Okay," Elle said softly, gripping my hand. "Take a breath."

I did as she said and felt my fears morph into sheer exhaustion. "He's just so perfect."

"Look, I know you think I'm on Team Hale and I am, but first, I'm the head cheerleader for Team Rayne. I love you, Ray. We all do. So stop acting like you're this unlovable person."

I reached for the cupcake wrapper and proceeded to lick it. Elle caught my hand.

"For the love of God, stop. I'll get you a cookie." She took the trash and went to the counter. A moment later she returned with a large chocolate chip cookie in a napkin. "Here."

"Thanks." I took a bite. "I know Hale loves me, but—" I paused and cocked my head. Then I spit the crumbled cookie onto the napkin. "Blah. No wonder I have trust issues."

"What's wrong with the cookie?"

"Raisins masquerading as chocolate." I shoved the cookie away. "I seriously miss the coffee shops back home sometimes." Oregon was the OG of hipsters and coffee shops. I sighed. "You'll help me, right?"

"Of course. I mean, I have school and work, but other than that I'm yours. And don't forget Tyler."

"Do you think it's bad he's not in the wedding? The planner said we could make him an usher or a reader. I suggested ring bearer, but…"

She snorted. "Were you thinking of making him wear a fanny pack full of flowers? He'd hate that."

"The idea crossed my mind. Isn't there some rule that you can't say no to a bride?" Tyler was our childhood friend and so obviously gay, but he'd never outwardly admitted his sexual orientation. He didn't like flash and he hated being the center of attention. But he also really liked staring at hot men.

"Maybe don't piss him off just yet. Tyler can be helpful when he wants."

"True." But he could also be negative. "Maybe he'll meet a sexy single guy at our wedding. I think Elara's nanny might be gay."

She lifted a brow. "Maybe we sit them next to each other at the rehearsal dinner."

"Sounds like a plan."

"So, do you think you're going to do it?"

Maybe my mind was already made up and this panic was just part of my process. "I don't want to wait two years." All I wanted was to marry Hale.

"Then I say do it. Life's just a series of distractions. You can either focus on the fun stuff or worry about everything that could go wrong. Either way, time is passing by."

She was right. I needed to start looking at this as an adventure. After all that was how the best memories were made.

I pulled out my phone and tapped the screen. Then I banged it on the table and blew into the charging port.

Elle frowned. "Are you having some kind of fit?"

"There's couscous stuck in my phone and it's not working right."

"Why is there couscous in your phone?"

"Because I accidentally dropped it in the toilet and the internet said to sit it in rice overnight, but we were out of rice. All we had was couscous.

Those little fucking balls got everywhere." I blew into the charger hole and finally got my contacts to open. I dialed Hale. "It's ringing."

He answered right away. "Hey, babe."

"Hey. Are you finished work for the day? I need to talk to you about some wedding stuff."

"Hello?"

"Shit." I shook the phone. "Hale?"

"Rayne?"

"Can you hear me?"

"Hello?"

I banged the phone on the table. "Stupid fucking couscous. I'll call you from the car!" I chucked the phone in my purse.

I'm in Deep Smit

MY PHONE WAS RINGING the moment I got into the car. I quickly plugged it into the stereo to activate the Bluetooth because, yes, my car was from the Stone Age. The screen of my radio flashed with the words *Big Dick Davenport* and I answered.

"Hey."

"Can you hear me now?"

"Yeah. Sorry. I was in a café and there was couscous and… Anyway. Are you finished with your calls for the day?"

"I have a few hours free."

Perfect. "Good. I wanted to talk while Elara was still at the park."

"Oh?" Hale's tone peaked with interest. He knew Elara being out with the nanny was code for sex. "*Talk* talk, or talk?"

"Talk. Nothing fancy. Just a shoes-on quickie." Hmm, maybe sex could be my pre-wedding stress relief strategy. Why go to the gym when I could bang out some exercise at home?

"Let's make it happen."

"Okay, but then we have to talk about some wedding stuff."

"Whatever you need, baby. Drive safe."

"Love you."

"Love you too."

The call ended and I found myself smiling. Hale got me. He really did.

With one eye on the road and another on my phone, I cued up my newest playlist, a montage of songs mentioning New York to help me get in the wedding spirit. My mood only got better as *King of New York* from the *Newsies* soundtrack blasted. Just as I was belting out the chorus, something caught my eye and I veered into the other lane.

"Shit!" Oncoming traffic swerved and beeped.

I searched the dashboard, certain I saw something with eight legs crawling around the vents. Assuming it was my imagination, I continued to focus on the road, but my singing had dialed back a notch on account of my feeling like I now had an audience.

I was almost home by the time Frank Sinatra was spreading the news when my little stowaway reappeared, dangling from a web and swaying right in front of my face. It just so happened I was also making a sharp turn and the difference between wearing a spider in my hair or not, came down to nearly crashing my car.

Frank crooned about *little town blues* and my car went careening over the median. Spider gone, I screamed and slammed on the brake, jerking the wheel and slamming the car into park before driving off the road.

My feet hit the pavement and I flipped my head, ransacking my hair and dancing like a lunatic on the side of the road as Frank's grand finale belted from my speakers and my screams yodeled through the air.

Out of breath, and unsure where the spider went, I panted. That was when I saw the wide-eyed police officer staring at me.

Crap.

"Ma'am?" he said, sounding both suspicious and cautious.

"There…" I panted. "was a spider. I swear I'm not drunk. I only had a macchiato."

He slowly approached, flipping open his little leatherbound booklet like I was a real perp in a crime. "You cleared the median."

I glanced guiltily at the divider and back to my car, which was humming and pinging a little more than usual, but I saw no real damage to the old girl. Nervously swiping at my face and neck, I looked up at the cop.

"You seem a bit agitated. Have you taken anything?"

Did he not just hear me about the spider? My finger dug in my ear, making sure the speedy little shit didn't go that way. "I'm fine. I just don't like bugs crawling on me."

His suspicious eyes shifted from me to the car.

If I knew how to flirt, this was where I'd use those skills. Unfortunately, my game with the opposite sex had always been mediocre at best, so I shrugged. "You want to see my license and registration, don't you?"

"Yup."

I clicked my tongue and shot him a finger gun signal. "You got it."

Twenty minutes and one speeding ticket later, I was back on the road with my hands safely positioned at ten and two. My sex window was getting smaller by the minute, so there was no time left to worry about the spider I still hadn't located. But I knew it was there. I just knew that little fucker was hiding in wait to sneak up on me again.

I shivered and swiped at a loose piece of hair hanging from my bun.

After some stress relief sex, my focus needed to move to Hale and the wedding. I mentally reviewed my laundry list of concerns I had about moving up the date. We needed to have a serious conversation and make a decision, because the uncertainty was eating away at my insides.

I planned to tell him my feelings and he'd come up with a solution. After he looked in my ear, of course. I scratched under the collar of my cardigan. *Gah, I hated spiders.*

As soon as I pulled into the driveway the front door opened. Hale waited as I rushed up the walk. "I need you to look in my ear before you can get inside of me." I lobbed my purse in the direction of the den

"Pardon?"

I waved a flustered hand. "There was an incident with a spider. Just a precaution."

Like a true hero, he whipped out his phone and turned on the flashlight. The moment he was close to me my hormones rallied. Just the mere touch of his fingers to my earlobe and his breath softly teasing my skin had me ready to take off my clothes.

"Good?"

"I don't see anything." Warm breath skated over my cheek as his mouth closed over my earlobe. My stress levels were already rapidly dropping as lashes lowered and my knees softened.

"How do you do that?"

He chuckled softly and dragged his fingers down my throat and kissed my temple before shutting off his phone. "Do what?"

"Barely touch me and make me melt."

Another chuckle. "Are you melting?" His fingers trailed up my thigh and hooked under my panties. "It seems so."

I toed off my flip-flops. "It's go time. We have to hurry. Elara and Andrew will be back soon."

"On it." He caught my arm and yanked me back, pegging my body to the wall as he delivered a brain-spinning kiss. His hands were instantly on me, sliding up my dress and pulling off my cardigan. My fingers raked through his sun-bleached hair.

Like a drug, the moment I had one taste of him I wanted more.

He broke the kiss and shoved my panties down my thighs, turning me to face the wall. "Fuck, Rayne." The click of his belt buckle sent a thrill reverberating right to my core.

Nudging my feet wider, he yanked the thin straps of my bra and dress down, freeing my arms. His fingers delved inside of me, deliciously swirling as his lips teased that sensitive spot where my shoulder curved as he crowded his body around mine, possessively holding me. I gasped as his fingers sank deeper, driving me to that razor-sharp edge. Needing the pressure, desperately craving his demanding attention which sometimes seemed the only thing capable of making me feel grounded, I gave him total access to my body.

"That's it, baby. So fucking wet for me." Hale gave constant reassurance in the boudoir, which was how he initially got me to sleep with him. He also excelled at the dirty talk. "You want my cock?"

"Yes," I panted, already near release.

Fingers working, he bit my shoulder, the scrape of his teeth tormenting me closer to climax. "Whose tight little pussy is this?"

"Yours. All yours."

For Hale, nothing was sexier than my devotion and loyalty. As long as I assured him that he was the only man I wanted anywhere near my body he was set.

"I love these thick thighs." Withdrawing his touch, he gave me no time to whine as he hitched my hips and flicked the skirt of my dress over my ass, then landed a possessive slap. I yipped and he squeezed my flesh hard enough to make me gasp.

Body folded forward, I leaned into the wall. Hale caressed every inch of bare skin he could reach, leaving me sensitized and ready to shatter. Aligning our bodies, he held me possessively. There was no time to worry that my boobs might be hanging like windchimes or that someone might walk in. All I cared about in that moment was getting him inside of me.

"Please," I begged.

The warm nudge of smooth, hard flesh stretched me and I rose on my tippytoes, sighing in contentment as he seated himself deep. Then, I was fully his. He knew it. I knew it. That's how it always was whenever our bodies connected this way.

"Jesus, Rayne." He bent forward, pressing a kiss to the center of my spine. "There's no place I'd rather be."

I moaned because words were hard when skewered by a massive cock. I didn't call him Big Dick Davenport for nothing.

He ground into me, letting the sensations build until I could take no more. "Hale."

He chuckled, then drew back and pumped hard, giving me little time to do more than feel how sharply his possession claimed me. I was unmistakably his and I'd have it no other way.

His hands closed over mine, pressing them into the wall and I rose on my toes with each hard thrust. He understood my love language perfectly and slowly started to move.

Resting my brow on the back of my hand, he pinned my other hand to the wall, our fingers lacing as his hard, slick body pounded into mine. My cries echoed off the foyer walls. There was a little thrill at knowing Andrew or the gardener could walk in at any moment.

His hand suddenly lifted and tangled in my hair, angling my body back into his. Harder and harder he fucked me, controlled me, shoved into me, and took from me, until there was no denying that I was his. His possessiveness did it for me in a big way and once those shivers started and my body clenched around his hard length, we were done.

He grunted and shoved deep as my sex fisted him like a tight glove. His legs stiffened and his body pulsed, deep inside mine. Tremors shook me from head to toe, every muscle tightening until it gave out in pleasure.

And then I heard him. That soft gasp of vulnerability that validated he needed this as much as I did. That finishing breath that whispered into my soul at a frequency one could only hear in the quiet safety of true intimacy that went beyond any ordinary throes of passion. Finishing with a silent whisper as he always did, those three meaningful words pressed into my skin and all the chaos quieted the moment my body felt his confession more than my ears heard it. "I love you."

He scooped my wilted body into his arms and carried me into the den. Lowering me to the sofa and cradling me to his chest, pressing kisses into my hair. "Is that what you needed, baby?"

"Mmm-hm," I hummed happily, too content to open my eyes.

He simply held me, his fingers combing softly through my hair as our bodies came down from such an exquisite release. I could fall asleep in his arms like that and be content to never wake up.

Cradled softly in the quiet moment, my thoughts drifted into delicate musings. Hale was the best anti-stress drug I'd ever taken.

"Tired?" he asked, stroking a finger delicately down the slope of my nose.

"Comfortable," I mumbled, eyes still closed.

"Take a nap." He pulled the throw off the back of the sofa and covered my legs.

My mouth curved into a smile at such simplified bliss. "Did you ever notice," I slurred, only half coherent. "That the older we get the more our childhood punishments seem like rewards?"

He chuckled. That deep rumble was a familiar comfort I craved to hear several times a day. "Such as?"

"Nap time was torture when we were kids. Now, it's like the biggest treat an adult can get."

"I think you like naps a little more than most." He teased my nipple and I nuzzled closer, getting a chill. "You're the one who taught me about *nappetizers*, after all."

I grinned. Napping before going out to eat just made good sense. That way there was less of a carb crash later.

"It's not just naps, though. Staying indoors used to be a punishment too, but now I'd give anything to avoid the outside world."

His hand stroked soothingly up my bare arms. "Thank you for finishing the meeting with Quinn today. I know that was a lot for you."

It was, and I appreciated him acknowledging that. "I want you to have the wedding of your dreams, Hale."

"I've already got the bride of my dreams."

Gah, he was so impossibly sweet sometimes. I sure hoped the latest wedding-gate news didn't ruin it.

I shifted to sit up, wanting to read the look in his eyes as I explained the situation. "Quinn found the perfect venue, but there's a catch."

"The wedding has to be in three months."

My jaw unhinged. "How did you…?"

"She sent a follow-up email. I read it in between calls."

"Damn, she's efficient."

He nodded with approval. "What are your thoughts?"

How had this come back to me? I wanted Hale to make the final decision so I could go along with whatever he wanted—which was the big, fancy wedding in the city. I knew that. But he also seemed interested in my thoughts.

"You decide."

"No, this is *our* wedding, Rayne. We both have a say."

I groaned. Pressure had a way of making me more indecisive than I already was. Okay, it was time to commit. I could do this.

I drew in a deep breath, looked him in those devastatingly grey eyes, and blurted, "I don't want to wait."

He smiled and I knew I'd made the right choice. "Me neither."

"So, I guess we're getting married in April."

"You sure you're okay with that?"

I hesitated because I was scared. "I am, but that doesn't give us a lot of time. Things will be more expensive—"

"Don't worry about that."

"Okay, but not a lot can change in three months."

He frowned in confusion. "What needs to change?"

I shrugged. "Me."

"Hey." He caught my chin, forcing me to look into his stern eyes. "I don't want you to change. I love *you*, exactly as you are. You're who I want to marry."

"Even if I'm just a big dork who will never be as sophisticated as your fancy friends and someone the tabloids will always poke fun at?"

"Fuck the tabloids. And you're my friend—my *best* friend—the only friend that matters. There are very few people I trust, but I know I can always trust you. That's everything to me. And as far as you being a dork, I happen to find you *adorkable*."

I stilled and smiled. "You know I can't resist you when you're *punny*."

"That's why I do it."

I hugged him. "Thank you."

"For?"

"Loving me."

As he pulled me into a hug, I wondered if he would always make me feel this way, calm but giddy, truly loved and eager to show love. He unraveled me and put me back together in a way that made the world a logical place for a while. I was incredibly lucky to have him, so lucky it inevitably freaked me out if I thought about it for too long.

I mean, what would happen if I lost him? Knowing life could be this good meant very little could ever compare. I could never go back to dating mediocre guys or putting up with crappy sex. No, thank you.

As far as Hale was concerned, I was completely smitten and I wanted to stay that way forever. It wasn't that I loved him. I also loved the way he loved me. No one else had ever gotten it so right. I was in deep, deep *smit*.

Reveling peacefully in the afterglow of great sex, we cuddled on the couch, watching the palms sway in the wind through the panoramic view of the back windows overlooking the Gulf. I loved these quiet reprieves when I felt safe and protected. That's how I thought of Hale. He was my protector.

"Are you stressing about the wedding?"

I glanced up at him. "I'm always stressing about the wedding. But I was also thinking about how nice this is."

"This *is* nice."

It had been a long time since we simply sat like this. The holidays had been busy and then Hale's job inevitably demanded most of his time. My job working for Remington also kept me on the go. Then there was Elara and school and just trying to make everything work at once. The idea of adding an enormous wedding into the mix overwhelmed me.

"Do we have any chocolate?"

He laughed. "I'm sure you have a supply squirreled away. If not, there's always your secret stash upstairs, the one you keep with your vibrator."

"Don't judge. It's my feel good drawer."

"I'm not judging. I like to see you happy."

I sighed. I liked that he liked that. I felt the same, which was why I wanted to go through with this extravagant wedding, so I could see him happy too.

He leaned over and pulled open a drawer. "Jelly beans?"

"No. I want chocolate." I sighed. "Why haven't they started making other candy bars large like Toblerone bars?"

"You're back on this?"

"I'm just saying, I would totally buy gigantic KitKats if they made them."

"I don't know."

"Bigger candy bars could be the solution for world peace."

"I'll notify Nobel." He toppled me to my back. "You think about candy far too much."

"Well, duh, it's candy. There are very few things better than chocolate in this world."

"I could think of a few." He tickled me and I squealed. I loved it when Hale turned playful. It was a side of him only I got to see.

Twisting and squirming, I tried to escape as he blew raspberries on my stomach. I scrambled to pull down my dress and shoved him away with a firm foot planted on his chest. He caught my ankle and laughed, playfully biting my calf.

Any moment we would be interrupted. The phone would ring or Andrew would return with Elara. I treasured these times alone when Hale and I got to simply enjoy each other like this.

That reminded me… "Are my panties still in the foyer?"

"They're in my pocket."

I relaxed. He never missed a beat.

There was still one thing we hadn't addressed and I dreaded even bringing it up. "Hale, I have to ask you something. I don't want to have a drawn out conversation about it. I just need to get it out of the way so I know what to expect."

He sat up, sensing the seriousness of my tone. I also scooted up and crossed my legs, tucking my feet under my knees and fixing my dress.

"What is it?"

"I know we're inviting a lot of people and I get that they're on the guest list because of business associations and political ties."

His brow creased. "Some are family and friends, too, Rayne. I want you to meet everyone."

"Like Noah?"

He gave an apologetic smile. "Are you upset I didn't clear that with you?"

"No. You can have whoever you want as a groomsman. I just never heard you mention him before."

"When Noah got married I was in his wedding. It seemed appropriate."

"It's fine. That's not what I'm worried about."

"What then?"

I should just come out and ask, but I knew there was no delicate way to drop her name into conversations. Every time she came up the atmosphere changed as if an atom were fractured open. "What about Jasmine?"

He drew back and scowled. "Why the fuck would she be invited to our wedding?"

"I don't know, because she's married to your father." That didn't help.

His scowl darkened. "Their marriage is a business arrangement. My father wouldn't dare bring her to what should be the happiest day of our lives."

Did he really expect the wedding to be our happiest day? The fact that he assumed I might also see it that way alarmed me. "Elara's birth was the happiest day of your life, Hale."

He took my hand and squeezed. "Then this will be my second."

I smiled, wondering what would be mine. Probably the day after the wedding when all the wedding stuff was over and we were finally husband and wife.

"Listen to me. Jasmine is no longer a part of our lives. She's living in Europe and that's where she'll stay. My father wants nothing to do with her and I want less. Don't worry about her. She can't touch our happiness. Trust me."

I did trust him, but after everything Jasmine pulled over the last year, trying to use Elara as leverage in a custody battle to get more money out of the Davenports, I would never trust her. That woman was more than Hale's ex who cheated on him with his father. She was evil.

She used her pregnancy as a meal ticket, at first expecting a large payout with a tidy visit to a clinic, followed by a lengthy vacation to recover. But when Hale stepped in, her expectations changed.

Despite his father's atrocious betrayal that resulted in pregnancy, he couldn't stand by and watch part of his family disappear. Hale did everything he could to protect Elara and see that she made it safely into this world, at which point he adopted her. After the delivery, Jasmine was supposed to be on her back-stabbing way. But like an unwanted chin hair that won't quit, the bitch kept coming back.

Jasmine saw Hale's unconditional love for

Elara and used it against him. She never wanted to be a mother, yet she threatened to take Elara away if she wasn't paid more. In the end, the cost of her silence and Hale's peace was steep. His relationship with Remington would be forever changed. And now, Jasmine was technically married to his father, in a cold, contractual, loveless marriage where they never saw each other, but Elara was safe.

"I just feel like that woman can't rest knowing you're happy. She always feels entitled to a portion of your joy."

"That bitch will get nothing but misery if she tries to come near me or my family ever again, understand?"

I swallowed and nodded tightly, relieved but also regretful I brought her up. It was the only time I saw Hale truly lose his composure. She was the root of his territorial nature and deep seated trust issues. That woman could transform his usually agreeable personality into a frigid wasteland at the drop of a hat, which was why I hardly ever mentioned her name.

No one knew what Remington had done. Barrett suspected, but never actually asked. Seraphina assumed Elara was Hale's biological daughter and Hale never intended to correct her assumption. As far as he was concerned, Elara was his. And, in all reality, she truly was Hale's.

Coming from a father who abandoned me in diapers, I recognized more than most the selflessness of Hale's actions. Elara might never fully know what an incredible thing her father had done for her.

"Will Remington bring Odette to the wedding?"

He scoffed. "If they're still together."

"It's in three months."

"He moves fast."

That was true. Jasmine was his fifth marriage and Odette had lingered longer than most. According to stories I'd heard, Remington's lovers typically had a very short shelf life.

"Well, I hope he does. I like Odette. I like the way your dad acts when he's with her."

"Baby, let me give you some advice. Never get attached to any of my dad's women. He changes lovers as frequently as most people change their shoes."

I curled my lip, disliking such a depraved view of the man I adored. "Gross."

Contracts Can Be So "Prey"

I HAD MADE the crucial mistake of bitching about the tabloids to Remington. As a man, Hale's father had very little patience for feelings and what he considered bullshit. As a boss, he only wanted to spend time addressing problems with solutions.

"Jesus, Meyers, that's what I call a cheap shot." He paged through the latest exposé of my contorted face against the backdrop of his beautiful son. "What the hell happened to your face in this one?"

I snatched the magazine out of his hands. "I was eating a jelly donut and I forgot napkins!"

His silver eyes rolled under his bushy grey brows. "Look, if you're going to be a part of this world, you need to anticipate an audience. Someone's always watching. Don't give them so damn much. Do your hair once in a while."

"My hair is done!"

He glanced up at my head and grimaced. "If your aim is a good photograph, fix yourself up and pay for one. Stop assuming the position of the victim and get control of the situation. Have an engagement shoot. Then sell the photos to the tabloids. Hell, if you were using your head, you'd realize you could even make some money out of their interest. Instead, you're sitting here, bitching to me about it in the middle of the work day. Get control of this thing before you give them all the power. You're going to be a Davenport for Christ's sake."

He was right. This was our wedding and our story. With a little planning and self-care, I could totally take control of the narrative and redeem my image so the world didn't think Hale was marrying Quasimodo on crack.

That night, when Hale got home, I told him about his father's suggestion. He rarely liked admitting Remington was right, but he also hated when I felt less than everyone else.

Hale was always game for boosting my confidence at any cost. "Would a professional photo shoot make you happy? We can have PR work up a few wedding shots to generate positive press."

"A tequila shot would make me happier," I joked.

"I'm serious, Rayne. We can arrange a shoot if that's what you want."

"I want *them* to understand why you love me and stop over analyzing all the reasons we don't make sense."

"We make perfect sense." He smiled in that bless your heart sort of way. "Baby, they don't want to understand. They want to sell headlines. You have to stop worrying about this."

"Says the man they adore. They act like you found me in the fish market shaking a tin cup full of rusty nails and coins."

He laughed. "Nobody thinks that."

"Well, they're trying really hard to sell a similar storyline."

"Then we'll have a photo shoot and offer an exclusive interview that clears the air. You can tell them whatever you want."

"Really?"

"Yes, but they're never going to understand why I love you or why I'm marrying you. This isn't real journalism. It's trash. They don't care about the facts. Please try to grasp that."

I sighed. In the past, there had been some less flattering articles about Hale, but since we started dating the papers changed their position on Remington Davenport's eldest son. Getting engaged seemed to put him in a more flattering light—a handsome, wealthy bachelor about to settle down.

Maybe Hale just had a thicker skin than me.

I considered the interview. Did I want all that attention? "Like a television interview?"

"We could do television or print. There are ways for us to leak whatever paints us in the most flattering light."

"But what if they twist things around?"

"Then we sue the balls off of them and make their life hell. Don't give them so much power, baby. They're following you because you're irresistible. You shouldn't doubt yourself."

My face pursed. "You're biased."

"Completely." He kissed the tip of my nose.

"But I'm not alone. Millions of men wish they had you. Which is exactly why I claimed you first."

I rolled my eyes and shoved him away.

I didn't want to be a weak woman who constantly doubted herself. Before this blinding spotlight on our life, I never used to be. And, deep down, I wasn't. I liked me. I liked my life, my job, and I especially liked my future husband. What I disliked was the light the media tended to cast me in. They had no idea who I was, yet they continued to tell the world about a character with my name they completely fabricated from assumptions and shitty pictures.

But maybe he was on to something. A photoshoot and polished article would give me a much needed sense of control where the tabloids were concerned. It would also give me a chance to show the world the lovable little sidekick I was.

"Okay. Let's do it."

Hale's schedule was gridlocked with meetings and travel for the next few weeks, but we managed to squeeze something in. The photo shoot would take place as soon as Hale returned from Tokyo.

I was feeling pretty calm and in control now that we had a plan. Everyone seemed to agree that an exclusive interview would redeem me in the critical public eye.

I'd called Seraphina for some fashion advice. "I love this for you, Rayne. I insist on sending you something to wear. Something to bring out the green in your eyes, but also something that doesn't strobe or clash with Hale's golden coloring.

I hadn't realized my appearance required such an in-depth strategy session. But I trusted Seraphina's taste and was happy to promote her clothing line publicly. "Whatever you think. Just remember, I'm still holding onto some holiday weight." And Thanksgiving weight, and baby weight, and new job weight, and there was the usual organs and flesh and bone weight. "It's probably wise to size up."

"I know your size, Rayne. I've dressed you before."

This was true.

Things were working out. The wedding venue was booked, and Quinn was currently on the lookout for a ceremony location to host the rooftop wedding Hale envisioned.

No one but me seemed concerned that it might rain on our wedding day. Or snow. And wasn't it colder at high altitudes?

New York only saw April snow about once every ten years. But once in a while, extreme blizzards blew through. It had been more than a hundred years since the largest recorded snowfall, so statistically speaking, a whiteout seemed overdue. Sure, those storms were freak incidences, but stranger calamities have been known to happen to brides on their wedding days, and calamities happened to me *every* day.

To play it safe, I told Seraphina to look for a fur shawl to go with my gown. Snow or not, fifty stories high had to be cold in April in New York.

When the clothing for the photo shoot arrived, I was pleasantly surprised. Phina sent multiple options with all the trimmings. She thought out every detail and her packages included everything from panties to earrings, plus a sweet little note telling me to keep the items I didn't use for the shoot for future events.

"I should have her work on my mood board," I told Elara as I lifted the various blouses and dresses from the tissue. "Your aunt has more style in her pinkie finger than I have in my entire body."

Elara babbled and pulled a crinkly caterpillar down from the bed. The brightly colored bug began to play *Mary Had a Little Lamb* for the hundredth time that day.

"What was Auntie Phina thinking with this?" I lifted a lace thong out of the box then several more. "These must be for your father."

Elara cooed and laughed and I bent forward to join the fun.

"Yes, they are! Because your daddy's a big pervert who loves to rip off mommy's undies!"

As soon as *Mary Had a Little Lamb* ended it started again. I needed to burn that toy.

The last box was full of tiny garments that looked sized for a small child. "What the hell is this?"

I tugged the industrial-grade spandex. The rubber-lined shapewear hardly stretched when I pulled it. No way this scuba gear was fitting over my ass. At the bottom of the box was another note.

"Just try it." I grimaced at the shapewear and tossed the note back into the box. Then I shut the door and looked at Elara. "You never repeat what you're about to see here today. Got it?"

She cooed and I took that as agreement.

The next ten minutes passed with me slipping and sliding from the bed to the floor as I tried to squeeze too much blubber into too little material. The tight fabric had absolutely no give. A woman would have to be a contortionist to get into such a garment smoothly.

The undergarment only covered half of my belly and my boobs were bursting from whatever torture device this was. Glancing at the mirror was a mistake. I looked like a partially exploded can of biscuits.

I couldn't get the thing off fast enough. But there was really no graceful way to quickly slip out of tight, rubber-lined clothes, so the exit was just as messy as the entrance.

When I finally pried it off and could breathe again, I collapsed onto the bed in a full sweat and panted. "Fuck that noise."

Why was the fashion industry so dead set on women's discomfort?

Over the next few days, I tried to get used to wearing thongs, but they felt like a constant wedgie. I was definitely more of a granny-panty kind of gal, and those lacey little slingshots were strictly for days when Hale was around. My sore ass was in full agreement.

I used the remaining time Hale was away to catch up on work. Remington had me reviewing reports for data leaks, and I had a term paper due for my finance course.

Pursuing my MBA gave me new insight at work. I wasn't sure I'd ever chase the life of a tycoon, but Remington did offer a substantial raise if I earned my masters, so I figured why the hell not. Besides, I liked school.

I never would have picked a business degree for

myself, but since working around the Davenports I discovered a lot of new interests. I now liked sex, playing the stock market, and sniffing out espionage—all things I never knew I enjoyed a year ago.

I didn't know why Remington loved me enough to take an interest in my future. He'd been that way even before I'd gotten engaged to his son. And he certainly didn't take such an interest in his other employees. But I was glad he did. I loved the grumpy old bastard and his interest made me feel important.

Sure, he still threw out insults and called me incompetent with the rest of them, but we also shared countless heart-to-hearts. I wasn't even sure he shared his feelings with his children the way he sometimes shared with me.

I loved him too. We trusted each other, and I knew I could go to him with any problem and he'd fix it, even though I wasn't supposed to do that anymore, on account of it really pissing Hale off.

Hale and his dad operated on a strange frequency of disapproval and acceptance, sort of like two magnets drawn together that could never touch. They were very similar, yet totally different.

Hale was selfless and loyal. Remington was self-serving and narcissistic. All of his children craved his approval, but the man rarely handed out praise. They'd deny it, but they all lingered in his orbit like a nest full of fledglings, mouths open and waiting for any crumbs of affection daddy might drop.

It was a sad sort of dysfunction, but the Davenports seemed incapable of operating any other way. I knew Remington loved his kids. He just didn't know how to show it. Unfortunately, he had no such struggles expressing his disapproval, so things were always a little off-kilter.

Elle came by after work for a fashion show. "I can't believe she just sent you all of this. Ray, this is like thousands of dollars' worth of designer clothing."

"Please don't tell me that." That sort of money was nothing to the Davenports, but to me it was the difference between a dependable car and the current death rattle I drove on a daily basis. "Now I feel bad. Do you think I should send them back?"

"No! That would be insulting."

I bit my lip. "Fine."

"Try on the green dress."

As I modeled each outfit, Elle gave me her opinions, but she kept glancing at her phone. "Are you texting someone?"

"No, I signed up for this dating app."

"What?" In that moment, nothing else mattered. "Why? What about Barrett? Are you guys okay? Did something happen? Why didn't you say something?"

"Ray, relax. Everything's fine. I'm just checking my options."

"But...why?"

She shrugged. "You never know."

Did Barrett know? Signing up for a dating app seemed extreme. "Are you just looking or are you actually talking to other guys?"

"I literally just opened an account this morning. So far, I've only gotten immature DMs. It's like tinder-garden out there."

I nodded. "So maybe just stick with Barrett. You two are great together."

She looked up at me but said nothing.

"What aren't you telling me?"

"Ray, you know how guys like Barrett are. They never stay for long in one place."

I frowned. "You're not just some random chick, Elle. Barrett knows you're my best friend. He would never do anything to hurt you."

"Because I won't let myself get hurt. It's wise to have options."

Everything about this seemed like a bad decision, but she had to have her reasons. "Just don't make any hasty decisions without talking to him first, okay?"

She sighed. That was the most I would get out of her in terms of agreement.

In the end, we both agreed the cream jumpsuit looked best with my eyes and hair.

"That, with those emerald earrings—stunning." Elle gave a chef's kiss to the air.

I chewed on the corner of my thumbnail, debating. "It's really white."

"So don't eat or drink while you're wearing it. It's a photo shoot and an interview, Ray. You'll be fine."

She was right. I could keep an outfit clean for an hour or two.

"Those earrings make the look. Does Hale have a matching tie?"

"Probably." He had ties and cufflinks in every color.

I grabbed the emerald earrings and headed into Hale's dressing room.

"Whoa." Elle stopped at the door and stared. "I'm getting heavy Fifty Shades vibes."

I snorted, no longer phased by the impressive French architecture, stunning glass cabinetry, dark wood, and ambient lighting. "His ties are over here."

I slid open a wide, shallow drawer and found a selection that would make Gucci himself swoon. Holding out the earrings, I tried to find a green tie in the right shade.

"How about this one?" Elle lifted a deep aquamarine that was more teal than green, but it looked great against the earrings.

"Perfect."

"Oh, look! He even has a pocket square to match." Her gazed scanned the masculine dressing room. "He's so organized."

"I know. Put everything back the way we found it."

"You should find a shirt that matches the cream of your suit."

"Good idea." I went to get the jumpsuit while Elle looked for cufflinks. When I returned, she was sitting on the upholstered ottoman reading something. "What's that?"

"I don't know. It has your name on it."

I hung up the jumpsuit and crossed the dressing room floor. "Where did you find it?"

"In that drawer. I was looking for cufflinks." She held the thick sheaf of papers out to me and I took them.

Flipping the document open, I lowered to the leather club chair. *This agreement is between Hale Dav-*

enport and Rayne Meyers, collectively the "parties" or indi-
vidually a "party"…

"It looks like some sort of contract."

I scoffed. "It's a fucking prenuptial agree-ment." My stomach soured as I realized he'd hidden this from me. "Why would he have this?"

"Isn't that self-explanatory?"

I shook my head. "But I'm not after his money."

"And I'm sure he knows that, Ray. This is just a precaution. More weird stuff rich people do."

I frowned and closed the packet. My stare locked on the cover page where both our names were typed. I slid it back into the manilla envelope. "Where did you say you found this?"

She pointed to a drawer. "In there. Are you going to tell him you saw it?"

"I don't know." Forgetting about the cufflinks and shirt, I left the dressing room.

Elle followed me down to the kitchen where I proceeded to rip into a tray of Oreos. My thoughts spiraled as I chewed through my emotions.

How long has he been hiding that?

When was he planning on springing it on me?

Should I read the whole thing before he comes home?

A cold sensation settled in my chest and I closed the cookies. "I think I need sleep."

"Okay." Elle grabbed her purse and stepped into her shoes. "Call me if you want to talk."

"Uh-huh." The door clicked behind her and I set the alarm once I heard her car start.

Good thing I had the foresight to take the cookies with me, because I couldn't sleep. My mind was going a mile a minute. And around three in the morning I found myself back in Hale's dressing room, reading over the entire contract.

I wanted to call Remington, but Hale was his son. He needed to take Hale's side.

I scoffed. This was probably Remington's idea. He was well-versed in gold diggers and betrayal. Somehow, I was dumb enough to think Hale and I were above that toxicity, but I guess I was wrong.

The next two days were spent working on wedding things. No matter what I found hidden in Hale's closet, I still wanted to marry him. But now more than ever I felt like I had something massive to prove.

And, if I somehow failed at this marriage, which was a pretty probable possibility being that not a lot of my big plans had panned out, the fallout would destroy me. Davenports had a habit of always coming out on top and I never wanted to be in an oppositional position to one, especially Hale. He could be so cold and cunning when his survival instincts kicked in. Could he be that way with me? I'd personally watched him pay people off and move on with nothing more than cold indifference. The thought of him treating me indifferently was my worst nightmare.

As much as I loved him, I knew he had a vicious side when pushed too far. I never wanted him to react to me the way he reacted to the mention of Jasmine or the other people who betrayed him. I just wanted him to love me.

I finally fell asleep around dawn, but those pesky fears lingered. Now I needed to decide if I should play dumb or confront Hale. Both options left me with a shitty feeling.

Don't Forget to Floss

HALE'S FLIGHT came in the morning of the photo shoot. His luggage had been delayed, so he told me to head over to the studio and start without him. How the hell was I supposed to take an engagement photo without a fiancé?

I packed our clothes and had Alphonse drive me there so that I could ride home with Hale. The closer it came to facing him the more conflicted I became. I wished I never saw that contract, but I had.

Maybe I was making too big of a deal about the prenup. Hale had a lot of money and I had none. It was just good sense to protect his assets. He'd been burned before. But I never betrayed him and it hurt to think that he needed that sort of insurance on our love.

Once I arrived at the studio, I was surprised to see television cameras and private dressing rooms. This was a lot more involved than anything I'd envisioned.

A man with a clipboard led me to a dressing room incorrectly labeled *Mrs. Davenport*. I was still Rayne Meyers.

As soon as I stepped inside, I was on sensory overload. An enormous bouquet of purple roses sat on the vanity beside a basket of artisan chocolates, a card stuffed deep within the blooms.

"Congratulations on your upcoming nuptials. Sincerely, The Dailey Crew." That sounded cold and impersonal.

"Knock, knock." A beautiful brunette came into the dressing room. "You must be Rayne. I'm Symone, your makeup artist."

"Oh. Hi." I hadn't realized I'd have someone doing my makeup, but that was fine because I must have done such a pitiful job that Symone hadn't realized my makeup was done.

As soon as I was seated, she began washing my face and applying some sort of cold mask she claimed was packed with vitamin C. "So," she said, once my face was wrapped like Hannibal Lector's. "What's he like?"

"Who?"

Symone laughed. "Hale Davenport, your fiancé."

Sexy, territorial, distrustful, endowed... "He's private, sort of reserved."

"Mmm, the strong silent type." She rubbed lotion into my hands and massaged my fingers. "Are we married to this nail polish? If you want, I can take it off and put on a fresh color."

I had just painted my nails that morning. "Sure."

"How about his brother? I used to have such a

crush on him. That one underwear ad he did on the beach in black and white—good Lord, I had some filthy thoughts that day. That man was the source of many sexual fantasies."

"Yup. All the ladies love Barrett."

"Is he nice?"

Protectiveness knifed through me. The Davenports weren't godlike to me. They were people. Family. And I didn't like gossiping about them. "They're all pretty wonderful."

When the hairstylist, Jenna, arrived, the attention was off of me for a while as the two women chattered about people I didn't know, people I suspected they worked with regularly.

By the time the mask peeled off, Jenna was knuckle-deep into my roots, massaging products into my hair and using various hot irons to give my drab brown locks some much-needed body.

I silently sat there, mostly staring at Symone's boobs as she worked on my face or looking her awkwardly in the eye as she gave short commands like *open, shut, look down.* I smiled, made fish faces, and puckered exactly when told and by the time they were finished, I didn't recognize the woman in the mirror.

"Whoa."

"Didn't realize you were such a bombshell, did you?" Jenna said, proudly packing up her tools.

"Mr. Davenport's going to love it. Should I send him in for a sneak peek?"

"Hale's here?" My heart tripped against my ribs and raced into a sprint.

"He's in the room next door. You know men.

They just have to dress. He's been waiting and is probably bored out of his mind."

Hale was here. Why did that make me more nervous than usual? "Should I get dressed?"

Symone removed the black cape that had been protecting my clothes. "Your clothes are all freshly steamed. Dress and I'll send him over in a few minutes."

Relieved to finally be alone, I examined my reflection. My eyes were smoked out with shimmering greys and dramatic black coal. The false lashes Symone applied were so heavy every blink clicked. They looked like caterpillars sleeping on my eyelids.

My hair swept into the full-bodied up-do of a dangerous CEO. I looked beautiful but scary, not at all like myself.

Stripping out of my clothes, I unzipped the jumpsuit.

"Rayne?"

"N—naked!" The door opened and I gasped, covering my front.

Hale quickly slipped inside, locking the door behind him. "Wow, look at you."

I blushed and looked away, embarrassed by how silly these lengths must appear to him. "It looks like I'm trying too hard."

He crossed the room. "No, it doesn't. Why are you hiding yourself?" He caught my wrists and gently pulled them to my sides so he could see my lace bra and panties. "These are new." His finger grazed my breast where the scalloped edge of the bra curved against my chest.

"Your sister sent me some lingerie."

"I'll be sure to thank her." He glanced at my ass where the thong disappeared between my cheeks and grinned with approval. "What's wrong?"

I found a prenup hidden in your closet, I wanted to say. But instead, I shook my head and said, "Nothing. Just nervous."

"About the interview? Don't be. I've done this a thousand times before."

"Gotten married?"

He chuckled. "No, been interviewed. It's like any other press. You give them a few juicy headlines and some good sound bites and they're happy."

I didn't like how he compared it to the interviews he did for business.

"Hey." He cupped my jaw. "You haven't even kissed me yet. I missed you."

Leaning forward, I gave him a chaste kiss on the cheek, worried I might mess up my hair or makeup.

He frowned. "What's going on?"

"Nothing. I need to get dressed."

He glanced at the jumpsuit hanging to my right. "I kind of prefer what you're wearing now." His hand cupped my ass, his fingers sliding dangerously close to business-town and I stiffened.

"Hale—"

"What?"

"My hair—"

"Looks beautiful."

"They're waiting for us."

"So let them wait. I haven't seen you in days."

I glanced nervously at the door.

He caught my chin and turned my attention back to him. "You're always like this whenever I'm gone for more than a few days." He pulled my back against his front. His hand slowly glided down my bare stomach, his words whispering close to my ear. "Shy." His fingertips edged closer to my panties. "Nervous. It reminds me of that first night we spent together. Remember?"

His thumb teased lower and I sucked in a sharp breath. "Yes."

"You were so set on not enjoying yourself I had to practically force you to let me kiss you here." He slipped his finger under the lace and I shut my eyes. "This always calms you down when you're nervous, doesn't it baby?"

"Me nervous?"

"You. Nervous. Like you are now." He slid the panties past my hips and they fell to the floor. "Relax." His mouth teased my neck, then my shoulder. His lips trailed softly over my skin as he slowly turned me.

"Hale, they're waiting for us."

"Let them wait." He kissed my breasts, teasing my nipples into sharp points. "I'm not leaving this room until I taste my future wife."

A stuttering breath skipped into my lungs as he pressed another finger inside of me. I gripped the vanity at my back for balance.

"That's it, baby." He nudged my thighs apart and purposely took his time to make his point. He was powerful Hale Davenport. The world waited for him. "There's my good girl." He sucked my nipples and slowly fingered me. "So wet. Did you miss this?"

"Yes."

"I missed it too. When I was in meetings, I'd find myself getting hard, thinking about how I wanted to eat you for breakfast, lunch, and dinner as soon as I got home."

We really didn't have time for more than a quick finger bang and an—Oh, he was going down. Okay.

The first swipe of his tongue had my knees buckling. He strummed his thumb over me and I moaned, my grip on the vanity searching for purchase as he pulled me closer. I caught his shoulders, gripped his neck, lost myself and forgot where we were as he made a feast of me. Moaning and arching, I angled my hips toward his mouth and fisted his hair, holding him close as he tortured me in the most delicious sense.

When it came to making me come, Hale was a fucking *vagenius*. The man could literally get left in the middle of the tundra, during a 1920's dust bowl, blindfolded with no compass or map, and he'd still find the G-spot faster than most men could find their own nose.

Moans morphed into sensual sobs as he pressed deeper. Fingers pounding deep, he groaned against my sex. Then I was coming.

Sloppy. Wet. Hale didn't care. As a matter of fact, he preferred it. The more I came, the more satisfied his groans of pleasure sounded. He lapped up every last drop, not pulling away until his lips glistened and the small dressing room reeked of sex.

I was useless. Slouched against the mirror, I sprawled before him, panting and twitching. Aftershocks ripped through my body, shooting shivers up my spine.

He stood, adjusting his suit into place with one sharp tug as he grinned at me with cocky satisfaction. Dragging a thumb over his lower lip, he sucked it clean. "To think, you almost told me no."

I rolled my eyes. "No one tells you no."

"That's right." He caught the back of my neck and wrenched my body forward, our mouths only a breath apart. "Now kiss me like you fucking missed me."

The second my lips parted his tongue stole into my mouth, possessive and demanding. The taste of my release mingled with his heady desire, and my body caught fire again.

My hand went to the front of his suit pants, stroking his engorged cock through the material. "Do we have time—"

A startling knock pounded sharply on the door, shattering the moment like a dart through a water balloon.

"Two minutes," someone yelled from the other side of the wall.

"Oh, my God." I turned to the mirror and gasped in surprise. My varnished hair and shellacked makeup still looked flawless, but my cheeks were rosy and my lipstick was gone.

I looked at Hale and pointed to his crotch. "You need to fix your hair and do something about *that*."

"You could do something about it."

"In two minutes? Doubtful. I still have to get dressed." I rushed from the vanity to get my clothes, but he caught my wrist.

"Rayne. I'm not going out there until you put my cock in your mouth."

"Hale…"

He arched a brow.

"Fine."

I tossed a throw pillow to the floor and dropped to my knees. He crossed his arms and chuckled.

Was he messing with me? "What's so funny?"

"Nothing. You're hot. I was just laughing at how lucky I am."

I blushed. And that's exactly why he got his way in moments like this. If I was hot it was only because he made me that way. "Are we doing this or not? I still have to get dressed."

He unzipped and stepped closer, cupping the back of my head and giving me little time to do more than part my lips as his hard cock slid to the back of my throat with purpose. He groaned and a delicious calm settled over me.

I actually loved doing this for him and regretted that we only had two minutes. I let him fuck my mouth like he wanted because I wanted that too, but after a few quick pumps, he was zipping up.

"That's it?"

"For now."

How did he do that? How did he cut himself off from pleasure and not even break a sweat? His discipline was mind-boggling compared to mine. I was the one blowing him, yet I felt ripped off.

He glanced over his shoulder. "They're going to knock again in about ten seconds."

"Shit."

He helped me off the floor and I rushed to put my panties back on. I quickly stepped into the jumpsuit. "Can you zipper this?"

"Take a breath, baby. Without us, they have no story."

That was true, but I still hated making people wait. I didn't want them to think we were rude or entitled or having sex in the dressing room.

Hale fixed his hair with a quick swipe of his fingers. I swear, the beautiful bastard looked like runway material on his worst day. So unfair. But he still had an enormous boner.

He glanced at me through his reflection in the mirror. "What are you grinning about?"

"Nothing. Just thinking how dreamy my boyfriend is." *And how embarrassing dicks could be.*

"Fiancé," He corrected, reaching into his pants and making a quick adjustment.

Another knock pounded, startling me again even though it was expected.

"Time," that same voice called.

"Ready?" Hale asked, before flipping the lock.

"As I'll ever be." The moment I stepped into the hall I realized my crucial mistake. "Shit."

Hale paused. "Problem?"

"I think I put my underwear on backward."

"I'll tell them to wait."

A woman with a clipboard appeared at the end of the narrow hall. "We're all set up this way, love birds"

I waved away Hale's concern and whispered, "It's fine."

Hale frowned. "Rayne, if you need to change, they'll wait."

I didn't want to cause any more delays. I also didn't want anyone to hear that I was such a hot mess I could put a thong on backwards.

"No. I'm good. Let's do this." Before he could argue, I headed down the narrow hall, the lace thong of my panties flossing my vagina with every step.

The photographer was a man named Viktor who took his job very seriously and spoke in a thick Russian accent. In his black wool turtleneck and pants, he looked exactly as a photographer should look in my opinion.

It was a lot of awkward posing and requests for unusual expressions. Apparently, smiling wasn't *en vogue* anymore. I tried my best to follow the photographer's instructions and take this seriously because the last thing I wanted was another picture of me looking like Hale's embarrassing sidekick, but there was a string chafing my clit, expectations made me sweat, too much direct attention gave me the shakes, and these five-inch heels weren't made for functionality. So overall, I think I looked like a nervous pickpocket with a glandular problem.

Occasionally, when Hale and I were instructed to stare into each other's eyes, a giggle slipped out.

"Try not to smile," Viktor said from behind the camera.

But being told not to smile only made me want to laugh more. It was like an intense staring contest. Hale's eyes creased at the corners as he seemed to challenge me in a game of who would break first.

"Great." The camera snapped several times.

"Rayne, now I want you to look at Hale as if he just proposed."

I thought back to that night and my shock.

"No, no. You're happy," Viktor coached. "You should look elated. Maybe you're in awe. Try not to look so scared and confused."

But I had been confused when Hale proposed. Then terrified, then saddled with the worst case of relentless imposture syndrome I'd ever experienced. Cinderella probably went through the same shit when she traded in her dustpan for pearls.

Hale—at ease like a fucking catalog playboy— met my gaze and smirked. "Try food," he said to the photographer while never taking his gaze off of me.

"Beg your pardon, Mr. Davenport?"

Why did it seem like everyone addressed Hale with the utmost respect and I was the tiresome toddler being lured with lollipops and shiny things?

"Talk to her about beignets. She loves food."

Great. I was now as trainable as a puppy.

"You like beignets, Rayne?"

Here we go… I narrowed my eyes at Hale. Food lust was private talk.

"Imagine you're surrounded by snowy powdered sugar and delicate treats."

I rolled my eyes, holding the awkward pose exactly how Victor positioned us. "I'm not sure I know what you want."

"We want to see your love for Hale. The audience wants to read the affection in your eyes. What is it you feel for him? Passion? Adoration? Gratitude?"

My brow creased and the feathered awnings

glued to my eyelids flickered annoyingly. This wasn't working for me.

I relaxed my pose and stood normally for a moment. "Can we have a minute?"

The photographer and crew looked bothered by my request, but Hale read the distress in my stare and ordered, "Clear the floor." A moment later we were alone. "What's going on?"

I picked my front-seater wedgie and held out my hands. "What are we doing?"

"We're having our picture taken."

I waved a hand at all the lights and billowing canvases. "But this isn't us. We don't stand like this and stare at each other like ice sculptures. None of this feels real."

Hale caught my hands and pulled me close, pressing a kiss on my knuckles. "That's because the world isn't interested in what's real. They want glamour and highlights starkly contrasted with tragedy and gore. None of this matters. We're only doing it to provide the press with content that doesn't stress you out. We can walk away at any time."

Even if we gave them the best photos and a perfect interview, they'd eventually go back to the gritty snapshots that robbed me of privacy and pride. "I hate that this matters to me."

"The only thing that really matters is that I love you and you love me."

I wanted to live in a world where the superficial judgment of others didn't faze me and I was immune to petty, hurtful headlines, but I simply wasn't that evolved. "Everyone thinks I'm not good enough for you."

"No one thinks that."

I leveled him with a stare. "Hale."

"Fine. But they don't know you. And they don't know me. They only know what my PR team and publicity handlers have intentionally chosen to show them. And I prefer it that way."

"So, was it your PR team that shared the picture of me in the purple hoodie and told them to call me Grimace?"

"I'm not talking about that crap."

"Well, that crap is why the world sees me as the embodiment of a purple milkshake." I rubbed my temples, convinced these professional photos would undergo the same level of scrutiny.

It had always been Remington in the news and Barrett blasted across social media, but never Hale. He was always the low-key one in the background, the tall silent type everyone missed. Now, I felt like I had to mark my territory before droves of gold-diggers showed up to steal the *other* hot Davenport son.

But I had him first. And I wasn't one for competition—mostly because I usually lost. "I wasn't prepared for this."

"What are you saying? I thought we both agreed we were ready for the next step. This is us."

"No, I'm ready to marry you. That's not the problem."

"Then what is?"

"This." I waved a hand at the expensive equipment. "Who are we? I don't even recognize myself. And why is everyone so obsessed with you lately?"

The side of his mouth kicked up. "Because you make me a more desirable man. It's not about me.

It's the beautiful woman at my side." He tucked a strand of hair behind my ear and rubbed my hands in his. "Baby, they're intrigued by our chemistry. Let them obsess over what they can't possibly understand. You get it and I get it. That's all that counts."

His words eased a bit of the pressure in my chest. "Thank you for saying that."

"It's you, baby. I'm far from perfect, and no one expects you to be perfect, but you and me…" He kissed my hands bundled in his. "We're perfect for each other."

"Right there. Don't move." The photographer rushed in with his camera and snapped several shots as I looked adoringly at the man I love beyond my heart's usual capabilities.

I didn't have pretty words to say back, and I was grateful that we were told not to move so there was no expectation for me to speak. But in my heart and in my head I made many promises. I vowed to love this man with every ounce of my being and then I made a mental promise to blow his doors off that night.

After the photo shoot, we were taken to a glass studio with a stark white conference table shaped like a boomerang with orange chairs. The overhead lights were clinically bright. Mugs of water were brought out, and we were told to wait for makeup.

"Why do we need more makeup? Isn't this a print interview?" I shifted uncomfortably in my seat, pretty sure this thong was giving my vagina rug burn.

"They're just covering their bases."

My toes were numb and I wanted out of these shoes. "What does that mean?"

Before Hale could answer we were both fitted with little paper capes to protect our clothing—the kind they used at the dentist's office.

Symone touched up my lip gloss as a man attached a tiny microphone to the lapel of my suit. Then a camera rolled close to the table.

"Hale," I whispered, fully aware that we were mic'd. "Are they recording this?"

He appeared completely at ease while I did camera math in my head. If the television added ten pounds and there were currently three cameras pointed at me like sniper weapons, how did that translate to smartphones and why the fuck were they videoing a print interview?

"Did we negotiate this?"

"It's a part of the option. They want to market the article on social media. That requires videoed soundbites and clips."

"But they're not airing the entire thing, right?"

"Correct. Only the good parts."

Or the embarrassing parts, I feared. My mouth was suddenly dry and the water in my cup was already warm from the overhead lights.

I squirmed, the lace strap of the thong buried between my labia like a cheese slicer carving through a wheel of brie. By the time this was over I was going to need to ice my cooch for an hour.

"Are we about ready to begin?" A young woman appeared, moving quickly to take her seat at the table.

She wore multiple earrings, an edgy vintage T-shirt screen printed with an old *Rancid* label, and a black blazer. Lowering into the vacant chair, she crossed her legs in a hip fashion that screamed youth and plenty of time for yoga in her life.

I instantly knew she was cooler than me. And while she appeared only a few years younger, she was so at ease in her retro eyeglasses and onyx nail polish, that I subconsciously blamed her for why women in their thirties were now called ma'am.

She held no notecards but glanced at a computer screen embedded in the table. The angle of the teleprompter was set so that Hale and I couldn't read whatever was on the screen.

"Ready when you are," Hale said, taking my hand.

Her gaze caught the gesture and she smiled. "Great. Rayne, I don't believe we met. I'm Frankie London."

Of course, she had a badass name to match her persona. This chick was aging me by the minute.

I shook her hand when it was offered and the moment she let go I dropped my hands onto my lap. Why were my hands always so awkward whenever cameras were around? Hale's looked completely natural folded together on the table.

Several red lights glowed from the equipment that the crew pointed our way. I reached for my mug, only to find it empty. Great. I was overheating and parched.

"Let's start with how you two met."

Hale glanced at me, but I had nothing to say. "Rayne was hired to help my father last summer after he suffered a fall."

"Are you a nurse?"

I shook my head. "I was hired as Remington's personal assistant."

"Remington, not Mr. Davenport? Are you two close?"

"He's still my boss."

"And, Hale, how do you feel about your fiancée working for your father?"

Did this woman know that this was a touchy subject? "Rayne and my father have a very special relationship."

"So, would you say he approves of the marriage?"

I frowned. Was this a Remington interview or a Hale and Rayne interview? As far as I was concerned, the world wasn't aware of Hale's rivalry with his dad, and I was one hundred percent sure he preferred it that way.

My protectiveness came out. "Remington is like a father to me."

Frankie grinned. "And soon he'll be your father-in-law. How does your biological dad feel about your relationship?"

I froze. There were very few things that triggered me, but my father was one topic I avoided like a minefield.

"Next subject," Hale said with the authority of a military leader.

"We'll move on." Frankie glanced at her teleprompter. "So was it love at first sight?"

Hale fielded the next few questions. I heard reminiscent mentions of *The Lady Parr*, Remington's yacht, hurricanes, ducklings, and many other bits and pieces from those earlier days of our relationship, but I wasn't fully listening until I heard him mention paprika.

No! My eyes widened as I watched in horror, his words coming out in slow motion as he detailed that humiliating night on *The Lady Parr*. My ears were in denial. He wouldn't tell that story!

But he was.

"She was adorable," he said, smiling at me with such innocence. "Half of her face was swollen to twice its usual size and her S's sounded like T-H's. I think I fell in love with her that night."

I was going to murder him.

Frankie smiled. "And Rayne?"

"Huh?"

"When did you fall for Hale? Was it that same night?"

I thought back. The only thing I could recall was how shocked I was the first time Hale made me come. But I couldn't say that. That wasn't even the moment. But it seemed all I could think of now that I knew it was the wrong answer. Where the fuck were all the right answers? It was like my memories just vanished. *Poof!* Gone. *Voila! Nada.*

"Um…"

Now, not only was Frankie staring at me expectantly, Hale seemed curious as well. Then he appeared concerned. And then hurt. How could I literally think of nothing?

"Flip-flops!" I finally blurted.

"Flip-flops?"

I nodded. "I was coordinating a birthday party on the yacht for Hale's sister and he brought me flip-flops."

"Rayne doesn't like wearing heels," Hale explained. "I also seduced her with ice cream."

Frankie laughed. "So would you say you're the aggressor in the relationship?"

"Definitely."

"As a Davenport, I assume you're used to getting what you want."

"For the most part, but not because I'm a Davenport. I get what I want because once I make the decision that I want something, I become relentlessly focused on the outcome."

Frankie grinned. "And you wanted Rayne."

"Very much."

She turned to me with a grin. "How does it feel to know that you were the central focus of a man as powerful and desirable as Hale Davenport."

It feels wrong, I thought. *Accidental. Make believe. Like the other shoe could fall at any second and my entire world would crumble and burst into flames.*

Thank God I kept my mouth shut long enough to think of a better answer than the first ones that came to mind. "It feels flattering."

She looked at Hale. "Do you find it challenging to manage so many business endeavors and a new relationship?"

"Rayne's the center of my world."

Did he have a cheat sheet or something? How did he always know the right thing to say?

"And how does that work with the other lady in your life?"

My head snapped back to Frankie. What other lady? She couldn't possibly know about Jasmine, could she? Or was she referring to someone else? Because I'd cut a bitch.

"I'm referring to your daughter, Elara," she finished and I instantly relaxed. Of course, she was talking about Elara. *Duh.*

"Rayne was with me the night my daughter was born and she's been a part of her life ever since." He took my hand and squeezed affectionately. "I'm very grateful that my daughter has such a kind and loving role model in her life. Elara and Rayne have an excellent relationship."

"Do you think of yourself as Elara's mother, Rayne?"

This woman had no qualms about getting personal. "I love Elara as if she were my own."

"And how does her biological mother play into your arrangement?"

Her question was met with dead silence. Hale's PR people knew what topics were permitted and which ones were off-limits. No way this woman wasn't provided a list before the interview.

Everyone knew Hale didn't have a baby alone. But no one suspected he wasn't Elara's birth father. Dropping any mention of Jasmine into conversation would forever be the equivalent of a church fart. Something everyone knew was there but most were too polite to discuss or acknowledge.

Frankie, however, just stopped the sermon to play a game of *Smelt It Dealt It.*

Hale wore a serene expression of professional indifference. But he was not unaffected by the mention of his ex. That impenetrable mask was harder than armor and only appeared when he was about to go to war.

Casually, he leaned forward and kept his voice low so Frankie also had to lean closer. In a cool but lethal tone, he whispered, "Stray from the approved questions again, and this interview is over—and so is your career. Do we understand each other?"

Her dark eyes widened as she looked up at Hale with palpable regret. "Y—yes, sir."

I exhaled, knowing there would be no more lines crossed at this table. Frankie might be cool, but no one was cooler than Hale. And if there was one thing Hale took very seriously, it was protecting those he loved.

The conversation turned to wedding plans and Hale kept his answers brief, stating that we were getting married on the East Coast in a non-disclosed location and the guest list would be extensive and exclusively high society.

I could tell Frankie wanted in on that action, but after her mention of Elara's birth mom, there was no way she was getting a press pass.

Ugh. The actual term press pass in association with my wedding day turned my stomach.

When the topic turned to business, Hale was truly in his element. The man could talk about water turbines for days.

I was looked to for simple responses and, honestly, I preferred it that way. If anything, this interview taught me just how uncomfortable and unprepared I was for a life in the limelight.

When that microphone finally came off my lapel I was relieved. Apparently, this was all very normal in the sphere of affluence. Billionaires didn't just do save-the-dates—they did press junkets and publicity tours.

The article would run sometime next week and the payout Hale's people had negotiated was substantial—more than the cost of an ordinary wedding, but probably just the tip on the bar bill at a monstrosity the size of ours.

As soon as we were allowed to change I rushed back to the dressing room and stripped out of the jumpsuit like it was on fire. I tore the thong off and sighed with relief. My poor lady bits were swollen and sore.

Champagne sat in a bucket of ice on the vanity. I grabbed the bottle, choking it by the neck, and shoved the chilled glass between my legs. *"Yahahahah."* I shivered with relief.

Thongs were clearly built for speed rather than comfort. From now on, I was sticking to my ergonomic granny panties.

When I left the dressing room in street clothes with my hair still done and my makeup still on, I felt oddly out of place. I could have washed my face and brushed out the hairspray, but I just wanted to go home. That was until I spotted the table at the opposite end of the hall.

I swear, angels sang and trumpets roared, then I was levitating on a cloud and being carried directly to the enormous display of desserts.

I'd been debating my diet a lot lately, strictly in my head, of course, but I found myself in a constant struggle of hunger versus bride. There was no law saying brides had to be a certain size, but the more I looked at photographs from high-profile weddings the more I realized most wives had waistlines the size of my thigh.

I'd been strongly considering asking Elle to train me into shape after all. But making such a request felt like signing up for an unnecessary root canal.

I stared down at the platter of cookies longingly, knowing there was also a tray of vegetables on the table. Shortbreads, macarons, biscotti, chocolate chip—they were all calling my name. I glanced at the celery and broccoli. The vegetables were strangely silent. Then I was distracted by a tower of cannoli.

"You ready?"

I jumped as Hale appeared. "I wasn't doing anything."

He frowned. "What?"

"Nothing. Let's go." I quickly walked away from the food table, and while I didn't eat the fucking cookie, I mentally debased myself for the next two minutes as if I had.

By the time I was sitting inside Hale's Rolls Royce, I was disgusted with my imperfect body and repulsed by the ongoing mind-fuck the fashion industry and diet culture put me through.

"You hungry?"

"I'm fucking starving!" I all but sobbed.

Hale gave me a concerned glance, then pulled into the parking lot of a pancake house. "Let's get you fed."

Over the next hour, I devoured a stack of buttery buttermilk pancakes loaded with chocolate chips, a side of bacon, and two scrambled eggs.

"Better?" Hale asked when I finally pushed my plate away.

"Yes."

"Let's get one thing straight, Rayne. I like your body exactly the way it is. I have no interest in fucking a bag of bones, and I don't feel like navigating hunger mood swings. I've lived that life before and I'm much happier with the way things are now."

Hale had always been intuitive, but I truly thought I'd been hiding my inner debate with food well. "How did you know…?"

"I can tell when you're denying yourself. One of my favorite things about you is that you're not afraid to indulge in life's little pleasures. So you can drop any notions about losing weight or cutting calories. I know what your body looks like and I happen to find it hot as hell. Got it?"

My lips pressed in a tight smile and I nodded. "Got it."

There was very few things in this world that gave me more pleasure than delicious food, but Hale was one of them. In terms of love, he would always take the cake.

Paging, Fairy Godmother...

CLEAN UP ON AISLE FIVE

SOME PEOPLE HAD *the eye* and some did not. As I stared out over the grey haze of New York City, civilization four hundred feet below, I wondered how this vacant, barren, concrete space was ever going to transform into the warm, romantic wedding space of Hale's dreams. I clearly didn't have *the eye*.

"It's perfect," Hale said. "Great work, Quinn."

The wedding planner smiled, but who wouldn't under such praise? "I was thinking we could section this area off for catering. There are open plumbing hookups in the wall…"

My attention drifted as they walked off discussing various hookups and logistics. This place was *eff*-ing huge. Hale could not possibly know this many people.

Back in Oregon, when couples got married, they typically rented out the fire hall, and even then a partition wall sectioned half the space off. This floor was roughly the size of a football field and Hale and Quinn were worried about making everything fit.

I pressed my forehead to the cold glass and stared down at the yellow cabs and people scurrying about like little ants. It sure looked cold down there. It wasn't much warmer up here and sometimes the wind would blow against the glass hard enough to stir unease in the pit of my stomach.

New York looked nothing like the version Hollywood depicted. I truly wondered why Hale was so set on getting married here.

After our meeting, the wedding planner left, and Hale took me to a private restaurant in Madison Square Park to eat. I really thought coming here would flick on some internal bride switch inside me, but I only felt more intimidated after seeing the space.

Quinn had made a few comments about my mood board being the inspiration for the reception —the mood board I had yet to create because my mood hovered around terrified every time I thought about the ever-growing spectacle of a show our wedding was becoming.

Did it really matter if I picked a pillow? Who would notice such a minor accent amongst the oceans of cold, grey unfinished floor, sprawling views of the endless horizon, or the sea of strangers, and let us not forget the rivers of bride tears shed in secret?

I was just about to tell Hale how I felt when an ear-piercing squeak broke the polite dinner chatter and I was tackled by a hundred pounds of fur-wrapped Cartier.

Startled and thrilled to see Hale's sister, Seraphina, I laughed in shock. "What are you doing here?"

"Did you honestly think I would let you two come to the city and leave without seeing me? When Hale told me you were visiting I insisted we have dinner."

The white-gloved wait staff immediately set a third place-setting and took Phina's coat and gloves.

"So, tell me all about the location. Did you love it?"

Hale looked at me because I was the bride and this apparently was my department.

"It's big."

"Of course. How's the view? April in New York is so pretty. The park's the most vivid shade of green and all the cherry blossoms are in bloom. You'll have the prettiest sunset, just as guests are finishing cocktail hour and sitting down for dinner. You haven't truly seen New York until you've seen it under a pink sky."

I suddenly had a brilliant idea. "Phina, would you like to help me with the mood board?"

Hale's sister gasped and pressed a hand to her chest. "Oh, Rayne, I'd love to!"

For the first time in weeks, I felt true relief. Why had I not thought of this before? Seraphina went to the best design schools in the world and she loved talking about the wedding. Not only that, she adored Hale. It was then that I realized how incredibly lucky I was that she approved of me and welcomed me into the family with open arms.

I glanced at Hale and he appeared to read my

mind. The moment I nodded, he flagged down a waiter and ordered a bottle of *Veuve Clicquot.*

When the champagne arrived, I held up a glass. "There's one other thing I wanted to ask you." Seraphina lifted her glass and smiled expectantly. "Will you be a bridesmaid in our wedding?"

She unleashed another enthusiastic squeal and rushed from her seat to hug us both. "I'm honored!"

Over the next hour, we discussed all things theme and function. The beauty of Seraphina—aside from her indisputable outward prettiness—was her non-judgmental eagerness to help. I had no problem voicing my worries to her and asking for her opinions on various styles and etiquette. The woman had the fine breeding of a debutante and the grooming of American royalty.

"Don't worry about a thing, Rayne. I've got you. The first thing we need to do is hire you a coordinator."

"Oh, Hale's already hired a wedding planner."

She waved away my words. "A coordinator's different. They come in during the final months, which—*ta-dah*—we're here. The coordinator arranges meetings and handles the bride's schedule to make sure you have plenty of time to attend every tasting, fitting, and approval that's needed before the big day. I have someone perfect in mind and I'll have them reach out to you tomorrow. Then you'll need a point person for the week of the wedding. Someone at your beck and call in case there are any last-minute requests."

She turned to Hale. "I assume you'll be staying at the Plaza?"

"I haven't thought that far ahead yet—"

"Well, Hale, the wedding's less than three months away. You need to make these decisions now." She turned back to me. "Daddy has the most divine suite. You'll love it. There's twenty-four-seven butler service and the view is sensational. You'll be right in the heart of Manhattan."

My head was spinning from more than the champagne. "Whatever you think."

"I think Fifth Avenue is a must. Have you finished your guest list yet?"

"We're almost done." I currently had eleven people on mine. Hale had close to three hundred.

"That needs to be your main focus. Now that we have the location, I'll work on the looks and come up with some options for a theme. You two focus on the guest list and I'll have Devyn—he's the coordinator—set up some appointments to interview musicians and whatnot. Then that should bring us to phase four: The Design." She steepled her fingers, wiggling them excitedly in front of her mischievous grin. "At that point, you should probably be staying in the city full-time."

My smile fell. "Wait, what?" I looked at Hale. "We're moving to the city?"

"Only temporarily," Phina said.

But I needed to hear this news from Hale.

He took my hand. "You know what my schedule's like over the next two months. I'll be traveling non-stop for work. Think of this as a vacation, a chance to enjoy the full bride experience."

That sounded absolutely horrific. It sounded like I was being shipped away to curate *his* ginormous wedding and all of this had been decided without even consulting me. I suddenly empathized with all those trust fund kids that got transported to boarding schools when their bazillionaire parents were busy building empires with no time to take care of their family responsibilities.

There was suddenly a totem pole and I was not at the top.

My eyes narrowed. "How long would I be here?"

Was it going to be just me and the butler? What about Elara? I didn't want to be a bride without the groom. Weddings were supposed to be together affairs.

"Just a few weeks."

"A few *weeks*?" Why was this necessary? And why had this been arranged assumed without my knowing?

The waiter appeared with a glass cart and hot plate that he proceeded to flambé. The slivers of bananas went up in flames like my prior calm, and I stared at my future husband wondering why he was suddenly trying to pawn me off on his little sister.

"Rayne," Hale leaned close and whispered, interrupting the fancy banana show.

I ignored him because I didn't want to argue in public.

"Stop ignoring me." His hand settled on my thigh and squeezed affectionately. "I haven't even made arrangements for your stay yet."

I pushed his hand away and buried my own in my lap. "I'm not a child."

He frowned. "No one said you were."

"You didn't even ask what I wanted."

"You didn't give me a chance."

I glared at him as the flambé flames shot into the air. Seraphina's attention was on the server. "It's bad enough I have to spend weeks apart from you because of business. I'm not leaving Elara for that long."

He studied me and a small grin curved the corner of his mouth. "Enough said." He sat back and watched as the waiter plated the Banana's Foster.

By the time we left the fancy art deco restaurant, I decided I didn't care for New York and I wanted to go home—my home that I would only be permitted to stay in until I was neatly moved by my many handlers to my new residence in the Big Apple.

On the flight back to Florida, Hale did that thing where he rested with his eyes closed and his hands folded tightly across his chest. I scowled at him, fully aware he wasn't sleeping and probably just sitting that way to avoid a confrontation.

Once the private jet was cruising at an altitude of around thirty thousand feet, I kicked his shoe.

"Really?" He opened his eyes and scowled at me. "What was that for?"

"When were you going to tell me about New York?"

"I planned to discuss it with you sometime this week."

"You're shipping me off like an unruly child."

"I've already explained that's not the case. No one is shipping you off."

"Sure feels that way."

He cocked his head as if I were totally making this up. "Rayne—"

"Don't Rayne me. Engagements include two people, Hale. A bride and a groom. Getting married in New York was your idea. If anyone should have to live there it should be you."

He sat up and flicked on an overhead light, which immediately signaled one of the staff to check on him.

He held up a hand to the attendant. "Not now." Turning back to me, he said, "Do you not want to get married there?"

My words jumbled in my throat in an impassible traffic jam. I just wanted to marry Hale. I didn't want to parade our life in front of a million strangers and have our relationship on display like some sort of exposé. This whole thing was turning into a circus. "What's wrong with a church?"

Deep grooves formed between his brows. "Is that what you want? When I asked you about your faith you told me Santa was cool and you loved Jewish delicatessens."

"I just don't see why everything has to be so grandiose. And I'm tired of decisions being made behind my back."

"Every single decision has been yours, Rayne. We're all waiting to hear what you want. When I suggested New York, you said you loved the idea. I hired Quinn to help bring *your* visions to life. This whole thing has been about creating your perfect day. How am I suddenly the bad guy being accused of secretly conspiring behind your back?"

When he originally suggested New York I loved the idea, mostly because of the way his eyes twinkled and how his smile lit up when he described his vision. I didn't have a vision, but I could share Hale's. I could picture him waiting for me at the altar, and that was the light at the end of the tunnel, the beacon I assumed would guide me down the aisle. I just never assumed I'd be traveling solo.

He pitched the idea and I agreed. Hale took my word at face value because that's how he typically negotiated big decisions.

My sudden objections probably sounded manic and out of the blue. They were valid and had been festering for some time, but he wouldn't know that since I actively tried to hide any irrational fears from him. I didn't want to shit on his parade and talk him out of his big New York dream, especially after Quinn had worked so hard to find the perfect place and I already agreed to move the wedding up.

"You're right," I said, lowering my stare. "I don't know why I'm acting this way."

"No one is keeping secrets from you, Rayne."

That wasn't true. He had a secret. A very thick, heavy skeleton in his closet, currently stuffed in a manilla envelope at the bottom of his sock drawer. He probably had that stupid contract drawn up specifically for reasons like this. Hale knew how crazy I could get. It was good sense to have an escape plan.

"If you don't want to stay in New York before the wedding, then don't." Irritation showed on his face as he dragged his fingers through his hair. "I just thought it would be fun for you to have a chance to fully experience the city since you've never been there before."

I hated arguing with him. Mainly because I always felt outmatched. Here I was, pissed and feeling discarded when he was only trying to treat me to a fun experience. He didn't understand that he was the secret ingredient to my happiness.

"I do want to experience New York, Hale, but I want to experience it with you." I nudged the side of his shoe with my socked foot.

His frustration morphed into understanding and then regret. "Baby, these business meetings have been planned for months. I can't reschedule."

"I know. And I appreciate you trying to make the best out of a difficult situation, but I honestly don't think I could enjoy an extended stay in such a big, foreign city if you and Elara aren't there to share it with me."

"Then you won't. We'll have the planners take care of everything."

I pouted, unsure if that was the best solution.

He moved to the seat beside mine and lifted the armrest. Reaching across my body, he un-buckled the seatbelt and pulled me into his side. "I love you. I don't want to fight."

I nestled into the crook of his arm. "I'm not trying to make things more difficult."

"You're not." His hand rubbed slowly up and down my arm as we sat in silence.

I realized then that I needed a break from wed-ding-gate. Just one day when we didn't talk about mood boards or gowns or anything else having to do with getting married. I just wanted to be plain old Hale and Rayne again.

I stared down at my hands, one ring finger glis-tening with a diamond large enough to take down the Titanic and another ring finger adorned with a platinum band and a delicate diamond anchor. My thumb caressed the anchor lovingly. Just a few more months and then these rocky seas would calm.

Man-splaining and Martinis

"GIVE ME SOMETHING ELSE TO DO."

Remington glanced up from his iPad, suspiciously gauging my motives over the narrow, rimless lenses of his Gold & Wood eyeglasses. "It's six o'clock, Meyers. Go home."

I'd checked in with Andrew an hour ago and informed him I'd be working late. He promised to give Elara dinner and a bath before putting her to bed. There was no real reason for me to remain at Remington's. Even Myles had clocked out and gone home. But I was operating in full-throttled procrastination and would rather work here than go home and work on wedding-gate.

I lowered to the sofa and sat beside my future father-in-law. "What are you watching?"

He glanced over at me again and frowned. "What's going on with you?"

I so badly wanted to talk to him about Hale and the prenup, but I'd made a vow—for the sake of my relationship with his son—not to concern

Remington in big relationship issues. At least not before giving Hale a chance to address matters first.

I was, after all, marrying Hale, not his father. Their relationship was already volatile and I didn't want to make matters worse.

Plus, Remington would probably view a prenuptial agreement as a necessity. He wouldn't see the issue from my side, or understand how such a contract could be so toxic to a marriage. So there would be no satisfaction in discussing such matters with him.

But I still wasn't leaving. We didn't have to talk about my problems for him to help me avoid them.

I shifted a pillow and made myself comfortable. "We hardly spend any time together anymore."

"We see each other every day, Meyers. I have parts of my own body I see less than your face."

I twisted my lips, unable to deny it.

Removing his reading glasses, he sat back and studied me. "Why don't you tell me what's actually going on?"

Sinking deeper into the sofa, I groaned. "I'm sick of talking about the wedding and if I go home, I'm going to have to face the huge pile of wedding crap that's suddenly become my life."

He chuckled, the gruff, craggy sound condoling and familiar. "I was wondering when you were going to crack." He slid his iPad away and sat back. "Doesn't my son realize you're the kind of woman who—"

I cut him off. "I swear to God, Remington, if you say something offensive that compares my situation to slapping lipstick on a pig or worse, I may cry. I'm overly fragile at the moment."

The engagement had made me hyper-aware of all my shortcomings and the last thing I needed was more criticism.

He rolled his eyes. "I was going to say, you are who you are."

"Oh." Well, that was rather sweet and accepting of him. "You're right about that."

"But if you need some fortune cookie bullshit to feel validated, here it is. A fox can turn from auburn to silver, but changing the coat doesn't change its nature."

I thought about the fox analogy for a moment, not finding it insulting. It was actually pretty accurate since I was being dressed up in furs and diamonds but underneath it all I was still just plain Rayne.

"See? You get me."

"Try not to act so feeble-hearted. The world has enough snowflakes. Rise above the emotional baggage, toughen up, and do what needs to be done. Leave your feelings at the door. That's how success is achieved."

"You think I should leave my feelings out of my marriage?" Of course, Remington would approach this like a business acquisition.

"Not the marriage. The engagement. They're two different things."

"But I'm a bride. Brides are supposed to love this experience."

"Why, because a catalog trying to sell veils and wedding bands says so? Don't be so damn impressionable. They're marketing so women in your situation feel pressured to think that way. It's an advertising scheme—a lucrative one. You should feel proud that you're not falling for the hype. It shows independent thinking and a sign of intelligence. Maybe even a sign that you truly love my son. Plenty of women get married to the wrong man simply because they want the fancy dress and big party."

"I just want to make him proud."

Remington sighed. "Meyers, if you're asking for relationship advice where nothing goes wrong, I'm afraid, even I, can't buy you that sort of assurance. This is marriage. It's a manic institution where the highs are euphoric and the lows can be as gory as enemy lines on the battlefield of the most brutal wars. Trust me, I've had five marriages and my current situation is by far the easiest."

I scoffed. "You never even see her."

"Exactly. Just the way I like it. Help me up."

I stood to offer him a hand, but when I retrieved his cane he waved it away.

I followed as he slowly wobbled into the dining room, heading straight for the bar. "I'd prefer to avoid the battlefield."

"If that's true, I feel bad for you. A peaceful marriage is a passionless one. I had one of those with Barrett's mother. Bored me out of my mind and right into Seraphina's mother's bed. Nothing wrong with a little fighting. It adds some heat."

I thought about the arguments Hale and I had. There had been some doozies. "We only fight when Hale gets jealous."

Remington chuckled.

When he reached the bar, he gripped the ledge

and caught his breath, more winded than usual. I retrieved a bottle of water from the mini fridge and uncapped it. "Here."

He took a sip and sighed, shifting his body onto a stool. "I don't know if Hale's capable of real trust anymore, and I'm sorry for that."

He should be sorry. He was responsible for his son's trust issues. "I'm not interested in anyone but Hale."

"You're young."

"I love him, Remington. I wouldn't marry Hale if I didn't plan to spend the rest of my life with him. I plan to take my marriage vows very seriously."

He studied me for a long moment then nodded. If he had any reservations about my loyalty to his son, he kept them to himself.

"Look, Hale loves you. He knows who you are and he knows what you're not. A wedding is just one day. If you're lucky—or unlucky—your marriage will last the rest of your life. I hope you both get what you want out of the deal."

I hated that he referred to my marriage as a deal.

He handed me a brass shaker. "Fill this with ice."

I scooped several cubes from the hidden freezer into the cup. Remington topped it off with a heavy-handed pour of Straka and added a dash of something from a decanter.

"Hand me two martini glasses."

"Oh, I'm okay—"

"Do as I say." He shook the mixer making too much noise for me to argue again.

I slid him two glasses that had been chilling in the freezer and watched as he poured. The vodka was cloudy and the surface shimmered with slender ice chips.

"There's cheese in the fridge. And get me the olives."

My stomach turned as I located the container of aged blue cheese and the jar of Spanish Queens soaking in brine that he had shipped in from Southern Europe each month. He skewered the olives on a silver pick.

Frowning at the slight tremble in his fingers, I wondered if he was taking the right dosage of his medicine. Since the heart attack, Remington was on blood thinners and several other drugs that could cause tremors. I preferred to think of his shakes as a side effect that could be corrected rather than a symptom of old age. I also intentionally ignored the darkening liver stains on his hands. In my mind, Remington was going to live forever. He had to. That was the only way he'd have time to eventually make amends with his kids.

"Here." He plopped a chunk of cheese into the glasses and slid one very dirty martini in front of me. "It'll put some hair on your chest."

"Oh, good. That'll go great with my wedding gown."

"Which I bet you haven't even purchased yet."

I twisted my lips, confirming his suspicions, and lifted my glass to take a sip. "Here's to passion without pain."

He chuckled. "Cheers."

The cold, briny concoction went down the

hatch like a sword on fire. "*Zoiks!*" I wheezed and sputtered a cough. "That's…something."

"Keep going. A few more swallows and you'll learn to like it."

Where had I heard that before?

Remington was the kind of man who liked to sit in silence with a good cocktail. He once told me too much talking spoils the taste. I couldn't see this martini tasting any worse, so I asked, "Where's Marta?"

"She has the night off."

"No Odette?"

"Not tonight."

"How are you two do—"

"Did you find me lingering around your living room fishing for advice? No, that was you. So let's keep the focus where it belongs."

"Jeeze. Touchy much?" I sipped my martini. My mouth puckered and my eyes instantly watered.

I planned to ask Myles about Odette the next time I saw him. It had been a while since she'd visited and I sure hoped she and Remington were doing okay. "For the record, I wasn't fishing for advice—"

"Yes, you were. You're just not allowed to say it."

I drew back and frowned. "*Allowed?*"

He gave me a pointed look. "Don't get your feminist panties in a twist. You said yourself, Hale has trust issues. Let's not pretend that he likes it when you confide in me."

"That's not why—"

"Sure it is. He doesn't want you to come to me with problems because he feels threatened."

"No."

"Then what is it?"

It was a lot to unpack. I blew out a vodka-scented breath, convinced once again I was a tequila girl.

Remington was the closest thing I had to a father. Unlike his real children, I craved his input.

He told it like it was, even if his views weren't always kind. I'd never met anyone who viewed the world with such singular and impersonal cynicism. He cut right to the heart of matters and that sort of directness worked for me.

But he was also incredibly self-serving and critical, especially where his children were concerned. I wasn't exempt from his criticism, but I also didn't take it as personally as his kids because I wasn't starved for his approval.

When he betrayed Hale, he broke something that might never get mended. It would take a lot of therapy and time for Hale to reach a place where he no longer wanted to punish his father for what he'd done.

Hale accepted my relationship with Remington, but disapproved whenever I confided in him about personal business. It made sense that his father would assume that stemmed from Hale's trust issues, but it had more to do with Hale's need to protect me than anything else.

In his eyes, Remington was untrustworthy, and that made him dangerous to *me* along with everyone else. Hale knew I loved the crotchety old bastard and he didn't want me to get hurt.

Maybe I needed his protection after all, because I naïvely believed Remington would never hurt me. At least not maliciously. Deep down, I knew Remington loved me—differently than he loved his children and very differently than he loved his wives. We were friends.

Hale was a jealous, territorial man. And while his father had betrayed him with women before, poaching directly from his son's bed without a single thought wasted on consequence, I was pretty sure Remington wasn't attracted to me.

But I did love the man and he loved me. Our relationship was paternal, yet safe. He wasn't trying to sculpt me into his image or shoulder me with a billion-dollar legacy. He only wanted to help me where he could and be slightly entertained by the minutia in between.

On some level, I think all the Davenport children were jealous of the way Remington doted on me. Sometimes he was kinder to me than he was to his own kids. But in all fairness, he hadn't raised me. He wasn't responsible for me, and he hadn't had thirty years to hurt me.

Remington wasn't the best father, but he tried his best. Unfortunately, there were times when his best was what better parents might consider the worst.

"Hale just wants to protect me," I finally said.

"You mean protect what's his."

"It isn't like that, Remington. You aren't a threat to him like that anymore. At least not where I'm concerned. He knows our relationship's different."

He turned his glass by the stem and sighed in retrospect.

I sipped my salty martini, with perpetual disappointment. No matter how much I wanted it to grow on me, every sip tasted like I swallowed a mouthful of ocean. But the alcohol was working, so I at least had that going for me.

"Hale wants to put on a big show so that he can show the world—and me—that he won."

I scrunched my nose. "Won what?"

"The prize sitting across from me right now fishing a lump of cheese out of her glass. Jesus, Meyers, it's for flavor not consumption. Leave it alone."

"Sorry." I sucked the vodka off my finger. I hadn't eaten in a few hours and that lump of cheese was the only food in sight.

"Hale thinks he has something to prove."

He was referring to Jasmine—the metaphorical church fart. Unlike the reporter, I knew how to respect a church fart so I silently let the reference pass.

"You came into my son's life just before the shit truly hit the fan."

"I'm sure you can find a better way to describe your granddaughter's birth."

"You know what I mean. Hale was in a bad way and I put him there. It was ugly. Ugly enough to literally trigger my heart attack. Then you showed up and somehow made him happy again."

I grinned. That was probably one of the sweetest things Remington had ever said to me. "Hale's easy to please."

He laughed, hard. "That's not even a little bit

true, but the fact that you think so says a lot about your relationship with my son."

I frowned because I did believe it to be true. Hale valued loyalty. Required trust. He loved physical affection. He hated it when I left sugar granules on the counter by the coffee pot. Sunday mornings on the floor with me and Elara were his absolute favorite. He liked his slippers by the door. These were not difficult expectations and when they were met, he was happy. I wished I was that easy.

Remington sighed. "He never talks with me anymore. He doesn't come to me for advice, and I can't recall the last time he looked at me as more than a business associate."

I smiled sadly. The older Remington became, the more he craved a relationship with his kids, and the more they were disinclined to have one.

They all craved his attention, but after decades of criticism, they'd learned to live without his praise. By not offering it, he'd inadvertently taught them not to need it, so their dependency on his approval was waning. More so for Hale, the eldest of the three and the one who'd dealt with Remington's high, sometimes unreachable, expectations the longest.

"Parenting's hard, Remington."

He glanced at me. "You seem to be a natural at it. So does Hale."

"Elara's easy right now. A high-pitched voice and a dramatic game of peek-a-boo get her laughing. Let's see how good we do once she's old enough to actually start making demands."

He patted my hand. "You'll do fine. You've always been quick on your feet."

I expected to make mistakes where Elara was concerned. So did Hale. But he did everything he could to avoid repeating his father's, which was why he always spoke with gratitude to those he loved. He didn't withhold praise or expect perfection. Remington could try the same, but he no longer had the opportunities he once had to make an impact. A lot of the damage had already been done.

"Your kids love you, Remington."

He lifted a grey, scraggly brow. "Even Hale?"

"Especially Hale."

"Yet he's determined to leave me." He shook his head. "He was the one I could count on. Phina's doing her thing in New York and Barrett…" He scoffed. "Who knows what he'll do once his looks run out."

He'd probably land a role in a soap opera or something. I wasn't sure where beautiful people got recycled once they aged.

"But Hale," he continued. "He was supposed to take over."

I frowned. "We're not going anywhere—"

"You can't say that when you've only ever lived in two places, Meyers. The world's large and you're young. You're in a position—financially speaking—to have whatever life you want. Don't set that aside for anything. Including me. Hale won't let you."

Because it was Hale's money and he'd have the final say. "I'm happy living here."

"Florida could never hold Hale's interest forever. He's built an empire that ensures he'll have global freedom outside of Davenport Industries. Why else do you think he's working so hard to negotiate with Tokyo? Next, it will be the UK, then France, then Germany. He won't stop until he corners the global market."

A wave of unease snaked through my stomach. "But I like it here."

"Come on, Meyers. Why do you think he wants you to fall in love with New York?"

He could have knocked me down with a feather. Was that what this was? Was Hale using our wedding as a billboard to sell me on moving to the business capital of America? Once again, I felt like the last to know.

My face felt numb and not from the vodka. I kept telling myself that after the wedding life would slow down. But according to Remington, things were only going to get busier and bigger. That sort of fast-paced living terrified me and I honestly thought all this travel was temporary. But what if this was what our marriage would always be?

I pushed my martini away. "I have to go."

He frowned. "You look a little green."

"It's probably the old cheese."

He glanced at my glass and sighed. "I told you not to eat it."

What the hell else was I supposed to do? He was dumping all this stressful crap on me, and I hadn't had dinner. I needed grief bacon!

When I got home, Elara was still awake. I lifted her out of her crib and sat with her on the glider, just rocking and thinking how much our lives were about to change.

"You like it here, don't you, peanut?"

She smiled and grabbed my mouth. I pulled my lips over my teeth and playfully bit her fingers while making monster noises.

She laughed and my heart lightened. "You're getting so big."

Soon, we would start researching preschools. Hale would only want the best for his daughter and what if the best was in New York? Or Helsinki, Finland?

Slowly rocking Elara, I realized I wanted the best for her, too. But what if the best was simply being surrounded by love? How much did a preliminary prep-school really matter in terms of a happy life?

She babbled and pulled at my hair. "Mah-mah-mah-mah." I looked down at her and she smiled, reaching for my nose. "Mamma."

My heart stilled and time stopped. "What did you just say?"

She smiled up at me, that fourth tooth had finally broken through. "Mah-mah-mah-mah."

It was the first time she said those sounds, and she said them to me. "Mamma?"

She grinned and gurgled in solidarity. "Mamma."

My eyes welled with tears. "That's right. I'm Mamma." I kissed her pudgy cheek. "And you're my little peanut."

In that moment I realized, it didn't matter where we lived. It was the people who created a sense of home.

"We need to work on your daddy and grandpop."

I wished there was a way to heal their relationship, because while I would go wherever Hale needed to be, I worried about leaving Remington behind. Yes, he had a full staff to wait on him hand and foot, but they weren't the same as family.

"Dada?" Elara chattered to herself, staring peacefully into Meep Meep's wooly face as her eyes grew heavy.

"Exactly," I agreed, stroking her hair and rocking her slowly to sleep.

Sometime later, I awoke to Hale lifting Elara out of my arms and carrying her back to the crib. He quietly returned to the glider, crouching low to kiss me.

He drew back and frowned. "Stressful day?"

"Sorry." I covered my mouth. "My dinner was vodka, olives, and old cheese."

He smiled and hugged me, resting his head on my lap as he knelt between my legs. "God, I missed you. It's good to be home."

My fingers combed through his hair. It had been a few weeks since his last haircut and his waves were more defined. "I'm glad you're back. How was the flight?"

We always ran through the same script to break the ice that formed in the distance we suffered. Was this how it would always be, Hale coming and going while I waited for him to return? When he was gone, life had a way of feeling like it was on hold, like I was only fully living when he was with me. I didn't want that hiatus to become our normal.

"Flight was fine. I slept most of the way."

Yet he seemed exhausted. "You still seem tired."

"Tired of being away from you."

I stroked his hair much like I had done to soothe Elara. "Well, you're home now."

He shut his eyes and hugged my waist. "No place like home."

Sometimes, when Hale's guard came down, he was so vulnerable our roles reversed. I laced my fingers in his and urged him to stand. "Come on. Let's go to bed."

I washed up and met him in his dressing room, smiling as he meticulously rolled up his tie. My gaze dropped to his sock drawer, but I didn't want to think about that right now. I just wanted a moment between us—no wedding talk, no work, no contracts or trust issues, just him and me.

Crossing the room, I stepped between him and the closet. Without words, I reached for him and pulled him down for a kiss. Hale's mouth met mine in a language that said everything I needed to know at that moment. No matter how far apart we drifted, we always came back to each other.

We fumbled our way out of the closet and tumbled onto the bed. His body glided over mine, our hands stroking and gripping, until he found his way home. There was no rush as we savored the familiarity we found whenever we came together as one. I arched into every intrepid thrust as his body filled mine. Sometimes he held me so tight I wondered if he feared losing me, like a dream that disappeared in a blink or a sudden sound.

"Rayne," he rasped, pressing his lips to my

throat and driving into me with deep strokes. His fingers laced with mine, holding me down as we slowly made love with intense purpose.

"I'm here, Hale. Yours." It was what he needed to hear. What he desired me to say.

"Yes, baby. Mine. Only mine."

"Forever."

Our whispered words were a consummation of our love. We understood each other's needs and we worked hard to fulfill them. Equally.

Before Hale, I had no idea relationships could survive on mutual respect. I always thought one person was inevitably a giver and the other was a taker, but that wasn't true. Hale and I both gave and we both benefited. It was the only explanation I had for how two extremely opposite people could share such an all-encompassing love.

Pulling my hands free, I wrapped my body around his, holding him tightly. My nails dug into his back and his shoulders flexed and bunched as the hard muscles of his stomach clenched tight. He trembled through his release, sinking his weight into me without crushing me.

"I love you so much, Rayne."

Our mouths dueled in a passionate kiss as our bodies remained connected. "I love you too." Looking into those gunmetal grey eyes, I realized I'd always love him a little more than he'd ever know.

Were there other things he'd never know? Was my avoidance possibly robbing us of closeness? No matter how much I disagreed with Remington, I worried he might be right about one thing. Constantly peaceful marriages were unrealistic.

If it was a choice between messy and fake, I'd take the messy every time. Was that what he meant about healthy fighting keeping the passion hot in a relationship?

What if confrontation was necessary? I would never fight with Hale just to get him hot. But what if secrets were hurting us in the long run?

How to Suck at Seating Charts

THE FOLLOWING DAYS WERE PEACEFUL. Maybe because Hale wasn't scheduled to travel for a while, or maybe because I was finally "*trying*" to come to terms with the fact that life was unpredictable and sometimes that was a good thing.

I liked uncertainty about as much as I liked commitment, so I was trying this new thing where I took life one day at a time. I was doing okay, considering that today was Day One of my new staying present philosophy. I might not be so accepting as the week went on and new challenges arrived.

Remington's health remained on my mind, so I scheduled a physical with his primary doctor and requested a full workup of his blood just to make sure everything was okay. When I asked Myles if he noticed any strange behavior, he confessed Remington had been smoking again.

Poor Myles. I had no choice but to throw him under the bus when I confronted Remington for such stupid behavior. "Are you kidding me?" I had burst into his office. "You're smoking again?" I ordered him to quit immediately. "Hand them over."

"This is my office, not an arena, Meyers. Lower your voice."

His avoidance wasn't going to derail my purpose. Angling my body over his desk, I lowered my voice to a chilling whisper. "Are you trying to give yourself another heart attack?"

"Why should I try when you seem set on doing that yourself? What are you thinking bursting in here like that?"

I flipped open his breast pocket and frisked him. "Hand them over, Remington."

He swatted me away, but not before I found his stash. "Meyers—"

"Don't Meyers me. You should be thanking me. I seem to be the only person in the room who gives a crap about your health."

He sighed. "You're a royal pain in my ass."

"The lighter too." I waited until he dropped it into my palm.

I pocketed the paraphernalia and planted my fists on my hips. "Don't you dare send anyone to the store to buy more." I turned in the direction of the hidden figures I knew were eavesdropping from the next room. "Do you all hear me? Anyone who buys him cigarettes or offers him a light will answer to me!"

In the kitchen I opened the trash and snapped every black Russian filter and crumbled the tobacco into dust.

"You should not let him get you so worked up,

niña," Marta said, her attention on watering the house plants.

"He thinks he's invincible and he's not. He deserved to get yelled at."

"But now he will be a bear to deal with. One or two a day can't be that bad for him."

I glared at her. "Marta, do not let him smoke."

She sighed and nodded, but then she muttered something in Spanish as she left the room.

Myles appeared and smirked. "That was impressive."

"If you catch him smoking, I expect you to yell at him, too."

He laughed. "Not a chance, Meyers. I'm not family."

"Neither am I..." My claim wilted as I realized how soon those words wouldn't be true. "Okay, fine. Then you call me and I'll handle it." I slapped the gold zippo on the counter. "Hide this where he won't find it."

When I told his kids their father had started smoking again—less than a year after a massive heart attack—none of them seemed concerned. Hale said Remington would do whatever Remington wanted to do. Barrett called his father an idiot. Seraphina suggested homeopathic aroma therapy paired with hypnosis to help him break the habit, which Remington later called *millennial cult voodoo*—and there went Seraphina's concern.

It was the first time I shared an actual conversation with Phina about her father and it was eye opening. I knew Remington could be a pain in the ass to his sons, but he caused a different pain for his daughter. There was so much expectation based on her gender, and we both knew he would likely never change.

"If it helps, I know your dad's extremely proud of you."

She'd smiled sadly. "I wish hearing that from other people was enough. What does help is learning to value my success without the validation or approval of others."

She sounded so healthy, speaking from that tender place of pain and peace that always gave away when someone had gone to therapy to heal a wound.

I wondered if Hale would ever consider talking to a therapist about his father's betrayal with Jasmine. It might help him work through his trust issues. Maybe I'd suggest that to him after the wedding. Maybe I could go to—Lord knew I had some issues to work through.

Phina's complaints about misogyny and closed-mindedness were valid. What threw her was the idea that I might be an exception to the rule. "He's different with you." She looked at me as if I had some magic solution where Remington was concerned. I did not.

"He's still the same man. The difference is I'm not his kid."

"But he…loves you like…" She frowned and I understood her confusion.

Remington withheld affection where his own children were concerned. Rather than praise them, he preferred to command and critique them and get frustrated whenever they didn't do exactly what he suggested. If he treated me like one of his children, he'd be a lot harder on me.

"Love can be expressed in countless ways. He might not say it out loud, but he does love you, Phina."

I felt closer to her after the conversation. She was incredibly humble and open in ways that most people couldn't manage. I saw her vulnerability and openness as extremely courageous.

Plus, she had proven to be my greatest asset in wedding-gate, especially since Elle canceled the last two times we had plans to '*do wedding stuff*'. My MOH was MIA, and I was starting to wonder if she was as overwhelmed by all this wedding talk as me.

So, yes, I was very grateful to have Seraphina's help and more than willing to listen to her sniffle through some frustrations about her father.

"He's just different with you, Rayne. It's difficult to not get envious when I see you together." It was the first time I ever considered that Seraphina might put herself and I in the same category.

It was never my intention to make her jealous. I didn't know why Remington and I had such an easy give-and-take. It just came about organically. "I'm not his daughter."

"But you're going to be his daughter-in-law."

Phina was the only girl and the baby of the family. I didn't want to intrude on her territory. "That's not the same. No one can compete with a father's daughter. She's the greatest love of a man's life."

My heart hurt a little as I said those words. In terms of Hale, they were true. He loved Elara like the moon loved the sun and he'd dotingly follow her shadow for all of eternity. But in terms of my dad, that was a bald-faced lie. There were plenty of things he loved more than me.

I wondered if, subconsciously, I was trespassing on Phina's "daughter territory" to fill a void in my own life. I adored Remington. And, as much as he could be a pain in the ass, I loved him like a father. But I wasn't out to steal him from his other children.

I made a conscious decision to push Remington to call his daughter more often so there would be no sense of competition between the two of us. It would do him good to put in some extra effort anyway. He could use the time he would have spent smoking to call them.

Seraphina never tired of the wedding plans. On the contrary, she seemed invigorated by every design challenge. She truly had a gift and an eye for beauty. I could claim no such thing.

As promised, Phina drew up several theme proposals for the wedding and emailed us a slide show for each one. Hale and I settled on the one she called *Traditional & Timeless Elegance.* We *finally* had our mood and theme.

The wedding would be a formal white-tie event, which I had never heard of before. I'd always assumed black tie was the top of the fancy cake, but nope. There was a whole other tier for white ties and floor-length gowns.

"So you'll have to select your gowns soon, Rayne. We're running out of time," Seraphina said during her latest video call.

"I'm sorry, did you say gowns, as in plural?"

"Yes. You'll need one for the ceremony and one for the reception. Something to wear to the rehearsal, and then there is your wedding week wardrobe and your send-off attire. We might as well conquer honeymoon outfits, too, while we're at it. What are you doing next week? I have Monday open."

I glanced at Hale, but he was preoccupied with poopy-gate, as Elara Houdinied her way out of another diaper. "I'll have to double-check with Hale's schedule."

Most days I felt like a clueless game piece that others moved around the game of Life. I opened the calendar on my phone to view his itinerary but got distracted.

As Seraphina went on about shoes and accessories, I smiled at the adorable picture of GQ Dad trying to negotiate with an oppositional six-month old that could squirm her way out of any situation. I loved watching them together, especially when neat-freak Hale would inevitably get taken down by doody. It brought out his human side.

My gaze drifted from *GQ Daddy* to *GQ Mommy*, my hand casually sliding the magazine from the pile to rest beside the laptop. Who was that couple?

It was us, but not us. Well, Hale looked the same. Me… I looked striking. Incredibly hot, like a woman with the confidence of a queen and the prowess of a true diva. She was stunning, but I honestly preferred the real me—soft, cute, sort of dorky.

I smiled at Hale. He preferred the real me too.

"Rayne, are you listening? If you can fly into New York next week, I'll block off my schedule now."

I pushed the magazine aside and returned my attention back to wedding-gate. "Hale leaves Monday, so that should work." I glanced at my planner, checking a few due dates for school. I could finish a few projects on the plane and, without Elara or Hale there to distract me, I'd be able to get some studying done. "I just have to confirm with Andrew that he can care for Elara."

"Ooh, yeah. Do that. I love my niece, but babies are not allowed in my boutique."

"Understood. I'll work something out with the manny."

"Any word from Josette about the rehearsal venue?"

Josette was my point person for the wedding, but I liked to think of her as the poison taster. She got to see and try everything first, and was currently running around New York searching for the perfect venue to hold our rehearsal dinner now that we booked a rooftop for the ceremony overlooking Fifth Avenue and Rockefeller Center.

Hale loved that he would be able to see the famous Prometheus statue when we said *I do*. I chalked up his obsession with the god statues to boys being weird and never outgrowing action figures. I loved that the rooftop could only fit seventy-five people, which meant the ceremony would be exclusively for close friends and family.

There was an almost militant chain of command for every decision. Josette scouted, then Quinn approved. At that point, a proposal came to us. Hale weighed in and I surveyed Phina and Elle. If the decision was approved, Quinn paired with Devyn to work out the details and Phina took over the attire. It was sort of like a play with a very involved stage crew. Hale and I were the cast. My only job was remembering my lines.

Since the article with the engagement photos published, Hale's phone had been ringing off the hook. It was amazing just how many people wanted to be a part of our wedding—or Hale's, I should say. I foolishly expected the article to ease some of the pressure I felt, but all it did was raise everyone's expectations.

Hale was going viral while I was fighting crippling imposter syndrome. His soon-to-be-taken status made him such a hot topic, there were even rumors circling that *People* was considering him for this year's *Sexiest Man Alive*.

Then there was me. Phina suggested I hire a PR person to help develop my persona, but I didn't want a persona. I just wanted all this attention and publicity to go away. Besides, the only person who called me about the article was my mom.

That reminded me… "Phina, do you think you would be able to help my mom with a dress for the wedding?"

"Of course! Send me her sizes. Do you have an idea of what she likes as far as cut and style?"

I shrugged. "She mentioned something about the Dress Factory—"

"I'll handle it. Kindly tell her to cease shopping at once."

"Will do." I mentally crossed *Mom's Attire* off my list.

Surrendering most decisions to Hale's sister seemed the wisest choice since she was in her element. The more I delegated the less I panicked.

Time was flying. We had a team of people helping us and I could finally envision something close to the final product. But no matter how many invitations, or menus, or mood boards I saw, what I awaited most of all was the look on Hale's face when we finally made it to the altar. The only thing that mattered to me was becoming his wife.

"Have you finished the seating chart yet?"

My eyes drifted to the enormous pile of index cards on the counter. Hale just added two more guests that morning, so the seating was far from finished. "We're almost done with it."

"Rayne," she said with a stern and knowing look.

"We'll have it finished before the weekend. I promise."

"Thank you. Oh, hold on, that's Josette."

I frowned. Why was Josette texting Phina before me? I was the bride. Then I remembered that this was what I wanted, and I quickly got over any sense of jealousy.

Seraphina read a text then squealed and clapped.

"What is it?"

"Josette managed to get Rarity Lockhart!"

Was I supposed to know who that was? "Who?"

"She's a famous New York photographer, Rayne. A great one! Hale knows her brother, Riley. After their father passed away, Hale bought his shares in some big New York company.

I reached for the stack of cards and shuffled my way to the L's. "Riley and Emma Lockhart?"

"Yes. Go ahead and mark Rarity as a vendor. She'll need a seat for herself and two assistants."

Great. More people.

Hale returned from upstairs, sans child, and a frazzled expression on his face. His cuffs were rolled to his elbows and he held the monitor in his hand as he went right to the wine fridge. Poor guy. Looked like the score was doody diaper-one and Dad-zero.

He lifted a bottle of chardonnay, gesturing to the label to silently ask if I wanted a glass. I nodded, because it was rude to let him drink alone.

"Phina, I'm going to let you go so we can work on that seating chart. Thanks for everything."

"Okay. I'll talk to you tomorrow. Kiss Elara for me."

"I will." I shut the laptop. "You look like you just got your ass kicked by a six-month-old."

"I'm not sure if she's teething or growing horns." He handed me a glass. "Cheers."

Little did he know, his adorable little demon spawn already had him wrapped around her tiny finger. He wasn't going to win any battles where she was concerned. Deciding that there was no way to salvage his night, I said, "Sorry to break it to you, but we have homework."

"What? No."

"Your sister wants the seating chart by the weekend."

"Fuck that chart."

"Hale. We have to finish it. She's doing so

much already. This is the only thing she asked us to do."

He growled and topped off his glass. "There are a million ways I'd rather spend my night off with you."

"Hey, these are your people. My guests are organized neatly at tables three and four."

He groaned. "Fine."

I grabbed the stack of cards and headed to the living room. "Bring the wine."

Hale reluctantly followed.

I pushed the coffee table out of the way and tossed Elara's toys into the bin. "I think this will work best if we lay everything out. I printed the names and cut and pasted each one on the front of an index card with any notes about allergies or enemies on the back."

"How very Ms. Meyers of you." Hale teased, using the name my students used back when I was a teacher.

"I might have geeked out a little over this, but let's not read too deeply into it. My affinity for childlike crafts doesn't lend itself to bouquets and bridal belts. I'm still me."

"What's a bridal belt?"

"That torniquet thing brides wear around their thigh."

He laughed. "A garter?"

"Whatever. Unless I need to carry a knife, I'm not wearing one."

"I think it's sexy."

I paused from cleaning up the toys, second-guessing my decision. "You do?"

"Yeah. And I get to pull it off of you with my teeth."

"Not in front of four hundred strangers."

"We're far from four hundred, and I'd rather save that part of the night for when we're alone."

Warmth spread from my chest up my throat. "Well, that doesn't sound too bad."

"See?" He crossed the room and hugged me from behind, distracting me with a kiss on the side of my neck. "Wedding traditions can be fun. You'll be dressed up like a cupcake and I'll get to claim you through all that crinoline and lace." His hand cupped my boob possessively and I sank into his hold. "*My* bride."

Sensing he was trying to distract me, I squirmed out of his arms. "Calm your loins or we'll never get done." I held up the cards. "Girls are in pink and boys are lavender."

"Why not blue for boys?"

"Because traditional colors create a gender stereotypes, and our wedding will be a progressively freeing affair." I pointed to myself, the most non-bride bride in the history of womankind. "Obviously."

"But you kept the girls pink?"

"Look, Elara's craft kit consists of finger paint and stamps. I had limited options and we're never going to get done if we don't focus."

"Gotcha."

I handed him a huge pile of cards that wasn't even half the guests. "Start with these."

He paged through the stack. "What am I doing with them?"

"We're arranging them in groups of ten. That's

how many guests can sit at one table. Where are you going?"

"To get more wine. No way I'm getting through this sober."

"Might as well crack open another bottle to breathe." I looked down at the cards in my hand and mumbled, "Because this is going to take all night."

Hale began spreading out names on the carpet as I worked on a cross-referencing system, something to identify sub-categories of guests so I had a better idea of who the hell these people were. We used mermaid stamps for Naomi's friends and anchor stamps for Remington's. Politicians got an American flag stamp, and business associates got butterflies.

"Who's Lucian and Evelyn Patras?" I asked, taking my job as card-marker very seriously.

"Business associates. You can put them with Shamus Callahan and Lucian's two sisters. Their names escape me at the moment."

"We're inviting people whose names you can't remember?"

"I know their names, I've just had a lot of wine."

I shuffled through the pile. "Antoinette Patras and Isadora Patras?"

"Yes, that's it."

"Uh-oh."

"What *uh-oh?*"

I read the back of Isadora's card. "It says here that Isadora's husband and brother don't get along."

"That's old news."

"This came from your father."

"Well, he's old. He doesn't keep up with that sort of thing. Sit them together. They'll be fine. And put Slade Bishop at that table too."

"That leaves three more seats."

Hale stood like a giant over a sea of scattered index cards appearing overwhelmed and ready to bolt. His fingers forked through his hair, leaving it standing on end. "Why is this so difficult?"

"Because someone wanted an enormous wedding." I took no pity on him. This was his doing, not mine.

"This is like trying to solve an impossible puzzle. Too many people have too many damn enemies. Can't they just suck it up for one night?"

"Would you want to share a table with people who screwed you over in business or someone who beat you in the last election."

He huffed. "We can't possibly accommodate everyone's bullshit."

"How about this? Every time you close out a table, I'll remove an article of clothing?"

His head shot up, a look of intrigue in his eyes. "Deal." He scanned the grouping of Patras guests. "Find Mason and Liberty Davis and add Sean O'Malley."

"Who are they?"

"Friends from North Carolina. We can put them at that table. Then you owe me a piece of clothing."

"Fair is fair." The wine was making me hot anyway. I stripped off my cardigan and draped it over the chair. I handed him the cards he requested and kept moving. "Who's next?"

Hale worked faster once I found the right incentive. By the time we were on the G's I was down to my bra and panties.

"Elliot and Nadia Garnet."

Hale clicked his fingers and pointed in the air. "That's… Uh… Roan! Put them with Asher and Scarlett Roan."

I crawled across the floor to locate the group with the Roans. "Found it." I looked over my shoulder. "Four more seats to close out their table."

His smoldering gaze locked with mine. "Fuck." He visibly swallowed. "Stay right there." His hand went to his collar as his stare drifted to my ass.

"Focus, Mr. Davenport. We have a hundred more guests to do."

"I'd like to do you."

"You can after you finish your homework."

His eyes rolled back and he groaned. "And when you use that teacher voice… I'm already hard."

I smothered a laugh. "A boner in class? Not very classy of you, Mr. Davenport."

"I would have had one every day if you were my teacher."

"Your assignment's not finished yet."

"Fine," he growled. "But once those panties come off, I'm done and so are you."

"We'll see about that." I tapped the pile of cards impatiently. "We need two more couples to close out Table Nineteen."

He pinched the bridge of his nose. "Did we place Alessio Di Vicci?"

"The Italian dude? Yes."

"Damn." He acted like he was on a game show

and a timer was about to go off. "Add Gage and Perrin King…"

"Two more."

"Shit." He paced, agitated and unable to think with the huge erection pressing against his pants. "Couples or seats?"

"Two seats or one couple."

He wracked his brain and fumbled through the cards. "I've got nothing but old people and politicians here. We need a young couple."

"What about the photographer's brother?"

"Yes! Riley and Emma Lockhart! Bra off, baby!"

I rolled my eyes and laughed at how excited he got. As if he couldn't see my tits whenever he wanted. "Find their cards."

While Hale rummaged through the various piles for the Lockharts, I sat up on my knees and unclasped my bra. The room had chilled and my nipples instantly puckered as the lace fell away.

He held out the cards and I knew we were done. Keeping my eyes on him, I tossed the cards onto the appropriate pile. "Nice work, Mr. Davenport."

He groaned. "You know it drives me mad when you look up at me like that. No more wedding stuff tonight."

"Good, because I was hoping we could practice for the honeymoon."

His nostrils flared and his hand went to the bulge in his pants, the zipper slowly lowering. "Crawl your sexy ass over here, Ms. Meyers."

I grinned and dropped to my hands and knees, creeping slowly across the room in what I hoped was a sexy crawl. Hale walked backward, safely away from the cards. One strong breeze and all of our work could be ruined.

I laughed when he kept going. "How far do you plan to go?"

He chuckled. "I don't know. I like watching you crawl to me."

"The sooner I reach you the sooner you get my mouth around Prince Everhard."

He stopped walking immediately and I closed the distance.

Seconds later, his hand was tangled in my hair as I took him to the back of my throat. He was bossy and demanding, but I didn't mind. When Hale had control, I could let go. The weight of worries and stress lifted as he told me exactly what to do, and I obeyed, happy to take care of him.

In the end, he always saw to my pleasure as much as I saw to his, so it was a win-win. I got off on his praise, and he got off on my surrender. It was the perfect give and take, a beautiful inter-change of desire and trust that satisfied both of us in countless ways.

His fingers caressed my cheek as he watched me. "Such a good girl."

I literally preened when he talked to me like that, and he reaped all the rewards that came with dishing out such praise.

Then he dragged his fingers down to my throat, tracing the bulge there, and said something I'd never heard him say during sex before and my panties were ruined. "Show me what a good fucking wife you're going to be."

Something came over me in that moment and

I graduated from exceptional to advanced placement honors. I was his, but soon I'd be more than that. I'd be his good fucking wife. And he would be my husband for all of eternity.

When he was close to finishing, my mouth released him. Gasping and panting, I looked up at him with tear-dampened lashes and swollen lips. Arching back, I let him use my body as a blank palette. His fist worked over his flesh and he grunted, holding me by the hair as he dragged my mouth back to his cock. "Take it like a sacrament."

His attention and desire hit like a sacred blessing as I opened for him. Heat spilled over my tongue and down my chin, trickling to my breasts.

His grip in my hair loosened and he gently caressed my throat. "Show me."

I licked over my swollen lips and swallowed, then showed him it was all gone.

His gaze dropped to my breasts. He swiped up a small drop and fed it into my mouth. "You missed a spot."

I sucked his finger clean and he groaned.

"You're going to be such a good fucking wife."

I rose on shaky legs and he kissed me, all his aggression and lust shifting into love and adoration. He led me upstairs and tucked me into bed.

"I need a shower." He kissed the top of my head. "I can't wait to see you walking down the aisle those last few minutes before you're officially mine."

I envisioned that moment, sharing his excitement, until dark inadequacy swept in, destroying the sweet image. While Hale waited at the altar, the perfect picture of tradition and luxury, I would be facing him and all the guests completely alone. A cold void pushed a shiver through my body.

He frowned, so in tune with my emotions he sensed the shift in me. "You okay?"

"Fine," I lied, nudging him toward the bathroom. "Just tired. Go shower."

As soon as the water turned on and I knew I was alone, the wave of inadequacy swallowed me whole. Brides were escorted by their fathers. Given away from one significant man to another. Sure, it was a dated and sexist tradition that held no real implication nowadays, but the symbolic gesture remained a part of American wedding culture, and I found myself wanting my dad's presence with a fierceness that rivaled every milestone that had come before.

It was my wedding after all. As the bride, didn't I at least deserve that?

The Definition of Insanity

PEOPLE SAY Einstein defined insanity as doing the same thing over and over again and expecting a different outcome. I wasn't crazy. I might be a general hot mess, but I was by no means cuckoo. I did, however, fit Albie's supposed definition.

As soon as I had some time alone, I unzipped my emotional baggage to try on some of my old bullshit. And, yup, those daddy-issue-demons still fit like a glove. Familiar and broken in, I slipped right back into my old unhealthy habits with no regard for my progress or peace of mind.

I had to. It was the only way to resolve the obsessive loop that had been running through my mind since I realized I'd be walking down the aisle alone.

I needed to contact my father.

I didn't mention this to Hale or Elle or anyone else who might try to talk me out of it. This was what I wanted. I didn't care how illogical or emotionally dangerous it might be. I had to try and I didn't want anyone stopping me.

I already knew the emotional dangers and what my friends' arguments would be. But the alternatives weren't the same as having the one thing I knew I probably would never get. I stubbornly and unrealistically wanted it to be my dad.

Yes, moms also gave their daughters away. Sometimes brides even made that final walk alone. But, according to tradition, it was supposed to be a dad's job.

After all of Hale's comments about the charm of tradition, I understood the appeal. In this area specifically, I wanted the fairytale, by the books, with father and daughter arm in arm.

I knew the origin of this practice was tied up with some patriarchal bullshit having to do with dowries and treating women like property, but my brain wasn't focused on the archaic roots. I could only see the symbolism of a beautiful tradition that evolved into something sacred and stood the test of time—something the little girl in me longed for deeply.

All I felt—all I wanted—was one symbolic gesture from my father to prove once and for all—regardless of whatever messed up history we shared—he loved me enough to be there on my wedding day.

Just this. That was all I was asking for. One. Simple. Walk.

And I knew it wouldn't happen.

The echo from years of rejection still stung and I welcomed the familiar, hopeless ache that hollowed my stomach every time I contemplated reaching out to him again. Of course I was going to try. I was a glutton for punishment. And, according to Albie Einstein, insane.

But it wasn't like I was broadcasting my unhinged bad habits for the world to see. Of course not. That's why I was hiding on the second floor, in the empty guest room, while Hale was downstairs making calls and Andrew and Elara were at the park.

My actions were harmless. The only person who would get hurt was me, and I knew exactly what I was getting myself into. I'd done this a hundred times before and every time I tried to contact him the blurry reality cleared a little more. He was never going to come back into my life. I knew this. As long as I stayed fully aware of the probable outcome and how impossible and unrealistic my hope was, I would be okay.

I'd send the message, wait a few days, then call Elle and she'd show up with a bottle of tequila and a bag of oranges and we'd drink until it didn't hurt anymore. Although, now, Elle would probably just eat the fruit, which was fine. More tequila for me.

My best friend wouldn't approve of what I was doing, which was why I hadn't told her my plans. As my ride-or-die-bitch-for-life she'd have no choice but to show up for damage control when it was over. She could lecture me then.

My dad had not responded to me in nearly sixteen years, and, before then, his correspondence had been impersonal and sparse.

I opened Facebook and swiped through my DMs until I stared down at the last ten messages I sent him. They quantified to about ten years of my life until I finally stopped reaching out. Each desperate request for any semblance of a relationship with the man who made me had gone unanswered. But they were read.

His privacy settings were tighter than a virgin asshole, so I had no way of knowing if this account that I assumed was my dad's was the correct Raymond Meyers. But all the other Raymond Meyers and Ray Meyers I found over the years had the decency to respond, kindly letting me know that they were not the man I was looking for, many of them wishing me luck in locating my real father.

This was the only Raymond Meyers who had read my messages and not responded. I knew, from the way my stomach twisted and my gut swooshed, that this Raymond Meyers was him.

His profile picture was a bald eagle and all his other photos were on lockdown. His hometown was listed as Darby, Pennsylvania, but no schools, workplaces, or marital status showed. However, Oregon was listed under places lived and that was exactly where he left us thirty years ago.

He used to keep in touch. I still had some foggy memories of hanging by the kitchen door as my mom spoke quietly on a landline phone. I was young and their conversations went over my head but I remember my mom mentioning money, which my dad never sent.

On birthdays I'd get a card—the small kind that was made of flimsy paper and only said two words inside. But those words, printed plainly in low-quality ink, were the best birthday gift I received every year. That HAPPY BIRTHDAY meant more to me than all the bicycles and balloons I'd ever received.

When I was twelve, I waited for the mailman to come, but when he filled our mailbox with sales papers and bills there was no card from my dad. All week I waited anxiously for his card to arrive. When it never did, I blamed the post office.

I wrote my dad several letters, letting him know the stupid mailman lost his card and making sure he had our address right. I told him not to write in cursive and print very clearly on his next envelope. All of those letters were returned.

There was a period when I thought something terrible happened to him. I searched the internet for mentions of his name but found nothing. I was eighteen when I gave up. Then social media came around, breathing life and hope back into my old obsessive search and I was back at it again.

None of my milestone birthdays meant as much as they should, because I was always aware someone was missing. I wanted to get over his rejection, truly I did. My dad's abandonment was a primal wound. It cut deep and would take more than one lifetime to heal. I didn't want to feel the things his abandonment made me feel, but I had no way to shut those emotions off.

Therapy helped. Self-help books worked for a little while. But then there were days I'd think of him and the scar would rip open and my heart would be left bleeding for days like it was bleeding now.

There was no choice. I needed to do this. I needed to try one last time. It was my wedding for fuck's sake.

While I'd not been the most cliché bride, I had been an agreeable one, making sure that Hale and the Davenports got everything they requested. Marrying Hale was enough for me to put myself through all the drama and excruciating attention, but if I could make one teeny, tiny wish, this was it.

I wanted my dad to walk me down the aisle.

For all the birthdays missed, all the father-daughter dances I attended with Uncle Rob, all the extra tickets to plays and softball games that went into the recycling, for the empty seats at both my graduations, this was the one thing I believed he owed me, so I was going to invite him to my wedding and I didn't want anyone to tell me not to.

I knew the likelihood of a response was slim to none, but I had to try. I braced for the self-deprecating spiral that would follow. I could already hear Elle's lecture. Although, since the damage from the accident, she might not remember how many times we traveled down this road, so maybe this time she'd say something different than, *Ray, why do you let him hurt you like this?*

Yes, I was hiding to avoid being talked out of something that would ultimately cause me pain. But also because I preferred to face my shame privately. Rejection was hard, but it was downright humiliating when others witnessed it.

Hale would comfort me when the time came, but I hated drawing his attention to that icky part of my past. There were two, possibly three, men who should love a woman unconditionally—her father, her husband, and, if she was lucky, her son. There was a very illogical but real part of my psyche that feared if Hale thought too hard about the first guy leaving me, he might cut and run too. I never wanted him to think I might be defective.

Chewing my lip, my gaze darted to the hall as I sat on the bed of the empty guest room, assuring I wouldn't be disturbed. I opened a new message.

Dad

I waited for the words to come but they were tied up in some kind of knot. My skin tingled and a woozy sensation sloshed through me.

Should I call him Dad? Did he go by Raymond or Ray?

I shook my head. I was being ridiculous. "It doesn't fucking matter," I hissed, then started typing.

Dad, It's Rayne. I'm writing to let you know that I'm getting married. My wedding is this April. I'd like nothing more than for you to be there. Do you think you could do this one favor for me? You wouldn't have to worry about travel expenses or anything else. If you're willing to do this, I'll take care of everything. I know we lost touch over the years, but you're still my dad and I can't imagine this day without you there. Please answer this message and please say yes. It's the only thing I'll ever ask of you. Love your daughter, Rayne

SEND.

"Oh God." I rushed from the guest room to the bathroom where my body drastically punished me for compartmentalizing years of stress and self-loathing. I had to exercise the demons and it was not pretty.

When I finally exited the bathroom I came face to face with Hale. He drew back and frowned in concern. "Are you sick?"

"My stomach was bothering me. I should be fine now."

He tsked and gave me space. "Do you think you caught a bug?"

"No. Just my usual stomach issues."

"Are you sure?"

"Positive." I doubted other couples discussed poo as much as Hale and I, but these were the joys of loving someone with IBS.

"Maybe it's something else…"

I frowned, then understanding dawned. "I'm not pregnant, Hale."

He smirked. "It wouldn't be a bad thing if you were."

I shoved him out of my way. "It would." Opening the nightstand drawer, I pulled out a candy bar. "We have enough on our plate with Elara and the wedding and school and travel."

"Should you be eating that—" When I paused and sent him a death look he held up his hands in a sign of peace. "I'm only saying that it might not be the best for an upset stomach."

I decapitated the chocolate bunny. "This is exactly what I should be eating right now."

For the rest of the day, I ignored my social media, then I moved the app into one of those little boxes on the last screen of my phone's display so I wouldn't obsess. I set a reminder on my calendar to check the message in two days and made a promise to myself not to look a minute before. But I had always been the sort of person to peek at Christmas presents so I broke that promise about five minutes after making it.

Viewing his unread message over and over again was the equivalent of being pecked to death by chickens. It was a slow death, but eventually, the misery would end.

The Beastie Boys Were Right

As Hale backed his Rolls out of the parking garage, I sighed. His hand rested on my knee, rubbing soothing circles at the hem of my sundress. "We'll find someone, baby. Don't worry."

"We're running out of time. All the wedding books say we should have an officiant booked by now."

"We have plenty of time."

"No, we have seventy-four days and if you subtract your travel dates that leaves us with roughly thirty nine. Thirty-nine days, Hale."

"Just because I'm away doesn't mean things can't get done."

"I know. You're very impressive. But when you're in a different time zone I have to field all of Quinn, Phina, Devyn, and Josette's questions on my own. Not to mention deal with my mother, who still thinks this is going to be a quaint affair."

He glanced at me. "Did you tell her it's white tie?"

"That means nothing to my people. She offered to pay for the flowers and I know she can't even afford the centerpieces, not to mention all the other stuff Quinn outlined."

He frowned. "Tell her not to worry about the cost. She's our guest. We don't want her to pay for anything. She only has to attend and have a good time."

"She wants to help."

He navigated the afternoon traffic, the WTF creases between his eyes deepened. "We'll come up with an affordable way for her to contribute so she doesn't feel left out."

The topic of my mother was a touchy one and I was being unfairly sensitive. My dad hadn't responded—shocker—and I now felt like my attendees were going to be overshadowed by Hale's ever-growing guest list, eight-foot topiaries, ice sculptures, god statues, and towering skyscrapers.

Like a growing shadow, the closer the wedding came the smaller I felt. "I feel like we're rushing."

"We're right on schedule."

"But we *are* rushing. Most couples take at least a year—"

"Rayne."

"I'm just saying, maybe we should postpone."

"Rayne," he said with limited patience and enough authority to command a boardroom. "The venues are booked and gears are in motion. We'll find someone to perform the ceremony. You have to trust the process. Everything's going to be perfect."

"See, right there. You use that word too loosely. Perfect's an impossible standard."

"Look, as long as you're there it'll be perfect. None of this other stuff matters."

"Well, if we don't have someone to marry us, we can't get married. I don't make the rules, Hale."

"We should look at the list Devyn sent again. Maybe some officiants are worth a second glance."

"Like who? They were all terrible."

"What about the first guy?"

"The one who kept looking at my zoomers?"

He glanced at me with a half-smile. "Can you blame him?"

"Fine. Hire him." I flashed him a nipple. "You were the one who crossed him off the list in the first place."

He grimaced. "No. You're right. Your zoomers are mine." He switched lanes. "What about the guy Josette found with the dove connection?"

"His prices were ridiculous. He totally started up-charging us the second he heard your name."

"Price isn't an issue"

"It's the principle. Plus, he was a flat earther."

"The guy with the beard?"

"Yes."

"Do we care?"

"Conspiracy theories aside, do you really want to be married by a chipper hipster who looks like a clerk at Trader Joe's? That's not really on brand with your vibe."

"Definitely not. You're right. Keep him off the list. What about the officiant out of Brooklyn from Josette's list?"

"No. He does clown gigs on the side. You know I suffer from coulrophobia."

"Right. No side hustle clowns at the wedding. I'll email Quinn for more suggestions. Maybe when you're in New York you can hold a few interviews."

Wonderful, more solo decision-making. "I need boots. Last time we were in the city my feet were freezing. Not to mention I'm leaving tomorrow morning and still have nothing packed. You know what that means."

Sensing the opening to yet another Production of *Rayne The Musical*, Hale sighed.

I searched my music and cued up the Beastie Boys. Poor Hale hadn't had control over his radio since his penis met my vagina. But he never complained.

As I belted out the lyrics of *No Sleep 'til Brooklyn*, I noticed we weren't taking the usual roads home. Hale made a slight turn and I stared at the unfamiliar surroundings.

"Where are we going?"

"I have a surprise for you." He pulled into a little parking lot near a brick strip mall.

"This wasn't on the wedding itinerary for the day."

He shut off the car and grabbed my hand. "You mean this itinerary?"

Officiant 11 am

was scribbled on the back of my hand in black ink. I shrugged. "I didn't want to forget."

"You'll like this." He came around to my door and opened it.

"What is this place? Why the secrecy?"

"If I told you, it would have distracted you all throughout our last meeting. I wanted it to be a surprise."

"Good surprise or bad surprise?"

I had flashbacks to my childhood when my mom would take me out for a fun day only to surprise me midway through with a trip to the doctor. I'd spend the rest of the day nursing a sore arm and sulking over a lollipop.

He frowned as if he'd never think to give me a bad surprise. "It's a good one."

"You could have told me. What is it? Are my clothes okay? Should I have brought anything?"

"This is exactly why I wanted it to be a surprise."

I huffed. "You act like I have no self-control."

He grinned as we walked hand in hand toward the back of a brick building. "In areas such as this, you don't."

Then I smelled it. "Oh, my God."

He tugged my hand. "Keep walking."

"Is this what I think it is?" The scent of sugar and carbs wafted from the fogged windows. I doubled my pace. "Holy shit. Are we having a cake tasting?"

"Yup. The owner of the bakery's been preparing all day."

"Oh, my God. But wait… If the bakery's here, how can we use them in New York?"

"He also has a location in the city. They're family owned and they've been in business for almost fifty years."

"How many cakes do we get to taste? Will

there be chocolate? I heard grooms get a chocolate cake. I don't know if that's just for the guys, but as the bride I think I should be entitled to taste every dessert. It's my wedding after all."

"There will be plenty of chocolate."

We rounded the building and entered from the front, despite the sign on the glass showing CLOSED, Hale walked right in. A delicate bell jingled overhead and the delicious scent of heaven drove me close to orgasm.

The bakery section was dim and empty. "The owner's waiting for us."

"It's a private tasting?" The displays were more seductive than porn. "Look at all of this, Hale." I turned and smiled at him. "I feel like the winner of a golden ticket."

Hale rang the antique bell on the counter.

A little old man wearing a white muffin top hat appeared. "Monsieur and the soon-to-be Madame Davenport, welcome!"

"Chef Dubois," Hale greeted, holding out his hand. "Let me introduce you to your soon-to-be-number-one-fan, my fiancée, Rayne."

The baker smiled, his dark eyes hidden by bushy, grey eyebrows. *"Bonjour, bonjour."*

He waved us toward a small table, intentionally placed in front of the window and dressed like it be-longed on a Disney set with a white tablecloth, two black wrought iron chairs, and a single yellow rose in a bud vase. Blue linen napkins had been folded neatly beneath several silver spoons. I was in heaven.

The stout chef carried a carafe of cool milk to the table with two glasses. "Make yourselves comfortable. I'm just finishing up some last-minute touches. *Excusez-moi* for a moment."

"Take your time," Hale said as he pulled out my chair.

I eyed the glass displays and all the colorful confections as I sat. "There's so many spoons."

"Excited?"

"Oh, come on. You know this is better than sex to me."

He arched a brow. "Should I be offended by that?"

"I'm just saying, a little chocolate play in the bedroom could go a long way." I rubbed my hands excitedly. "Thank you for planning this."

He caught my hand and traced his thumb over my engagement ring. "It's good to see you smile. You seemed down these last few days."

I had tried to hide my disappointment about my dad, but it was hard, especially when Elle was so busy. I hadn't even had a chance to tell her I reached out to him. Maybe it was time to tell Hale. "I did some—"

"Let us begin!" The baker burst from the back carrying three plates of freshly baked, beautifully iced, full-body, orgasmic slices of wedding cake. "Monsieur Davenport tells me you have a sensitivity to paprika. Not to worry. I do not keep the stuff in my kitchen."

My mouth widened in a gaping smile as he set the cakes in front of us. "There are so many."

"This is only the beginning. I've started you off with the more traditional *crème au beurre* and white butter cakes, but not to worry. I have many more unique options in the back if you want something more creative."

I picked up a spoon then hesitated. "Do we just dig in?"

Chef Dubois nodded and laughed. *"Bon appétit."*

I went for the frothy one with shavings of white chocolate first. "Holy mother of Godiva. What is this?"

"It's an old family recipe. We call it *Grand-mère's* vanilla ganache."

"It's incredible," I mumbled over a mouthful of sugary decadence. "Hale, you gotta taste this."

He carved his spoon into the dense cake taking a much daintier sampling than I had. He was the well-mannered tortoise to my spastic hare. I watched as he tasted the cakes the way a somme-lier might sample a three thousand-dollar glass of wine.

"It's very good."

"Hale, detergents or vacuums are *very good.* Cake—*this* cake in particular—is a work of art." I picked up a clean spoon and tasted another one, but there was really no point. I was certain I wanted Grandma's ganache until the new flavors of the next slice melted in my mouth. "Uh-oh."

"What's wrong?"

"Is there a problem?"

Both men looked at me in concern and I frowned, then whined, "This one's just as good." My hand thumped on the table causing the silver-ware to rattle and I closed my eyes. "Are you kid-ding me?" Creamy frosting and decadent, perfectly fluffy butter cake burst over my tongue, a flawless combination of sweet and rich. "You're not a baker. You're a wizard!"

Chef Dubois laughed. "*C'est bon!* You like this, you'll love what I have in the back." He disappeared through the kitchen door and I looked up at Hale, tears of joy prickling my eyes.

"He's going to bring out something better than this? Can we get married here?"

He laughed. "There's a reason he's been in business for nearly fifty years."

"I'd say." I shoveled another bite into my mouth. "Everything's so moist you don't even need milk."

Hale grinned in his pristine, unwrinkled suit jacket and bazillion-dollar tie as he leaned closer to wipe a dash of icing off my lip. "You're too sexy when you eat."

I snorted. "You're crazy."

"For you."

I hid a smirk. My boyfriend was so dreamy. "Seriously, you need to taste this one before I eat it all."

"You know, you make the same sounds in bed."

"You have a dirty mind, Monsieur Davenport." I laughed around my spoon. This cake could give Hale a run for his money in the boudoir.

"Don't fall in love with the Chef. He probably has grandchildren older than you."

"Yeah, but he can probably make a woman come with eggs and flour alone."

"And a very soft stick of butter."

"Don't be jealous," I teased, leaning over to give him a sugary kiss.

Chef Dubois returned with more samples.

How was I going to pick just one? Every bite was better than the last. I wanted all the Dubois cakes. After thirteen samples—a full baker's dozen—I was ready for a nap and thoroughly confused about which one I liked best.

"*Qu'aimes tu, mademoiselle*? Do you have a favorite?"

"The raspberry. No, the almond. Wait! No, the lemon butter. All of them! I don't know. I can't choose!"

Hale glanced at the wide-eyed baker and laughed. "You know your bride well, *monsieur*."

I looked at Hale in question. "Why? What does that mean?"

"I had the remaining cakes delivered to the house. You can sample them again when we get home. I figured you'd need more time. That way, you can run an actual experiment. The one you destroy first will obviously be the favorite."

This was not part of the engagement diet. Other brides were having things nipped and tucked and living off celery juice two months out from their weddings. My fiancé just had thirteen cakes delivered to our door. That was our kind of love.

"Wait. Thirteen cakes are really waiting for me at home?" This man, this miraculous god of a man, had just delivered heaven to my house. He could just as easily be the devil himself. I snickered. "I have a fitting tomorrow."

"So?"

"So…nothing." The fact that he didn't see a problem made me fall for him even more. "I seriously love you."

"Ah, you see?" Chef Dubois cheered. "You are happy, so your groom is happy."

"Amen to that." I dusted the crumbs off my clothes and stood. People hugged their bakers, right? Screw it. I flung my arms around the pudgy man and—oh my, he smelled like childhood and world peace and cupcakes. "Thank you. This was the best day ever!"

He laughed and patted my head, which only made me love him more.

On the drive home, I couldn't stop smiling. And every time Hale glanced at me, he chuckled.

"You know how some couples finish each other's sentences?" I asked.

"Yes."

"We're not like that. We're totally opposite, but you know what?"

"What?"

"You get me more than anyone else in this world."

His fingers laced with mine and he squeezed. "I just like to see you happy."

Lifting his hand, I kissed his knuckles. "*You* make me happy. Very, very happy."

As soon as we got home I started packing but before I even organized my underwear my phone buzzed.

"Hello," I answered, still on a pleasant sugar high.

"Meyers," Remington's brisk voice wailed over the line. "Those pigeons are back. They shit all over my car. Get down here with something to clean it up."

"Remington, it's Sunday."

"Exactly. Alphonse is off."

"So am I."

"Meyers, don't piss me off." He was especially prickly and looking to punish me, probably for taking all his cigarettes.

"Fine. But you're going to have to wait until I wrap up what I'm doing."

"Good enough." He hung up and I frowned. "That was weird."

I only had so much winter clothes, so it didn't take long for me to finish packing. When I carried my suitcase downstairs I stuck it by the door. "I have to go to your dad's."

Hale looked up from the couch where he sat with Elara. "For what?"

"Something about bird shit."

He scowled. "Tell him to handle it himself. It's your day off."

"It'll be easier to just go over there. I won't be long." I kissed his cheek then Elara's head. Ah, the fancy life of a glorified assistant.

It was easier to walk down the beach to get to Remington's than to drive this time of day, so I left through the back. The lights of the guesthouse were on so I assumed Andrew was home and en-joying his night off.

When I reached Remington's house, I braced for his usual cigarette-withdrawal pleasantness. Last time I was there I threatened to muzzle him with a nicotine patch right over his mouth.

Plugging the code into the keypad, I entered through the sliding door. "Remington?"

The house was quiet and dark. He better not be out front smoking. I grabbed a bottle of window cleaner and a roll of paper towels, then headed to the front. When I opened the door, I came up short.

"What the fuck…?" A white Rubicon Jeep sat in the driveway, not a drop of bird shit on the exterior. Did he have company over?

I moved toward the garage and called for him again, "Remington?"

Hale stepped out from behind the Jeep, Elara perched on his hip, rattling a set of keys. "Surprise!"

What the hell was going on? I looked at the garage, but the door was closed. "Huh? Where's your dad?"

"He's in New England with Odette."

"But he just called me…"

"Ma Ma Ma Ma," Elara called as Hale crossed the drive.

"Do you like it?"

I looked at the Jeep and then back to him. "Um, sure. But I'm a little confused. Did you buy this?"

"With the money from the interview." He took the keys from Elara and handed them to me. "It's yours."

My jaw dropped. "What?" I'd never owned a brand-new car. And I wasn't used to big surprises —at least not the good kind. "You got me a car?"

"Take it for a spin."

"You got me a…*car*. Like, for real, an actual car."

He laughed at my shock. "You needed something more reliable."

And something spider-free. I looked back at the

Jeep and at him again. *"You got me a car!"* I rushed to the door and pulled it open. Buttery white leather with blue piping covered the seats. "Look at this radio!" I finally had cordless Bluetooth. "You even got a new car seat for peanut!"

I flipped buttons and turned dials, scrambling around like a squirrel on crack. Hale stuck by my side, vicariously enjoying my excitement.

"The interview really paid for this?"

"For the most part."

I shook my head. He was like a money magnet. "I love it. Thank you."

"Here." He dropped the fob into the cup holder. It was attached to a glittery unicorn key-chain. "Let's go for a spin."

Once Elara was fastened safely in her seat, I backed out of the driveway. The Jeep was much larger than what I was used to, but surprisingly smooth on the road.

Hale took my phone and hit a few buttons. A moment later, my music synched with the vehicle's system and The Emotions *Best of My Love* came on. I couldn't stop smiling as we drove with the windows down, the wind blowing in my hair.

"Does the top come off?"

"It opens. When it's warmer and Elara's not in the back you can try it out."

"Hale…" I looked at him, in awe of his thoughtfulness. "This is the nicest gift anyone has ever given me."

"Technically, you bought it for yourself."

"No, I didn't." If the magazine had only inter-viewed me I would have barely been able to afford an inflatable raft. Everyone in the world wanted a piece of Hale and the rest of the Davenports. This was all him.

"Rayne, when are you going to realize that everything's changed? People want to know you. They want to love you as much as I do."

My smile faltered, but I quickly forced it back into place. That wasn't true. Nosiness wasn't the same as affection. Those people didn't know me and they wouldn't hesitate to judge and crucify me if they found me lacking.

"We received an offer for the wedding."

I looked at him, confused, as I navigated my way toward Mallory Square. "What do you mean, an offer?"

"Several magazines want to cover it. We could make a decent amount."

My foot eased off the gas. "Since when do you enjoy being such a public figure?" When I met Hale, he was extremely private, especially about his private life. "Is this about your dad?"

"What?"

"I'm just trying to understand why you would even entertain the idea of letting reporters in on what should be one of the most intimate moments of our life?"

It was bad enough we were sharing our wedding day with three hundred strangers.

"What the hell would my dad have to do with it? If I was thinking of anyone, I was thinking of your mom. We could buy her a house with the money they're willing to pay."

I wanted to say we could buy her a house anyway, but I still didn't know if my financial situation would change with my name. There hadn't been a good time to bring up the prenup and I sort of just hoped the whole thing would go away if I didn't mention it.

"My mom has a house."

"A house near us, Rayne."

Dear God, did I want my mom living that close again? What was I thinking? None of this mattered. "I don't want a bunch of video cameras and reporters intruding on our wedding day. The answer's no."

"Fine."

"Fine." I pressed my lips tight. "And next time it would be nice if you didn't spring this stuff on me."

"What are you talking about? I just told you."

"But you knew before now. This is exactly why I hate surprises."

"You hate surprises?"

"Well, no. But I don't like the bad ones."

"I was communicating with you, not trying to surprise you with bad news. You said no, so it's a no. End of story."

"Do *you* want cameras there?"

"I want you to be happy. How did this become a fight?"

"It just seems like there's been a lot of secrecy lately. I'd prefer it if I wasn't always the last to know."

"Are you kidding me? I surprised you with a tasting and a car and I'm somehow the bad guy? You act like I'm making deals behind your back."

Because he was. He'd met with his lawyer and had a prenup drawn up without even discussing it with me. Between the car, the bakery, and now these offers he was getting from reporters, he'd proven how oblivious I could be. And why this sudden concern for my mom? "If you're worried about me or my family spending all your money, don't. We're perfectly stable on our own."

The air of the Jeep chilled. His voice was low and cold. "What the hell does that mean?"

I shook my head, unable to form the words I wanted to say. He said it himself, *I* technically bought this car. Was he already allocating our assets? "No one is after your money, Hale. I'm not Jasmine."

The moment her name left my mouth I winced. What the hell was wrong with me?

"That's enough," he said with frightening calm. "Pull over up here."

"Where?" There were only privately owned parking lots in this area.

"Just stop the fucking car, Rayne."

I immediately pulled over, worried I'd gone too far. "What are you doing?"

He got out of the Jeep and slammed the door. "I'll get a ride home."

"Hale."

He turned and walked away. I lowered my head onto the steering wheel and cursed, only to jump when a horn beeped.

When I got home I carried Elara in and took her up to her crib. Hale wasn't home and I didn't know if I should call him or make dinner or what, so I texted him.

I'm sorry.

AN HOUR PASSED and he still hadn't responded.

The longer I waited, the more I felt like a complete schmuck. What was wrong with me? He treated me to a fantastic day and ended it with a brand new car. What kind of woman turned that into a fight?

That damn prenup was making me crazy. Why hadn't he told me about it yet? Was it a power play to wait until the last minute? I hated the thought that he might have a strategy—mostly because such toxic thinking had more to do with my own personal insecurities than anything Hale had done, but I'd taken it out on him all the same. I wasn't sure how I felt about the contract, but I hated that he was keeping secrets.

I tore through three slices of cake and called Elle. But there was only so much I could explain in regard to Jasmine, so she didn't understand why Hale got so triggered.

"That seems like an extreme overreaction to mentioning his ex. They broke up. She married his dad. He's got you. Maybe the issue should be why he cares so much about a woman he's no longer with."

He cared because it was much more complicated than hopping Davenports. Jasmine had used Remington to get pregnant when she learned Hale wasn't the sort of man to make such careless mistakes. Then she'd used Elara to blackmail the Davenports. But she didn't stop there. Once she saw Hale emotionally invested in Elara, she went for the jugular. Remington's offer of marriage was the only thing that stopped her from bleeding Hale dry.

In my opinion, Remington owed his son that much, but Hale hated that his father had once again involved himself where he didn't belong. Either way, those details were top secret. No one, not even his other two kids knew that Elara was really their sibling and not Hale's biological daughter.

"I can't believe he bought you a car."

"And I ruined it."

"No, you didn't. Couples fight. He'll come home and you'll explain why you said what you said."

"I hate feeling like the last to know."

"Ray, surprises are meant to be secretive. That's the point."

"He wants to let reporters into our wedding."

"No, he doesn't. You said no and he said fine."

"I know Hale. If he doesn't want something, he's direct and to the point. He would have told them no right away if he wasn't considering it on some level."

"He was just weighing options, Rayne. It's sort of sweet he was thinking of your mom."

"Don't you get it? He's trying to keep our finances separate. That's why he wants me to have this money."

"I think you're reading way too far into this. It was just an idea."

"It sounded more like a suggestion."

"What does it matter? You said no and he dropped it."

I licked my spoon, jumping between the ganache frosting and the butter cream. "He's going to spring that prenup on me. I know it."

"Did you ask him about it?"

"No?"

"Why not?"

I didn't have an answer. "What if he has it because he doesn't fully trust me? Why else would he have a backup plan? If he needs an escape route, maybe we shouldn't get married in the first place."

"Hale trusts you, Ray. But he has a lot of assets and divorce can get really messy."

"Gee, thanks." This conversation wasn't helping. I wiped my eyes and stared over the box of mini cakes at the bedroom door, my feet under my knees. "This isn't like him. We both have to travel this week. Where is he?"

"He's angry. Give him time."

I didn't have time. "Are you sure you don't want to come to New York with me?"

"Ray, I can't."

"Are you sure? Barrett's there on an underwear shoot."

"I can't."

I sighed, hating how needy I felt at the moment. "There's something else I have to tell you."

"What?" Elle asked uneasily.

"I contacted my dad."

"Rayne, no!"

"I know, I know. But it doesn't matter. He didn't respond and I'm over it. I just couldn't get married without at least trying."

She sighed. "Are you sure you're okay?"

I sniffed and dashed away a tear. "I'll be okay. I know the drill." A few days of feeling bad for myself, a week of eating my feelings, then anger, then distraction. "Look at it this way, when I get to the angry stage, you could probably get me to take one of those kickboxing classes at the gym with you."

She didn't laugh and neither did I. "Did you tell Hale?"

"There's nothing to tell." I was a big, fat, secret-keeping hypocrite.

"Maybe that's why you were so prickly with him this afternoon."

My head snapped up when I heard the front door open.

"Hale's home. I have to go."

"Have a safe trip to New York. Text me when you land."

"I will. Bye." I tossed my phone under the covers and stared at the door, waiting for Hale to appear. When he didn't, I frowned and climbed out of bed. At the top of the stairs, I heard him listening to something on his phone.

I tiptoed down and paused at the landing when I saw him sitting on the couch. "Hale."

He seemed to purposely avoid looking at me. "I'm tired, Rayne."

His rejection hit like a bullet to the chest. "Are you coming to bed?"

He sighed and shut off his phone, dousing the house in silence.

I waited several seconds for him to move or speak, but he stayed quiet.

"Hale, I never should have said what I said. I'm sorry."

His head shook, but he didn't look at me. He just stayed seated on the couch. "Have I ever made an issue out of your financial circumstances?"

My stomach twisted with guilt and shame. "No."

"No. And have I ever bitched about taking care of things?"

"No."

"So why would you assume I—"

"I saw the prenup." The air chilled and when he didn't respond, I further explained. "I wasn't snooping. It was in your drawer. I saw it when I was getting your suit together for the photoshoot."

His head lowered and his shoulders lifted with a deep sigh.

"Why do you have that, Hale? And why were you hiding it in your closet of all places."

"I wasn't hiding it."

"Because you normally keep important files in your sock drawer. Come on, Hale."

"Fine. Maybe I was. But only because I…" He hesitated. "Maybe I was hiding it from myself."

"Do you think I'm after your money—"

"No, I don't think that."

"Then why—"

"I don't have a say in it, Rayne."

I drew back. "What?"

He shook his head. "There are trusts of mine that have certain bylaws I can't override."

"Trusts from Remington?"

"Who else?"

So Remington knew about the prenup. I wasn't

surprised, but I thought assuming as much would make it hurt less.

"Do you want me to sign it?"

His fingers raked through his hair. "I know you're not marrying me for my money, Rayne."

A tear tripped down my cheek. That wasn't exactly a no.

Stepping into the living room, I went to the table and pulled open a drawer and found a pen. Having a healthy relationship meant full transparency, even when the reality hurt.

"I hate when there's secrets between us, Hale. I'll sign whatever you need me to sign."

"Put that away."

"If it's because of Remington, then it's because of Remington. I believe you." Why was he looking at me like that? "That's what it is, right?"

The longer he hesitated the harder it became to guess what he was thinking. Did he really have a problem with the prenup or did he think it was a sound contract with unfortunate side effects? A *take your medicine and get over the bad taste so we can move on* situation?

I honestly wasn't sure if I wanted to know his feelings now that we were staring this in the face. It was easier to blame Remington. At least then it wouldn't reflect a lack of trust on our part.

"I don't want to fight, Hale. Today was perfect and I hate that I ruined it. Do you want me to go get it?"

"It's not here."

"Where is it?"

"My lawyer's working on it."

"With Remington?"

He shook his head again. "Not yet. We're looking for loopholes."

Knowing Remington, he wouldn't find any. "It's okay—"

"No, it's not," he snapped, then sighed. "I hid it from you because I know you love him."

He was hiding it to protect my feelings for Remington? The ache in my chest spread.

Hale spent most days trying to disentangle his life from his father's. My business association and love for the man created an obstacle that complicated his exit plans. While Hale tolerated our bond, I knew he'd prefer it if I cut ties, but he would never ask that of me.

Hale could have used this to prove how cold and manipulative Remington could be, but he hadn't. Instead, he tried to shield me from any pain his father might cause.

I lowered into the club chair. Remington didn't draw this up to hurt me. Chances were it was drawn up long before he even knew of my existence. When it came into play, he might have hesitated to consider the impact, but he would have done the necessary thing in his eyes and left emotion out of it.

I could almost hear him saying, *Marriage is a business deal, Meyers. It has nothing to do with love.* Somehow, that made this feel less personal.

"He won't budge on it," I said, trying to view it through the eyes of a businesswoman.

When a man like Remington Davenport drew up a contract, he made sure it was according to his terms and legally binding from all angles. His legacy was for his children and his children alone, not even his wives got a piece of what he had ear-marked for them. I would be no different.

"I'm sorry, Rayne."

I looked up at him. "Why are you sorry? You didn't do it."

"I'm sorry he hurt you. I wanted to prevent that from happening. I wanted to protect you from…him."

My heart broke, not because of Remington and his stupid contract, but for Hale. "He didn't do this to hurt me. This is just what he does."

"He systematically complicates our lives by inserting himself—"

"No, Hale. This might hurt me, but he did it to protect you."

"You defend him too easily."

"Those conditions existed long before me. Don't let this be one more wedge between you two. It's fine. I'll sign whatever you need me to sign and we'll put it behind us."

His gaze held mine as he studied me for a long moment. "Just like that?"

I nodded.

What else was I going to do? I worked for Remington. I'd seen firsthand how firm he could be when he felt strongly about something. It was only a thing if I made a thing about it. "I'll sign whatever you need me to sign."

That night, as I lay in bed beside Hale as he slept peacefully, I realized two things. First, money complicated matters as much as it fixed them. And, second, Hale no longer had a secret, but I did.

Concrete Jungle

WHERE BRIDES ARE MADE OF...

"Do you have all your flight information?"

Since Hale was catching an international flight, he left me the jet. It was a straight ride to the Big Apple once I made it onto the tarmac. "It's the long, shiny tube that looks like a Tylenol with wings, right?"

"You're hilarious." He fisted the lapels of my cardigan and tugged me close for a kiss. "Do you have your coat? It's still in the mid-thirties there."

"Yes, Daddy."

He yanked me to his chest and swatted my ass, then he kissed me hard. "Text me as soon as you land."

"You'll be in the air."

"Text me anyway."

"And give your regards to Broadway?" I threw out some jazz hands, but I was too exhausted to go into full cancan *a la* Rockette.

He laughed. "By now your playlist must have every song to ever mention New York."

215

I had to do something while up night after night with insomnia. "I might have downloaded a few more while you were sleeping. Besides, life's better when you live like the main character of a musical."

"I love you."

"I love you too." I shouldered through the excruciating ache that always came with goodbyes by pretending I was unfazed by our parting. Elara was a great distraction until I realized I would be leaving her too. "No growing while I'm gone, understand?"

She grabbed my nose and squeezed.

"I arranged a car service, so you don't have to deal with cabs."

I swooned with the vapors, going full-on southern. "Why, I do declare, however, would I survive without all these big powerful men in my life makin' every little decision for me? Such dangers could befall a woman on her own in the big city."

"I'm serious, Rayne. I don't want you walking alone at night. And I don't want you getting into cars with strangers."

"Is this a service through the hotel or a Davenport employee?"

"This is a private arrangement. He's a man named Martell Sharoski. He'll take you wherever you need to go. I already programmed his name in your phone."

I never mastered that cool double-fingered whistle trick they used to hail cabs in the movies, so I appreciated having a driver. "Thank you."

"If you have any problems while you're there,

Sharoski will handle it. He's highly trained in tactical driving and unarmed combat."

I snorted. "Am I joining the cast of *Fast and Furious*?"

"The city can be dangerous, Rayne. Sharoski will keep you safe."

I batted my eyes. "Aren't you afraid I might pull a Whitney and fall in love with this bodyguard slash driver? You are leaving me all alone, after all."

He pinched my chin. "Not funny."

"Is he cute? Tall? How's his smell?"

"I think you'll find him about as personable as a longsword. Cute if you don't mind scars. Taller than most. And he never lets anyone close enough to smell him."

"Sounds like a real peach."

"He's very good at what he does. I'm trusting him with your life."

"All right, Hale, now you're making me nervous. I'm only going to New York."

"A place you've only visited once."

"Yes, but I'm going to be staying in one of the poshest hotels in the country. And your sister's there. So is Barrett. I'll be fine."

He pressed his lips tight and I realized he was truly uncomfortable leaving me.

"Hey." I hugged him. "Nothing bad's going to happen. Focus on your work and before you know it we'll be together again."

He tucked a strand of hair behind my ear and looked into my eyes. "What did I think about before I loved you?"

"I imagine acquisitions and mergers. Nothing

nearly as sexy as this hot mess." I shimmied my boobs against his chest and he laughed. "I love you. I'll be fine. You're going to miss your flight if you don't get moving."

After several more kisses and goodbyes, I was on my way.

Once I boarded the private jet, the captain gave me a rundown of the flight like they usually did with Hale. I thought we were going to La-Guardia but this time we were landing in a private airport I'd never heard of. This made me more anxious than I already was when I traveled.

I texted my new travel companion, Martell Sharoski, letting him know when and where my flight was scheduled to land. Good old Marty responded right away, confirming that he would be waiting on the tarmac when I arrived.

Seraphina texted me several times that morning in an attempt to hype me up, but I was running on minimal coffee and no sleep, so no matter how many times she reminded me that New York was the beating heart of the fashion industry and her boutique had everything I needed, an exaggerated *Yay* and a few emojis were all I could muster.

Her store was right on Madison Ave, not far from the hotel, so I imagined I'd go there first. After checking in, of course.

I napped a little on the flight and that helped matters, but I still needed to find coffee. Martell was waiting by a dark town car when I arrived on the tarmac. When Hale said the driver was taller than most he wasn't kidding. Sharoski was an oak tree of a man with a long, jagged scar carved from his eye to his jaw.

Feeling a little like an underdressed Eva Gabor and about as important as Jackie Onassis, I shaded my eyes from the jet's boarding stairs and took a moment to process that this was my life.

"Let the adventure begin," I mumbled, taking the steps carefully as the cold February wind whipped against my clothes. I was not cut out for these northern climates anymore.

"Rayne Meyers?" Sharoski said as I approached the sleek town car.

"That's me. You must be Martell."

"Yes, ma'am." He immediately relieved me of my bag and opened the back door. "Welcome to New York." He replaced the W of welcome with a V in a deep voice that would make any woman shiver—both with fear and awareness.

Yowzers. This man was a man-man. The sort who could nick himself with an ax and barely flinch. The moment he had my luggage stowed in the trunk and he was behind the wheel, we were on our way.

"With morning traffic we're looking at about an hour's drive to the Plaza."

"Thank you." I texted Hale even though he wouldn't get the message until he landed in Tokyo late that night.

Phina had texted me another three times with pictures of champagne on ice and reminders to bring any meaningful accessories. I had no meaningful accessories aside from the two rings Hale had given me.

Within minutes my anxiety hit the crescendo

of a fast ticking time bomb even my music couldn't calm. I wasn't sure why I was so nervous. Maybe because this meant the wedding was actually happening. Or maybe because I would be on my own making crucial decisions and I was worried others might take issues with my choices. Either way, I really wished Hale or Elle had come with me.

"Hey Marty, is it possible to stop and get some coffee on the way."

"Absolutely, Ms. Meyers."

Ugh. Ms. Meyers was a woman I hadn't been in years. A name that wouldn't exist after April. "Call me Rayne."

"Yes, ma'am."

He was very formal. If we were going to see a lot of each other, I wanted to break the ice. He should learn right out of the gate that I was the chatty sort—especially when I was anxious. "How long have you known Hale?"

"I've driven the Davenports for years."

"Oh. Cool." I glanced out the window, eager to get to my destination and nervous about the day ahead. "So, where are you from?"

"Many places."

Marty was not a talker.

We stopped at a Dunkin and I insisted Marty get something as well. He reluctantly accepted once he realized I wouldn't back down. His body language and vigilant demeanor indicated extensive military training, but I had a special gift for making uptight men let down their guard.

"Do you like your hot chocolate?"

"Delicious. Thank you."

I could tell he wasn't used to passengers talking

to him this much, but he was my only friend in New York at the moment and my only distraction from the grumbles in my stomach.

"You should try the home fries before they get cold."

He didn't respond but I knew I'd eventually crack him.

New York had a way of taking me back to childhood. Not that I ever visited the city as a child. But once, when I was a little girl, I got lost on a crowded beach and the experience caused the same nervous ball of uncertainty in my stomach.

I still recall how the strange adults towered over me like skyscrapers, blocking the sun. No matter how hard I looked, I couldn't find my mom or our familiar umbrella and blanket. Manhattan was sort of like that. Big, intimidating, unfamiliar, daunting, always bustling, and big. Did I mention it was big?

A cab honked its horn and Marty muttered a slur in Slavic language. In my head I had narrowed him down to Russian or Czech, or maybe he was Polish. Not that this mattered, but trying to pinpoint his homeland based on the eight—maybe ten —words he said in the past thirty minutes helped me not to freak out about encroaching surroundings.

A man jaywalked just as a traffic light was about to change from green to red and Marty hissed a few non-English words again. I was pretty sure he said something profane as we missed our chance to turn.

Our eyes met through the rearview mirror and the corner of his mouth twitched. He could so easily be a hitman, but that little winky-smirk threw me off. Leave it to me to buy an assassin hot cocoa. Holding his intimidating stare in the reflection, I laughed nervously.

We pulled up to the Plaza. A checkerboard walkway bordered a set of red-carpeted stairs. Doormen, dressed in timeless livery, assisted guests and carried luggage to gold bell carts. One opened my door and I flinched, not used to such rapid service.

Marty abandoned his post behind the wheel and began barking orders about my luggage. He took his job very seriously, his stern voice and dictator-like manner making about as much fuss as a motorcade. For a moment, I felt a little like an underqualified Princess Diana, overwhelmed by empathy for all the times her prince had abandoned her.

Then I frowned, not liking that scenario at all.

What was wrong with me? When had I become this needy co-dependent accessory to a man? Had my life become so sheltered in the short time I lived with the Davenports that I forgot how exhilarating it could be to live spontaneously?

Exhilarating? Maybe nauseating was a better term.

Misremembering how I used to live as a single woman had to be a sign of how deeply I'd embedded my life with the Davenports. It was like I completely forgot how to make decisions on my own. Maybe this trip was a necessary part of becoming more autonomous.

For the next few days, I'd be Rayne Meyers. Not Rayne, Hale's fiancée or the future Mrs. Davenport. Not Rayne, Remington Davenport's personal assistant. And not Rayne, Elara's…whatever I was to Elara. Step-Daddy's fiancée? No, that wasn't right. Pre-step-parent? Whatever. Today, I was neither. I was just good old Rayne.

Before Hale, I did everything alone. I took risks and flew through life by the seat of my pants. Sure, there were some crash-and-burn moments, but I survived. I needed to tap into that Rayne Meyers and stop making such a big deal out of one little trip on my own.

Breathing a deep lungful of that fumid New York air, I prepared to exit the car. "This is a fun trip," I reminded myself, scooching toward the open door.

Marty supervised the luggage transfer so I never needed to touch more than my purse. He even tipped the bellman so I didn't have to.

"You have my number if you need to go anywhere."

"Yes. Thank you." I reached into my bag and withdrew my wallet.

He waved a hand. "Mr. Davenport's taken care of everything."

"Oh. Okay." A car beeped and I flinched again.

Marty's friendly expression turned into a scowl as he eyeballed the driver. Then he smiled at me and I noticed the large gap in his otherwise straight teeth. This man had definitely buried a body before.

"Right. Okay then. Well, thanks."

With a nod, he returned to his sleek town car

and pulled away. I wondered where he went. Did he just camp out in a parking garage nearby?

"Ma'am, if you'll follow me I can show you to the front desk," said a bellman, dressed head to toe in a literal gold-trimmed uniform. He wore white gloves. *White gloves!* I was living in an Annie musical.

Heat gusted from the grand entrance as hotel guests entered and exited the building. I stood on the red-carpeted steps, my gaze angling up, up, up, up the stonewalls to the cathedral-like angles of the enormous French Renaissance hotel. A year ago, if someone told me this was where I'd be standing I would have bet a million dollars they were wrong.

I verified my name with the front desk and told them I was staying in the Davenport suite. At that point, they pulled out all the stops. A woman in a sharp business suit explained the hotel layout as we skirted our way around guests and up to the twentieth floor.

"You have full use of our butler service. If there's anything you require during your stay, please feel free to ask." She opened the door to the penthouse and my jaw nearly hit the polished, herringbone floor.

Central Park was the focal point of the two-story skyline view. There was a brief tour, but I was on sensory overload, so not much sank in. The lavishness of the living room alone had some of the most opulent fixtures I'd ever seen.

"Holy shit."

Her training must have been impeccable because she didn't bat an eye at my trash mouth. "The master bath is through this door."

A gilded floral motif complemented mosaic floors. Gold-plated fixtures surrounded the shower and tub. This shit was Disney princess fancy, and not cottage-core village princess either. This was screwed-the-beast, get-the-library, and inherit-the-castle next-level-shit.

"The wet bar is fully stocked, and if there's anything particular you require, we can have it delivered."

I was on overload. How much did a place like this cost? Who could afford this? New York was beaucoup bucks to begin with. This suite-penthouse-tower-whatever-you-called-it was straight-up insane.

"Is there anything else you require?"

I peeled my gaze away from the beveled moldings and jumped. There were three of them—the woman, the man with my luggage, and another man in a tux, his gloved hands folded at his waist. Where were they coming from?

"Um… I think I'm good." Literally feeling like Kevin McCallister, I fumbled through my pockets and pulled out a crumpled Dunkin receipt. "Hold on. Don't go anywhere." I rushed to dig out a few dollars from my purse and handed each of them a tip.

The woman nodded and exited the suite while the bellhop carried my luggage to the master bedroom and then left. The other guy with the white gloves grinned.

I looked behind me because I wasn't sure if he was waiting for someone or something else to appear. So I smiled—super cheesy with a lot of teeth to hide my awkwardness and nerves.

"Can I make you a drink, Ms. Meyers?"

Was this guy from room service? I was so confused. "What are you serving?"

A drink sounded phenomenal, but it was barely past ten. Was this a New York thing? Maybe he meant coffee or some sort of brunch cocktail.

"I can offer water, *Pellegrino* or non-sparkling, French pressed coffee or espresso, or perhaps something stronger. Mr. Davenport suggested margaritas on the rocks. I have Casa Dragones Blanco, per his request. He mentioned it was a favorite of yours."

This guy had done his research. "And, who are you?"

"I'm your majordomo."

My brain instantly filled with images of Barbie, going straight to Ken's mojo dojo casa house. "And a majordomo is a…?"

"Butler, ma'am. I'll be your steward during your stay. I attend to any of your personal needs."

Oh, my God, I had a real Jeeves. "What do I call you?"

"You may address me as Mr. Purcell, if it pleases you, ma'am."

"Okay, Mr. Purcell. First rule, I'm not a big fan of ma'am. You can call me Rayne or even *hey you*. But please don't feel the need to be so formal. "

"As you wish. Have you decided on a beverage, madam?"

Tricky. I didn't have the same adverse reaction to madam as I did to ma'am, so I let it slide. "Sure.

I'll go with option C, and let's make it a double, Percy."

His cheek twitched, but he didn't correct me for shortening his name.

I watched as he got to work at the wet bar, uncorking the tequila and setting out several limes. Keeping his gloves on, he sliced the fruit and pressed it onto a glass juicer. Holy crap he was making the margarita from scratch—totally James Bond. No bottled mix or anything.

I approached the bar. "Do you do this for everyone, Percy?"

He smirked again, but remained focused on his work. "Everyone who stays in the penthouse."

Did he sleep here too? "So… If I needed something, like a sandwich or a soft pretzel…"

"I'd see to it." He poured the juice into a shaker over ice and added the alcohol and a few other ingredients. Using only two fingers, he set out a margarita glass, holding it only by the stem and poured. "Would you like your cocktail in the sitting room?"

I laughed, sort of outside of myself. "Sure."

He transferred the margarita to a silver tray and carried it into the other room, waiting for me to select a seat. My butler was serving cocktails in the sitting room and my life had become that of a game piece in Clue. This was fucking nuts.

Skipping after him I plopped down on the French Renaissance settee. "Why thank you, Percy." I took the margarita with two hands and sipped. "Uh—mazing." My lips snapped at the delicious tartness. "Wow. This clearly isn't your first tequila rodeo." The smooth blend of lime and salt tasted like it came right out of Barcelona.

"If there's nothing else…"

"Oh." I wanted to get to know him if we were going to be hanging out over the next few days, and he seemed less intimidating than Marty my driver. "Why don't you make a drink for yourself?"

He smiled. "Thank you for the offer, but I must decline."

I studied him for a long moment. He looked to be in his mid-twenties, but he talked like he was torn fresh out of a Victorian novel. No millennial was that serious. I bet he had tattoos under that tuxedo.

"I won't tell your boss if you have a drink. Relax. I'm probably the easiest guest you'll ever have."

"Thank you, but I must decline."

Hmm. He was going to be a tough nut to crack. I sipped my margarita. "You sure? It's really good."

"Positive, madam. I'm pleased you like it."

"I guess I have everything I need then."

He nodded. "If there's anything else, you can ring the bell." He pointedly tipped his gaze toward the antique end table.

I followed his stare to a small bell—so very Queen Elizabeth. "Okeydokey."

After Mr. Purcell—I couldn't call him that. It was too formal. He was Percy—After Percy left the sitting room—not quite sure where he went—I stared at the furniture.

A few minutes later I was slurping the last few drops out of my cocktail and crunching on the lime-flavored ice cubes. Not quite ready to head out into the world of traffic and bridal veils, I texted Hale.

> This hotel is insane! I just housed a margarita at 10:23 in the morning. My butler made it. I have a butler!

IT LOST a little of the sheen when there was no response. I glanced at the time. Hale wouldn't be landing for hours. Eyeing the bell, I considered asking Percy to make another margarita just so I could have his company again. I only hesitated because I didn't want to be trashed when I left for Phina's boutique.

Setting my glass aside, I drummed my fingers on the arm of the settee, debating if I should let Hale's sister know I'd arrived. The moment she knew I was here it would be full-throttle wedding-gate for days, so it made more sense to procrastinate a while longer.

I picked up my phone and dialed the second contact on my speed dial

"Meyers," Remington answered briskly. "Did you make it to the hotel in one piece?"

"Rodger dodger. How much does a place like this run a night?"

He gave a gruff laugh. "What did I tell you about price inquiries? A real man never brags about how much his luxuries cost. And a classy woman should automatically assume—whatever it is—she's worth it."

"But seriously, Remington, how much? Did you know the tub spigot is plated in fourteen-carat gold? *Real* gold!"

"Why aren't you on your way to Madison Ave.?"

"My appointment's not for an hour."

"Oh, please. You're family. Get your ass downstairs and have Martell run you over to Phina's. New York isn't in a penthouse. Get outside and experience it."

"Hey, about Martell, where did you find him?"

"He's Hale's guy."

"But you use him too, right?"

"When I'm in the city."

"So, what do you know about him?"

"He's a goddamn chauffer, Meyers. Why the hell would I want to know more than the fact that he knows his way around the city?"

I tsked. "Everyone has a story, Remington."

"Some stories aren't interesting or worth my time—or yours. For God's sake, stop hanging around the staff and make real friends."

"Remington, *I'm* staff."

He grumbled, unable to argue with the truth. "Go shopping, Meyers. Try to do something ladylike for a change."

I sighed. "Fine. Tell Odette I said hi."

"She's still in be—" He caught himself and grumbled again. "Tricky, Meyers."

I grinned, relieved by the confirmation that he was in fact with Odette and things seemed back to normal where their relationship was concerned. "Bye, Remington."

"Goodbye. Say hi to Phina for me."

"You should call her and say hi yourself."

"Goodbye, Meyers."

"Call your daughter!" I hung up.

It was bride time.

When I stood, the alcohol had taken effect. "Whoa. Hey, Purce, do you have a bat phone that connects directly to my driver or should I just shoot him a text?" I wasn't sure if there was some sort of chauffer-butler-etiquette or interconnected communication switchboard I wasn't aware of. "Percy?"

Crickets.

"Mr. Purcell?"

I glanced at the bell and tapped it with two fingers.

"Yes, madam?" The butler appeared out of nowhere.

Too weird. I decided to play it up. "Be a darling and ring Mr. Sharoski to pull the car around. I will be leaving presently for my bridal appointment."

He didn't even flinch. "Yes, madam."

A Garter is Not a Headpiece

"THERE'S MY FUTURE SISTER!" Seraphina rushed to greet me the second I entered her posh boutique situated appropriately on Madison Ave.

I grunted as she flung her arms around me and propelled me toward an elegant display. "Hey, Phina."

"I'm so excited you're finally here!" she squealed as if anyone could have mistaken her enthusiasm for a lesser emotion. Excited might have actually been an understatement. "I've had gowns sent in from all over the world for you to try on."

The boutique was her flagship store and her first brick and mortar location, but I assumed the Davenport name outfitted her with impressive collateral when it came to calling in favors with other designer brands. I wasn't a designer girl—per se—but I knew who Oscar de la Renta and Vera Wang were.

I stepped into the connecting room and stilled.

Holy crap, there was more than a million dollars of tulle surrounding the dressing room.

"I'm so thrilled you came here for your gown, Rayne. More than excited. Truly flattered."

No matter how privileged Hale's sister's life had been, she managed to stay humble enough to get away with saying sweet stuff like that and still sound completely genuine.

Lacing her arm in mine, she pulled me across the white marble floor. "Now, Hale tells me this is a stress-free shopping spree, so whatever you want you get. We're going to have so much fun." She spun to face the woman folding lingerie at a granite counter on the other side of the store. "Lilly, will you pour a glass of champagne for our special guest?"

"Of course." Lilly set down the ivory panties to do Phina's bidding.

Even the littlest Davenports had an intimidating edge to them.

"So…" Phina fanned out her fingers and breathed in as if she could detect my taste through the scent of smell alone. "What sort of gown did you have in mind?"

"Uh, a white one."

Hale's sister laughed. "Well, no kidding. What sort of bodice? Are we thinking traditional or modern? Minimalistic or something divinely couture and beaded?"

Lilly returned with a silver tray, two champagne flutes fizzing softly. I instantly wondered if she knew Percy.

"To sisters." Phina held up her glass. "I've always dreamed I'd have one, and I'm so glad my brother found you. We're going to be best friends, Rayne. Cheers."

Oh, boy. I instinctively sensed Elle's head perk up from thirteen hundred miles away.

"Cheers."

As I sipped the champagne, it occurred to me that Seraphina already had a sister, but she would never know. To her, Elara would only ever be Hale's daughter and her niece.

"I have the entire afternoon blocked off, so we're in no rush today."

We sat on a set of white leather chairs as Lilly hauled out another long rack of white gowns. There were so many.

Seraphina, who could never sit longer than a few minutes, sprung to her five-inch blush heels. She was styled and stunning enough to be a Kardashian, and there I was sitting in my jeggings and boots looking like a Han Solo reject. I should have been sipping my champagne through a straw because my fashion sense sucked.

"What do you say we start with the more traditional gowns? You'd look so elegant in a long train with Italian beading and lace."

"Okay, but nothing too complicated." I was prone to tripping over my own feet.

"Of course. I know just the one."

Ten minutes later I was lugging around an impossibly heavy dress that fit about as comfortably as a beaded strait jacket. "I think this is a bit much."

"There's no such thing as too much when you're a bride."

I didn't agree with that. "I think the Princess of

Wales had a shorter train. How about something more ergonomic?"

She laughed. "It's a bridal gown, not an office chair, Rayne." Unhooking the top clasp, Phina followed me back into the dressing area. "But I hear what you're saying. We want your gown to look and feel like it was made specifically for you. Let's try something more contemporary."

Sure, because I screamed nifty and new-age. I was starting to sweat under the weight of beaded lace.

I'd been forced out of my own undergarments and squeezed into an ivory dominatrix bustier with more bones than the human body. It was cutting off the circulation to my ribs and my boobs were smashed into uplifted conformity. When I looked down all I saw was a butt crack of cleavage on my chest.

"I think this corset might be a size too small."

She stuck her finger between my skin and the ungiving silk as casually as a seasoned grandmother might wedge a thermometer up a baby's ass.

"Um, do I have a fever?" Her finger was literally buried between my tits.

"Nope, you're fine. It's supposed to be tight."

"It's crushing my chesticals."

She paused and then did a quick adjustment of my boobs. "If that's what you call your breasts I can only imagine what kind of other stuff my brother hears." She smiled as she adjusted the heavy silk. "I honestly think you're the best thing to ever happen to Hale. He's never been this happy or at ease. You singlehandedly pulled the stick out of his ass and turned him into a normal person."

I quickly learned there was no privacy when shopping with Hale's sister. She didn't hesitate to manhandle my private parts and gave no warning before cutting off my oxygen to cinch each bodice tighter than a hangman's knot.

As she tied off the next dress I thought my eyes might bulge out of my head. She literally pulled the tapes so tight the air was forced out of my lungs.

"Take a look."

I walked to the pillar of mirrors and stared in horror. "I look like a giant cupcake."

"You look gorgeous."

This could not be what girls were wearing these days. Could it? "How do you even sit down in something like this?"

"You'll be dancing and talking to guests all night anyway. You can sit once you're married."

"What if I have to pee?"

"Your bridesmaids will help you."

There was no way all this tulle and a bridesmaid would fit comfortably in a bathroom stall. "I don't think this is my style."

She pouted. "But you look so pretty and once your hair and makeup are done you'll be perfect."

Hale didn't care if I wore makeup and I typically didn't do more than Chapstick and mascara, so I wasn't sure if I'd be able to pull off the dramatic image she had in her mind—or if I wanted to.

I stared at my basic brown hair in a lopsided bun. "How do you think I should wear my hair?"

Her grey Davenport eyes met mine in the mirror. "You haven't picked an updo yet?"

"Phina, the wedding's two months away and I'm just now trying on dresses. I've never done this before."

She paced and took a long sip of her champagne, thinking and then regrouping. "You're lucky you came to me."

That wasn't an answer to the hair question.

"Lilly, call down to the salon and see if they have an opening for Rayne. Tell them we need an emergency consultation tomorrow." She released the ties of the gown and my insides expanded much like an inflatable life raft unfolds. "Don't wash your hair tonight. Updos hold up better when hair's a little dirty."

"Okay."

"While you're here, you can squeeze a salon visit in between a fitting and a makeup consultation. I'm guessing you haven't selected a cosmetologist yet either."

Was this another person I needed to headhunt? "Um…"

"On second thought, Lilly, call Devyn. He can book all of Rayne's appointments."

I was juggling three event coordinators and one bossy soon-to-be-sister-in-law.

Already missing Elara, I said, "I wanted to be back to Florida by the weekend."

"Then we have a lot to cover."

Those magic words unlocked my compliance. Sixteen dresses later I was exhausted and defeated. Nothing looked right on me. I wasn't fancy enough for gowns and the moment I tried one on, it showed.

"What if I wore a tux? That would be funny, right?"

Phina scowled. "You're not wearing a tuxedo on your wedding day. Hale wants to see you in a gown."

"Did he say that?"

"He didn't have to say it. I know my brother. He's traditional and boring."

"Hale's not boring!"

She waved a hand. "Whatever. He's … by the book. I know we have something here that you'll like. We just have to keep trying."

I openly sulked. I didn't want to try on any more dresses. I wanted to eat my feelings and put on some elastic-waisted pants, preferably made of fleece.

As she passed over several gowns, flicking through the selection. I refilled my champagne. It was past lunchtime and I was getting cranky.

"Wait! What's that one you just passed?"

Phina backtracked as she swiped through the rack of designer gowns. "This? You don't want this one. It's too plain."

I set my glass on the veneer table. I'd consumed enough champagne to no longer care that I was walking around like Princess Dominatrix Ivory Underpants in what was essentially a public setting. "Let me see it."

She sighed and lifted it off the rack. "It's very low cut, Rayne."

But it was simple. Spaghetti straps. All white

silk. No beads. A delicate crisscross open back. "Can I try it on?"

"We'll have to tape your boobs."

"I'm sorry, do what now?"

"Tape your boobs. Lilly, get me a box of rose petals."

Before I could ask another question, I was turned and sucking in a much needed breath of fresh air as the hooks of the trap-corset came undone. Lilly handed Phina a pink box.

"Okay, face me."

The cool air against my skin filled me with awkward embarrassment as my nipples were exposed. Phina pulled away the corset.

"Whoa." I covered my jubblies.

"Rayne, I need to see your breasts to fix them."

Fix them? "What's wrong with them?"

"You're thirty."

Offended, I scowled at her. "My boobs are perfectly fine."

"Of course they are, but a dress like that shows everything. And you're not what I'd called buxom, so you have to work for a nice décolletage."

I pouted. "Your brother *loves* my boobies." They weren't anything to write home about, but I was working with a nice C-minus in the cup department.

"I definitely don't need to know my brother's thoughts about your breasts. But I can guarantee, he's going to love them more when I'm finished perking them up." She batted away my hands and tore open the pink box.

"What is that?"

"Tape. Stay still."

I frowned as she slapped one sticky, flower-shaped pad over my nipple. She cupped my boob, lifted it, and readjusted the adhesive.

"Ah, careful!"

"The trick is making them match." She pulled out the other flower and repeated the process.

"You should really serve something stronger than champagne to your customers if you're going to molest them on the first date. At least offer dinner and a movie or have some sort of a fluffer on hand."

"Don't talk. I'm trying to get them even. Try not to breathe."

"Are my boobs uneven?"

"Shh." She adjusted the tape and I whimpered.

"You're pulling at some super sensitive skin there."

"Perfect."

I turned and faced the mirror. I had to give it to her. She basically gave me a boob lift in under five minutes. "What happens after the wedding when I have to take them off?"

"They just peel right off. Arms up."

I lifted my arms and she slid the dress into place. After a few seconds of adjusting the silk and tweaking the straps, she turned me to face the mirrors again.

My breath hitched.

"I have to say, this one does suit you, Rayne."

It was perfect. Simple, sexy, and white. "This is it." I laughed, shocked that we found something. "This is my wedding gown."

"Thank God." Phina let out an exhausted

breath. "Let's try it on with some shoes and find you a veil."

"Do I need a veil?"

"*Yes, you need a veil!* My God, what happened to you as a child? Most girls can't wait to pick their wedding veil."

I rolled my eyes. "Fine. But nothing that makes me look like a beekeeper and no heels over two inches." If I had my way, I'd wear flats—preferably flip-flops.

She groaned and left me standing alone in the back. I faced the hexagon of mirrors and smiled. A little tipsy and happy, I dug my phone out of my purse and texted Hale then Elle.

> I found my dress!!!

PHINA RETURNED before I got a response. "Try this on."

When I saw the flash of rhinestones I took a step back. "No crowns."

"It's a tiara."

"No tiaras."

"You're killing me, Rayne."

That was when the words finally left my mouth. "It's *my* wedding. You can wear a tiara when you get married."

The room silenced and we both paused. I hadn't meant that to be offensive, but I had to draw the line somewhere.

Rather than take offense, Seraphina tipped her head in a sort of admiration. "You finally sound like a bride." She put the tiara aside. "I'll see what we have as far as subtle veils."

"Something pretty but not in my way, please." I didn't want candids of me swatting at my face all through the ceremony.

"Take out your bun. We need an idea of what your hair will look like with accessories on the day of the wedding. How about wearing it half up half down?"

I removed my hair tie as Phina stood on the pedestal step, fussing with my cowlick and part. In less than a minute she created a hairdo prettier than anything I could manage in hours.

"How did you do that? It's perfect."

"This dress is so pretty and simple I think a shoulder-length blusher might be all you need."

"What's a blusher?"

"It's plain. You'll like it. Lilly, bring me the blusher from the display case in the front."

But as soon as she put it on I felt like I was in a fort. "I can't see."

"If I can see you, you can see us, Rayne."

"It's too much."

She sighed. "You're not making this easy."

"Says the woman *not* wearing a headdress. I don't want to hide my face."

She shook her head then snapped her fingers. "I've got it!"

"What?"

"Lilly, get that off of her. Where's the birdcage?"

"You want me to wear a birdcage on my

head?" This was getting a little too *Extreme Runway* for my blood.

"It's a veil style. Very chic. Very understated." She returned a moment later with a small scrap of beaded lace. "Come here."

I tipped my head forward and she did her magic. The moment the veil was attached I looked in the mirror and I was in love. It was simple, vintage lace, sewn wide enough not to cover my face but still add an element of mystique.

"That's it. Nothing else."

"You still need shoes and a garter belt. The closest I have to flats are two-and-a-half-inch heels."

Ugh. I was going to break my face in heels. "I can get shoes somewhere else."

That earned a scowl.

"I want to be able to walk down the aisle, Phina." *Especially since my dad wouldn't be there to hold me up.*

She huffed. "Fine, but I forbid you to wear flip-flops."

"Why?"

"Because it's your wedding day!"

I rolled my eyes. "Whatever. Ring me up."

"You need a garter."

I didn't object to the useless accessory because Hale mentioned finding them sexy. I looked forward to watching him pull it off with his teeth—when we were alone of course.

She led me to a glass display. "The gown shows a lot, so you'll want a discreet design. Pick one from this side."

I was more drawn to the simpler styles anyway. "That one?"

"Perfect." She removed it from the display and handed it to me. "Make sure it fits."

While she examined the shoe selection, I slipped the lace garter onto my head like Olivia Newton-John and began to aerobicize, doing my own rendition of *Let's Get Physical.*

Phina laughed. "You're so opposite from Hale."

I grinned and kept dancing. "I know. That's why he loves me."

She grinned and studied me for a moment. "You look really pretty. Even while wearing a garter on your head and dancing like an idiot."

"Not wanting to crush my veil, I removed the garter and slipped it under my dress. I couldn't believe I was asking this… "Can I wear the gown a little longer?"

Phina smiled. "Of course." She adjusted the garter.

"It seems odd to have a garter on one leg and not the other. I don't get it. Do people put money in them or something?"

"You're a bride, not a cancan girl."

As I followed her around the main area of the store shoppers complimented how pretty I looked. Attention wasn't usually my thing, but in that moment I felt like a superstar, so I ate it up.

"Thank you," I gushed, fanning my hands with all the drama of an old Hollywood socialite. "I'm the future Mrs. Davenport."

"Rayne, try these on." I let Phina slide a pair

of three-inch heels onto my feet, which—*not gonna lie*—elevated the look.

I continued to flutter about the boutique, using my best Ava Gabor accent. "My fiancé's so dreamy. Please, darling, give our regards to Broadway."

"Who is she talking to?" Lilly asked.

Phina shook her head. "I think herself."

I sipped my champagne, talking to my reflection at every mirror I passed. "Thank you for coming," I purred. "You're so kind." I turned and showed off the elegant back of the gown. "We're so glad you could make it. Why, yes, my ass does look fabulous. Thank you for noticing."

"The models are back," Lilly announced, carrying a large binder to the register that conveniently faced the front window where a stretch limo parked.

"If you don't want Barrett to see you in your gown, Rayne, you better head to the dressing room."

"Barrett's here?"

I sort of wanted his reaction to help me gauge Hale's. Not that they went for the same type of women. Barrett only dated blonde bombshells and I was more of a brunette blunder-fuck. But he was a heterosexual male with an active penis who also happened to share Hale's DNA, so it was worth a preview.

"He's doing a photo shoot for our men's line."

Lilly tilted her head toward the front window where the limo idled at the curb. A chauffeur helped a leggy blonde out of the car, and then I spotted Barrett.

"Is he wearing makeup?" I asked as the sun glinted against his chiseled cheekbones. Damn, he was too pretty for a boy. His carved facial features were only more pronounced by the man-bun twisted at the back of his head.

Lilly stationed herself by the front window with a clear view of him. "All the models wear makeup."

"Rayne," Phina said, less distracted by her brother's arrival. "I still need to get your exact measurements."

Phina pulled out an enormous ledger. As things got intensely businesslike at the register, I wandered toward the door to surprise Barrett.

Another female model with legs up to her neck climbed out of the limo with astonishing agility and two-foot high heels. She brushed a familiar hand over Barrett's arm. My smile faltered as the willowy creature leaned close to whisper something in his ear.

"What the fuck?" There was something off about the way they looked at each other. Something more intimate than being mere co-workers.

Barrett brushed her blonde hair behind her shoulders and angled his head, smiling and edging closer until his lips brushed hers.

"Oh, hell no!" I shoved my champagne glass onto a display and pushed through the doors.

"Rayne!" Seraphina yelled. "You can't wear that dress outside!"

I practically hip-checked Barrett off the sidewalk with the force of a Canadian hockey player. "What the hell are you doing?"

"Rayne?" His startled eyes dropped to my gown. "Whoa. You look incredible."

"Don't try to sweet talk me, you man-slore. Why the hell are you putting your tongue into other people's mouths!"

"Okay, just calm down, Meyers."

The model looked from me to Barrett. "Excuse me, who are you?"

"I'm his future sister-in-law."

She squinted and cocked her head in confusion, as if trying to solve a math problem way beyond her grade level.

I scoffed, losing patience. "I'm marrying his brother." I turned back to Barrett, hiking my thumb in the model's direction. "Seriously?"

"Rayne, you have to come back inside with the dress," Phina spoke frantically from the door.

Cabs honked and people bustled by, nudging me this way and that.

The model looked around nervously for an ally. "Why don't you call me later, Barrett?" She edged toward the limo.

When Barrett moved to hug or possibly kiss her goodbye, I snapped, "Don't you dare!"

"Jesus, Meyers, knock it off!" Barrett barked, quickly apologizing to the woman as he helped her into the limo. "Sorry about this. I'll call you later."

"No he won't!"

He shut the door and scowled at me. "What's wrong with you?"

"What's wrong with *me?*" I scoffed. "What the ever loving fuck, Barrett? You're supposed to be with Elle!"

"Rayne, if anything happens to that sample

dress you're going to have to buy it, on top of your actual gown. It's Parisian silk."

"Yeah," Barrett said, face irritated. "Why don't you take it inside, Meyers?"

"Why don't you tell me why you were just kissing that Amazon when you're in a relationship with my best friend?"

He held out his hands. "Look, I didn't know you were here."

"Like that's some sort of excuse? What would you have done if I hadn't interrupted?" I reached for my phone but remembered I didn't have pockets and was in my wedding gown. "I'm calling Elle."

He caught my arm before I could escape to the inside of the boutique. "Don't."

"Barrett!" Phina snapped. "She needs to get out of that gown."

"Don't tell Elle."

"She deserves to know the truth. God, what is it with you Davenport men? Can't you be satisfied with one good woman?"

His face darkened with fury. "Watch it, Meyers. I'm not my father. And don't forget, you're marrying one of us." He looked me up and down.

"Hale's not like the rest of you people."

"You people? I didn't do anything wrong."

"You're literally wearing that woman's lip gloss."

"Rayne, the dress…"

Glancing back a Seraphina, who looked about ready to cry, I hesitated, torn between ripping my slutty future brother-in-law a new asshole and preventing my future sister-in-law from having an embolism.

I returned my glare to Barrett. "I warned you not to hurt her." Then I punched him—right in the junk.

He dropped to his knees and I left him there, marching past his sister and into the back of the store.

Phina rushed in after me. "Let's get this gown off before anything else happens to it."

I turned and scowled at the mirror as she carefully fiddled with the straps and hidden zipper. As soon as the veil and dress were off, I stepped into my jeans.

"How could he do that to Elle?"

"Barrett's Barrett," Phina said, as if that was any sort of excuse. "He's always been a womanizer. Your friend probably knows not to expect monogamy from him."

I hooked my bra around my waist and twisted it so the cups were in the front. "He had his tongue down that woman's throat!"

"It was just a kiss, Rayne."

"Everyone knows kissing is a gateway drug."

"I think you might be overreacting. Maybe you should talk to your friend."

"Maybe I should punch your brother in the dick again." Hitting him felt really good.

"Hold still." She yanked the tape off my boobs.

"*Mother fucker!*" My hands flew to my chest.

Phina stepped back. "Don't hit me."

I growled. "So glad I had my nipples removed before the wedding. What the hell, Phina! You said those things wouldn't hurt when they came off."

"They usually don't. You're sweating. We'll have to have the dress cleaned."

"I'll pay for it." I stuffed my wounded tits into my ordinary cotton bra and winced. "Seriously, my nipples are on fire."

"Maybe you should wait here until Barrett leaves."

I shoved my arms into my shirt and coat, too angry to sit still. "Do you need anything from me? Credit card? A check?"

"Hale's got it covered, but I need your measurements." She glanced down at my wrinkled clothes and sighed. "We can get them tomorrow."

"Great. Thanks for everything."

Swinging my purse over my shoulder I marched through the store. As soon as Barrett spotted me he sprung out of a chair and followed.

"Meyers, wait up."

I lifted my middle finger and kept walking.

"Rayne, please, I need to talk to you."

"I have nothing to say to you, pig."

Pushing through the doors I scanned for Marty. Shit, was I supposed to call him? I pulled out my phone but Barrett grabbed it.

"Are you texting Elle?"

I glared at him. "What if I was? Give me my phone back."

"Don't text her, Rayne. Please."

"Oh, suddenly we're friends? If you don't give me back my phone I'm going to dick punch you again."

"Please don't."

I held out my hand and he reluctantly placed the phone in my palm. "Thank you." I texted Marty to let him know I was ready, then walked to the corner. "Go away, Barrett."

"Look, I know you're pissed, but I didn't do anything wrong."

I spun on my heels and faced him. "Are you kidding me? Ten minutes ago you were counting some chicks teeth with your tongue."

"So what? Elle's doing more than that with that douchebag from the gym!"

I stilled. "Wh—what douchebag?"

"The one she's been seeing for the past few weeks."

That couldn't be right. If Elle was seeing another man I'd know. We were best friends and, as such, we told each other everything. It was the law. "You're lying."

"I'm not."

"If Elle was interested in someone else, I'd know about it."

"Are you sure?"

"Yes, I'm sure. We tell each other everything."

He cocked his head as if to say he could prove me wrong. "Think about the situation, Meyers. You're marrying my brother. Maybe she didn't want to upset your plans."

"How would her dating life affect my plans?"

He shrugged. "We're both in the wedding. There are a lot of parties scheduled. She probably didn't want to add more complications to your plate."

"So she lied to me?" I scoffed. "If she dumped you for someone else, why are you defending her?"

I couldn't wrap my brain around how she might have failed to mention such a thing to me.

He shrugged. "Call it trying to be the bigger person."

"So…you weren't the one to suggest seeing other people?"

"Hell no. Why do you think I took a job in New York? I needed to get away."

"What does this mean? Are you two broken up?"

"We were never officially dating."

"You've been sleeping together for months!"

He held out his hands and shrugged. "Don't take your frustrations out on me. This wasn't my decision. I was having fun the way things were. But I'm not going to sit around while she spends all her time with some dope named Paul."

Paul? Nope. Elle never mentioned any Paul to me. "When did this happen?"

"Around New Year's. I sort of flipped out, so I figured it was best to get away for a while."

My mind returned to my last conversation with Elle. Me asking her to come to New York. Me raving about my new Jeep. Me, talking about the wedding and my hair and the wedding. Me, being a total me monster blabbing about me, *Me*, *MEEEE!* "Oh, crap."

"What?"

Feeling small and ashamed that I could be so preoccupied with my own world that I'd somehow miss such massive drama in my best friend's life, I quietly asked, "Why didn't she tell me?" But then I heard the *me* in my question and I felt sick. "This wedding's turning me into a total narcissist."

"No, it's not. I've seen other brides run around for months acting worse than Mussolini. You barely bring up the wedding."

Maybe not to Barrett, but it had been the focus of most of my conversations with Elle lately. "What kind of friend am I if she can't even tell me about her breakup."

"Well, it's not necessarily a breakup."

"Semantics."

The black town car pulled up and Marty stepped out to get my door. Barrett seemed to recognize him but didn't say hello.

"Rayne, please don't tell her you saw me kissing someone else. We both understand the rules. Telling her will only make things worse. It changes nothing."

I hesitated. "I wish I hadn't seen you."

He rubbed the back of his neck. "For what it's worth, I'm sorry. And you looked really pretty in your dress."

The truth was, I couldn't deliberately do anything that might hurt Barrett. He was a slut but he was also a big softy. I growled, frustrated that I now had knowledge I couldn't openly share without Elle wondering how I acquired it. "Fine. I'm sorry I punched you in the meat and veggies."

Doing the Dirty

IN MY MOJO DOJO CASA PENTHOUSE

NEW YORK WAS manageable when a girl had half a dozen handlers. Devyn made all of my appointments. Josette scouted the best delis for the most delicious New York bagels—I told her we were testing them for the wedding. Quinn handled my timeline. Seraphina ordered my wedding attire, Percy kept me hydrated and fed, and Marty drove me anywhere I needed to go.

I had called Elle the day I saw Barrett, careful not to bring up anything wedding-related, but she still made no mention of the other guy or her breakup. Since she was clearly avoiding the topic, I decided not to bring it up. I just didn't understand why we were suddenly keeping things from each other. Her secrecy hurt my feelings as much as it pissed me off.

Every day, when I talked to Hale over video chat, he sounded more groggy than the last. The jet-lag from so many short trips from one opposing time zone to the next was wearing on him.

His schedule was almost twelve hours behind mine so it always felt like I was delivering old news. We talked every morning, Tokyo time, which was usually around dinner time in New York.

I told him about my dress and the salon trips and how I'd caught Barrett making out on the street. Hale, the picture of diplomacy, saw nothing wrong with the situation.

"They're both adults, Rayne."

Just once I'd like him to respond to drama like a regular irrational person. Instead, he remained unshakably calm and acted all lukewarm whenever I had hot tea to spill. "That may be true, Hale, but Elle lied to me about it."

"Lied or exercised her right to privacy?"

"Um, hello? She's my best friend. There is no privacy."

"Well, maybe in this case there is."

I scoffed. "Don't confuse things with logic. She should have told me."

"If you're so upset about it, maybe you should confront her and ask her why she didn't tell you when it happened?"

Confront my problems head-on? *Ick.* No, thank you.

I turned the focus back to Barrett. "I'm actually a little worried about your brother. He seemed oddly…sensitive about the whole thing."

"Barrett? He's usually pretty casual about his dating life. I wouldn't read too much into it."

"I don't think I am. Trust me, he's not himself."

"You caught him kissing a beautiful woman. That sounds pretty typical for Barrett."

"Hale."

"Okay. I'll give him a call."

Elle, on the other hand, seemed so unfazed by their breakup she hadn't even mentioned it. Five days in New York, six phone calls, and God knew how many texts, and not once did she bring it up.

My concern morphed into resentment the longer her avoidance continued. I trusted Elle with every little detail of my life yet she, apparently, trusted me with nothing. Like a dog with a bone, I couldn't stop wondering why this was, so the next day, after I finished all my bride tasks, I called Barrett. Not something I usually did, but I was desperate to understand why my bestie was being shady.

"Meyers?"

"Hey, are you still in the city?"

"Why?" He sounded so suspicious.

"Because I'm bored, avoiding studying, and I need a few hours that have nothing to do with wedding plans or sizing. Want to get some lunch?"

The seamstress stuff was really wearing on me —no pun intended. Fittings made people assume they could say whatever they wanted about my body and diet. Not that I expected to gain twenty pounds in the next two months, but everything was measured and marked down to the centimeter. It was needling my commitment issues and provoking my urge for defiance.

"Um… yeah. Sure."

"Cool. I can meet you in twenty minutes."

This was new territory for me and my future brother-in-law. We met at a fast food chicken restaurant in Time Square. I ordered my usual while Barrett looked like he'd never seen a takeout menu before.

"Just pick something. It's all delicious."

When my food was ready, I carried the tray to one of the tables by the window. Barrett followed, appearing completely out of his element.

"For the love of God." I ripped open a packet of the special sauce and set it in front of him. "Eat a nugget."

He hesitantly dunked a nugget and tasted it, lifting his brows as his tastebuds approved. "Pretty good."

"Duh, it's deep-fried chicken." I sipped my frosty. "So, have you talked to Elle?"

He frowned. "How did I know you would bring that up?"

"What else would we talk about?"

"Plenty. We could talk about you and Hale or how the wedding plans are going. My niece, your new Jeep, what it's like to work for someone as chronically dissatisfied as my dad, the upcoming election, how you're enjoying your time in New York."

"Yeah, that all sounds totally stimulating, but I really just want to know what's going on with you and Elle. Since you won't let me bring it up to her, I have no way of getting information. It's only fair that you fill me in."

He brushed the crumbs off his fingers. Davenports always had impeccable table manners, no matter the setting.

"There's nothing to tell. I'm not really sure what's going on. We're sort of in hiatus since I'm here and she's there."

"But you're going back to Florida, right?"

Barrett was the least rooted, so he frequently moved from one five-star hotel to the next, basically living like a *bougie* gypsy.

He shrugged. "Eventually."

That didn't sound promising. "What's the other guy like?"

"Well, last night when we were painting each other's nails—Come on, Meyers. Do you honestly think we're hanging out? I couldn't give two shits what he's like."

"But you care that he's with Elle."

"Well…" He dunked a fry and looked me in the eye as he chewed. Yeah, he cared.

I sighed. "Did she say anything about me when you were together?"

"Find another spy, Meyers."

I knew I was pushing my luck, but this whole thing felt like I was being shut out. I didn't feel welcome to go to the source. "Fine. How do you like the nuggets?"

"I'm going to have to run three extra miles to work them off. Why are they so good?"

"You cannot run three miles."

"I can run six."

"Shut up."

He leaned back and smoothed his palm down his fitted shirt, strumming his evident six-pack. "This takes work to maintain."

I never considered that Barrett's job might come with challenges. I just assumed beautiful people had everything handed to them. "So, eating like this…"

"Definitely not my norm."

"We could have gone somewhere else."

"You said you wanted to eat here. Don't worry. I'll work it off."

"By running? That sounds miserable."

He laughed. "I like it. Nothing beats a running high."

I arched a brow. "Nothing?"

He met my stare with a half-smirk. "Well, aside from fucking."

I cleared my throat and finished my fries.

After lunch, we walked around for a while. It was nice to see the city without the pressure of a schedule for a change. It helped me appreciate New York from a less-overwhelmed perspective. However, I would have enjoyed it more if it wasn't so damn chilly.

"It's colder than a witch's tit out here."

"Stop being a baby. This is the nicest day we've had in weeks."

I scoffed. "You're a…baby."

"Great come back."

Barrett was Fort Knox when it came to sharing classified information regarding Elle, so I made do talking about other things. We ended up having a decent time. He was good company, easygoing, funny, and way more laid back than Hale. His chill vibe helped me unwind and relax. In an odd way, he reminded me of the old Elle, before the accident changed her.

"What was that little sigh?"

I frowned. Had I made a noise? For appearing so nonchalant, Barrett could be surprisingly perceptive. "I was just thinking about how much things have changed."

"How so?"

The Davenports truly had no concept of how the other half lived. "Well, for starters, I'm currently residing in a penthouse overlooking one of the most expensive zip codes in the world. But also…"

"Also…?"

I sighed again. Explaining how much I missed my old friend Elle felt selfish. Barrett missed her too, but he didn't know the old Elle. The Elle who sat beside me all through grade school and the Elle who had a playbook of my entire sexual history before Hale. He just knew the new Elle, a woman I was still trying to figure out.

"I don't know. I guess I miss Hale."

He glanced at me and grinned. "That's good. You should miss him. Don't be one of those wives that counts down the days until her husband goes away on a business trip."

"I could never."

"You could. I feel like that's the majority. But you and Hale are different."

"We are?" I became instantly curious about how he saw us. "How so?"

"You're loyal to him even when you could get away with less."

"That's oddly specific and cryptic."

He looked up at the sun peeking over the clouds and skyscrapers. "Remember when you caught me with Elle the first time?"

"Yes."

"I was hiding in the closet and, at first, you didn't realize I was in the room."

"Naked. I remember."

"Well, a good view is hard to forget." He chuckled. "But while I was in the closet I heard you two talking. You were upset about something that had to do with Hale. Elle asked you to explain, but you said you couldn't."

I remembered that day. I wanted so badly to tell my friend how complicated Hale's situation was with Elara and Remington and Jasmine, but I'd given Hale my word not to share his secret. I didn't know that Barrett was listening. At the time, I assumed I was having a private moment with my best friend who I trusted more than anyone in the world. Yet I didn't break my promise because I didn't want to break Hale's trust.

"That was the moment I knew you loved my brother."

I grinned. "Really?"

He nodded. "I don't know what you were fighting about, but the fact that you wouldn't betray his trust—even in secret—proved you were different than all the other women who've fucked over Davenport men before."

"One look at me should have given that away."

"I'm serious, Meyers. Money changes people's perception. It also alters how people act around us. Do you know how many assholes have tried to pretend they were my friend over the years just to use me for my name, status, or wealth? How many women have fucked us because they thought dating a Davenport might somehow elevate their careers?"

"I don't know what you're talking about. Hale was a virgin before me."

"Sure he was." He chuckled. "It gets old and it

gets lonely. Elle never wanted anything from me other than an adventure. The days we spent at sea, sailing and fishing, they were some of the realest days I ever had with a woman."

My heart broke for him. I knew he wasn't okay about their breakup. "I'm sorry she broke up with you."

He sighed. "My point is, you're real with Hale. That's a rarity in our world. You don't love him for his money or status. You love him for who he is on the inside. I never would have picked someone like you for my brother, but I honestly believe you're perfect for each other."

I didn't know what to say. That was possibly one of the greatest compliments I'd ever received. So I bumped him with my shoulder. "Thanks."

He grinned and broke eye contact before the moment grew too heavy to bear. "You're also a hot mess, which Hale deserves after spending his entire life living like an immaculate tight ass."

I laughed. I certainly was that.

"I bet you're a firecracker in bed."

"Stop."

"Too far?"

"*Way* too far."

"Fair enough."

He led us through a detour where some of the trees had started to bud. The finicky weather was definitely causing nature to gamble with survival. Leaves were blooming and casually shifting the world from grey to soft shades of green.

Just when I was convinced that nothing could shake Barrett from his calm, he flew into a fit in the midst of a busy crosswalk. "Look out!" He took a quick step backward, his arms swatting spastically as people jumped out of his way. "Bee!" He ducked, berserk with fear, as if the thing was about to kill him.

His panicked response set me on full alert. "Are you allergic?"

It was just a fuzzy little bumble bee, but Barrett acted like he was being terrorized by a killer hornet.

"No, I just don't like bees."

"Don't hurt it!" I caught his arms and rolled my eyes, gently waving it away from his face. "Poor thing's probably all confused from global warming."

He made a sheepish sound and covered his face. "Is it gone?"

"Relax, Thomas Jay, your acrobat days aren't over yet." I swept the little guy toward a tree.

Barrett peeked through his fingers, then looked around, relieved as the bee flew away. "That was close."

"Yeah, you almost overreacted." The crowd had crossed the street and a new mob of pedestrians appeared.

"Bees leave marks. I can't have a swollen face while I'm still shooting."

I supposed blemishes were an occupational hazard in his industry. Another reason I was glad I decided not to be a model.

"I never knew you possessed such dramatic depth. Maybe you should've been an actor."

Back to casually walking with his hands in his pockets, he admitted, "I've thought about it."

I glanced at him and smirked. "Your performance back there was like a dramatization of Katniss Everdeen trying to escape the jabberjays in the Hunger Games."

"All right. You've made your point.

I snickered, enjoying the ball-breaking banter we shared. I never had siblings and this felt nice. Easy. When we got to the Plaza I thanked him for such an enjoyable afternoon. "This was actually fun."

"Yeah. You're not so bad, Meyers. Call me if you want to do it again."

When I reached the penthouse, I was relieved to have nothing on my schedule until tomorrow morning. I was well overdue for a pants-off weeknight, but then I thought about Percy. The man hid in corners like a stealthy little shadow. I dreaded him catching a glimpse of my hoo-ha or hiney, so I opted for keeping pants on but settled for my coziest leggings and a hoodie I snatched from Hale's hamper. Not quite as liberating as no pants, but comforting for other reasons.

I put in a call to Elara, who didn't have much interest in seeing me through a screen, but I still made Andrew hold the phone up to her for a good five minutes. I missed my bed and I missed my peanut. And I really missed Hale.

In for the night, I debated what to eat. While many people crossed state lines to dine at Manhattan restaurants, I really wasn't much for fuss, so I settled for soft pretzels.

I rang for Percy and he was happy to see to my needs. "How many, madam?"

"Six should be good."

"I'm sorry, did you say six?"

"I had a light lunch and I like to have leftovers."

He made no further comment and returned a while later with my food. I couldn't figure out the hotel remote, so I took my pretzels and iPad to the master bedroom and climbed into bed.

Glancing out at the glowing skyline as lights flicked on across the city, I noted how romantic everything looked from a distance. But without Hale to share such a view the reality just seemed covered in slush and pigeon shit. New York definitely hit differently with a buddy system. At the moment I was in a buddy recession.

I was also in need of sleep, because even I was getting on my nerves. Setting the iPad on what would have been Hale's side of the bed, I shut my eyes and let Phoebe, Monica, and Chandler talk me to sleep.

Poor Chandler…

When I next opened my eyes, the screen was asking if I wanted to continue watching and the sky had faded from sapphire to pitch black. Realizing I was still in New York and estranged from my people, I flopped onto my back and groaned. Napping had not improved my mood. I knew then, I wanted to go home.

Reaching for my phone, I dug out another pretzel and called Hale. He answered on the second ring and, for once, we had a decent connection with no echo.

"Hey, beautiful." He seemed to be handling this long-distance crap way better than me. "How's it going?"

I took a bite of my pretzel. "Stupid. I miss you

and Elara. Can I be done with wedding stuff for a while? It's no fun doing these things without you."

"I thought things were going well."

"They are, but I'm ready to go home. I miss my regular life."

He sighed. "I miss it too."

I slid off the massive king size bed and went to my suitcase in the corner. I sure hoped Percy wasn't around, because I stripped off my pants during my nap and I wasn't in the mood to put them back on. "Did you talk to your brother?"

"I did yesterday. You were right. He's pretty banged up over Elle."

I stopped rummaging and stood up straight. "I don't get it. She won't talk to me about this and I don't understand why she'd break up with him. She was obsessed with your brother long before ever meeting him. I thought they had something real."

"So did Barrett. But sometimes people invest too much into the assumption and a person doesn't live up to the expectation. Maybe her crush was more fun than the reality."

After my afternoon with Barrett I found it hard to see him as the shallow, pretty boy I'd once thought him to be. "If anything, I think she would have discovered Barrett can be refreshingly deep."

"My brother?" Hale laughed. "That might be reaching. Why don't you just tell her you know and ask her what's going on?"

I tsked. "Sometimes I think you know nothing about women. That's not how we operate. She'll tell me when she's ready."

"Tell you something you already know?"

"Exactly," I mumbled around the thick end of a pretzel pinched between my teeth like a cigar. "I don't officially *know* until she tells me."

"What are you looking for?"

I took a bite of the pretzel and stopped ransacking my clothes. "I don't even know. I'm bored." Now I had to fold all this crap again.

"Well, you're ass looks great."

I laughed. "How would you know?"

"Because I'm staring at it."

"You're—*wha*—" I spun and sucked in a huge gasp, instantly choking on salt and spit when I saw him lounging against the doorway, phone in hand. *"Hale!"* I tossed the pretzel and bolted for him.

He grunted as my body slammed into his with the grace of a rabid carabao. "That's the greeting I hoped for."

"I can't believe you're here!" I ran my hands over his long, cashmere topcoat, admiring the familiar sight of his Brunello suit as I peppered kisses all over his face. He laughed, silver eyes smiling as he looked every bit like my perfect wet dream.

"Easy. Easy." He caught my face and kissed my mouth.

I was too shocked to kiss back so I continued to blather against his soft, full lips. "What are you doing here? How? When? Why didn't you tell me? I can't believe this! Am I still dreaming?"

"This isn't a dream." He pinched my butt and I squeaked. "You're wide awake."

I angled my hips closer to his. "God, I've missed you."

His hand slipped under my panties, cupping my ass cheek. "You have no idea." He crossed the room and dropped me onto the bed, following me down. "Stay still so I can kiss you."

I laughed and squeaked with unrefined excitement, shoving back his coat and latching onto his body like ivy climbs over stone. "You're wearing too many clothes."

His hand went to his belt, the metal clip loosened and he gripped his engorged length. Sometimes there was nothing better than a fully dressed quickie to take the edge off. He yanked my panties aside and I caught his wrist.

"Wait!" I shoved a hand against his chest "Percy."

"What?"

"Mr. Purcell, my mojo domo guy, he'll hear us. He's everywhere!"

"You mean the majordomo?"

"Yes, the butler of my mojo dojo casa penthouse."

He laughed. "I'm so glad the *Barbie* movie made such a lasting impression on you."

"Hale, the *Barbie* movie is life, but that's not the point. We can't have a situation with the butler in the penthouse with the sex. It'll be like Clue-themed porn, and super awkward next time I send him out for my bagel."

He cocked his head in confusion then laughed. "Relax, baby. He's gone for the night. I sent him home."

"*Ohhh.* Then, by all means, proceed." I hooked my leg around his ass and pulled him down for a kiss, my hands roughly yanking his tie to get the knot loose.

"Rayne," he rasped. "Choking me."

"Sorry." I abandoned the tie to jerk other things that needed attention.

He only got one arm free from his jacket before he drove deep inside of me. His pants never hit the floor.

My eyes closed at the familiar fullness and I sighed, all the pieces of my chaotic mind settling into their designated corners. I moaned and stretched beneath him. Hale's touch had a way of calming my entire nervous system.

"Fuck, Rayne, I missed this." He cupped my breast and pressed his face into my neck.

"Oh, you have no idea. This distance crap is for the birds. Let's never separate again."

"Deal. I'll sell my houses and we can by a yacht. I'll quit my job and we can spend years sailing from island to island and living off the sea and land."

"Perfect."

When he kissed me again, I tasted his longing and reveled in the idea that anyone could desire me with so much intensity. His obsession was my drug of choice. I got high off his need to have me and I loved feeling so deeply wanted. His addiction had become my own. Hale bottled up his feelings, but there was no holding back his emotions when we came together like this.

Once I managed to strip him of his clothes, we rolled across the bed and he seated me on top of him.

"Take this off." He tugged at the oversized sweatshirt I'd smuggled from his hamper. I stripped it away and threw it onto the floor. He ran his finger under the hem of my *I heart N.Y.* tank top. "This is cute."

"Thanks. I got it from a guy selling hotdogs on the street. But it's not very authentic. It was made in Indonesia."

"Figures." He chuckled.

Strong hands held my hips as he guided me over him. I loved riding him this way because of the added sense of connection that came when he looked into my eyes. "I missed you, Hale."

"You have no idea, baby. The last few days apart were torture."

My face pressed into his touch as his fingers ran through my hair. Every caress eased away the homesickness that had haunted me over the last week.

We took things slow for a while, simply enjoying the leisurely way our bodies fit together so perfectly, but then passion got the better of us as it always did. As he pumped into me with hard, demanding strokes and told me in the filthiest terms just how much he missed me, I grew ever grateful that the butler was sent home.

My moans echoed against every gold fixture and shook the chandeliers as I cried out in impassioned pleasure, coming hard. But Hale was far from finished.

"Another. Show me how much you missed this. I'm not letting you go until we're both soaked."

He thrust faster, holding my body open as he touched every sensitive secret place and I was screaming through another release. His finish came in a fury of hard need and dark satisfaction.

In short, he once again ruined me for all other men.

As I lay sprawled out beside him, panting like a dog in heat and wishing I had something to drink, he watched me the way an art connoisseur might admire a masterpiece.

By no definition of beauty could I have looked remotely hot in that moment. I was sweating like a pig, wheezing like an asthmatic, and too tired to aesthetically pose myself in a manner that hid my rolls and folds. Yet, still, he stared.

"You're staring." I blew out a long breath and pulled the sheet closer to cover my stomach.

"I can't help it. You're gorgeous."

I grinned. Hale's opinion of my beauty would always make me laugh. The guy was an Adonis who literally dated runway models and heiresses before me.

"Stop."

"Stop what?"

"Rayne." He rolled to his back. "I can always tell when your brain's going into a spiral of self-doubt."

Ah, I loved our post-coital discussions. Was I really that transparent?

Time to think about something else. Sex awakened the philosopher in me, so I delved into one of life's greatest mysteries. "Do you think Batman secretly loved Robin?"

"Are you asking if I think Robin got into the Batcave?"

I chuckled. "No way was Batman a bottom. More like a bat getting in the robin's nest."

A low laugh rumbled from his chest. "I love where your mind goes after sex."

"Well, think of how tempting it must have been, fighting all those villains while Robin pranced around in that green speedo and those pixie boots." I draped my body over his chest and grinned. "I'm so glad you're here."

"Me too." He glanced at his watch. "What do you say we get dressed and go find something to eat. I'm so jetlagged I'm wired, but eventually I'm going to crash, so we need to get moving before I fall asleep."

That was Hale, always so regimented and intentional. "We can order room service."

"I was thinking something nicer."

"Oh. I didn't really pack fancy clothes for this trip."

"I saw a box with your name on it in the sitting room. Maybe you should check it out."

I perked up. "Prizes?"

When he smirked, I knew he'd brought me a gift. "Better go see what it is."

Give My Regards to Broadway

I RUSHED OUT of bed and raced through the penthouse. "Manhattan just got a glimpse of my bare ass!"

"For shame!" Hale chuckled as he lounged in bed.

I spotted the large red box and squealed. Carrying it back to the master suite, I jumped onto the bed and smiled. "*Valentino.* You must have been to the thrift store."

Hale pulled the ribbon. "Very funny."

He loved surprising me with fancy clothes, and thank God he did, because otherwise I'd live out of hand-me-downs and old college rags. I never asked the prices, because the cost of such spoils would probably make me puke, but I also never said no to a present.

The lid lifted off with a soft whisper of opulence.

Dropping my bare butt to my heels, I pulled apart the tissue. "*Oooh…*" Cream and mauve silk rippled about delicately sewn green patterns. I lifted the elegant material and gave him a cheeky smile. "Thank you."

"Do you like it?"

I stood, pulling the bohemian-style dress fully out of the box. It was floor-length with a deep V neckline. "I love it."

"Good. Put it on. We're going out." He rolled out of bed, enough spring in his step that no one would ever assume he was jet-lagged, and left the room.

"Where are you going?"

"I forgot something." His voice carried from the parlor.

"There's more?" I admired the dress, holding it to my body and turning to face the gilded mirror behind the vanity.

He returned a moment later and set a gift bag on the bed. "Your shoes, my dear."

I nosed through the tissue paper and found a simple pair of ballerina flats. Seriously, the man knew me better than anyone. I held them to my chest and smiled up at him. "Hale, these are my perfect size! How did you know my heel height?"

He kissed me then swatted my ass. "Shower. I'll use the guest bath."

Hale finished getting ready before I was even out of the bathroom. Music played softly as I did my hair and makeup. The clink of ice meeting crystal told me Hale was mixing himself a drink.

Once my hair was done, I slipped the dress over my head and it slid perfectly into place, no bra needed. Everything fit like a glove. I chuckled and yelled, "How do you know my sizes so well?"

He stepped into the master bedroom holding two cocktails. "I have your entire body memorized."

"Stalker."

"Your one and only." He set down the drinks and circled me, admiring the gown. "I knew you'd be breathtaking in this. The green reminded me of your eyes." He brushed his fingers over the tip of my nipple and I sucked in a sharp breath.

My boobs were especially tender. "Oh, by the way, your sister tried to rip off my nipples."

"Are you telling me to be more gentle?"

I laughed. "No. I'm telling you because I think your sister's a sadist."

"That's a visual I think I could live without. Here." He handed me the rocks glass. Something creamy and coffee-tinted swirled around the ice. "It's a white Russian."

I sipped, pleasantly surprised by the gentle flavor. "Yum."

"I thought you might like that."

His glass contained something that looked a few grade levels above my palette. But I was used to Hale being the more sophisticated one. And he never made me feel like I was less for preferring something sweeter.

I took a bigger sip. "This is like chocolate milk."

"It's a bit stronger."

I shivered when his fingers traveled over my hip to my ass. Our eyes met, something dark and suggestive hidden in his.

Lowering my glass before I guzzled the whole thing, I arched a shoulder. "What?"

"What do you mean what?"

"I know that look, Mr. Davenport. You promised me food."

"And I plan to feed you."

"But…?"

When he arched a brow I knew we would be late for our reservation. "What do I have to say to get you wet."

"Um, that."

He sipped his cocktail, watching me over the rim in that intense predatory way that unraveled everything feminine inside a woman and made her melt. "That's all?"

He had no idea how potent he truly was. "Yeah, that's all."

He set down his glass. "Show me."

"Show you what?" I nervously laughed.

"Are you wet? Lift up your dress and show me those panties."

He was lethal and he knew it. My body clenched as his words melted my insides. Before Hale, no one ever spoke to me like that. Maybe that was why I became someone else when it was just the two of us like this. When he looked at me like that and told me exactly what he wanted from me, I'd give him everything.

My gaze dropped to the carpet as a thrill tingled from my belly straight to my clit. I glanced at the open door and bit my lip with a smitten giggle. "You want me to take off the dress?"

"No, leave the dress on. Lift it up. Show me your panties. I want to see a dark spot where you're wet. Then I want to make you come in sixteen thousand dollar silk."

My heart raced as my fingers brushed over the gown, lifting it at my thighs. The delicate material whispered across my skin, exposing my bare legs and showing him exactly what he wanted to see.

"Look at me, Rayne."

My head lifted and I met his gaze. He stepped closer, never breaking eye contact as he teased a finger over the damp spot of my panties. I sucked in a sharp breath as he grazed that sensitive ache that needed to be set free. He loved teasing that razor's edge of pleasure and need, and I was more than willing to beg if that's what he wanted to hear.

"Mission accomplished, Ms. Meyers."

I bit my lip. "Well, there's a really hot guy in my bedroom, Mr. Davenport. And he's touching my panties."

He slipped his hand into the silk, cupping me possessively and sinking a finger deep inside. "I've got you now." Cocking my hips forward, his mouth found the sensitive spot on my neck, as his finger remained hooked inside of me. The scent of vodka mixed with his cologne as his breath teased my cheek. "Let's try two."

My breath hitched again as he stretched me, his fingers now pumping slowly.

My eyes closed as I leaned into the vanity, my thighs spreading wider. "I thought we had reservations."

"They'll wait." He nudged my knees wider. "Sit."

Boosting me onto the edge of the vanity, he pulled my panties aside and fed another finger into me. Knuckles slick with arousal, he gently worked deeper until he had complete possession of my body and I was deliriously begging for more.

"So fucking wet for me." His filthy words and the quick clap of his penetrating touch, paired with my breathy moans and the jostling furniture, creating a sensual tempo that beat against the walls of the suite and only added to the eroticism. "You love it when I touch you like this, don't you, baby?"

I was lost, completely under his spell. "Yes." Cosmetics rolled and fell to the carpet with a soft thud.

"Did you touch yourself while I was away?"

"Hale." My cheeks burned. I couldn't do the sexy talk like him. I never knew what to say and I didn't want to ruin the mood.

"Tell me, Rayne. Did you finger your tight pussy and pretend it was me? Did you rub your clit until your fingers were soaked and your body ached for mine?"

I lacked the technique to make myself come, but that didn't mean I hadn't tried on those nights I missed him most. Still, I had a hard time confessing such things. Even to Hale. "Maybe."

He caught my hand and pressed it between my thighs. "Show me."

Panicked and frozen, I looked at him. "I can't."

"Yes, you can. It's us." He sucked two of my fingers into his mouth, pressing the wet tips over my clit and holding them there with his palm as two of his fingers remained buried inside of me. "Show me."

My body clenched and I rubbed, but I knew I wouldn't give him the finish he was after so I quickly gave up. "I can't make myself come, Hale."

"Just touch." There was no disappointment in his voice. He caught my chin and kissed me. "Slide your fingers along mine and feel how sexy you are."

I shut my eyes, entwining my fingers with his, letting him lead. He made me feel my body, the arousal, the swollen bud of my clit. It was about sensation more than penetration, and my body responded to every caress.

He dragged the gilded chair closer and sat down, pushing my knees wide, a clear view of Broadway.

"Wh-what are you doing?"

"Taking care of you. Lean back." His mouth closed over my clit and my spine arched.

"Hale!"

My useless fingers forked through his soft hair as I gasped and moaned. He was the true Lawrence of A Labia. Giving myself over to the pleasure, I surrendered to his touch as he edged me closer and closer to another release.

"Fuck, I could eat you for breakfast, lunch, and dinner." He devoured me like a man starved. Feasting and licking over my most sensitive parts then greedily demanding things of my body I could not demand myself.

He finger-banged me to completion. Then he drank from me and demanded I give him more. It was lunacy, what this man could make me do. His understanding of my anatomy blew my mind, and when I wasn't screaming out in pleasure I was staring in awe.

He owned me.

"You're mine, aren't you?"

"Yes…"

"Well, I'm not done."

He growled, and pulled my legs over his shoulders, lifting me half off the vanity, as he buried his face between my thighs once more. I cried out, my arms angling back to support my weight as his wicked tongue delved between my folds and his thumb pressed precisely where I needed pressure most.

Again, he strummed me to climax, playing my clit like a maestro caresses a mastered instrument. I came in a slur of vulgarity and broken prayers, my body tightening like a bow only to shatter the moment ecstasy burst from every nerve. I trembled and wilted, but he caught me before I could fall.

"God, you're so fucking sexy."

"Only for you," I whispered, eyes closed and weak as he pulled me to his lap.

His cock was out and he lifted my limp body over him, his length sliding into me like a sword fits back to its sheath. "Just let me hold you like this for a little while."

I clung to him, needing a minute before I could do more.

His lips pressed into my temple, curving against my skin. "Only for me," he whispered, flexing his hips and hugging me tight to his body.

Soft gasps fled from my lips to his ears as he fucked me slowly. It was beautiful. Contrastingly gentle and perfect. When he finished, he held me as if afraid to let our bodies come apart.

"I don't want to spend another night without you, Rayne."

I sighed, resting my cheek on his shoulder and pressing a kiss to his neck. If only it was that easy. Still, I pretended with him that it could be.

"Then don't."

His sigh matched mine. "We should get moving if we want to make dinner."

Fate wouldn't allow us to stay that way, but Hale was always there to make sure we made the most of the precious moments we had. It was amazing we found the energy to do more than sleep after that, but he was determined. He ordered two espressos from room service while I cleaned myself up, and then we were on our way.

Some people knew how to do origami and others knew how to build empires out of nothing but sand. My fiancé knew how to do New York.

First, we had dinner at Per Se, then we went for a horse-drawn carriage ride around Central Park. We didn't have time for a show, but Hale promised to take me to Broadway during one of our upcoming visits when he had more time.

"I want to be there for all your firsts," he said as we walked under the bright lights of Times Square.

While Hale had not been the guy to punch my V-card, he was the first to steal my heart. He was my first love, the first man to show me how to make love, and the first man to truly love me for the woman I was.

"I want all those firsts with you," I confessed, lacing my fingers with his.

My love for Hale had formed a codependence

I didn't want to cure. But that's what marriage was supposed to be, right? A partnership should be equal and reliable, shouldn't it? Hale was my everything guy, and there was no coming back from how deeply I loved him.

As we walked, I wondered if my obsession with Hale had somehow pushed Elle away. As soon as I got home, I needed to spend some one-on-one time with her. If she could still keep secrets while looking me in the eye then there was no denying we had problems.

"I want to take a detour," Hale said, turning left on 48th. "Are you warm enough?"

It wasn't too cold of a night, and Hale had also bought me a long dress coat for the evening, so I was comfortable. "I'm fine."

We had left Marty a few blocks back and I wasn't sure how far we were from the hotel, but I was once again grateful for my flats.

Keeping his arm laced with mine, he veered me away from the bright lights. "Look."

I smiled over the ice rink at Rockefeller Center. "This is Thirty Rock! I feel like Tina Fey might pop out at any moment."

"I want to show you something." He steered me toward the building.

Many flags whipped overhead as we tried to dodge the wind. Hale led me closer to the mammoth skyscraper.

When I saw the neon lights for *The Tonight Show* my excitement and curiosity doubled. "Holy crap, are we going to see Jimmy Fallon?"

"Better."

The lobby doors opened, welcoming us into

the warmth of a gold and ruby showcase that featured godlike sculptures and enormous works of art. Pillars climbed to the ceilings, reminding me of Olympus. I was finally starting to understand Hale's obsession with this place as an almost tangible sense of power and possibility drifted around us.

"It feels magical, doesn't it?"

I stared up at the breathtaking walls and cavernous ceilings. "It really does."

"Mr. Davenport?"

Startled that someone here might recognize him, I turned. Hale shook the security guard's hand. "Charles, thanks for meeting us. This is my fiancée, Rayne."

The guard nodded a polite hello. "Nice to meet you. You can follow me this way."

We trailed Charles toward an escalator and veered into a bank of elevators. "Where are we going?" I whispered.

Hale squeezed my hand. "It's a surprise."

We rode the elevator to the sixty-seventh floor. When we stepped out, Charles paused. "I'll be waiting right here."

"Thank you." Hale released my hand to tighten the lapels of my coat, sliding the buttons through the slits. "It's colder up here."

He reclaimed my hand and led me through a set of double doors into a tented area outside of the building. At this altitude, I could hear the wind howling through the alleyways of buildings, but the noise of the city was silent from so many stories above.

"This is it," he said, leading me down a set of

wide steps. "This is where we're going to say our vows and become husband and wife."

In the quiet openness, stripped of all luxury and blanketed only by the stars, the space was still an impressive sight to see. Stone parapets and hedgerows lined the perimeter and the spires of the St. Patrick Cathedral speared into the blue night sky.

"Wow, Hale."

"It's perfect, isn't it?"

It was everything he wanted. "Yes."

"We'll be standing over here, by the reflection pool." He towed me toward the edge where a large grassy courtyard dominated the space. "I'll be waiting here. Our family and closest friends will be seated there and there." He pointed to either side of the rooftop garden. "And you'll come from those doors."

I could see it. Our friends. His siblings. My mom and his. Remington. It wasn't about the flowers or the architecture for me. It was only about the groom.

"It's beautiful."

He faced me and took my hands in his, as he looked into my eyes. "I know everything's been moving fast and I've been putting a lot of the planning on you, Rayne, but everything is going to work out. I feel it. For once in my life, I know—without a doubt—that I'm doing the right thing. You make my life make sense."

I laughed that he could hold that sort of faith in me, because my life was a complete cluster fuck on most days. How I could make sense of anyone else's was beyond me.

He placed his hands on my shoulders. "Are you getting cold feet?"

"No, my feet are toasty warm."

"Then what? I know that look. If there's something you don't like, tell me."

Dropping my gaze, I sighed. "I really thought my dad might want to walk me down the aisle. I know how stupid that sounds. I haven't heard from him in years—"

"Hey, that's not stupid. He's your dad. Of course you'd want him here."

Part of me wished I didn't. Part of me wished I could accept his rejection and reject him right back, but I wasn't built that way.

His brow pinched as he looked into my eyes, sincerely measuring my pain. "Have you thought about asking him?"

"I tried contacting him."

"You did?" The shock on his face was tinged only by his worry. "When?"

I shrugged. "A few weeks ago. Nothing came of it." My dad would always be the one thing I couldn't get right.

"Why didn't you tell me?"

Gross inadequacy slithered through my stomach. "It's embarrassing."

"Rayne, we're getting married. You never have to be embarrassed in front of me. We're in this together."

And while I appreciated his sentiment, I knew that wasn't completely true, at least where my dad was concerned. Just as I could never fully feel the pain Remington caused Hale, he would never fully understand the pain my dad caused me. The most we could do is show each other empathy and compassion, so I hugged him. "Thank you for bringing me here."

He rested his chin on the top of my head and rubbed his hand up and down my back, spreading warmth through my coat. "There's no rule that says a dad has to give his daughter away. People are there to see you, not him. No one will miss him if he's not there."

Except me, I thought.

"I know. It's just taking me more effort than I expected. It's like this officially ends something I always assumed he'd eventually fix."

He hugged me. "I'm sorry, baby."

"Me too."

My mind leapt to a different wedding, far away in the very distant future, as I imagined Hale coming out of a set of doors and me watching from the front. Elara, dressed in a cascading white gown, walking by his side. There were good dads and then there were duds.

I no longer wanted to waste energy on the duds.

Truth or Glare

WHEN I RETURNED TO FLORIDA, I joined the gym for three reasons. One, I had a wedding in a few weeks, and no matter how much I tried to escape the social pressures and wedding stereotypes, working out on sweaty, metal equipment seemed the bride-like thing to do and the only way to escape the guilt.

Two, my best friend was avoiding me and keeping secrets about a gym rat named Paul. I hoped to meet Paul by accident while at said gym, then Elle would have no choice but to admit to their clandestine love affair and all would be right in the world of BFFs again.

And three, they had a smoothie bar.

I fiddled with the controls of a treadmill that lured me in with the promise of Netflix.

Look, I said I would go. I didn't say I'd give it my all. I was obviously following the *Lazy Bride's Guide* to the altar.

Elle walked on the machine next to me. Her

short hair now long—thanks to extensions—and her perfect blonde ponytail swinging side to side above her svelte little hips and toned ass. If I didn't love her I'd want to punch her for being so damn pretty.

Then there was me, trotting and stumbling along as if someone was tugging me forward by a rope. I fiddled with the controls, setting the speed back to just above standing still.

"So…"

Elle wore ear buds but I was pretty sure she could still hear me as she cranked up the speed and started to jog. There were a lot of men at the gym and none of them wore name tags. I followed her stare to see if she made eye contact with anyone, but she just looked straight ahead.

"So?" she repeated, looking as radiant as a woman in one of those lying tampon ads that portrayed serene females smiling through cramps and the added pressure of a volley ball game.

My eyes narrowed as I studied her. If I stared long enough I assumed I could penetrate this fake façade. It had been weeks. There was avoidance and then there was deception. This was deception and I'd had enough.

Old Elle burped, cursed, ate raw cookie dough, loved celebrity gossip, and even shoplifted once. This one looked like butter wouldn't melt in her mouth, when I knew for a fact it would.

Why was she acting so fake? This superficial phoniness created distance where truth and closeness once existed. Why couldn't she just be herself around me?

And what the hell was my Netflix sign in? *Gah,*

sometimes I wished we were microchipped so I didn't have to remember this shit.

Giving up on the television options, I sipped my banana smoothie and stuck to a geriatric pace. Elle continued to bounce along, already closing in on a mile, while I had barely moved.

"So what's new with you?" I yelled, hoping she could hear me over her music and rapidly thudding footsteps.

She shrugged without losing her rhythm. "Me? Nothing."

"Nothing? Really?"

"Nope. Just the *ushe*."

Glaring at her perfect arm formation as her elbows swung back and forth with every loping step, I lost my patience. I'd given her more than a dozen opportunities to tell me and she still hadn't said a word. Enough was enough.

Stepping onto the unmoving tracks, I hopped off the rotating tread and stared at her. "That's funny, because I heard you and Barrett pulled the old Ross and Rachel."

She frowned. "What?"

"You're on a break."

Elle's finger shot out and she dropped the speed of her machine, slowing down to a walk. "Who told you that? Did Barrett talk to you?"

"He's going to be my brother-in-law, Elle. We do see each other on occasion."

She frowned. "I told him not to say anything."

"Why would you tell him that? We used to tell each other everything. Now you're lying to me."

"I wasn't lying, Rayne. Don't be dramatic."

"Hey." I pulled the plastic safety key out of her

machine and it shut down. "Don't gaslight me. I asked about your relationship and personal life a bunch of times and every single time you basically said you had nothing new to share. That was a lie. I think I deserve to know why you didn't confide in me when we used to tell each other everything." It occurred to me that this was no longer about her choices with Barrett but more so about her behavior with me. "We're supposed to be best friends, Elle."

She shrugged. "I didn't want to cause any weirdness before your wedding."

But now there was weirdness. "Why aren't we communicating the way we used to? Even when I text you, it takes a decade for you to respond. What's going on? Did I do something?"

"*Nothing* is going on." I might have believed her if she didn't sound so defensive and bothered by my concern. "We're not allowed to carry our phones on the floor when we're working."

"Okay, but seriously, what's going on in your life?"

Her frown deepened. "Nothing. I'm just working." She hopped off her machine.

Were we done talking? What the hell?

A second later she was back to wipe the treadmill clean. No way was I letting her off the hook that easily. She was obviously keeping secrets from me. I needed to know why.

I followed her to the next row of equipment and climbed onto the step machine beside the one she selected. If she was trying to avoid me through physical activity it wasn't going to work. I would just have to tap into some inner boot camp mentality and power through whatever routine she had planned.

I stared down at the cockpit of controls. "How do I use this thing?"

She leaned over and hit a few buttons and my dashboard lit up. Then the hydraulics kicked in and I was sinking.

"I'm going down!"

"You have to step."

I pushed one leg and the other lifted, sort of like a seesaw. "Well, this is incredibly boring. How long am I expected to climb like this?"

"I usually do thirty minutes."

"Thirty *minutes?* Of *this?*" Dear God, why?

I would be lucky if I could accomplish thirty seconds. I strained to bend my knees as Elle casually managed to climb like the bionic woman. Did she have lungs made of metal? Mine were on fire.

"So…" I panted. "Catch me up on your life. What's going on?"

"Nothing much."

Were we really back to that?

"Well, what have you been doing since you haven't been spending time with Barrett?"

She still hadn't mentioned the other guy.

"I've been here most of the time, and hanging out with friends from work after my shifts."

I was her friend. We used to share any side friends and only bring people into the circle after careful consideration. Yet, I didn't have a clue who these friends were. Nor was I invited along for any of these so-called hangouts.

My knee started to click. That couldn't be normal. The second I slowed my steps I sank back to floor level, but I couldn't climb anymore. "What friends?"

"I told you about them. Nick, Paul, and Raj."

Ah, there was the infamous Paul.

"Nope. I would have remembered you mentioning them. Are my legs supposed to hurt this much?"

Maybe I wasn't eating enough bananas. I remembered reading somewhere that bananas helped with Charlie horses. Or maybe I was eating too much ice cream. Last night I finished a pint of Ben and Jerry's while using a Snicker's bar as a spoon—once again falling off my bride-or-die meal plan.

"You have to pace yourself. It takes time to build up stamina."

I scrunched my nose, not easily seduced by the idea of discipline. "I think my butt's falling asleep."

"You don't have to do everything I do, Rayne. We can do different things."

Her tone pricked at something tender I hadn't realized needed protecting. I no longer felt like we were talking about gym equipment.

I grabbed the remainder of my smoothie and sank on the machine. If I wanted to stay on her level I was going to have to hike my ass up there. With a deep breath, I climbed some more. "Tell me about your new friends."

"They're just guys from work."

Sweat rolled directly into my eye and I blinked rapidly. "Do any of these guy friends have something to do with you and Barrett breaking up?" It was like pulling teeth. Pretty soon I was going to have to call in Homeland security and go full-on inquisition.

"We were never dating. You can only break up if you're in a relationship."

"Pardon me if I'm wrong, but his penis was in your vagina many, many times, correct?"

"Jesus, Rayne," she hissed and looked around nervously.

I followed her stare. Who was she looking for? Was he tall? Bald? Tattooed?

"Sex doesn't mean we were in a relationship."

"It means you were in *something*." If it meant nothing, Elle wouldn't have felt the need to tell Barrett she wanted to see other people.

"We were just messing around."

The stench of her bullshit stunned me. I could not believe her pretended nonchalance when I had been there through all the heavy emotional conversations about Barrett being the hottest guy she ever kissed.

Then there were the talks about how much fun she had whenever they hung out. And how she loved going on adventures with him and learning new things. She once told me she liked him so much that he could make nautical knots interesting, and I believed her because Elle had become obsessed with sailing the moment she and Barrett started sleeping together.

I was getting a neck ache from looking up at her but my body was literally giving out on me. "Seriously, you do not do this for thirty minutes. I'm dying." Nothing was worth this pain. Why climb if it took you nowhere? I sank to the floor again. "Can you just be honest with me, Elle?"

"Sometimes I do less than thirty—"

"Not about the machine! About you and Barrett. Just tell me the truth."

She scoffed. "Fine. We broke up. What does it matter what we call it? It's over."

My heart pinched. "I just…don't understand. Why?"

She shrugged and looked away. "Barrett was great after the accident. When I first moved here we had a lot of fun sailing and snorkeling."

Was snorkeling code for fucking? "You cared about him."

"So? It was never going to be more than a fun fling."

That didn't sound like my typically confident friend. "How do you know?"

"Because he's Barrett, Rayne. Look at the life he leads."

I worried a lot about his lifestyle when they first started fooling around, but then they started to make sense together and now it just seemed like a wasted opportunity. Plus, Barrett didn't want this. He wanted Elle. "I thought you were falling in love with him."

"I'm not stupid, Ray."

"I never said you were."

"Then why are you questioning my judgment?"

"I'm not! I'm just trying to figure out what's going on with you."

"Stop saying that!"

"Saying what?"

"What's going on with me. It sounds like I have

a problem. There is no problem. Sometimes relationships simply have a shelf life."

I wondered if ours did, because I didn't understand any of this. While we were discussing her breakup with Barrett I couldn't ignore the fact that it felt like she was also breaking up with me. The distance between us was spreading, even when we were standing right next to each other I could feel her putting up boundaries and using half-truths to push me away.

"Elle, Barrett seems pretty banged up over this."

She laughed. "I doubt that."

"I'm serious. He——"

"He's just sulking. Soon enough he'll have his tongue down someone else's throat."

She had him figured out there. But a rebound didn't guarantee getting over someone. This would make much more sense if she just admitted to having a relationship with mysterious Paul. Maybe I should just confess I knew there was another guy.

I didn't know what to do. Her lies made me feel like I should lie, when I was always much more comfortable with honesty.

Unsure how to proceed, I opted to take a break and collect my thoughts. "I have to pee."

I left her to her workout and chucked my smoothie cup. Then I bought a bottle of water at the vending machines because it gave me a chance to nose around in the lobby of the gym where Elle now spent all of her time. I don't know what I was looking for, maybe a bulletin board that showed all the employees' pictures by name.

Elle's shady behavior was starting to really piss

me off. As much as I hated confrontation, I loved Elle more, so I knew what I needed to do.

I went back to wipe off my machine and she was still going. "I feel like you're not telling me something."

She looked at me, appearing stunned that I was still on the topic of her love life. "Why are you being like this?"

"Like what?"

"Nosey."

I drew back. Was she kidding? I was only being nosey because she was being secretive. How did my concern make me the bad guy?

Fuck this shit. "I didn't realize taking an interest in my best friend's life was so intrusive. Forget I asked."

"Rayne…"

I walked away, pissed I'd even wasted an afternoon beating up my body when I had so much other shit to do. Work was piling up on my desk, I had a paper to finish for school, and Elara had a doctor's appointment in a few hours.

When I got to the locker room, I shoved my bag on the bench and looked for my keys. The fact that my vision was blurring with unshed tears was a total inconvenience. When I found them at the bottom of my purse I turned and came face to face with Elle.

"Jabberwocky!"

"Rayne, you can't get mad at me for living my life."

"No one said you can't live your life, Elle. I just thought I was a part of it."

I refused to cry in front of her, which was

weird because this was Elle. But Elle no longer felt like Elle. She no longer felt safe. On the contrary, she made me feel very unsure and confused. She felt like a stranger I couldn't trust. A stranger who assumed I had less than her best interest at heart. A stranger who just hurt my feelings by calling me nosey when I was only concerned and trying to take an interest in her personal life.

So I lied, "It's fine."

"It's not. You're upset. I shouldn't have said it that way. Please don't be mad at me."

Said it that way? What the hell did that mean? What was she trying to say? Butt out?

As her supposed best friend I no longer understood my place. "Being concerned does not make me nosey."

"Well, sometimes your concern feels like judgement."

"How could you say that? I've always supported your choices."

"You overthink everything, Rayne. Sometimes I don't feel like having my life under a microscope. Of all people, you should know what that's like."

"Are you comparing me to the paparazzi?" I wasn't sure if there was a lower insult.

Just that morning the tabloids had published another picture of me and Hale. This time they zoomed in and circled my double chin in red so no one missed the fact that I had flaws.

"I'm just saying I'm allowed to make my own choices without justifying myself to you. You're not my mother."

In no way did I want to play that role. I wasn't even the responsible one.

"Are you kidding me? Elle, I do not try to mother you."

"Well, I don't need you to take care of me."

I scoffed. "No shit, but you were in an accident. I was there when they were going to put you in assisted living. I moved home to make sure that didn't happen. I saw to your bills, watered your house plants, and made sure you didn't lose your home."

"And now that's over. Can we please move on?"

My jaw dropped. I was stunned by how easily she could minimize what had been one of the most traumatic events of my life. I thought she was going to die. I had never been so terrified.

"Maybe you're over it, but for someone who consciously watched it happen I need a little more time." It hadn't even been a year and she still struggled with cognitive issues from the crash. "It feels like you're punishing me for caring and dismissing everything I did to help you."

"See, you're too dramatic—"

"I left my job to take care of you, Elle!"

"Your job working for Hale's dad."

I scoffed. "Fuck. Off." I could not believe she would diminish what I sacrificed by acting like it wasn't a real job.

That time had been incredibly difficult for me. Yes, it happened to her, but it deeply affected me, and she made me feel selfish for being so impacted by the thought of losing her. I'd never felt so helpless or worried. Sometimes I still had nightmares that she was back in a coma.

I feared, not only losing my closest friend, but

that Hale and I might not survive the distance or what the crippling anxiety was doing to me. We were new and fragile, but Elle needed someone to watch over her and see that she got the best care. So I left Florida and flew back to Oregon to sit by her side, day after day, night after night—for her. I risked losing everything to watch over her when she had no one, and that took a toll.

Her own brother hadn't bothered to visit her. Every day I felt like I was in over my head and drowning, but I couldn't give up on her.

"You have no idea what that accident put me through. It didn't just happen to you, Elle."

She rolled her eyes. "And here we go, somehow making an accident that happened to me all about you."

"What the fuck is wrong with you?" Now, I was pissed. "That accident was a tragedy that happened to all of us. Tyler couldn't even look at you most days, but he showed up anyway and did his best to be there for you. I lost sleep crying at your bedside for weeks, terrified you might never come out of that coma. We were all in pain."

"Well, I was the one lying in a hospital room with my head split open and half my memories gone!"

"What do you need me to say here? You win? Fuck, Elle, I was physically sick over the fear that I might lose you. It was agony. And now you're throwing it in my face, like I somehow did something wrong by caring for you? Like I'm some sort of narcissist for letting your pain affect me. That's not narcissism, it's love! I'm sorry if I can't just shut it off when you suddenly decide you don't need a best friend anymore."

"I didn't say that."

"Well, you're certainly acting like it. You're keeping secrets and avoiding me."

"You were in New York!"

"So what? We have phones! You were super sketchy every time I called. And now, you're acting like I'm smothering you by simply asking about your life."

"Wanting to make some decisions on my own has nothing to do with you, Ray. I don't need you to weigh in on every choice."

"Fine, but did you ever think that I might still need you even if you don't need me?" I gathered my belongings, my hands trembling violently as I rushed to get out of there. "Our friendship is one of the most important relationships of my life, and I feel like you're cutting it into pieces without even giving me a say."

"Maybe I'm not your best friend anymore."

I staggered at the door, her words stabbing into me with no warning and nearly dropping me to my knees. Denial choked me. But I couldn't argue her accusation because part of me knew she was right.

Tears fell down my cheeks. I couldn't face her.

Elle's voice lowered. "You have Hale now. You don't need me. Not like you used to."

"I still need you."

"Things were always going to change, Rayne. I didn't do this. It just happened."

My head lowered. I wasn't ready for this conversation. I didn't want it.

"Rayne, this year… A lot's changed. We're different now. Both of us. Why can't you accept that? It's unrealistic to expect me to go back to being a girl I only partially remember. Just as it would be unrealistic of me to expect you to have the same time for me as you had before Hale."

Tears rolled down my face as a steady ache seemed to pry open my chest. "Maybe things changed, but I never pushed you away. Can you say the same?"

She sighed. "Rayne, when you wanted to change careers, I supported you. Did I think it was a mistake? Maybe, but I still thought it was an experience worth having. A few months ago I woke up in a hospital bed with half my hair and who knows how many memories missing. I thought we were still in high school and my parents were still alive. I thought my brother was still…my brother. But none of that was right. You're getting married, Chris is on drugs somewhere, and my parents are in a cemetery someplace I can't remember. I can hardly keep track of the things I'm supposed to remember, and why should I when they hurt me? Some days I just want to leave it all behind and move on. It feels…lighter to be someone new. You have no idea how heavy it is to carry everyone's expectations around every day and worry I'm going to disappoint all of you."

She truly forgot who she was talking to. "Elle, my only expectation is that you're honest with me and that we remain friends."

"I think it's a little more than that, Rayne."

"Maybe I've been a little preoccupied with the wedding—"

"This isn't about your wedding!" she snapped. "It's about me finding my independence."

Everything I said seemed to be the wrong words, so I shut up.

"Look," she said in a calmer tone. "You're getting married. Hale's going to be your husband and Elara's going to be your daughter. I'm okay with that. But I'm not sure you are. Before you get to the altar, I think you need to examine what you're really agreeing to. No one else is going into this marriage with you. I can't be there for every decision and disagreement."

Hurt, insulted, it all started to blur into unwanted pain. Wanting her input was different from needing her to decide for me. Ultimately, I knew it was Hale and I. When did valuing her opinion become a character flaw? Maybe it wasn't my flaw after all. Maybe this was her issue.

I should have left. I should have walked away then and there and given us both a chance to cool off, but I didn't because I would never understand why new beginnings sometimes felt like unwanted endings.

Giving up on hiding my tears, I faced her. "Things don't have to change if we don't let them, Elle."

"Yes they do. Without change, we aren't growing. I want to grow, and so do you."

"That doesn't mean we have to grow apart."

"I can't drop everything to fly off to New York on a moment's notice."

"I never asked you to."

"You ask all the time."

And that was a bad thing? It seemed every step

I made to get close to her she interpreted as some sort of threat or crossing of personal boundaries.

"New York is your journey, Rayne. The Davenports are your people. I appreciate having a place in that world, but it's not mine. I need to make my own adventure."

My entire world was shook. What was she saying? Were we breaking up? If I hadn't confronted her, would she have told me any of this? I was blindsided and confused, unsure what this future with or without Elle would be.

"Are you still going to be my maid of honor?"

"Of course, I'm going to be your maid of honor," she said as if it was crazy to wonder such a thing. "I just need a little space and I can't sleep with the best man anymore. It was different when he was just your boyfriend's brother."

Was she saying she broke up with Barrett for me? I didn't want that. "Elle, I'm fine with you dating Barrett. I mean, it was a little weird at first because I was afraid he'd take advantage of you, but it turns out he's actually much deeper than I realized—"

"Rayne, stop. You're putting way too much thought into this. We all know Barrett never stays with one woman for long. It was time to end things."

The dishonesty needed to stop. Frustrated she was pinning her breakup on Barrett's reputation when there was another man in the picture, I finally called her out. "I know about Paul."

"How?"

"Does it matter? The point is this isn't just about Barrett's reputation. Why won't you admit there's someone else? Can't we just be honest with each other?"

She lowered her stare. "He's just a friend."

"But you like him?"

She blushed and shrugged. "We're just sort of hanging out right now but, yeah, I like him."

When she first told me about Barrett, she couldn't wipe the smile off her face. I still remember how giddy she'd been. This felt very different, but I wanted to understand. I still wanted to be a part of her life. "Does he like you?"

"There have been some signals."

I had a terrible fear she was going to ask—

"I was actually wondering if he could be my plus one at the wedding."

My insides instantly cramped as a bowling ball seemed to settle in the pit of my stomach. "Oh, um, I'll talk to Hale."

Hale was always my scapegoat in a pinch. I'd learned that from getting out of boring work things Remington sometimes wanted me to do. While I wanted to support Elle's choices, I wasn't sure I wanted to invite this guy to my wedding where Elle would be sitting directly next to Barrett.

"Thanks. You'll like him. Maybe we can all go out sometime so he can meet you guys and you can get to know him. I think you'll really like him."

That seemed so much safer than inviting him to the wedding. "Let's do that."

Unfortunately, like after any battle, the damage could not be undone. While we found our white flag and called a truce, words had been hurled. I left the gym sore and wounded in ways that had absolutely nothing to do with the machines and everything to do with the girl who used to be my best friend.

I knew it then.

We were over. Something in the security we shared had changed.

I felt our ending like a slice through bone. But I denied it all the same. I wasn't ready to amputate just yet, so I let it fester as I waited for a miracle to come.

She was my Elle. Plenty of others in my shoes would have done the same.

Douche-Canoes

NOT RECOMMENDED FOR OFF-ROAD TRAVEL

THE FOLLOWING FRIDAY EVENING, as soon as I turned in my assignments for school and finished the last of my work for Remington, I showered, dressed, and ran Elara to her grandfathers.

Hale came home, bent to kiss me, and scanned the unusually tidy living room. "Where's my daughter?"

"Marta's watching her at your dad's tonight."

He frowned. "All night?"

"Yes. We have the double date with Elle and Paul, and Andrew was unavailable. Go change."

"Did you clear this with my father?"

"Of course not. Besides, It'll do Remington good to spend some time with his granddaughter. Marta's the one who volunteered to watch Elara anyway. Relax. It's handled. We have to leave in thirty minutes."

He eyed me curiously. "Let me get you a glass of wine."

"I don't need wine." Hale typically offered wine whenever I was especially…uppity.

"You seem…tense." He rubbed my shoulders. "It's just dinner with Elle, Rayne."

It was more than that. I hadn't been myself since the fight at the gym. The things Elle had said consumed me.

Hale didn't have anything comparable to my relationship with Elle in his life, so he didn't get what this fissure in our relationship was doing to me. *Everything* was riding on tonight going well.

He kissed my head. "This guy's the one who has to worry about impressing you."

"I know."

Whenever anyone hurt my feelings, Hale took a protective stance. While he'd always liked Elle and enjoyed having her around, he was not happy about the things she'd said to me. Hale hated when I cried and her words had left me weepy for days.

"You sure you don't want some wine?"

Maybe I was a little anxious. I pinched my fingers in the air. "I guess I could have a smidge before dinner."

He kissed my cheek then drifted into the kitchen. "Do not let this guy intimidate you."

"I'm more worried about Elle."

His silence spoke volumes.

He wasn't happy with my friend, but he respected our relationship enough to hold his negative commentary until we worked through this little tiff. He handed me a stemmed glass.

"Thanks."

Lingering by the steps, he studied me. I could

tell he wanted to protect me from getting hurt, but also respected that I needed to do this.

I couldn't just let our friendship die on a do-not-resuscitate. If it was going to die, it was going down in flames and screams. That was the only possible way I would ever accept that our relationship of more than twenty-five years was over. Hopefully, that wasn't the case.

But it felt like the case.

The things she said to me the other day… Not only did I feel like I didn't know her, she seemed to completely forget who I was. I didn't know or recognize the Rayne she saw. And I hated the needy part of me that couldn't bear to be misunderstood or disliked.

Maybe Paul wasn't the solution, but he seemed like the only life-raft within reach. "I just want tonight to go well."

"He's just a guy, Rayne. There will probably be many more we have to meet."

That was a terrible dating attitude. Didn't he understand women wanted accuracy when hunting for a mate.

Women rarely dated by chance or picked a man all willy-nilly. We observed our prey, stalked, collected data, mounted, and tagged. We had standards, and would never simply sample a random penis-toting male that passed by. There was skill involved. Goals! Very rarely did a woman spend time on a man for simple shits and giggles.

If Elle wanted this guy, she wanted him for a reason and I needed to understand her logic. Besides, this wasn't about the stupid guy anyway.

I sipped my wine, lacking the bandwidth to

explain all of that to Hale. "We're going to be late."

Hale sighed and went upstairs to change. A minute later he yelled, "I'm not wearing this."

"Yes, you are!"

Of course, he didn't wear the screen print T-shirt and jeans I put out. Instead he came down stairs in his usual button down dress shirt and designer slacks.

"At least roll up your sleeves."

"I don't know why what I'm wearing matters."

"Because you have to put yourself on Paul's level. We're working on a love connection."

"Between Elle and Paul?"

"No! Between you and Paul. As best friends it's crucial that our men get along. Keep up!"

When we reached the restaurant, Hale searched for the hostess and paused, startled by the enormous shark head on the wall. There wasn't an interior designer anywhere capable of explaining how the giant fish complemented the snow skis mounted to the left or the upside down cat clock hanging to its right.

Yup, this tacky place was Hale's hell.

"I think we just seat ourselves."

He frowned, as if the concept of not being formally seated somehow broke the laws of propriety.

"Oh, there they are." I waved at Elle who was sitting next to a guy in what might as well have been a toddler's T-shirt. "Holy muscles," I mumbled under my breath. "Paul's got bigger boobs than me."

We reached the table but they didn't rise to greet us on account of it being a booth. I wasn't sure Hale ever dined in a booth before, so this would be an interesting experience for everyone.

"Hi!" I greeted, smiling at Paul. "I'm Rayne. This is Hale."

The guys shook hands. No real sparks flying yet, but it was still early. I settled in across from Elle, forcing Hale into a conversational-corner with Paul.

"What are you guys drinking?" I asked, reaching for the cocktail menu.

"Water. We're on a cleanse."

I paused. "A what?"

I knew what a cleanse was, I just never understood the purpose. Denying the pleasures of food and alcohol went against my belief system in every way. There were only so many carnal pleasures in life. In my opinion, we needed all of them to balance out the stress and anxiety and general cases of *The Mondays*.

"It's this thing Paul and the guys are trying. I thought it would be fun."

Ahhh, the guys…

"Sooo, you're not eating?"

"No, we can eat, just no meat, dairy, gluten, or sugar."

"What else is left?"

"Detoxifying the organs is known to heighten other senses," Paul explained with an air of arrogance. "Hale probably knows what I'm talking about."

I looked at Hale. His poker face was in full effect so I couldn't tell if he agreed or disagreed with Paul's statement, but I thought I knew him well enough to assume he wasn't the type to deny himself of life's pleasures.

He gave a tight lipped grin as a reply.

Hale didn't lust for food the way I did, but he enjoyed indulging in life's little pleasures. I cared nothing for moderation and he loved that about me. Hale loved overindulging me, to the point that he sometimes got off on it. I, too, got off on his let's-spoil-Rayne-kink. He turned me into a total whore for carbs, coming, and fancy clothes—sometimes presenting me with all three at once.

Those were the days that life was truly worth living.

While Paul continued to talk about the joy of depriving the body of pleasure, I mentally compared him and Hale. Hale's lean, athletic build was a combination of potent Davenport DNA, innate sex-appeal, frequent morning jogs, a strong metabolism, and his endless thirst for adventure. Paul looked like someone had literally pumped him up with hot air.

Okay, that wasn't nice. I needed to reset, so I opened a menu. *What was I going to eat?*

"I appreciate a life of moderation, but I also recognize the need for duality," Hale said when Paul finally took a breath.

"Duality? How so?"

"Saintliness cannot exist without sin. We're designed to be a mixture of both."

Was it just me, or was he totally hot when he said philosophical shit like that?

Champagne and caviar were in his blood but he also loved earthy pleasures. Hale felt shamelessly entitled to whatever he craved, be it steak, pasta, pastries, or pussy. He was a walking aphrodisiac, a potent mixture of masculinity and propriety. And I was getting hot just thinking about how sexy he could be.

As if sensing my arousal, Hale slowly turned. His eyes creased ever so slightly as if he knew exactly what I was thinking. Then his hand landed on my thigh.

"Right, but it's our job to control the balance. That's where discipline comes in." Paul continued to ramble about purifying the body while Elle stared up at him adoringly.

I didn't have the first clue what she found attractive about this guy.

My knees locked as Hale's palm glided up my thigh. "It's my experience that too much rigidness leads to breaks. There's something freeing about giving up control, don't you think, Rayne?"

His touch nonchalantly traced the seam of my jeans and I inhaled sharply. I looked up at him, casually disguising the fact that he was cupping my crotch under the table.

Uncertainty formed an awkward smile on my face. This was new territory. Also, he was full of crap. Hale was the biggest control freak I knew.

"I think it all depends on the circumstances. Sometimes a little recklessness is fun and sometimes it's totally inappropriate." I locked my thighs around his wrist and he chuckled as I shot him a withering look of death.

I was by no means graceful enough to pull off incognito sexy time in public. What was he thinking?

"Paul's one of the most disciplined people I've

ever met. Tell them about your schedule," Elle said.

Hale pinched my crotch through my jeans and I pressed my nails into his skin as a warning. He needed to stop.

He chuckled softly, so only I could hear the sound, then he pulled his hand away. "That's interesting," he said to Paul as he casually checked his phone. "Pardon me. I have to answer this." He typed out a text and discretely slid the device back into his breast pocket.

A moment later my phone buzzed from the abyss of my purse. I looked at Hale suspiciously, but his focus was strictly on Paul as he detailed every mundane facet of his workout routine.

I discretely checked my phone.

I'm going to eat you for dessert.

HIDING A SMIRK, I stashed the phone back in my bag and sat up straight. *Okay then.*

Paul was still pontificating like a blowhard about things that did not interest me at all. I tried to care—for Elle's sake—but something about the guy felt off. He was a know-it-all who hadn't said two words to me but seemed fully infatuated with himself.

After more than twenty minutes of only Paul talking, I got annoyed. Didn't he know I was the friend he had to impress?

"So, plant-based," Hale confirmed. "I've read good things about that."

"You'd be amazed how many athletes are cutting out meat and dairy. Take Arnold Schwarzenegger, for example."

Elle looked enthralled. I was utterly bored and admiring all the tchotchkes nailed to the walls. Was that really Axl Rose's guitar?

When Elle finally smiled at me, I lunged for that fragile olive branch, diving into conversation that revolved around something other than juicing and supplements. "Did you look at the email I sent you about the dresses?"

"I did. I love the dark blue."

Relieved she liked it, my smile grew. The weight on my shoulders was getting lighter. "You always look great in cool tones."

Sapphire was our accent color, because it reminded me of the ocean and our days on the *Lady Parr* when there was nothing but cerulean sea and blue skies for miles. That was where I fell in love with Hale, so blue seemed a fitting wedding color.

When the waitress arrived with our cocktails I eagerly accepted my margarita. Hale had ordered a Manhattan for himself, but based on the ambiance I knew he wasn't going to be happy with the result. This was the kind of place that put maraschino cherries in everything. When he sipped I caught his subtle wince at the alcohol quality.

Paul looked disappointed. "Wait a minute."

The waitress paused and looked at him expectantly. "Did you change your mind about cocktails?"

"No. This water has ice in it. Can you please bring us room temperature water, no ice?"

"Of course." She took the glasses away.

Paul gave a tight-lipped smile that screamed intolerance. "Cold beverages shock the liver. It's an American habit that's not doing us any favors."

"I come from the school of beliefs that alcohol kills everything," I joked, licking the salt off the rim of my margarita. "Germs and stuff."

"That's not true."

I was going at my cocktail like a horse on a salt-lick. Did this guy honestly think I looked like someone concerned with scientific fact at the moment?

He grimaced at my delightfully toxic beverage. "If you knew how much sodium and sugar was in that margarita you might feel differently."

"Oh, Paul," I teased with feigned patience. "Let's not spoil the things that bring me joy, okay?"

"That's the problem with the health in this country. No one wants to do anything until it's too late."

I opened my mouth to respond, but my mind blanked. The fading sunlight coming from a nearby window glinted and my attention snagged on the enormous fake diamond in Paul's ear.

Wow. P Diddy called and he wants his rock back...

I had to force myself to look away.

Thankfully, Hale saved me. "So, Paul, how long have you worked at the gym?"

"Nine years. I'm their best trainer, sort of like the boss on the floor..."

As he spoke, my eyes narrowed on his beard. Was that a beard? It looked more like the strap of a birthday hat, but made out of hair. How did Elle go from Barrett to this?

I tried not to judge, but the dude was a total me-monster. His ego was sucking up all the air, and since he gave no one else a chance to talk I had nothing better to do then pick him apart mentally as I drained my margarita. I knew it was destructive and unkind, but I also knew a douche-canoe when I met one.

What I didn't know was why or how Elle liked him. There had to be something I wasn't seeing, so I looked harder. But the deeper I examined his shallow persona the more I realized there was absolutely no depth to Paul.

"…the gym would have folded if not for me bringing in so many clients on a regular basis."

He shifted in his seat and my nose twitched at the scent of drugstore cologne.

"You work out, Hale?"

"I live an active life."

Paul eyed him shrewdly. "You work a desk job, right?"

I nearly scoffed. Was he honestly taking Hale's measure? Who did he think he was?

Hale spent a lot of hours seated at a desk, but he had several corner offices and owned numerous companies, many on the *Fortune 500* list and a few in the one hundreds. It wasn't like he was wasting away in some cubical not experiencing the world. Didn't Elle tell this guy anything about us?

Hale didn't flinch under his intrusive inspection. "I wouldn't categorize my career as sedentary. I own several global operations. I'm on the road, at sea, or in the air most days."

Or in bed with me, I thought smugly.

I swore Paul flexed his arms. "You work for your dad, right?"

Uh-oh.

"No. He and I are associates. I work for myself." While he corrected Paul's assumption with straight facts, there was no missing Hale's disenchantment and thinning patience. Paul was quickly approaching some thin ice.

Wanting a shield, I re-opened the plastic menu that was roughly the size of a pirate map. It parted with a sticky sound that assured Hale would not touch his. To save him the trauma, I angled mine so he could read over my shoulder.

It was time for a subject change. "So, what's good here? Have you had the mozzarella sticks?"

Crickets.

I turned another sticky page. "Ooh, onion rings. It's been a minute since I've had a good fried onion."

"Fried foods are loaded with saturated fats. Chances are you're also getting synthetic food-like ingredients in those over processed options."

A stiff smile locked on my face. Oh, good, the food police was back. If Paul was opposed to ninety percent of the menu, why the hell did they pick this place?

Hale eyed the condiment caddy like he wanted to drop it into a biohazard container and wash his hands. I patted his thigh. Moments like this really exposed his quirks and I took sympathy on him as much as I enjoyed watching him squirm.

There was a true inner-battle of germaphobia and OCD versus propriety and self-control taking place beside me. But on the outside, he appeared completely unfazed and calm. *So very Hale.*

"Day-um." Paul grabbed my hand, nearly yanking me across the table to examine my engagement ring. "How much did that set you back, Davenport?"

Hale went into full reserved gentleman mode and silently met Paul's stare until the man had the good sense to release my hand. Realizing he overstepped, Paul lowered his gaze.

I hid a smirk behind my enormous menu. Sometimes nature organized itself like that. *An alpha's gonna alpha and a beta's gonna beta...*

Unfortunately, Paul was the type to ramble through his nervousness. "I have a friend that just threw down six G's on a ring for his girl. You ever see *Blood Diamond?*"

Oh, thank God, the waitress.

We placed our orders. Hale requested a medium rare steak and I ordered some deliciously homogenized synthetic cheese dipped in lethal frying oil. Elle and Paul ordered rabbit food, sans everything with flavor.

"So how long does this cleanse last? You'll be eating by the wedding, right?"

"We can send you our list of restrictions," Paul said and I tensed.

My question had been directed to Elle, since she was an approved guest on our list. But Paul assumed my question included him.

Elle had asked about bringing Paul to the wedding, but I never gave an answer. My mind went to Barrett. How would he react to seeing her with this guy?

Honestly, it might help him get over her. Paul was no competition. If anything, Barrett would see him and feel good about himself. *Ugh, I could be so mean.*

I remembered I was supposed to be getting to know Paul so he and I could be friends. "Have you ever been to New York, Paul?"

Elle smiled at my effort to take an interest in this man-shaped tit. "We're coming early to hit some of the sights like the Empire State Building and maybe catch a show at Madison Square Garden."

She was coming early to catch a show with Paul? I would also be there early, likely taking care of all the last minute things that needed to get done. It would be nice to have my maid of honor there with me, but so far Elle had no time to visit New York so I just assumed she'd be arriving last minute.

Yet, for Paul, she was wide open?

I smiled tightly while swallowing down a gulp of my margarita.

I hadn't confirmed Paul's name on the guest list yet. I mean, it wasn't like adding one more person was going to create a financial strain. We had the room. But I'd hesitated because of Barrett.

Now my gut was telling me not to invite him for other reasons. I instinctively felt the need to erect boundaries, but my heart demanded I do everything to make Elle happy, so I was torn.

I wanted to be happy for Elle. Truly, I did. But she was blowing me off left and right, telling me she had no time to take off from work or school, except when Paul was involved she became a total hypocrite. She had all the time in the world.

Maybe I was being selfish. Or maybe it was normal to expect your best friend to make time for the wedding plans as the maid of honor. I didn't think I was a bridezilla. I'd made no outlandish demands. I was paying for all her expenses. This was the problem with being an over-thinker. I never knew if my feelings were valid or wrong.

I could feel myself melting down and I was almost out of margarita.

I needed to say something. "It's going to be a really busy week. I don't know how much time there will be to go sight-seeing before the wedding." She was supposed to come to New York to support me, not to catch a production of *The Lion King* or impress Paul.

"Exactly. It'll be nice to have Paul there to help me with everything."

Help *her* with everything? What about me, the bride?

What the hell was going on?

As I sat there, stewing over my margarita, I honestly wondered if I wanted her there at all. She was acting so shitty and down-playing what was going to be one of the most important days of my life. And god forbid I say that, because she'd only call me self-centered again.

I wanted to leave. I no longer cared about getting to know Paul or waiting for my food. I just wanted to get the hell out of that booth and scream into a pillow.

"A wedding's what? Two hours?" Paul said. "Then the party. If you can't squeeze me into the guest list, I can always crash after the cake's cut." He laughed.

Elle leveled her stare with mine, using her BFF-telepathy to strong-arm me. "Rayne can fit you in. Can't you, Ray?" She smiled sweetly, but there was no sweetness banked in her eyes.

The wedding was a monumental, life-altering moment in my life, and Paul had just summed it up as a two-hour party. Hurt and angry, I forced a smile. "Sure, anything for you, Elle. We'll just order more red plastic cups."

Dear God, what was happening to us?

Thankfully, the waitress cut the tension by delivering our food, but once we started eating the table grew awkwardly silent—Hale's knife scratching against the cheap china and my deep-fried cheese oozing under the judgmental stare of Paul and his ridiculously large arms.

"Oh, they put dressing on my salad." Elle flipped a few lettuce leaves, noting the way the greens were slathered in what looked like butter-milk ranch.

"Nah, babe, you aren't eating that." Paul pushed the plate away from her the way a human might take something from a pet and I frowned. "Excuse me," he practically shouted to the nearest server.

"That's not our waitress," I hissed, mortified by how uncomfortable this dinner was getting.

"Can you grab our waitress?" Paul shouted, disrupting the conversation of diners seated around us.

I wanted to crawl under the table. This meal couldn't end fast enough.

Our waitress returned. "How is everyth—"

"Yeah, we ordered no dressing. Hers is slathered in crap."

I kept my eyes on my plate, discomfort ruining my appetite.

"I'm sorry. I'll have them remake the salad and be right back with a new one."

"We'll just wait." Paul folded his big arms, and as she hurried away he muttered, "Because making a salad is hard."

My stomach was instantly upset. "Want one of my mozzarella sticks, Elle?"

"Thanks."

"What are you doing?"

The table froze, as did Elle's partially extended hand. I held out my olive branch of a cheese stick as it wafted the delicious scent of battered bread and gooey goodness across the table.

Take the stick. Take the damn mozzarella stick.

I held her stare. If she didn't stand up to this micromanaging, probably steroid-induced micro penis, he was going to take over her whole life.

I needed her to eat that fucking mozzarella stick more than I needed my next breath. It was a matter of female independence and solidarity. A fuck you to toxic diet culture and the oppressive body-shaming men who made women feel like they had to be less to have more or deserve something as basic as acceptance and love.

Even Hale paused, watching to see what she would do.

Her hand drew back and utter disappointment swamped me. "I'll just wait. My food should be right out."

I wanted to scream. This was not my friend. This was some brainwashed, self-deprecating, *hungry,* waif who thought she needed to change to be worthy. And for what? This guy?

I glared at Paul and snapped the tip of the mozzarella stick off with my teeth. *Fuck you, Paul, and your little dick, too.*

When the waitress returned with the dry salad, Elle squeezed a lemon over the leaves and hummed happily at the first bite, cutting some of the tension at the table. We ate in silence for several minutes, but Paul eventually ruined that too.

"You ever hear of P-Cubed Supplements, Hale?"

"Out of Silicon Valley?"

"Right. Well, I got a friend whose cousin went to school with the guy whose brother started that company. He's pretty interested in this Kickstarter I'm doing. You could be a shareholder if you're interested in making some money."

"Your friend's cousin's classmate's brother? Say less." It was hard not to laugh when Hale actively patronized Paul. Sarcasm wasn't Hale's go to, but when he whipped it out I found it hysterical.

Smirking around another bite of hydrogenated cheese, I watched to see how this sales pitch might unfold.

Paul, however, was too involved in inflating his own ego to identify condescension, even when it smacked him upside his dumb-ass head.

The more he talked the more I realized something. There was no way Elle would stay with this guy. He was an intolerable egomaniac, a know-it-all. He had to be a stage, a future regret she needed to suffer for some twisted masochistic reason. He was a pothole on her path, not the whole journey.

"Paul's going to change the way people view fitness."

I frowned. Or maybe I was wrong and Elle was in it for the long haul.

She gobbled up every dumb word this guy said. Where was the appeal? He hadn't said one nice thing to her since we sat down. As a matter of fact, he had a way of poking her insecurities without actually putting her down, like when he reminded her of every consequence to anything that might be remotely pleasurable.

Was there a name for that?

Maybe the accident had knocked her confidence loose. What if she took his crap because she didn't believe something better existed? That's when it hit me. I needed to save my friend. I needed to tell her that I was here for her and she didn't have to settle for this loser.

"I have to use the restroom. Elle, do you want to come with me?"

She looked up from her salad, sensing that wasn't a question. "Sure."

Hale shot me a warning look not to take long. I set my napkin on the booth and he grudgingly stood to let me out.

"We'll be back in a minute."

The moment we entered the bathroom I turned on her. "Okay, *what* is going on? You can't possibly be into this guy."

She drew back. "What are you talking about? You don't even know him."

"I know enough. Come on, Elle. He's a total wanker." I caught her shoulders and looked her in the eye. "Look, I know I've been pre-occupied, but you've got my attention now. I'm here for whatever you need. If it's not Barrett, fine—"

"Oh, my God, stop making this about Barrett!"

"That's not what I meant. I'm saying, if you need to find a new job or go on a vacation—"

"What the hell, Rayne?" She flung my hands off of her and scowled. "Every complication can't be resolved by running away. That's how you solve problems, not me."

"Elle, come on…" I honestly thought if we had a real moment of straight talk she'd revert back to being honest with herself. "This isn't your guy."

"How do you know?"

"Because I know you!" I practically laughed. "We used to make fun of guys like him. You're way out of his league, yet you're deferring to him like he's your cult leader."

She scoffed. "Gee, thanks, Rayne."

"I'm just concerned." I held up my hands, unsure what more there was to say. To me, it was all very obvious. This guy was not for Elle.

"Well, thanks for the concern, but I'm fine."

"What's with him restricting what you eat?"

"It's called self-control and discipline. Maybe if you had some, you wouldn't call me with a new calamity every other day."

I drew back as if she slapped me. "Excuse me?"

"Paul's being supportive because he knows what I want."

"To starve?"

"I'm not starving! Plenty of cultures avoid over-indulgence. It's one of the Dharma principles and a key factor in holistic clarity."

"Oh, right. Like Paul's going to be your guru on the path to some spiritual awakening. Ten bucks says he shoots his ass full of non-organic steroids every morning."

"When did you become so judgmental?"

"When did you decide to live a life of suffering?"

"Probably about the same time I got bored with your ignorance! It's the same thing, over and over again with you, Rayne. Not everyone wants to live their life on the merry-go-round of self-destructive coping mechanisms."

Holy shit, she wasn't pulling any punches. I panicked and yelled, "This isn't about me!"

"Well, maybe it should be!"

Our voices rose, bouncing off the tile walls and ricocheting around the hollow chamber of the restroom.

"Take a pulse, Elle. You aren't happy."

"I'm working on myself! It takes time and discipline. Not everyone has Prince Charming on speed dial! Some of us have to figure things out for ourselves."

"What the fuck?" Who was this woman?

"You know it's true. You have one little hiccup and Hale comes running to your rescue."

She had no idea the day-to-day challenges I faced that did *not* include Hale. Hale had nothing to do with my job or my education. He worked eighty hours a week. Most of the times it was *me* deciding what to do with Elara because he was on a call or in a meeting. But all of that was beside the point.

She made it sound like I was still some dumb kid making stupid choices without ever thinking about the consequences. My bowels alone could prove how much I stressed over the possible fallout in my day-to-day life. I lived in a chronic state of anxiety, worrying that things might not work out as planned, fearing that I might disappoint those I loved.

"There's nothing wrong with having a support system. Depending on Hale from time to time doesn't make me weak."

"No, but marrying a Davenport has certainly blinded you to their privilege."

I scoffed. "You were dating his brother!"

"And I got out before I became dependent on something that wasn't mine."

"I'm not with Hale for his money or lifestyle."

If anything, his stature made me second guess myself. She, more than anyone, should know that.

"Maybe I do rely on Hale from time to time. So what? I'm allowed! How could you villainize me for that when my entire life has been riddled with trust issues when it comes to men? Of all people, you should be proud of me finding a partner I can rely on. Where is this resentment coming from?"

"I know you didn't fall for him because of his money, but let's not pretend his wealth hasn't had an impact on your life. You never have to worry about anything ever again, Rayne. You're set."

"I worry all the time!"

"About dumb stuff. Do you even realize how

lucky you are? How much your life and the lives of your children will change because of him?"

My eyes prickled, but I refused to cry in a restaurant bathroom. "Hale helps me because he's going to be my husband. We're partners. And I might be the broke one, but believe it or not, I help him too. Not everything is about money. Sometimes it's just about love."

She knew I was upset but made no move to comfort me. Instead, she popped her fists on her hips and looked hard at the pain she'd caused. "It doesn't feel good, does it?"

My breath skipped as if she'd stabbed me. Was she purposefully trying to hurt me? "What are you talking about?"

"I'm talking about feeling judged. Having your man measured unfairly for being exactly who he is."

Was she really trying to compare her inflated crush on Paul to what I felt for Hale? Was that even relevant? I couldn't get past her admitting that she intentionally just tried to hurt me.

"Wow." I didn't recognize her. I didn't even care why we were fighting anymore. I just wanted this to be over.

My brain flashed over a lifetime of memories. Swing sets and tree houses. Breakups and crushes. How had we gone from that to this?

I remembered painting her nails when she was in the coma. I could still feel the cannonball weight of worry I'd carried in my stomach for her during those months.

Maybe I just always loved her more than she

ever loved me. "What did I do to make you so angry—"

"Oh, please, Rayne. You're the one trying to fit us into a mold we both outgrew a long time ago. Why can't you accept that things changed?"

"I do accept that! I just don't understand what happened to you."

"I can't be old Elle for you anymore!" She pointed to the scar on her head where her face had broken the windshield. "I'm never going to be the pretty hairdresser again. I can't even cut paper in a straight line. Yet you somehow expect me to rush to your rescue whenever life gets complicated. This is my first time living, too! I don't have the energy to worry about my problems and then take on your first-world meltdowns about heel height, *apéritifs*, turbulence on your fiancé's private fucking jet, or whatever other calamities you're facing at any given minute of any given day!"

Her words literally knocked me back a step. I talked about those things because that was the mundane bullshit Elle used to enjoy discussing. I didn't bring them up to whine or brag, and I had no idea she resented my life so much. No clue that she resented *me*.

Oh, my God… This was it.

This space between us… There was no bridge back.

I was losing her. No. She was already lost. My best friend was gone.

The urge to bolt welled up inside of me. My ragged heart, the one she just tore into tatters, raced as if I were being chased by a bear. Then I exploded.

"*Me,* judgmental? That man out there that you're obsessed with has critiqued and scrutinized every fucking thing you've put in your mouth!" I drove the conversation back to Paul because the things I really wanted to scream were too heavy. "Why are you letting him control you, Elle? It's like you've been brainwashed!"

"Oh, you've got nerve! You haven't made one decision for yourself since the Davenports came into your life!"

"That's not true!"

"It's one hundred percent true! If not for them, we wouldn't be standing here right now."

"We're here because Paul picked the shittiest restaurant in a fifty-mile radius!"

"I mean Florida!"

"Fine! But *I'm* in Florida because of the choices *I* made. I applied for the job. I'm going to school—"

"Because they're paying for it! Can't you see how much control you've given them? You didn't even pick out your car."

I scoffed. "Because it was a gift."

"Think about that, Ray. Do you hear the privilege in your words?"

My chest hurt. I couldn't help that the Davenports were rich. That wasn't why I loved them.

"What was I supposed to do, Elle? Say no? Tell Hale to take it back?" She was punishing me for things I didn't choose.

"I see you and Hale passing judgmental looks back and forth. You're not subtle."

Was she calling me a snob? "It's hard to be polite when you're sitting across from a self-involved egomaniac! The guy hasn't stopped blowing himself since we sat down! You can't get mad that we don't instantly love Paul."

"This isn't about Paul. This is about you supporting me, the way I support you, no matter who's sitting by my side."

Support me? She just crucified me for falling in love with a wealthy man who enjoyed spoiling me.

I felt trapped, like she'd invited us to this specific restaurant and made things difficult with her restrictive diet to set us up.

Elle was in a position of privilege, too, since selling the house. She could afford days off and nice things. So why was she punishing me for enjoying the same?

"Why did you invite us here, Elle? It's not like they're known for the food you're eating."

"See? The old you would have never said that. You think you're better than—"

"No! You do not get to twist this up to make me look like a spoiled princess because I know we can do better."

"I'm angry because you think your relationship makes you better!"

"*What?*" I shrilled. "Have you met me? I live in a vortex of self-doubt and personal beratement. I do not think I'm better than anyone!"

"You and Hale are the result of luck and lust, not your ability to make the right choices, so stop acting like you have life figured out. You were stranded at sea, he was there, and shit happened."

"*Shit* happened?" Was that how she summarized the most epic love of my life?

I shook my head, literally speechless. This was

so much more than my issues over her relationship with Paul or the pressures of work and education. This was deep. Way deeper than I ever suspected.

"You're jealous," I finally said, speaking mostly to myself. I couldn't believe it.

"Excuse me?" She laughed without humor. "I am *not* jealous—"

"Then what?" I snapped. "Getting you to help me with the wedding is like pulling teeth. Yet, you get snitty whenever I mention hanging out with Phina or when I do stuff without you. Even when it's not about the wedding, you're always too busy to hang out. You never have more than a few minutes to talk. And you leave my texts on *read* for entire days before responding with the shortest reply possible. I'm beginning to think you even broke up with Barrett to break up with me."

"Wow." She took a step back. "Once again, you find a way to make everything about you."

"Oh, shut up."

"You shut up! Does it ever occur to you that I'm busy because I have bills to pay?"

"You have more money in your savings account than I have in mine. Stop acting like you're destitute!"

"That's my savings. It's different."

"Yeah, well, you can thank the Davenports for that. Anyone else would have charged a fortune to do what Hale did for you. So don't act like you haven't benefited from my relationship as well."

"My parents died, Rayne. That house was all I had aside from my drug-addict brother. How could you throw that in my face?"

Was she kidding? She just attacked every insecurity I had and categorized the greatest relationship of my life as a lucky-and-lusty-gold-digging-fuck-fest-at-sea. I was speechless.

Her gaze dropped from my face to my feet. "You look like a mannequin for Seraphina's clothing line."

Now she was criticizing my appearance? What the fucking fuck?

I had the bizarre urge to do something completely inappropriate like rip out her hair extensions. But I was better than that. I would not drop to her petty level.

My finger pointed to the door and I hissed, "Why are you with him?"

"He makes me happy!"

"How? How does *he* make you happy?"

"You don't know him!"

"I don't know you!"

The door opened and I gasped when the wood touched my back. For a split second, I recalled we were in a public place. Then Hale poked his head into the lady's room, his expression displeased.

"Your voices are carrying and the manager is about to get involved." He looked at me, his annoyance morphing into concern. "Rayne?"

Adrenaline had my insides quaking. Hale saw how badly I was shaking and reached out, but I evaded him. If he touched me, I'd shatter.

I looked back at Elle, not recognizing her as the safe person she'd always been. She was dangerous. A stranger. I might never understand what made her think so cruelly of me, but I couldn't lose one more piece of myself trying to bring her back.

It became a choice of her or me, and I knew I needed to save myself.

"Fuck this." I yanked open the door and stormed out.

On the way past the table, I snatched my purse from the booth without saying a word to Paul. No point in pretending we liked each other. I was probably one of the *unhealthy things* he convinced Elle to cut out of her life.

I waited at the car door for my rage to simmer. Hale must have stayed back to pay the bill, but he was out a moment later and the car unlocked.

I clambered into the front seat and crossed my arms—way past sulking and onto seething. Hale slid behind the wheel with perfect grace. He didn't ask if I was okay, because he knew I wasn't.

Once we pulled onto the road, my breath started to shake. The lump in my throat grew until it choked me. I blinked, unable to see past my rage-induced tears.

Hale held out his hand, palm open between us, and waited for me to lace my fingers in his. Only when his fist squeezed protectively around mine did he say, "I'm sorry she said those things to you."

A tear fell down my cheek. I had to mentally command my body to physically unclench. I had never been this angry before. I didn't know what to do with all of these sharp, heavy emotions. But the moment I felt his love radiate up my arm in that tight squeeze that said *I've got space for you and everything you're feeling right now*, the dam holding back my sadness collapsed and a guttural sob ripped out of me like a wounded animal cry.

There was no hiding my sorrow. My friendship

with Elle would never be the same again. Whatever it would become of it, I couldn't predict. But whatever it had been was over.

He pulled the car onto the shoulder and collected me in his arms, hugging me tight as I cried.

"I'm sorry, baby."

But no one was more sorry than me.

Virginal Behavior

CAN EAT A DICK

My life was in flux. When I was in New York, my heart was in Florida with Hale. When I was in Florida, Hale was in Tokyo or Hong Kong or California or New Jersey. Seriously, the man got around. And when Hale and I happened to be in the same state at the same time, his mind was on work and my mind was on Elle.

Elle.

Elle.

Always Elle.

The woman had become my Roman Empire—the thing I subconsciously obsessed over and thought about at least once a day.

Fine, once an hour, but who was counting?

How could she have said those things? She had the secret code to the safe where I kept all of my insecurities and she'd used that code to bust out my demons and sic them on me.

She hurt me. Deeper and harder than anyone ever had. She was the one person I trusted above all others to accept my ugly insecurities and keep me safe from the mean people of a sometimes uglier world. Never once did I assume she would become the person I needed protection from most.

I couldn't stop replaying her words in my head, inflicting the emotional trauma she caused over and over again until I broke down and cried. But sometimes I wouldn't cry. Sometimes, I became so overcome by fury I couldn't function, so appalled by the hurtful things she said even food brought no comfort.

I was down one dad and now one maid of honor.

I'd written out several texts. Some rehashing. Some apologizing. They all got deleted because in the end, they all felt more like justifying, which I didn't want to do.

Then I would deflate. The constant internal badgering wore me down like a steam roller until I felt flat and lifeless inside.

Hale's concern increased as the weeks passed and no reconciliation came. He didn't know what to do and his instinct was to help.

"You've got me," he said, late one night as I lay on my tear soaked pillow. "I'll be your best friend."

"Thank you." I smiled, more grateful than ever to have such a good man at my side. But Hale and I both knew a best friendship with a spouse wasn't the same as the one shared between two girls.

For his sake and mine, I forced myself to put my emotions about Elle aside. If I didn't get control of my feelings, they would distract me from the fact that I was getting married. This unearthed a new appreciation for wedding planning.

I had an outlet. A purpose.

To cope with my breakup with Elle, I focused on my job during the day and my upcoming wedding at night. I even read the bajillian articles Phina emailed me that had been sitting unopened in my inbox for weeks. That was how I stumbled across one specific article about the lure of romantic mystique.

"I think we should stop having sex," I said over dinner one night.

Hale paused, his fork suspended midair between his plate and his open mouth. "Excuse me?"

"Until the wedding."

He scowled. "Why would we do that?"

My reasoning stemmed from the article I read about waiting until marriage. That ship had sailed for us, but there was something intriguing about a chaste bride and groom sharing a wedding night.

What if our wedding night just felt like any other night? I wanted it to feel special, like the way the virgins described theirs.

"It could be fun."

"Not having sex? That sounds like the exact opposite of fun, Rayne."

We had done every position known to man. At least I thought we had. "Abstinence could freshen things up."

He cleared his throat. "I'm sorry, have you been bored? Because last night you came so hard I think your screams called a few ships into harbor."

"Ha. Ha. I'm just saying, a little waiting could spice things up. Remember how hot it was when we used to have to sneak around the *Lady Parr?*"

"If I recall, I wore you down in a matter of hours."

"No one likes a bragger, Hale."

"No one likes abstinence, Rayne."

"*Ugh*, you can be so difficult sometimes." I stabbed my fork into the broccoli. "If I say no, there's nothing you can do."

"I think we both know how that would end."

"In court?"

"Oh, please." He laughed. "You enjoy it too much. Five minutes and I'd have you drenched and begging."

"You make it sound like I have no self-control. A lot of couples stop having sex during their engagement."

"I'm not giving up sex, Rayne."

"Well, your fiancée is, so have fun with your hand."

Unimpressed, he set down his fork. "This is ridiculous. We have a healthy sexual relationship and we both benefit from that strong intimate connection. Why would you want to tamper with that?"

He was adorable when he used the right words and high emotional IQ to communicate his needs. Hale was so evolved compared to some of the men I'd met early on in life.

"We can still do other stuff—"

"Blow jobs?"

I glanced over at Elara who repeatedly whacked her bowl on the tray of her high chair.

"I meant kissing and making out. Nothing with penetration."

He rolled his eyes and reached for the baby

food. "This is the most asinine thing I've ever heard. Did I do something to piss you off? Have you not enjoyed yourself?"

"Hale, you know I always enjoy it."

He eyed me suspiciously. "Women fake orgasms."

I snorted. "I'm not stage trained. Besides, you would totally be able to tell if I faked it."

The baby spoon rattled against the glass jar as he swiped up a spoonful of green goop and grumbled something under his breath.

"Why do you force her to eat that sludge? She doesn't like it."

He spooned another mouthful of strained peas into Elara's mouth and the poor child grimaced, spitting it down her chin.

There goes another bib.

Hale scraped the slime off her face with the rubber coated spoon and pushed it back into her mouth. "She needs vegetables."

"She likes the sweet potatoes." I had to look away, unable to bear the pleading look she sent me.

He tried for another bite and she spit the green goop all over the highchair tray. "Hand me a napkin."

"Her poop's gonna be nasty if you make her eat that whole jar. I'm not changing it."

"This is what babies eat."

I nearly gagged every time I smelled the nasty sludge. "Have you ever tasted it?"

"I don't need to taste it to know it's good for her."

"Taste it."

He gave me an unimpressed look and I laughed.

"See, you don't want to eat it either."

"If I taste it, you have to feed her the next time. Vegetables. Not fruit."

"Deal." No way would he put that disgusting shit in his mouth and still argue it was good for her. I was a taster of everything, so I knew how gross it was.

Rolling his eyes, he scooped out a bite and hesitated. When he put it in his mouth, I smiled.

"Tastes about as good as what's going to come out the other end, doesn't it?"

His face contorted. "Ah, hell." He stood, wiping the mouthful into a napkin. He carried the strained peas to the trash and tossed the jar and napkin inside. "What is that stuff?"

"Told you."

After Elara finished her dinner of delicious sweet potatoes and carrots, Hale cleaned the kitchen. I gave peanut a bath and read her a story. When we finally made it to bed, Hale tried to get in my pants.

"Um, excuse me." I caught his wrist. "This is a no fly zone."

"You're serious?"

"I told you, I'm converting to virgin until the wedding."

"Virgin isn't something you convert to, Rayne. You either are one or you aren't." He tugged me over him and caught my ass in an unbreakable grip, forcing me to straddle him.

"Hale…"

"One of the sexiest things about you is how

unvirginal you can be." He pulled me down for a kiss and I tried to resist, but he was a really good kisser.

The moment I softened, he forked his fingers into my hair and whispered against my mouth, "I've fucked every inch of you." He bit playfully at my lips. "This mouth." He pinched my nipple. "Your breasts." He flexed his hips, grinding his erection against my panties. "Your needy, wet pussy." His hand shifted and his finger glided along my ass crack. "Even your tight little asshole. And you loved every filthy, fucking minute of it."

Okay, this was harder than I expected. That was extremely tempting and my body was already responding to his nearness and words. But I was determined, so I forced myself to roll off of him.

"We can have sex again on our wedding night."

I expected him to argue, maybe even get a little bent over my sternness. But, instead, he nuzzled close to my ear, kissed my neck, and whispered, "I know you're already regretting it." His hand slid to the front of my panties, teased me there then vanished. "Have fun fingering yourself to frustration. When you're ready to come, you know where to find me."

With that, he rolled onto his back, leaving me horny and annoyed.

For the next hour I debated if this decision would help or hinder our chemistry. To be honest, there had been nothing wrong with our sex life, but I needed a challenge so I had something else to obsess over besides Elle. It was working. Now my brain was on dicks. Dicks and Elle. But mostly dicks.

Hale's dick.

It was a good dick. Solid. Firm. Everything a girl could ask for where men were concerned. And I wanted to restrict this, why?

Remington often warned me that men who were unsatisfied at home would stray. Those traitorous thoughts, while not always accurate, lived in my head rent-free.

What if this was a mistake? What if sex was such a huge part of our relationship that cutting it out endangered us in some way?

And, if that was the case, what did that say about us? We needed to be more than good sex if we expected our marriage to last. Or maybe I needed to take a more handsoff approach since I had a habit of destroying good things while everything Hale touched seemed to turn to gold.

"Oh, my God, just do it!"

Hale, who I think had been sleeping, sat up and turned on a light. "What?"

"Sex. Just have sex with me. I don't want to break us."

He frowned. "Rayne, I'm over it."

Over it or over me? I was such a headcase. Sex was the one distraction I had to keep him from realizing he was marrying a total nut-job. What was I thinking, taking sex out of the equation?

"I never want you to feel like you have to go somewhere else for booty!"

"Hey." He caught my face and made me look him in the eye. "That would never happen. I love you. I don't want anyone else. And if this is something you need to do, then we'll do it. I'll wait as long as it takes."

"Really?"

"Really. I don't like it, but if you need this right now, I'll support you."

My heart melted. I wasn't sure if it was something I needed or something I needed to prove, but I appreciated his blind support. "I love you."

"I love you too." He closed the distance and softly kissed me. "And I've never been more grateful that we opted for a short engagement."

After a few nights of no sex I was over my vow of celibacy, but Hale started to get into it. I'd proven what I needed to prove and my squirrel-like attention span was ready to move on to a new goal. But Hale… The man loved a challenge.

He'd kiss me and get my blood pumping only to pin my exploring hands to the bed and firmly tell me, "No."

Somehow, his denial of my pleasure made me want him all the more. Not having sex had led to some of the hottest make out sessions of my life. Hale—the expert of edging that he was—literally had me begging for it.

"Please? I need you inside of me. I'll do anything you want."

He bit my nipple right through my shirt. "I know you will—when you're officially my wife."

"I hate you."

Not only was I the one regretting our arrangement, which I'd manufactured all on my own, Hale was getting off on my desperation. So much so that he amped up his usual sexting while I was at work.

I'd be dealing with Remington when a text would come out of nowhere, depicting some of the most vulgar, lewd, perverted things I'd ever read. It was totally hot. It was also incredibly cruel. What-ever the girl equivalent of a classroom hard-on was, I was walking around with one. Hale made sure I rocked a lady-boner twenty-four-seven with no relief in sight.

He'd even confiscated my vibrator as part of our no penetration rule. "This is contraband," he said, tossing it in the safe and twisting the dial.

"I know the code to get in there."

One hard look from him and we both knew I wouldn't dare open that safe. "Dick."

"That's right," he said, diving onto the bed and kissing me slowly. "The only *dick* that's going to bring you relief—when it's time."

He knew I was inept at making myself come. He was torturing me on purpose. I even tried using the water massager, but only ended up squirting the ceiling fixtures and burning my clit.

Meanwhile, he'd been taking extra-long showers at all hours of the day and walking around whistling showtunes in a way that bragged without words that his pipes were clear.

I'd had enough. If he didn't bring me some relief I was going to order the biggest vibrator I could find and make him watch as I finished the job once and for all. I was determined to get my husband back inside of me.

No way was I taking no for an answer again. As we kissed the following night, my legs coiled around him, locking his hard body against mine as I arched and moaned.

"Please, Hale." I pushed his hand between my thighs. "I need you." My body strained to get closer even though we were as close as humanly possible without actually having literal sex. "Please..."

"Baby, we can't."

His cock pressed through our clothing, nudging at all the right places. He'd become a master of outercourse, rocking against my body and forming delicious friction until I hung on a precipice of pleasure and pain ready to scream. I could come if he kept moving his hips that way.

"Are you close?" His lips teased my throat as his warm hand cupped my breast, pinching my nipple through the shirt ever so slightly.

I moaned, my body arching and trembling as I came closer to sweet, sweet release. "Please." The tip of his hard cock nudged me through my soaked panties. "Hale..."

Hands squeezed my ass, my breasts, and even pulled my hair. I was shaking like a leaf, more sensitized than I'd ever been. He caressed my throat, my ears, every touch carried a tantric weight. The slightest ripple of clothing slammed through me like a gong. And then it happened.

I don't know how, or what exactly he touched to send me off, but I was suddenly shattering in his arms. It was subtle yet undeniable. All the little aftershocks were there, but rather than feel replete and drained, my body wanted more. Only, I couldn't handle more. The slightest caress proved too much and I gasped every time he touched me.

He chuckled. "That was something."

It certainly was. "I think you're a wizard. I'm not even sure how you did that."

He nuzzled closer and kissed my throat. "Good things take time."

When he brushed his fingers over my panties I flinched and gasped. His low chuckle teased my skin as he kissed his way back to my mouth. Another touch and I reflexively darted my hips away. It was too much.

"You've turned me into a teenage boy." He pressed the hard bulge in his briefs against my skin.

I gasped. "You're wet."

"It's been more than a decade since I shot a load in my pants. Do you see what you do to me?"

I groaned. "This is killing me. I've learned my lesson. I don't want to be a virgin bride anymore. I want to be a happy little slut again. No more waiting. Please make it stop."

Another low chuckle. "I get so fucking hot thinking about our wedding night. I can't wait to finally get inside you again."

"No, no waiting. I want it now. Forget my stupid rules. Only virgins say those things because they don't know what they're missing. I've tasted the good stuff and I want more. I need it, Hale. Do you hear me? I need the sex!"

"Not until we say I do. Then I'm *really* going to come. Again…" He rolled on top of me, pinning my body open beneath his as he ground himself against me. "And again."

He thrust his hips.

My body trembled, falling into another delicate spiral.

"And again."

That time when I came, he didn't let up. He ground his hips as if we were actually fucking, and I rode out the friction in a combination of pleasure and misery.

Abstinence had sharpened my desires to an unbearable edge and I became super-sensitized to the slightest caress, but nothing would ever feel as good as having him inside of me. The wedding couldn't come fast enough.

Neither could I.

No matter how much he touched me or how many times he made me come that way, I would always want more.

He'd spoiled me and this little experiment proved I would never be able to go back to a sexless life. I was shamelessly addicted to Hale—the man, the massive cock, the legend.

When we were both as finished as an undercooked rare steak, Hale slipped out of bed. "I need a shower."

The water bill was going to be outrageous this month.

I smiled and stretched, my body buzzing but my bones heavy as I reached for my phone. No text from Elle—*shocker there.* I frowned, not at the empty text box but at the little red flag pinned to my messenger app.

My body went numb.

Was this it?

No. *It could be from anyone.* It probably was spam.

But what if it wasn't?

What if that little red flag was him?

I sat up.

Only one way to find out.

My gaze darted to the bathroom door then back to my phone. I swallowed, mouth dry and heart racing.

Don't overthink it. Don't get ahead of yourself—

Too late. I was already picturing my father welcoming me back into his life with open arms, knowing full well that would never happen.

I clicked on the app icon and held my breath. It took forever to load. Then, in bold print at the top of my private messages, just below his name, was the first line of his response…

Hi Rayne, It's great to hear
from you…

Casting Call For Steve Martin...

STEVE, PLEASE PICK UP YOUR SCRIPT

WITH ONE EAR tuned to the running water as Hale showered, I opened the message. My heart pinched and pulled in so many directions I wasn't sure if I wanted to scream with joy or throw up.

My dad had responded! He actually wrote something back! I was in such shock, I had to take a deep breath before I could make any sense of the words on my phone.

Hi Rayne, It's great to hear from you. Not a day goes by that I don't think about my little girl and wonder what kind of woman she's become. It sounds like things are going well for you. Nothing makes me happier than to hear that. Congratulations on your upcoming wedding and thank you for letting me know about this for letting me know about this important milestone in your life. I know I haven't always been there for the big moments, but you've never left my mind and you've always held a place in my heart. I have a lot of regrets. The main one being that I don't know you. I don't know what you do for a living or what movies you like. I don't know how you spend your free time or even what your laugh sounds like. Those are all things I believe a father should know, and I deeply regret that I don't. I'm also extremely touched, that after all these years and missed moments, you still think of me. I know I haven't always been deserving of your patience, but I am grateful that you have such a forgiving heart. I would love nothing more than to connect with you. Where do you live? I'm in Pennsylvania, and I can travel by car if it isn't too far. Would you like to have lunch? I understand if that's asking too much, and if writing to each other is all you can manage at the moment, that's perfectly fine. It's a start. I would have responded earlier but I rarely use Facebook and I didn't find your message until this

find your message until this
morning when I signed on to list
something on marketplace.
Anyway, I'm sorry it took me so
long to respond, to this message
and many others. I promise not to
make you wait again. If you have
it in your heart to write back, I'll
answer right away. Love, Dad

"RAYNE?"

I looked up from my phone with tears in my eyes and found Hale watching me from the bathroom door, a towel clinging to his hips and steam billowing at his back.

Still in shock, a stuttered breath filled my lungs and I held out my phone to him. "It's my dad…"

He crossed the bedroom and took the phone, frowning at the screen. "He responded to your message?"

I nodded. This was so unexpected I didn't know what to feel.

"That's…great." He looked up at me and then back at the phone as he continued reading. "He sounds sincere."

I laughed, sort of outside of myself. There had been a hundred—no, a *thousand*—other moments when I wished my dad would answer me. I never imagined it feeling quite this way.

I was elated and confused. Sick to my stomach but also excited.

Dizzy, as if I just stepped off a rollercoaster I'd

been locked on for the majority of my life. I didn't know what to say or how to walk. I just knew my dad was there and he wanted to hear from me again.

All of my bottled-up emotions from the past week burst out of me in a giddy sob. Finally, someone I loved cared that I was getting married.

"I can't believe it." More tears fell and I actively began to weep with joy.

"Hey, hey, hey," Hale said, coming to sit on the bed with me. "Don't cry."

"It's okay." I sniffled. "This is a good cry."

There was such an incredible, indescribable feeling of relief. I thought about my twelve-year-old self and how badly she'd wanted this moment, but it was so much heavier than I'd ever imagined it would be. I wasn't sure a little girl could process this much emotional baggage at once. Or maybe it was heavy because I'd been waiting for him to answer me since I was a child.

"I just can't believe this. I never actually thought he'd reply. I mean, I hoped, but I was prepared for disappointment. I was frustrated when weeks passed with no response but I was getting over it. This…" I shook my phone and scoffed with a smile, still in shock. "I *never* expected *this*."

"But you're happy, right?"

I gaped at him. "Happy would be an understatement. He wants to get together with me, Hale. I'm going to hang out with my Dad!"

I jumped off the bed and paced. I wanted to pack and leave that minute, before he could rescind the offer and make this amazing feeling go away.

"He's on the East Coast. It's perfect. I'll be in New York and he's right in Pennsylvania. They're pretty close, right? Drivable?"

"I read that. You should go. And yes, Pennsylvania's only a short drive from New York. When you go back to the city you should plan a day with him. Martel will take you wherever you want to go."

My heart did a cartwheel. "Oh, my God, I'm going to meet my dad!" Pressing my hand flat on my stomach, I paced the bedroom. "I think I'm going to be sick. This is like the night before Christmas when you're a kid waiting for Santa." I blew out a breath. "Wow. I don't know what to do."

"Enjoy it." Hale laughed, probably so relieved to see me happy again. "He's the lucky one. Trust me."

I had no actual memories of the man behind the birthday cards and phone calls. Just a voice from random phone calls and the fact that he always capitalized his Es, even at the end of handwritten words like Rayne.

"I feel like I need to do something." I didn't want sweets or snacks. I didn't want to sleep. I honestly felt like I could run a mile, and that was something I simply did not do. I wasn't a runner. Was I? No. Definitely not.

"This is a good thing, baby. Don't overthink it. Write him back and set up a lunch date."

"What's your schedule this week?" Now that we finally booked an officiant we both liked who didn't stare at my boob and was also willing to travel to New York, we were pretty wrapped up on wedding homework.

"I fly out on Wednesday, but you don't have to wait for me to leave. Go meet your dad, baby. You waited a lifetime for this moment."

I was going to meet my father. Another wave of excitement hit with the sensation of rolling down a hill. "Holy crap. What should I wear?"

"I don't think that matters—"

"It'll be his first impression of me as an adult, Hale. Of course, it matters. The last time he saw me I was smaller than Elara. I'm a thirty-year-old woman now. He might have certain expectations."

"Maybe put your expectations before his in this case, Rayne."

I stopped pacing when I caught an edge of skepticism in his voice. "What do you mean?"

"You're an incredible woman. It's *his* loss that he missed the first half of your life. Remember that. The fact that you're willing to forgive his absence is a big deal. He's the one who should be trying to impress you."

The waves of uncertainty dispersed and I smiled at Hale. "How do you do that? How do you always know exactly what to say to calm me down?"

"I don't *always* know. But I do realize how lucky I am to have you in my life. I know that I'd do anything to protect you and I'd suffer any injury if it saved you a moment's pain. I'm happy for you and I hope he's everything you're expecting, but I'm also nervous. Most people tend to let us down long before they lift us up."

I tried to decipher how much of his words

were good advice and how much was him projecting his own bad experiences with his own father.

I sighed and returned to the bed, taking his hand. "Hale, your dad hurt you because he was close to you. I'm not saying he had a motive, but that's the reason why his actions caused so much pain. You trusted him and he betrayed that trust."

"I didn't say that to make this about my father. This is your moment."

"I know. But our situations are different." I rubbed his hand, because whenever I brought up his personal relationship with Remington, Hale tended to run for the nearest escape. "You work together and see each other every day. Even if you argue constantly and rarely see eye to eye, you two are extremely close. Even now, after everything that's happened, you're still closer to him than Barrett or Phina could ever be. My dad's missed thirty-years of my life, and the ten he had when he called on the phone and sent greeting cards, well, if I'm being honest they weren't anything I'd categorize as real in terms of what a father and daughter should share. I don't think it's possible for us to ever be as close as you and Remington, so I don't think it's possible for him to hurt me that deeply."

He lifted our hands and pressed a kiss to my knuckles. "Just take it slow."

I knew what he was saying. My dad had a pattern of ghosting. Rejection was like bullet wounds. Getting shot more than once didn't make it hurt less. Sometimes, repeated injuries hurt worse than the initial ones because the prior damage never fully healed.

"I will. I promise. Right now, I'm just happy to have a reply. If I get another one, I'll be happy again. And if we wind up going to lunch or even just talking on the phone…" I briefly envisioned what that might feel like and a chill raced over my body. "Well, that would be a miracle. I promise not to get ahead of myself."

We both knew that was a vow I was definitely going to break, but I couldn't help it. I waited my whole life to feel this excitement. I didn't want to shut it off.

Hale kissed my forehead. "Your dad's going to hate himself once he realizes what he gave up."

I smiled. I wasn't looking for retribution or justice. I just wanted to know my father. We straightened the covers and climbed into bed. Hale shut out the lights, but sleep evaded me.

Once Hale passed out, I happily stared at the ceiling, watching a kaleidoscope of visions play through my mind. I saw my dad at lunch sipping coffee, ordering from a menu, laughing at a silly thing I said. I tried to picture him, but his features were always a little blurred. But the more I imagined, the stronger my certainty grew. This changed everything.

I couldn't envision my wedding day without seeing him there. By the end of the week we'd be drowning in inside jokes and precious moments.

He'd be with me the morning of my wedding day. He'd kiss my cheek and tell me how beautiful I looked and how proud he was of me. I could picture us in the limo on the way to the ceremony, envision our arms lacing together before I set foot on the aisle.

Would we share similar features? Maybe have the same fingernail shape or slope to our noses. I wanted to know what soap he used and smell his cologne—things a daughter should recognize about her dad.

The entire vision felt perfect—*right*—when so many things had been feeling wrong lately. We would toast and dance, and suddenly I knew my wedding would be the fairytale it was meant to be.

I replied to his message that night and awoke to the beautiful reassurance of his reply. And so it began. On and on, we messaged back and forth until all my insecurities disappeared. My dad was going to be there for my wedding and that certainty healed something huge inside of me—something bigger than I'd ever wanted to admit.

That Monday I flew back to New York. Seraphina had some shoes for me to try on and we needed to have a fitting for the final alterations of my gown. But this trip was more than just finishing touches. This was a trip for new beginnings.

The invitations had gone out and the RSVPs were flooding in, so Quinn was playing a constant game of seating chart roulette whenever a guest declined, but ninety-nine percent of the responses were yeses.

My anxiety over whether or not I'd have a maid of honor by my side was overshadowed by my elation to meet my dad. We had a lunch date scheduled for Tuesday afternoon at a little Italian restaurant about an hour and a half outside of New York.

After my fitting with Phina, I asked her to help me choose an outfit for our upcoming lunch.

"You've never met your father before?"

I shook my head. "Nope. Not since I was a baby. I have no memory from the few months or weeks he lived with us, but he used to send me cards on holidays and call from time to time."

"Rayne, this is incredible! How are you so calm?"

I think I was having a fight-or-flight response. We had messaged each other several times over the last few days. Each response brought another wave of intense excitement and cemented him more in my future.

Turned out my dad loved the show *Blacklist*, had hearing loss in his left ear—a result of years of working in loud construction, he ate two fried eggs every morning, drank his coffee black, and drove an old Chevy pickup. Our back and forth was still in the question and answer stages, but I was beginning to piece together a picture of the man whose DNA I shared.

"I think it's nerves," I finally said. "Although, I have been oddly chill for the last two days." Even New York wasn't causing the same angst I typically felt when visiting.

"You're happy."

Was that it? I had always dreamed about this moment. Was this what contentment felt like?

"I *am* happy. The wedding plans are mostly finished, all of our vendors are booked, the linens are ordered, there's nothing left but the final touches."

Final touches and Elle, but I didn't want to think about her right now.

"And you."

"Huh?"

Seraphina smiled. "The final touches are all about you."

Maybe that was it.

"So!" Seraphina clapped her hands and steered me toward the dressing room. "Let's get you out of this gown and find the perfect outfit for you to meet your dad. I'm thinking a trip to Bergdorf. Champagne first, because this definitely calls for a celebration. And then shopping!"

Shopping with Seraphina rivaled the Olympic games when it came to intensity. The girl knew how to spend and she took control of every store they visited. Who knew there were personal shoppers available to fulfill a customer's beck and call? I certainly didn't. But everywhere we went someone was there to wait on us hand and foot.

Hale's sister strategically put together a complete outfit—including every accessory—for when I would meet my father.

"Clothes impact confidence, Rayne. They're our armor. When we're dressed properly, we can handle anything the world throws at us."

I wasn't sure if Phina owned a pair of sweatpants, but I was pretty sure if she wore them the value would increase.

"Nothing too fancy. It's just a lunch. And nothing too CEO-esque. I don't want him to get the impression that I'm cold."

"No one could ever think that about you. You're

one of the most down-to-earth people I've ever met. You give a very warm and welcoming first impression, Rayne. He's going to love you instantly."

I hoped so.

In the end, I settled on a cream sweater with a rolled turtle neck and a taupe, cashmere skirt with brown leather boots. It was dressy, but understated. Phina insisted on pearl earrings—something I never thought I'd own—but she was right. They added the perfect degree of understated luxury. Simplistic, yet elegant.

"You should have your lashes done."

"No—"

"It'll save you the hassle of putting on mascara every day."

"Really?"

I hated makeup. I wasn't good at applying it and I didn't have the patience to take my time or practice so I could improve.

She was already dialing. "It only takes an hour. Believe me, you'll appreciate the time it saves."

Were women losing hours of their lives applying mascara? Sometimes I really thought I was missing some big-picture details about being a girl.

Seraphina, like her brother and father, wasn't afraid of throwing around the Davenport name to make the wind blow whatever direction her life needed at the moment. The salon *moved some things around* and fit us in that afternoon.

The lash extensions were pain free, but not nearly as relaxing as Phina promised. While I did get to sit in a comfy chair and let a woman carefully touch my face for an hour, I couldn't quite relax with someone that close to me.

In the end, it was worth it. My eyes looked defined and sexy. I sent Hale a picture right away and he instantly wrote back that he missed me. He was getting a lot of silly texts since I'd been incommunicado with Elle which was starting to unearth his playful side as well.

"I'm taking you to dinner tonight," I told Phina as we left the salon. "My treat."

She smiled. "Aw, Rayne, that's sweet. But you don't have to. I'm happy to help you with this stuff."

"I want to. After everything you've done for me with the wedding and now this, it's the least I can do to say thank you."

Her smile grew. "No thanks necessary. That's what sisters are for. And Hale will get my invoice at the end of the month, so let's not assume I'm completely selfless, though I do like doing these things with you."

It was going to be a very expensive quarter for Hale. I smiled. "I enjoy hanging out with you too."

I took Phina to a little hole in the wall pub I'd passed not far from Times Square. We sat on the second floor overlooking the street and drank from big mugs of beer while a game played in the background. It was March madness so no matter where you looked a hot basketball player was on a screen.

"I told Josette to schedule your countdown appointments. You want to make sure you're buffed and shined for the big day, but you also want to give your body time to heal?"

I frowned. "Heal?"

"Adapt," she amended, but it was too late. I already heard the word heal and anticipated pain.

"What kind of appointments?"

She pulled out her phone and read from a list. "You need a gloss treatment on your hair and the split ends trimmed. Your brows are desperately in need of some manicuring. You'll want to have a facial, but nothing too intense and nothing within two weeks of the wedding. You should really consider reducing your sodium intake as well. Maybe even cut out alcohol during those last weeks."

"That's not happening." I'd already given up sex. There was only so much a girl could go without.

"You also want to make sure you're getting plenty of beauty sleep."

"Ha! My body does not get tired under stress. Insomnia is real, my friend." I sipped my drink before anyone thought to take it away.

Cut out alcohol. Yeah right.

People got nuts about weddings. Didn't they know alcohol and marriage had a strong relationship for a reason?

"Then you should consider getting a lymphatic massage to help reduce any stress. It will also relieve some of your puffiness."

My fingers brushed under my eyes. "Am I puffy?"

"We're all puffy. Are you planning on getting a spray tan for the wedding? If so, you should do a test run. You'll need to account for a few days to get the full effect. The color needs time to develop and you'll want to wash off any extra before you put on your dress. We can use a test tan to judge how your body reacts and what day would be the best day for a wedding tan. I find day three looks the most natural."

My mind was on overload. "Do I look pale? I live in Florida."

"It's not about looking like you just returned from a holiday. Spray tans give you that extra glow. Plus, it'll even out your pigment and cover any blemishes or tan lines left over from summer. Have you scheduled an appointment with your PA?"

I cocked my head. As a personal assistant myself, I didn't think I qualified to need my own. Especially when I already had half a dozen wedding handlers. I had to be misunderstanding the meaning of PA.

"Remind me, what's a PA?"

"Your physician's assistant."

"You lost me. Do I need a physical for my marriage license?"

She laughed. "No, silly. For Botox."

I gasped. "I do not need Botox!"

She reached across the table and patted my hand. "Honey, we *all* need it eventually."

I studied her perfect face. "Have you…?"

"Yup. Started when I turned twenty-seven. Here, here, here, and here." She pointed to various places about her flawless face. "I also get filler in my lips, but you don't need that. Your lips are already full."

I was shocked. "I just thought you naturally looked like that."

"Well, I do. The injections just keep things from creasing or sagging."

My fingers blindly dragged across my features

as if I were reading a secret message in braille. "Do you think I need—"

"Yes."

"You could have at least pretended to think it over."

"Six months ago, I would have. But these things need time to heal and we don't have much time left. I'm texting Josette and telling her to make you an appointment ASAP."

There went my self-esteem. I guzzled the rest of my beer.

That night, when I returned to the penthouse, Percy was waiting to see if I needed anything else. Originally it felt strange having someone wait on me, but my mojo dojo casa butler appeared truly happy to fulfill any request when it came to my comfort or needs.

"Is there anything else you require, madam?"

"I'm all set, Percy. Thank you. Have a good night." I shut the door to the master bedroom and left him to locking up.

The following morning I woke up to a delivery of fresh flowers from Hale with a card wishing me luck on this momentous day. I texted him to say thank you, knowing I'd have news for him as soon as he was waking up on the other side of the globe.

As the hours passed my nerves started to jangle. It was a good thing I got my lashes done, because by the time I put my makeup on I could barely keep my hand steady enough to apply lip gloss.

Once I was dressed, I met Marty outside.

"Good morning," the driver greeted in a thick accent.

"Morning." I tried to smile brightly but my nerves made me question the contents of my stomach.

I would forever be cursed with a nervous bladder that made me impulsively want to pee before any noteworthy life events. Staying intentionally dehydrated helped curb my unintentional delusional habits.

The closer we drove to Pennsylvania the more I feared something going wrong. He was going to cancel or there was going to be an accident that would close down the interstate. A meteor was going to hit the planet—not huge, just enough to take out the tri-state area and prevent me from getting to lunch so I could finally meet my dad.

None of that actually happened. We made it to the restaurant with little traffic and parked with several minutes to spare.

I looked at the cars in the parking lot, trying to pinpoint my dad's Chevy truck. I didn't know what color it was, but that didn't matter. There were no trucks to be seen.

Oh, my God, he's standing me up!

Sick to my stomach, I dug out my phone. The last message I had from him was from last night. It said he couldn't wait to meet me. If he bailed on me, would he at least have the decency to tell me, or would I end up sitting all alone like a ditched blind date?

"Shall I walk you inside?" Marty asked.

I looked out the window again, my brows pulling tight. "You don't have to."

"I was merely asking if you were ready to go

inside. I have strict instructions from Mr. Davenport to accompany you at all times."

"What? Why?"

Marty had driven me all over New York and he never followed me into restaurants or stores. What was different about Pennsylvania?

"I'm merely following instructions."

Was this because of my dad? What was Hale expecting?

Overkill or not, Marty wasn't going to disregard a direct order from Hale. I checked my reflection in a compact and took a few deep breaths. Great, I had to pee again.

"I'm ready when you are."

Marty exited the car and came around to my door. I crossed the parking lot on stiff, shaky legs.

Inside the restaurant, most tables were empty and the air smelled of maple syrup. The soft clatter of metal spatulas working over a griddle carried from the back. A man in a black golf shirt appeared with a stack of menus in his arm.

"Can I help you?"

"I'm, uh, meeting someone."

"Name?"

Did he mean mine or my dad's? I assumed my dad's since he'd been the one to make the reservation.

My voice was small and overcome with fear. "Meyers. I'm meeting Raymond Meyers."

Always Do the Sweet Stuff First

THE MAÎTRE D' scrolled his finger down the screen of an iPad. "We have you in the back. You can follow me."

I glanced at Marty and he nodded for me to go. "I'll be waiting right here."

Did Hale expect me to get kidnapped? The whole bodyguard thing was throwing me off.

I followed golf shirt through a maze of empty tables to a glass room off the side of the restaurant. There, in the back, sitting by himself, was a man with rounded shoulders, a shiny bald head, though he wasn't fully bald, and green eyes like mine. He wrung his hands nervously and looked up the moment I approached.

"Rayne?"

My heart jumped into my throat. "Dad?"

He stood and took a step toward me then hesitated. "My God, you're beautiful."

I couldn't speak. My eyes took in every detail from the thick brown hair that encircled his head behind his ears to the way his nose looked like it had been broken a few times. His fingers were fat and creased in a way that told me he worked with his hands. He wasn't a heavy man, but a stout one. He wore a button-down flannel as if it were a dress shirt and something told me it was one of the nicest he owned.

"Can I…hug you?" he asked and I smiled, my vision blurring with tears.

I threw my arms around him, breathing in the scent of Old Spice and tobacco. There was something else too. Either mouthwash or he'd had a drink that morning. I couldn't blame him. The thought of tossing back a shot had crossed my mind more than once that day and it wasn't even noon.

But none of that mattered. Every negative preconception I held about this man vanished the moment he wrapped his arms around me and all was forgiven. My entire life, every monumental moment, faded to make space for this.

When we released each other we both had tears in our eyes.

He glanced at the table and laughed as if we both forgot we were standing in the middle of a restaurant. "Here." He rushed to pull out my chair. "Sit. How was the drive? Did you have any trouble?"

Such a perfectly dad thing to ask. "No. No trouble." I stowed my purse under the table. "I, uh, had a driver."

"Oh." He frowned then nodded. "All the way from the city?"

"It's a…private service." I didn't know how to

explain Marty so I moved on. "Are you far from here?"

"About forty-five minutes."

That surprised me. "We could have picked a place closer to you—"

"Nonsense. This place is nice. I like their desserts."

I smiled. I liked desserts too. Was that something I'd inherited from him? My mom always picked a salty chip over a sweet. But I was all about the sugary goodness.

A waitress appeared and filled up our waters. My hands were shaking so I folded them in my lap.

"Our lunch specials today are a braised…" She recited a few options. I missed every single one.

"I think we need a few minutes," my dad said and the waitress nodded and left us alone. "I can't get over how much you look like your mom."

"She says I look like you."

He grinned. "The green eyes and dark hair, sure. But you've got your mom's face." He chuckled. "Good thing, too, because it's not easy pulling off a mug like this." He pointed a stubby finger at his crooked nose. "You gotta have character."

And he did. In just a few words I could tell he was an easygoing guy who could talk to anyone.

I had so many questions a traffic jam formed in my brain and not a single one could get out. Why did he leave? Why did he stop calling and writing? How did he get that divot of a scar on his cheek? What was he doing on April fourth?

I drank my water, wondering what was appropriate to ask and what might scare him off. I couldn't believe I was sitting across from him.

"So, tell me about this fella you're marrying. Good guy?"

Of course Hale would be the perfect subject. I grinned, fluent on the topic and certain I could talk for days about all the reasons I loved my future husband. "Hale's…perfect."

"Perfect, eh?" He whistled and the cartoon-like sound made me laugh. "I didn't know they made men that way."

"Oh, don't get me wrong. He can be a gigantic pain in the ass. We're complete opposites, so our life is certainly interesting. Hale's a neat-freak and compulsively prepared. He hates disorder and is never late."

"And you?"

"I'm the extreme opposite."

He smirked and I noticed the wide gap in his front teeth. More character. "Yeah, sometimes love works out that way."

"Somehow, Hale puts up with my calamities and never loses patience with me."

"Do you push him? It's important for a man to feel challenged."

"Oh, I'm definitely challenging." I smiled. "We, uh, have a daughter."

His face fell. "You're a mother?"

"Stepmother. Well, soon to be. She's Hale's— from a previous relationship. But I've been in Elara's life since the day she was born. Her biological mom's out of the picture. Do you want to see photos?"

"I'd love to."

I pulled out my phone and went to this Sunday's photo dump. I always took a ton of pictures whenever I left town for more than a day. My heart instantly lightened when I saw her chubby cheeks and smiling face.

I handed him my phone. "Swipe left."

He scrolled for a while and chuckled at a few. "Where are these taken? I see palm trees."

"That's at our house in Key West."

"You live all the way down there? What made you get married in New York?"

I didn't remember telling him about New York, but we exchanged so many messages over the past few days I might have dropped it into conversation. "Hale wanted a big, traditional ceremony but at a destination everyone could get to."

He handed me back my phone. "Looks like you've got some life, kiddo."

Kiddo…

I'd forgotten how he used to call me that in his cards and sporadic phone calls. It was strange how so much of this was brand new, but there were little hints of familiarity, like the way he cleared his throat every few minutes and dropped the Rs at the end of words.

The waitress returned and we both ordered a cocktail. A margarita on the rocks for me and a Jack and Coke for him. When the waitress left, we opened up the menus.

"What do you like to eat?" he asked, perusing the options.

"I'm thinking if the desserts are good enough to drive all this way, we should start there."

He flipped to the last page. "My kind of girl. Do you like chocolate?"

"It's one of my basic food groups."

"Then order the hot house brownies over ice cream. They're to die for."

"Say less." I shut my menu.

In my life there had been a lot of situations and people I always felt out of rhythm with. My peers always seemed more informed than me, and I went through most stages of life feeling like I skipped an important chapter. But my dad wasn't like that.

With him, I felt like we were both on the same page, as if a switch that had been shut off for decades suddenly flicked on and everything worked fine. We were instantly in sync. We clicked. Our easy chemistry made my heart full and warm, and any worries I had that this might be a mistake disappeared.

My dad knew a lot about desserts, concrete work, movies that involved Robert DeNiro, and carburetors. "That's what I did back in Oregon, fixed cars."

We annihilated our desserts and then moved on to burgers and fries. "Do you miss it?"

"Being a mechanic?"

"Oregon."

"Oh." He popped a fry in his mouth and chewed thoughtfully. "I did for a while. Missed you, your mom… But Oregon wasn't right for me. I wasn't right as long as I was living there. My life had always been here, on the East Coast."

He left me for a coast? "Is that why you left?"

"Yes and no." He pulled another fry from his

plate, but didn't eat it. Instead, he just repeatedly dipped it into the pile of ketchup while looking down at his plate. "We were young. Especially me. Your mother wasn't worried about being a parent. It came naturally to her. But for me… You were just so fragile and small. I was terrified I'd break you."

It was hard to hear his reasons for leaving, but at the same time, I got it. "I felt the same way when Elara was born."

"So you know."

I nodded. "Hale's a natural with her. Sometimes he tosses her around and gets her belly-laughing so hard. I could never do that. I'm too clumsy."

He pointed to his nose. "Me too."

When we finished lunch we ordered another round of drinks. I wasn't ready to leave. Not without asking him.

"Dad…" I took a long sip of my second margarita. "I know this is still new and I'm not giving you much notice, but…do you think you might want to come to my wedding?"

He studied me for a long moment without saying anything. Then he asked, "You're sure you want me there?"

His presence was literally the *only* thing I wanted besides Hale's on my wedding day. "Positive."

He gave a wide gap-toothed grin. "Then I'd love to be there."

An enormous weight lifted off my shoulders and I smiled into my glass. "We'll have a seat reserved for you in the front."

"That's very kind of you, kiddo."

"Or… When you get there—if you want—we could walk to the front together, so you don't have any trouble finding your seat."

He set down his Jack and Coke. "Are you asking me to walk you down the aisle?"

I met his stare, my entire body suddenly made of glass. *Please don't break me.* "Yes."

"Wow, Rayne. That's…" He cleared his throat. "I mean, I'm flattered. I just thought there might be someone else you might prefer."

"You're my dad."

He stopped blustering and seemed to comprehend how much this meant to me. He nodded. "Then it would be my honor."

I tried to swallow but my throat was malfunctioning. Nodding tightly I tried to express my gratitude. When I could finally talk, I wheezed, "Thank you for today and for…."

He briefly squeezed my fingers. "I just hope I don't let you down."

I desperately hoped the same.

I paid the bill and took my time preparing to leave. As we walked to the front of the restaurant, I promised to take care of all the details.

"I'll schedule an appointment for your tuxedo fitting, and hopefully Hale can fly in so you two can meet before the week of the wedding. The guys are having their tuxedos custom-made."

"Custom?"

"Yes, the wedding's white tie, so everyone will be wearing tuxedos and gowns."

"I don't even own a suit. To think I'm gonna have my very own tux…" He whistled and I smiled. I loved that that little sound was his thing and I loved that I knew it was a quirky thing he did.

"I think you'd look handsome in one."

He gave me a shoulder bump, the epitome of secret handshakes, and I stopped in my tracks.

"You okay, kiddo?"

The shoulder bump was one of my first moves when I fell for Hale. It was a big freaking deal and my code for saying I love you. Did he view it the same? I took a moment to catalog this as one of my favorite experiences in my whole awkward life.

I tried not to smile too brightly, but my insides were bursting with gleeful goo. "I'm great."

We continued walking. "Is he yours?" My dad angled his chin toward the front of the restaurant where Marty stuck out like a sore thumb.

"Yup." I hated having to say goodbye. "Can I put my number in your phone? It might be easier to text than talk through private messenger."

"Sure." He pulled out his cell. "What's your number? I'll send you a text now so you also have mine."

I recited my number as he typed it in. A minute later, my phone vibrated. The message on the screen flashed: *It's Dad.* And my heart did another cartwheel. "Got it."

Marty held open the door and we walked outside.

"Hey, I didn't see your truck."

"I have Laura's car today. She needed the truck to help Tiffany transport a set of rocking chairs."

I frowned. "Who's Laura and Tiffany?"

"Oh, Laura's my wife, and Tiffany's our

daughter. She just bought a house in Upper Darby, a few miles from us."

My insides chilled as all those warm gooey feelings turned to ice. "You have another daughter?"

"Two—well, three if you count you."

If?

I could only imagine the expression on my face. I was numb from my lips to my eyelids. "How long ago did you... When..."

"I should have said something at lunch. I just assumed your mother told you."

"Mom knows about them?"

"Well, not the girls, but I'm not a bigamist. We had to make the divorce final eventually, so I could..." Realizing my shock, his words tapered off.

I couldn't feel my legs. "When did you get married?"

He looked down and I braced myself. "A few years after I left Oregon. The girls were born just before the wedding. Twins. Tiff and Trace."

I couldn't feel my legs. "I have sisters?"

"Well, technically, yes."

Technically? Oh my, God. "Do they know I exist?"

He had the grace to look ashamed. "I wanted to see how this went—before I told them." Seeing I was upset, he quickly said, "Believe me, kiddo, I plan to tell them about you. I was just waiting for the right time."

I nearly choked. He had thirty years. "Your wife, Laura, she got pregnant when you were only dating?"

"That's correct."

"And you stayed with her?"

"Like I said, I was a different person in Oregon."

I couldn't breathe. My margaritas, burger, and chocolate brownie all seemed to settle in the pit of my stomach like tar. "I think I need to go."

"Rayne." He rushed after me. "We had such a nice lunch. I should have told you about them sooner, but I didn't want to spoil our time. Today's been incredible. I'd still like to come to the wedding if you want me there. Please don't let this change things."

My spine had disappeared and I could barely hold myself up straight as his request tried to knock me down. This changed everything.

Marty held open the door to the car. I debated what response was appropriate before climbing in. Nothing came to me. I was too blindsided to think.

You stayed with them, I wanted to say. *You were there for their recitals and tea parties, their first days, and school conferences. How many of their scraped knees and booboos got kissed while mine never fully healed?*

Tiff and Trace got a lifetime of dad jokes and memories while I got nothing but abandonment issues and a pair of green eyes that looked nothing like my mom's.

But I didn't say any of that. I just climbed into the car and looked up at him, wondering if this man would ever stop breaking my heart. Then I said, "I'll text you when I get home."

He looked like he wanted more, but Marty stepped in front of him and closed the door. Whatever was said next, I couldn't hear, but I knew Marty said something he didn't want me to hear.

My dad nodded with disappointment and walked away.

"What did you say to him?" I asked as soon as Marty got into the car.

He backed out with practiced ease. "I told him that you would contact him when you were ready and he is not to interfere in your life until that happened."

I didn't know if I should be grateful for his high-handedness or outraged.

Maybe I wanted my dad to fight for a relationship with me. Maybe he owed me that much. Or maybe this would save me the frustration that came with waiting for my dad to want to spend time with me when he was already so busy with his other kids.

"Mr. Davenport asked me to intervene if anything upset you. You are upset, no?"

"I guess."

I was what I originally expected to be.

Disappointed by my dad.

It was upsetting indeed.

Hide and Go—Ooh, Tequila!

For once, I was relieved Hale was tied up in meetings all day. What would I say when he asked about lunch with my dad? Would Marty have already filled him in on parts?

Hale hadn't texted yet, so I assumed he knew nothing, which was better. I preferred to keep my confusing feelings private until I made sense of them.

Maybe I was being childish…

I couldn't fault my father for moving on. People got divorced for that very reason. I just didn't understand what was so good about his other family that I apparently lacked.

"Would you like me to order dinner, madam?"

I looked up at Percy, discomforted by the idea of having a steady audience while I deconstructed every inadequacy of my life back to the days of in utero. "I'm not really hungry."

His eyebrows lifted. "Would you like me to fetch a doctor?"

My head cocked. "Was that a joke?"

"Perhaps a slight one."

I appreciated what was truly an attempt to cheer me and as much as I enjoyed that, my butler used words like perhaps and fetch. "Do you have access to a time machine?"

"Perhaps. I'll look into it straight away."

He left me to my own devices as I stared at today's Wordle. Flustered with my inability to solve a simple word game, I swiped the app shut.

Not being able to reach Hale made me want to call Elle, but that would be a mistake. Would she ever know what I went through today? Would she care?

Like a festering wound, the mere thought of our dysfunction turned my stomach. The idea of her learning that the lunch with my dad didn't go so well left me really... tender. I just couldn't take her judgement or *I told you so* comments right now, so the urge to call her faded faster than expected. Maybe I was finally coming to terms with our situation.

Did she honestly expect this to just blow over by the wedding? When Seraphina told me Elle ordered her dress I was shocked.

Was she getting a fitting? Did she have her shoes? Fuck if I knew.

I wasn't going to apologize for being happy, nor was I going to let her say those terrible things to me because my relationship with the Davenports made her uncomfortable. Those were her problems talking, not mine. I just wanted to be her friend. But even that was becoming less appealing as the distance continued.

After scrolling through my contacts and discarding every possible person I could text to distract me from thinking about my father's other family, I let out a huff. I needed to get out of this hotel and do something. Blow off some steam.

I glanced at the door then listened for Percy. As much as I enjoyed playing princess in the tower, I didn't feel like being around people. A hard thing to accomplish when sitting in one of the most populated cities in the world.

I quietly stuffed my phone in my bag and checked that I had cash and out the door I went. Just as the elevator pinged I heard Percy call my name, but I dashed inside before he could stop the doors from closing.

The lobby was buzzing for late afternoon and several cars waited out front at the valet. I slipped out the entrance and spotted the black sedan idling on the corner. A plume of cigarette smoke surrounded Marty's head as he turned and our gazes met. He frowned, probably wondering why he didn't get a call that I was leaving, then he tossed his cigarette on the ground and strolled toward me.

I don't know what came over me, but I ran.

Well, I jogged.

He called my name, then doubled back to get the car. I cut through a group of tourists snapping photos in front of the Pulitzer Fountain and dashed down 58th. Cabs intercepted traffic and clogged the intersections as pedestrians moved about the busy walkways.

When I spotted the familiar sedan coming around the corner, I made a quick left and went back toward Fifth Ave, knowing Marty would be trapped in gridlock for a minute or two.

From there I walked. I walked until I could no longer see the spires of The Plaza peeking overhead. I walked through construction zones and busy intersections and some sort of business district. When I hit the entrance to the train station, I turned—no real clue where I was heading, but I continued to walk until everything looked unfamiliar.

My new boots were beginning to hurt my feet and I regretted not changing into more comfortable shoes after my lunch date. I looked for a restaurant that might serve booze so I could rest for a while.

Following signs to a rooftop establishment, I snuck into an aged building and took the elevators to the top floors. Black and white polished checkered tile met with deep blue walls. Dangling crystals cascaded from the ceiling as the stunning display of liquors illuminated on the far wall called to me like a mecca.

"Can I help you, miss?"

I turned to the woman I assumed was the hostess. "I'd like a seat near the bar."

"Right this way."

She led me to a red velvet sofa and placed a narrow cocktail menu on the white marble table. I glanced over the options and when a server arrived I ordered something called a Caribbean old fashioned, delighted when it arrived quickly.

I sipped the spiced drink, letting the rum and sugar work their way toward my frayed nerves. My phone buzzed and my mother's name flashed on the screen. I sent the call to voicemail.

Part of me wanted to tell her about meeting my dad, because she, more than anyone, knew what I'd gone through with him. But another part of me was pissed.

How could she have gone my entire life without ever mentioning that he'd remarried? Had I known my dad had a new wife, the possibility of him also having other kids might have crossed my mind, and I might not have wound up sitting in a bar at age thirty blindsided and hurt.

It wasn't my mom's fault. But my emotions were a little hard to manage at the moment, and I didn't want to take my shitty feelings out on her, so it was best to avoid her for now.

I was just beginning to unwind when a feminine laugh caught my ear. I followed the sound and my gaze collided with a familiar set of gunmetal grey eyes.

Shit. My shoulders tensed.

Barrett—with another blonde bombshell plastered to his side—stared back at me. This was not the ambiguity I was seeking.

His easy expression darkened as his brows came down. I dropped my gaze and fiddled with my cocktail napkin. No chance he'd figure it was normal for me to travel across the city alone and drink at a place like this midafternoon.

He'd assume something was up, and then he'd alert Hale before I had a chance to get my thoughts together. Not that I wasn't allowed to be there. I could go wherever I wanted, but not without Marty.

My flight or fight instincts kicked in and I felt the urge to flee again. I wasn't sure where this hunger for defiance came from, I just knew I needed to feel untethered for a moment so I could be alone with my thoughts. This obviously wasn't the place to do that.

Chugging back my drink, I threw a few bucks on the table and headed toward the restroom. A quick pee and then I'd move on to a different watering hole.

But as I exited the bathroom I came face to face with Barrett. "Meyers."

"Hi, Barrett."

"You alone?"

"In the bathroom? Yes, that's usually how that works."

He frowned. "What are you doing here?"

"Same thing as everyone else. Drinking."

"By yourself?"

"Yes. By myself. I *am* of legal age, which usually means I can do so without other people's permission. Did you want to see my license?"

He frowned. "You okay?"

"Fine."

His eyes narrowed suspiciously. "Why don't you join us?"

I glanced past his shoulder to the ninety-pound woman with lips the size of bike tires. She somehow managed to send flirtatious glances at Barrett while also giving me the stink eye.

"No, thanks."

He looked back at his companion and she smiled, sweetly, cocking her narrow shoulder out.

"You're sure?" Barrett asked, appearing reluctant to let me pass.

"Positive. I was just leaving." Before he could stop me, I said, "Have fun on your date."

Walking past him, I reached the elevators and paused. Barrett returned to his table, but he didn't sit down. He said something to the woman and she pouted. Then he was coming toward me again.

"Come on," I hissed, poking the call button of the elevator. But Barrett got there first. He stood silently at my side and I looked up at him. "What are you doing?"

"Going with you."

"Aren't you on a date?"

He shrugged. "I told her we'd reschedule."

The elevator arrived and we each stepped in. Neither of us said anything on the entire journey to the ground floor. When we hit the sidewalk he kept pace silently at my side.

"You didn't have to come with me," I said, annoyed by his company. "I don't even know where I'm going."

"Have you had dinner?"

"No." But I still wasn't hungry. This no appetite thing was uncharted territory for me.

"I know a place up here." He led me around the corner and we popped into a bustling pub.

The blue lit restaurant was simple with brick walls, a varnished bar, and beers on tap. The air smelled of burgers and fries so I didn't object when he asked for a table for two.

"We'll start with a round of shooters," he told the waiter. "Bring us your best tequila."

"You're feeling ambitious."

"I don't feel like playing guess the mood. In my experience, tequila's the fastest way to get a woman bitching about her problems. And you look like you have something on your mind you need to bitch about."

"I don't need to bitch."

"Sure."

Thirty minutes later I was three shots deep, hunched over a plate of sweet potato fries spilling my guts.

"He just dropped that bomb on me, like he was talking about a sort of coffee pot he owned or a pair of boots he liked."

"So you have sisters. Why is that necessarily a bad thing?"

"I do not have sisters. I have a father who abandoned me to live his best life in Pennsylvania with his *new* family since his old one didn't meet his standards for whatever fucking reason."

"Did he give you a reason for leaving?"

"He said Oregon never felt right." I shoved a fry in my mouth. "We could have moved! As a family!"

The waitress approached, but before she could interrupt my meltdown, Barrett swirled his finger in the air silently ordering another round. "I'm sorry he disappointed you."

I scoffed and flopped back in my seat. "It's not even him. I expected this to be complicated and emotional. It's everything else."

"Are things okay with you and Hale?"

I waved a hand. "We're fine." When he waited for me to go on, I confessed, "Elle and I had a fight. A big one." I held out my hands like I was measuring a trout, then extended them as far as my arms could reach. "Huge."

"About what?"

"Her dumb ass boyfriend." I didn't think it would be helpful to mention that the fight also had to do with the Davenports.

"She's dating him now?"

I stilled and looked up, noting the tension that now bracketed his eyes. Fuck. On account of the tequila I wasn't selecting my words carefully. "I'm sorry, Barrett."

"It's cool. We're not together anymore. She can fuck whoever she wants."

Ouch. "If it's any consolation, he's a total tool."

The corner of his mouth twitched. "It's not."

I studied him for a long minute, still not fully understanding why two people who obviously liked each other couldn't work their shit out.

The waitress arrived with more shots and I lifted mine. "To alcohol," I toasted.

Two hours later we had relocated to a tavern on 59th. I could barely walk, but Barrett proved an excellent holder-upper.

"Are you jealous of all the attention Hale's getting?" I slurred, chasing my straw with my mouth as it dubiously escaped.

We were piled into a booth that faced a stage. Instruments were set up as if a band were about to play but there were no musicians in sight. Classic rock pumped from the speakers.

"Jealous? Of Hale?"

"They're talking about making him *smexiest* man alive." I sloshed my cocktail, too smashed to recall what was in my cup. "He's very dreamy, you know?" I snorted. "I'd do him."

"No way is Hale making the cut. I've been on that list for years and never won."

I laughed, because he was clearly jealous. Barrett had always been the pretty one—or the hot one, as Elle used to call him. Now, Hale was stealing his thunder.

"The world's wondering what the hell he's doing with me." So not to spill my drink, I leaned forward and sipped from my straw without actually lifting my glass off the table. "I'm his Lord Farquaad, which I'm pretty sure is supposed to sound like Lord Fuck-wad."

"Who?"

"This short king dude on *Shrek*. Hale's the perfect princess."

"You didn't really pay attention during that movie, did you?"

I shrugged. "Why? Do you think I'm more of an ogre?" The tabloids had said as much.

"What are you talking about? You're the hot factor. Before he was with you, he was just boring old Hale. You elevated him."

"I'm not an elevator."

He laughed. "You know what I mean."

I shut one eye and squinted at him. "Not really."

"The world wants what they can't have, Meyers. You took him off the market and made him more desirable."

"I did that?" I asked, plastering my hand to my chest.

"You did that."

My insides turned warm and gooey. "Well, the world can eat a dick. He's my Hale. I found him first."

His mouth curved ever so slightly as he studied me. "He's always been lucky."

I cocked my head. "How come you're not so drunk as I—*hic*—" I hiccupped. "Feel?"

He patted my shoulder, "Because I actually ate my dinner and you've had all of three French fries tonight. We should get something else in your stomach."

I hiccupped again and laughed. "I'm not supposed to be eating this crap. Everyone keeps saying I need to watch my figure for the wedding."

He frowned. "Who said that?"

"The people." I took another sip of my drink then mimicked. "Go to the gym, Rayne. Don't eat fried foods, Rayne. Cut out sodium, Rayne. Here's some ass fat to inject in your elevens."

"What the hell are you talking about?"

"My elevens." I swung around to face him and pointed to the *oh fuck creases* between my eyebrows. "These indents right here."

His silver eyes rolled upwards as he looked where my fingers pointed. Then he glanced down at my mouth. We were very close.

Barrett looked so much like Hale in so many ways, yet they were completely different. He had a rugged style about him, stubbled and outdoorsy. Hale was all smooth lines and sleek luxury. Both men had incredible bodies, but carried themselves in completely different ways.

"You don't need any of that shit," he said softly. "You're beautiful just the way you are."

I meant to say thank you but it came out as a burp. I turned my head and blew out a breath. "Sorry."

"Jesus. Stay away from open flames."

Just then, my phone vibrated and I gasped. "It's Hale. I'm in trouble."

"Why?"

"I ran away from Marty."

"Who the fuck is Marty?"

"Martel. My driver."

"You mean Sharoski?" He laughed. "Please tell me you call him Marty to his face."

"Of course I do!"

He laughed harder. "Meyers, the guy's an ex mercenary."

"Well, he's my buddy. I bought him a hot cocoa and potato tots."

He nearly doubled over with laughter. My phone buzzed and vibrated across the sticky table-top. Barrett grabbed it and answered, laughter in his voice. "She's with me." He paused and scowled. "It's Barrett, you maniac."

I giggled, only able to hear a slight chirp on the other end.

"She's had a bit too much to drink. You're lucky I found her."

"No!" I hissed, covering his mouth.

He pulled away my hand and laughed. "She escaped Sharoski and was running around New York unsupervised. That's the fastest way to lose a fiancée, Hale."

I gripped my head and plopped my elbows on the table.

"No, we're not far. I'll see that she gets home

safely. Do you want to talk to her?"

Alcohol curdled in my empty stomach as he handed me the phone. Drunk guilt was the worst because I was usually too intoxicated to remember why I felt guilty in the first place.

"Hi, babe," I said, sheepishly taking the phone.

"Rayne? Are you okay?"

"Yeah?" That wasn't supposed to come out like a question. "Jussa lil tipsy." I pinched my fingers in the air and squinted.

"Why aren't you with Martel?"

I didn't have an answer that wasn't complicated and at the moment my brain was a little too pickled to think. "I just needed to be alone."

"With Barrett?"

"That wasn't my plan."

"How did it go with your dad?"

I shook my head. "I can't do that talk right now. My—" Distracted by the musicians, I gasped. "Ooh, the band's about to start!"

"Rayne?"

The drummer slammed down his sticks and noise erupted from the stage. "Hale, I gotta go. It's getting real loud in here and I can't hear you."

"Rayne, wait—"

"I'll love you later. Call you." I handed the phone off to Barrett.

"Hey." He covered his ear to listen to whatever else Hale had to say. "I will. Relax. I'll personally make sure she gets home safely. You got it. Bye." He tossed the phone on the table and mumbled control freak under his breath, stretching to loop his arm over the back of my chair. "This band better be good."

Detox and Tuxedos, Oh My!

I woke up to the piercing sun shining through the windows of the penthouse and my body sprawled across the bed. I was still in my clothes from the day before, but my boots were off.

I coughed and winced. "Oh, God." My mouth tasted like ass and my head throbbed. I turned my face into the pillows and groaned. "Percy?"

"Yes, madam?"

"Do you have some sort of magic bullet for a hangover?"

"Right away." He disappeared and ten minutes later I was sipping some citrus concoction and washing down two little white pills.

"Mr. Davenport left this note for you." Percy handed me the slip of paper and I frowned.

"Hale was here?" Then I looked at the handwriting and realized he wasn't talking about that Mr. Davenport.

> *Meyers,*
>
> *You're going to feel like shit tomorrow. Take it easy and call your dad. Life's too short to waste being pissed about the things we can't change. Rule number one about fathers—they usually suck at the hard stuff. At least he's trying.*
>
> *And call Hale.*
>
> *—B.*

MY BRAIN NEEDED a moment to detox before I could handle any of that.

After a long shower and another citrusy drink from Percy, I was feeling slightly human again. I called Hale, knowing it was after midnight in Tokyo. He answered right away.

"Rayne?"

"Hi."

"Are you home?" He sounded groggy.

"Yes. At the hotel."

"What happened last night?"

"Nothing. I went out and ran into Barrett. I had too much to drink."

He sighed in that silent way that said he didn't approve. "Why didn't you take Martel?"

"I wanted to be alone."

He shifted and his voice sounded closer. "I'm guessing yesterday didn't go as you hoped?"

I still didn't want to talk about it, but then I thought about everything Barrett said, and tried not to waste energy being upset about the things I couldn't change. I focused on the positive.

"We had a really nice lunch. He's coming to the wedding and he's going to walk me down the aisle."

"That's great, baby. I'm happy for you."

"Yeah. I'm happy too."

"Are you? It sounds like there's something else you're not telling me."

"It's just a lot to process. I made certain assumptions in my head and, well, you know how that goes."

"Just remember, he's human. He probably made assumptions too."

Ugh, that didn't help. Now, I was preoccupied with wondering if I somehow didn't meet my dad's expectations.

Hale cleared his throat and yawned. "I can't wait to hear all about him."

"I was hoping you two could meet when you come back."

"Bad news, baby. Some of our investors got delayed and I have to stay longer than expected."

Dread tunneled through my stomach. "How long?"

"Another week."

My heart instantly seized. "That's cutting it really close, Hale."

"I know. But I promise this is the last trip until after the honeymoon."

That meant he wasn't going to be able to come with us to get my dad's tux. "I'll miss you."

"I already miss you, baby. A lot."

I sighed. "Get some sleep."

After hanging up with Hale, I called Andrew to check on Elara. They had a full day scheduled with a visit to the petting zoo. I was jealous I wouldn't be there. Hale suggested flying them out to New York, but I wasn't planning on staying long. I just needed to get my dad situated then I could return home.

I texted the new man in my life and he seemed happy to hear from me. Was he sitting beside his wife? Having breakfast? Had he told his family about me yet? I wondered if he was even aware of how much his announcement screwed with my head.

We decided to meet tomorrow for another lunch and then a visit to the tailor. This time he was driving into the city to meet me—because he owed me that much.

I ordered room service and enjoyed a large breakfast. It felt like I hadn't eaten in weeks. Then I made the call I was dreading.

"Hi, Mom."

"My goodness, Ray, I've been leaving you messages all week."

"I know. I'm sorry. My schedule's been nuts."

"Are you getting excited for the wedding?"

We spent the next several minutes discussing the details of her dress, which Phina had shipped to her last week so she could handle the alterations in Oregon.

"I don't think I'm going to wear the shoes Dina sent. They're a little too pointy."

"Her name's Phina, Mom, not Dina. Short for Seraphina."

"Oh. Gosh, I hope I didn't call her the wrong name when we spoke on the phone."

My mom didn't have a mean bone in her body but she often rambled without a filter. "Josette made you an appointment to get your hair touched up when you get here."

"Touched up?"

"Highlights and a trim."

"Do I need all that?"

"I want to treat you. You'll have fun."

"A New York salon? They must charge a fortune."

"It's fine, Mom. I said it's my treat."

"Rayne, you sound a little stressed. Is everything all right?"

I debated bringing up my father and decided now was not the right time, but impulse was a bully and my common sense tended to be a big, fat wimp. "Why didn't you tell me Daddy got remarried."

The line silenced. "Where did that come from?"

"Did you know?"

"Yes, I knew. Honey, your father and I haven't been together for nearly thirty years."

"Did you know he has other children?" Silence. "Mom?"

She sighed. "Have you been talking to him?"

She knew. She knew and she kept it from me. "We had lunch the other day."

"Oh, Rayne."

"What? Why is that a bad thing? He's my father. I'm allowed to have a relationship with him."

"Of course you are, but I know your father and I know what he's like."

She couldn't know him that well. "You haven't been in his life for thirty years, Mom."

"Well, I'm in yours. I know you, Rayne. You always see the best in people and then you're devastated when they disappoint you."

"What's been disappointing is not having a father in my life. You should have told me he had another family."

"That wouldn't have made a difference, Rayne. It only would have made you question yourself more, and his actions have always had nothing to do with you. Oh, I wish you would have told me you were thinking of contacting him." She sounded so certain that my choice had been a bad one.

"Why can't you be happy for me? We're finally connecting."

"Your father's a complicated man, sweetie. He's not the most dependable person and he can be very selfish. I just don't want you to get hurt."

My defenses went up. "Just because your relationship with him didn't work out doesn't mean ours won't. He's been with his other family for three decades." I winced at how accusatory that sounded. I hadn't pointed that out to make my mom feel inadequate. "What I meant to say—"

"Well, it sounds like you have everything all figured out then."

"I'm sorry, Mom. That was mean. I'm tired

and hungover and yesterday, well, it was a lot to process. I just wish I would have been more prepared."

"You're right. That was mean. But it's also true. People change. For your sake, I hope he has."

"Please don't be mad at me for wanting this."

"Ray, the only thing I've ever wanted was for you to be happy."

"Thank you."

"Just…be careful and don't put too much stock in any promises he makes."

Nothing like ending on an ominous note. "I just wanted you to be prepared to see him at the wedding."

More silence. "I should go."

This entire conversation needed to end. "I'll call you when I get home."

The following day, I waited for my Dad at an upscale steakhouse while staring at a large photo on the wall of a woman who resembled Marilyn Monroe. My nerves were a wreck this time, so I ordered a glass of white wine to calm myself down.

My dad arrived five minutes late, but he made it.

"Parking's a nightmare," he said, dropping into the seat across from me. "I thought I gave myself enough time, but…" Realizing that he hardly said hello, he sighed. "How are you, kiddo?"

"I'm…okay." I smiled tightly. Did he call all his kids kiddo?

He frowned. "About the other day, Rayne… I thought about how that must have come off and all I can say is I'm sorry. There are a lot of things I wish I'd done differently in my life, but I can't undo what's been done. All I can do is move forward."

"I was just a little shocked."

He nodded. "I know it doesn't erase the last thirty years, but I'd love to have a chance to start over with you. I want you in my life."

I wanted that too. So much so I couldn't understand why I was allowing this barrier between us. "You're right. We can't rewrite history."

"But we can work on a better future. If that's what you want."

I looked down at the table and nodded. Then I looked up at him. "I do. I really do."

He smiled. "I do too." His hand reached across the distance and patted my fingers. "I won't let you down."

We ordered lunch and by the time the appetizers arrived we were back to chatting easily and even laughing at random traits we had in common. Not only did we both possess a sweet tooth, we could also roll our tongues and we both sneezed whenever we looked at the sun.

"So, I had to Google white tie," he confessed. "This wedding of yours is going to be pretty fancy, huh?"

I sensed the idea of a formal wedding made him anxious. I could relate. "The ceremony's private—just close friends and family. The reception's going to be a circus."

"Big guest list?"

"It's over three hundred."

His eyes bulged. "Dear Lord."

I laughed nervously. "The Davenports have a

lot of friends. I think my side accounts for eleven people. You make twelve."

He looked as if he had something to say, but hesitated. I thought about Elle asking to bring Paul and realized he'd probably want his wife there. I wasn't sure if I could handle that. It was my wedding day. Couldn't he just be there for me and we could do the whole awkward meet and greet another time?

As if reading my mind, he nodded and let the topic of the guest list drop. "I'm looking forward to it." Pushing his food around his plate with the tines of his fork, he said, "This, uh, tuxedo... How much do you think—"

"Oh, don't worry about any of that. I'm paying for it."

He frowned. "That doesn't seem right."

"Believe me. It's fine." Now it was my turn to reassure him, so I patted his hand.

He grinned. "Thank you."

When the bill came, I stuck Hale's black AMEX in the pocket and stood. "I have to use the restroom. I'll be right back."

As I washed my hands I thought of my mom's warnings. She was wrong about my dad. So what if he had another family? He was still my father and we both deserved a second chance.

Once I made up my mind to put the past behind us, I instantly felt lighter. That made me think of Elle. Maybe we were both too lost in our feelings and overcomplicating something that didn't have to be complicated.

I loved my dad and I wanted a relationship with him. So we chose to accept the things we couldn't change and moved forward with a relationship. It was that easy.

Couldn't Elle and I do the same since we also loved each other? I dried my hands and pulled out my phone. It had been eons since we spoke.

> I love you and I don't want to fight anymore. I'm sorry for all the shitty things I said.

SEND.

There. I was making leaps and bounds in the maturity department today.

When I returned to the table I smiled at my dad. "Ready?"

He stood. "Don't forget your card."

"Oh." I quickly grabbed the credit card and signed the bill. "Let's go get you a tux."

My dad was a lot more jovial than I anticipated. He said silly things that made me laugh and lament for the moments we missed together.

"I was thinking," I said as the tailor drew on him with chalk. "What if—after the honeymoon— you come to Florida for a visit?"

He stilled and I could tell my invitation surprised him. "I guess that depends on the cost of flights."

"We can fly you out." I really needed him to do this. I wanted him to see our house and spend time with Elara. I wanted to take pictures and have something to put on my wall that told the world I had a dad. I was willing to compromise almost anything to make it happen. "You *and* Laura could visit," I said, sweetening the deal.

"That sounds…incredible." He smiled but something sorrowful flashed in his eyes.

Maybe he didn't believe I'd follow through with my promise to get him there. "Consider it officially on the schedule. Will there be any issue with getting off work from your job?"

"There shouldn't be an issue."

After lunch I took him back to The Plaza to show him the penthouse and treat him to some accessories in the gift shop. I think the level of opulence overwhelmed him.

"The faucets in the bathroom are gold," he said after visiting the restroom.

"I know." I laughed at his expression, because I'd had the same reaction. "Rich people do weird shit."

"What does your mother think of all this?"

"She hasn't spent enough time around the Davenports yet. She's only met Hale. This will be her first time meeting the family. Wait until you meet Remington! He's such a character. Sort of a cross between Mr. Potter from *It's a Wonderful Life* and an angry badger with a soft spot for anything female."

"That's Hale's father?"

"And my boss. We're pretty tight."

He processed that bit of information without comment.

When we returned to the lobby I insisted he let me buy him a set of cufflinks from the boutique.

He'd been eyeing them earlier and he needed a pair for his tux.

"You've done enough, Rayne."

"Dad, don't worry about it. Hale told me to get whatever we needed and you need cufflinks."

"You're sure?"

"Positive. Which ones did you like best?"

He glanced at the display case. "I suppose those are nice."

"I like them too."

The attendant wrapped them up and I told her to charge them to the room. After that, it was time for my dad to go. This time when we parted, I had the courage to hug him goodbye.

"Thank you for today."

He drew back. "I'm the one who should be saying thank you. You paid for everything."

"But you were here. You said you'd be here and you showed up."

His green eyes looked into mine then he awkwardly looked away. "That's everything then?"

"I think so. Your tux will be waiting when you arrive for the rehearsal. We'll be staying here, so I'll have it sent to your room."

I'd already explained that we would handle the logistics. His presence was the only thing I needed from him.

"Okay then." He looked at me one last time. "Take care."

"Bye, Dad. Drive safely."

The rest of my day was a whirlwind of packing, checking in with Remington, emailing the wedding handlers, and boarding the jet. Elle still had not responded to my text, but even that was not enough to spoil my excitement to get home. I smiled through the entire flight just thinking of kissing Elara's sweet face.

The moment I walked through the door, I went straight to the nursery. The house was dark and Andrew was staying in the guest room as he usually did when Hale and I were away.

Elara heard me enter the nursery and immediately sat up with a smile. I swooped her into my arms and hugged her tightly. "I missed you, peanut."

"Mamma," she chattered, smiling back at me.

Andrew appeared at the door of the guest room in his robe. "Welcome home."

I turned and grinned, happy to be home. "Did I wake you?"

"It's fine. I wasn't expecting you until tomorrow."

"I couldn't wait. New York's lovely, but there's no place like home."

"She missed you too." He watched as Elara played with my hair and cooed. He glanced behind him into the dark guest room. "If you don't mind, I'm going to stay until morning."

"Of course." There was no need for him to relocate to the guesthouse at this hour.

"Goodnight."

I perched Elara on my hip and carried her into my bedroom. "Did you miss Mommy? I think that calls for a sleepover, don't you think? Yes, it does."

She cuddled into me, staring into my eyes with mirrored love. Realizing how much it pained me to leave her for only a few days made me think of my dad. Maybe that was why he left right away and why he rarely called. It was probably easier not knowing everything he missed.

I kissed her precious head and breathed in the sweet scent of her baby shampoo. "I could never leave you, peanut. Never."

Cue the Cramps

OVER THE NEXT two weeks I was plucked, waxed, buffed, stuffed, painted, and dyed until I resembled Calamity Barbie more than myself. But in truth, I looked damn hot so I had no complaints.

While my weight remained drastically unchanged, mostly because I opted to do nothing to change it, the rest of me went through a massive upgrade. I didn't get any injections but I did go for the spray tan. Aside from smelling like a dirty sock for a day, I thoroughly appreciated my new glow. Even my caramel highlights looked amazing against my dark hair, which had been freshly trimmed.

Hale was having a hard time keeping his hands off his hot, soon-to-be wife but we somehow kept our word about abstaining from sex. After making it this far, he was going to have to wait until the very end to put his dick in my dowry. Rules were rules.

"What's this?" he said, holding the tip of the oddly-shaped charger that plugged into the wall.

"A cord."

"This is the cord to a vibrator. Have you been cheating?"

My new vibrator, otherwise known as Thor's Hammer, had been a minor investment that proved to be worth every penny, especially on the nights when Hale was away and insomnia kept me up until three.

"Hale, it's not cheating if I google myself. Besides, it's not the sort of toy that penetrates."

"If by google you mean making yourself come, I assure you it's cheating. We had an agreement."

I rolled my eyes. "Like you haven't diddled."

"I don't diddle. I jerk off."

"Well, pardon me. Like you haven't jerked off."

"I haven't!"

My head slowly turned. By the tension around his eyes and the lack of sarcasm in his voice, I had the urge to believe him. "Good God, man, it's been weeks!"

"I fucking know, Rayne!"

"You've taken a hundred long showers! What the hell have you been doing in there, caulking the tub?"

"I've been decompressing!"

"Is that like googling yourself?"

"Not even a little. I thought we had rules!"

"I never said anything about not masturbating!"

"You said no sex or penetration!"

"Sex, Hale. Since when has anyone gotten pregnant from a hand?"

He marched to the nightstand and pulled open the drawer. "This is not a hand it's a power tool." Wading through the uneaten candy bars, he knocked several pieces of chocolate to the floor as he yanked the vibrator free.

"Hey, watch it. You're crushing my Ferrero Rochers!"

He pointed Thor's Hammer at me accusingly. "Did you order the biggest one?"

I pursed my lips, dropping my chin to my chest. "They didn't advertise it next to a peanut or a penny, so I had no idea it was going to be that big. What are you doing?"

"I'm taking this." He wound the long cord around the handle. "You can have it back after the wedding."

"Hey!" I rushed after him as he disappeared into his closet. "Hale, you can't keep confiscating my vibrators. That's like taking a kid's blankie! It helps me sleep."

In the end, I had to blow him to get it back, but that was fine. He would be in a much better mood after clearing out the pipes, and this gave him a chance to see how Thor's Hammer actually worked.

While I took care of him, he also took care of me. I think he pushed me to the max to punish me for sneaking in orgasms behind his back. I never took that thing past a two but Hale cranked it up as high as it could go.

He had me buzzing like a telephone on a 1950's switchboard. Seriously, by the time he was done, I'd survived a new kind of electric shock therapy. But that no-fuck-zone-closet-mess-around was exactly what we both needed to relieve some of our pre-wedding tension.

"Not on my skin!" I yelled at the last second, just as Hale tipped his head back and gripped his cock like he usually did when he prepared to come.

"What? Why?" His fist tightened as he held that thing like a grenade with a loose pin. One wrong move and he was going to blow.

Kneeling before him on the floor of his dressing room, I searched for something he could finish in. A sock. A towel. Literally anything would do.

"Rayne," he growled my name through gritted teeth. "It's been *weeks*."

I panicked. "Don't you keep tissues in here?"

"Why can't we finish the way we usually do?"

"Your semen could discolor my spray tan! I can't walk around with a giant splotch of man shame on my chest!"

"Rayne," he growled again, losing patience.

"Hale, I'm not going to look like the Hester Prynne of porn. I still have fittings."

"Then open your mouth."

Well, that also worked.

A moment later, I exited the closet and wiped my mouth—Thor's Hammer in hand.

The final days before the wedding were flying by. As much as I looked forward to the wedding, I knew I'd be equally relieved to see it pass. I missed when it was just the three of us and we didn't have this big project looming over every decision.

Remington kept me busy and preoccupied during work hours while I split my free time between studying, playing with Elara, and making sure all the last minute wedding plans were set. When evening rolled around each night, I was too exhausted to do more than cuddle up with Hale and watch a show.

Our weekends were reserved for everything we needed to get done so that we could enjoy the time off during the wedding festivities. I couldn't imagine Hale not working, but he swore he was keeping his calendar open for the next two months while we got married and honeymooned our asses off. I was going to need a B-12 shot for all the sex I planned to have after we lifted the sex-ban.

Things were moving fast and, while it started as a short engagement, it ended more rapidly than I'd expected. We were one week away and even though all the big things were done and the little details were handled, I couldn't shake the feeling of overlooking something, but Hale assured me we were ready.

There would be no more traveling overseas before the wedding. However, Hale still had one more trip to make up north to meet with Clayton, his lawyer.

"You scheduled a meeting during wedding week?" I pouted, looking over the itinerary on the iPad as I sipped my coffee in bed.

"It won't take long. I'll leave in the morning and be back to New York by evening." He exited the bathroom in a billowing cloud of steam and disappeared into his dressing room.

"But isn't Clayton coming to the wedding? Can't you talk about whatever you have to discuss when he gets to the hotel?"

"I'm not doing business during our wedding, Rayne."

"Then why is our entire guest list made up of business contacts," I grumbled into my mug.

He poked his head out of the dressing room. "What was that?"

"Nothing."

He tightened his tie. "Rule number one, never mix business with pleasure."

"Um, then how do you explain me?"

He adjusted his cuffs. "You never worked for me."

"But we were on a business trip the first time you took me to bed."

"What's your point? Are you planning to report me to human resources?"

"Maybe." I glanced back at the iPad. "If you're meeting Clayton, I'll be the one welcoming everyone. I don't know these people. Can't I go with you?"

"Not this time. And it's only one afternoon. You won't even realize I'm gone."

"Sometimes I think you don't know me at all."

He exited the dressing room and leaned down to give me a kiss. "I know you better than you realize."

I grabbed the front of his shirt, purposely wrinkling it. "One day your looks will fade and so will your power over me, mister."

His hand slipped under the covers. "I have other methods of getting what I want."

I squirmed out of reach and flipped to my stomach. "None of that. We have to go over the rest of this itinerary."

He sighed. "Rayne, we've been over this. Andrew's flying out with us tomorrow morning. Your mom and Tyler should be there by the time we arrive. My mom gets in late tonight, and my dad won't get there until Monday evening."

I frowned. "Monday evening's the welcome dinner."

"You work with him every day, Rayne. Does he really need to be welcomed?"

"That's different. And most of the time we talk on the phone." I was already dialing him. "He's family, Hale. He needs to be there for all the things."

Remington answered on the first ring. "What is it, Meyers?"

"Remington," I snapped. "The wedding festivities start tomorrow evening and I expect you there on time."

"Why are you bothering me about this? I have assistants who handle my schedule. Oh, right, that's you."

"Yes, that is me, and I told you to be in New York by tomorrow afternoon at the latest."

"I'm arriving at six. Dinner's not until seven."

"That's not enough time."

He grumbled. "Damn it, Meyers, then move my flight. I'm in the middle of something here."

I paused, trying to guess what he might be doing that had him so preoccupied on a Sunday morning. His schedule was currently open. "What are you doing?"

"Nothing."

I didn't believe him. "Is Odette with you?"

"She's shopping."

I switched the call to Facetime, but he didn't answer. "Pick up the Facetime, Remington."

"No."

"Are you smoking?"

"I'll see you Monday." The call went dead and I growled.

"I'm going to murder your father."

"Get in line," Hale mumbled, adjusting his jacket.

Registering that he was dressed for the office on a Sunday, I frowned. "Where are you going?"

"I have to run an errand."

"In a tie? What sort of errand?"

"Don't worry about it."

He crossed the room like a runway model for GQ and kissed my head. I was still in the wrinkled T-shirt I slept in the night before and rocking a bird's nest sort of bed head.

"I'll be back in a few hours."

"But…"

He was already out the door before I could muster up a distraction to keep him a while longer. As his car pulled away, I went to get Elara from her crib.

Once I plopped her in front of the television and put on *Curious George*, I grabbed some dry Cheerios for her and relocated to the living room.

Where would Hale have gone? I looked at the wedding list, but everything was done. We had no appointments or anything scheduled for the day, so I called Elle, unsure if she'd even answer.

We had moved past radio silence into tepid texting. Still not ideal or anything remotely close to our old normal, but I was doing my best to push us past this funk.

"Hey."

"Hey. Hale just left."

"So?"

"He wouldn't tell me where he was going. It was all very cloak and dagger."

Elle snicked her tongue against her teeth but didn't laugh at my joke. "He probably had to run an errand, Ray. Go back to bed."

Sometimes I forgot that other people didn't wake up with babies at the butt crack of dawn. Elle sounded like she was still half asleep.

"Who's calling you this early?" I cringed at the sound of Paul's voice. That confirmed they moved on to sleeping together.

Since apologizing, I decided to hate Paul silently. For the sake of our friendship, I supported Elle's choices and expected her to support mine. But there was still an invisible, icky film of judgment and distrust stuck to our relationship that neither of us seemed capable of removing.

"Maybe went to pick up your wedding gift."

I stilled. Wedding gift? What the fuck was a wedding gift?

"But... He's the groom. We don't buy the presents."

"The bride and groom always send a gift to each other the morning of the wedding."

"No one told me about this!"

"It's sort of common sense, Ray."

I frantically paged through my notes in the wedding binder, scanning for any mention of this stupid tradition. There it was, right after crochet hook and straws.

GIFT. FOR. GROOM.

"Why didn't someone say something to me about this sooner? And why the hell do I need a crochet hook?"

Elle sighed. "The hook is for your dress. It helps with the bustle and the buttons."

"My dress doesn't have buttons or a bustle." She would have known that if she'd attended any of my fittings like a normal maid of honor.

As always, she was silent whenever I mentioned something that drew attention to her lack of involvement.

I turned the page, wondering what other things I overlooked. "No wonder I didn't know about the groom gift. It's on this list that might as well be called Shit I Don't Need. *Gah!*"

"Some people are trying to sleep," Paul growled in the background.

"The wedding's not for six days, Rayne. Go online and order something for Hale. Then have it expedited to New York."

"Fine." The way she minimized my frustration only aggravated me more. "Sorry I woke you." I hung up the phone, irritated by her patronizing tone and the fact that Paul kept telling her to call me back later.

She didn't get it. Hale was the best gift buyer in the world. He was thoughtful and knew all my sizes. He always added special touches while I sat there like a moron, explaining my gifts by saying dumb shit like, "It's a blanket that looks like a burrito."

I dropped my face into my palms and groaned. This was going to be the Christmas fiasco all over again.

I spent the next hour panicking as I shopped online. The more desperate I became the worst my options seemed. Hale was getting me something nice. He only wore ties when he visited upscale boutiques. That meant jewelry or maybe a designer bag.

I searched the internet for men's jewelry. I was already getting him a wedding band. Wasn't that enough? I paused as a large Superbowl type diamond ring filled the screen. Then I scoffed and scrolled on.

"He's not a used car salesman, Rayne."

Biting my lip, I tapped my foot nervously. What the hell was I going to get him? I needed to know what he got me.

Throwing a few more Cheerios in front of Elara as she sat mesmerized smiling at the monkey on the television, I backed out of the living room and tiptoed into Hale's office. I rummaged around his desk for receipts in the most tidy way possible. He was very organized, so if anything was out of place he'd suspect something.

In the bin on the corner of his desk I spotted the credit card bill. "Perfect."

Skimming over the charges for the wedding, I looked for something out of the ordinary. Then I frowned.

"What the hell is Crypto Casino?"

There were several charges. Some for hundreds of dollars and others for more. My brows lifted when I spotted one charge for four thousand dollars.

"What is this?" Lowering into his chair, I opened his laptop and typed in *What is Crypto Casino?*

A spammy looking ad with a spinning slot machine popped up and I quickly exited out of it. "Shit." I should not be looking such things up on Hale's work computer.

I put everything back as I found it and left the room. By the time Elara's movie was over, I was thoroughly out of ideas for a wedding gift and concerned my future husband might have a secret gambling habit.

But that didn't seem right. Hale liked pragmatic order and dependability. He didn't indulge in games of chance and often disapproved of senseless investments. My gut told me Hale was not a degenerate.

Or was he? Did he have a problem?

There were several thousand dollars of charges on that bill, all beginning around the same time. Something wasn't right.

Why would Hale make so many transactions. Even if he wanted to play a few games with the online casinos, he would have done so once and been done with it. It wasn't his style to feed unhealthy habits. He was too disciplined and controlled to allow such temptations to enslave him.

My stomach started to cramp. I knew Hale. He wasn't a gambler. No one else, aside from me, had access to his account.

Or did they?

I thought about how many times I swiped that

little black card in the last three months. I'd spent a small fortune getting things for the wedding. It was possible the card was hacked. But wouldn't the company contact us if they suspected suspicious activity?

For charges to get approved, especially with such a high price tag, wouldn't they require more than just a credit card number. The signer would need the expiration date and secret code on the back—things that were never written out on any sort of statement.

Another wave of cramps hit my stomach. I shifted uncomfortably as Elara banged her sippy cup on the table.

Who had access to the credit card? Seraphina had it on record at the boutique but she would never use her brother's card for something like that. Would her employees?

The wedding planners all used invoices to get reimbursed and Hale paid them with checks. Who else could have made those charges?

I wouldn't allow myself to think the thought. I couldn't. But I did.

My mind went to that time at the steakhouse when I almost forgot my credit card. I'd paid the bill before running to the restroom and I'd only been gone a few minutes, but it was the only time I could recall ever leaving the credit card unsupervised.

"Don't forget your card," my dad had said as he rose from his seat. I'd bent down to quickly sign the bill, sliding the card safely back into my wallet.

I didn't want to think it, but my mind kept replaying that moment. How long had I been in the bathroom? Long enough to text Elle and wash my hands. Long enough for the waiter to run the charge and return the billfold.

He could have looked. He could have written down the numbers or taken a quick picture with his phone.

I opened up our text messages and paused. What could I say?

Dad, did you steal my credit card info and go on an online gambling spending spree?

He wouldn't do that. Would he?

Of course not. I was obviously missing something. And if I even made the slightest accusation of such untrustworthy behavior it could ruin our fragile relationship. I didn't want anything to spoil the tenuous bond we'd formed over the past few weeks, especially so close to the wedding.

Oh God, what if my father was a total degenerate? Not only that, but what if he was the kind of man to steal from his own kid?

I thought back to how he mentioned the wedding being held in New York before I shared such details. Or was I misremembering? I still couldn't recall mentioning the destination in any of our prior messages, but I needed to check to make sure, so I went back to our earliest communication thread on Facebook, scanning every word for any mention of New York.

"Come on," I whispered, searching frantically.

I told him we were getting married in April and that I would pay for him to attend, but I never mentioned the location. Looking away from my phone in disgust, my gaze fell upon the magazine sitting on the coffee table. The headline read, *A Wedding Suited For American Royalty.*

My heart sank to the pit of my stomach as I looked at the date the article published. It came out a few days before my dad responded to my private message. A response that came after weeks of silence.

I flipped open the cover and paged through until I got to the photos of me and Hale. Words jumped from the text. *Opulence. Lavish. Limitless. Luxury. Net Worth. Davenport. Davenport. Davenport.* Then I saw it. *New York.*

The glossy pages fell from my hands as I stared blankly through the memories playing in my mind. He knew. He fucking knew I was marrying into wealth and *that* was why he answered me.

Did he steal my credit card information? Was he using me? No. I couldn't fathom anyone doing something so selfish and heinous, especially to their child!

He hugged me. That was real.

But then I heard my mother's voice.

I needed to get to the bottom of this. I needed him to look me in the eye and tell me this wasn't him, that he didn't fucking steal from his own kid after robbing her of having a father for thirty fucking years.

I called Andrew and told him to come to the house right away. Then I called the number for the jet and requested they have it ready in one hour.

Hale had opened the statement, but maybe he didn't go through the charges yet. No. He would have done that right away. Right? Hale didn't believe in putting things off. He probably already had an investigation underway. But wouldn't he have asked me about it first? I didn't know what to think or what Hale might be thinking.

"Oh, my God," I muttered to myself as I frantically threw toiletries into my carryon. "My husband's going to have my father arrested."

I needed to fix this. Or at least prove him innocent before police got involved. If it was my dad, I was sure there was a good explanation. Maybe he was sick and desperate. Maybe he was confused.

Gah, no excuse justified this. I had to be wrong.

I threw a few extra items in my bag for New York and zipped it shut, all the while envisioning swat teams storming my wedding ceremony and knocking down topiaries as doves swarmed overhead like props in an Alfred Hitchcock film.

When Andrew arrived I apologized for bothering him on his day off and gave him quick instructions. "Hale should be back soon. Tell him I had to leave early and I'll call him later. Elara had some cereal, but she's probably hungry again. There's yogurt in the fridge."

As soon as I was seated on the jet, I opened my text messages to my dad and stilled. He hadn't answered my last three. Something was definitely going on.

I opened my text thread with Hale.

> Had to fly out early to deal with bride drama. Nothing major, but had to go. See you there.
> Love you.

. . .

HE IMMEDIATELY STARTED TEXTING BACK, but I set my phone to airplane mode. I wasn't letting him talk me out of this, and I was too mortified to explain what was going on until I had some real answers. If my father had actually done this—actually stolen from me and Hale—I wasn't sure what I would do. But I knew, before anyone else, Elara and Hale would always come first.

Avoidance is in my DNA

MY LEG BOUNCED the entire drive from New York to Pennsylvania. Martel had been surprised to hear from me, but he arrived right away when I asked him to drive me to my father's.

Hale had texted me several times asking what was going on, but I couldn't find the words to tell him. Not until I knew for sure what the reality of the situation actually was, so I just kept responding that I'd explain later, which was not a satisfactory response in his opinion.

I could only handle so much. I felt like the earth was crumbling beneath my feet. I was also dealing with severe stomach issues because all of my drama always landed there.

I'd texted my dad several times but received no reply.

It didn't take me long to find his address now that I knew what town he lived in, and once I spotted the old Chevy truck I knew we arrived.

"That's it. Just pull over here."

"I'll find a place to park—"

"Don't bother. I won't be long."

"This neighborhood isn't—"

"This neighborhood's fine." This wasn't up for debate. I was getting out of this car and I was handling this on my own. "I'll only be a few minutes." I opened the car door as soon as we stopped moving.

The houses were wedged together and covered with mildew, faux brick, or weathered metal siding. Several were in disrepair and the yards were mostly dirt and grass that wouldn't grow.

I looked for the house number that matched the address I found online, then spotted where the worn off numbers once hung, enough of a shadow for me to make out the twenty-five.

I lifted the metal latch of the chain link gate and followed the cracked path to the door. Boxes were piled on the chipped porch and an ashtray overflowed with cigarette butts, several of the sun-bleached filters piled on cement around the leg of a broken chair.

I rang the bell, but it didn't work, so I knocked on the storm door and waited. A moment later, the latch flipped and a woman appeared. "Who are you?"

"Are you Laura?"

"Who's asking?"

"Is Ray here?"

She frowned at me. "How do you know Ray?"

"I'm Rayne."

"Who?"

My brain buffered. She didn't know. He lied.

Again. He never told her he had another daughter. "Is he home?"

She eyed me suspiciously, never fully looking away as she yelled over her shoulder. "Ray, someone's at the door for you!"

The interior door opened and she stepped back, tightening the lapels of her ragged housecoat.

"Rayne?" He appeared shocked to see me at his home. Maybe if he would have answered my text we could have handled this differently.

"I need to talk to you."

His wife scowled at him. "What's this about?"

"Laura, go inside."

"Not until I find out what this woman's standing on my porch for." She slid a long cigarette out of a pack and proceeded to light it as if she had all the time in the world. "You pregnant?"

Oh, God. I looked at my dad. "I need to talk to you. Now."

He stepped outside. Laura didn't move. "I've, uh, been a little busy. I was going to text you later today."

I just wanted to get this over with. "Did you steal my credit card information and use it to gamble thousands of dollars online?"

His face paled.

"Jesus Christ, Ray," Laura said, as if this was nothing new. She shook her head, confirming my suspicions. "Again? I've had it." She scoffed, chucking her cigarette into the pile of butts without extinguishing it. The storm door slammed behind her.

A tear fell from my eye. "It's true then?"

"Rayne…" He reached for me.

"Don't touch me." I stepped back. "I trusted you. I believed you wanted a relationship with me."

"I do."

"Then why did you steal from me?"

He looked away, shaking his head then he sighed. "I barely took anything. A few hundred bucks. That's nothin' to people like them."

People like them?

The wind cut across the porch, stealing the breath from my lungs. He was still lying. "It was more than a few hundred. And those people are my family."

"I'm your family. They'll chew you up and spit you out as soon as they're done with you. But you and I… We share blood."

My jaw trembled. "You're nothing." I drew in as much air as I could manage to get the words out that I needed to say but a lump formed in my throat making it nearly impossible to speak. "The sad thing is, if you needed money, I would have helped you. I would have done anything just to know you." My face chilled as another cold gust of wind whipped against my cheeks where tears had fallen. "What a disappointment."

I turned, no longer able to look at him.

"You're the one who contacted me."

I paused. "That was a mistake." Meeting his gaze, so there would be no misunderstanding, I said, "Don't come to my wedding. And don't ever contact me again."

My vision blurred as I navigated the decaying path. Martell was there holding open the car door.

As soon as I was inside, I looked down. My dad followed me, but Martell intercepted, not allowing him within ten feet of the car. They exchanged a few words and my father eventually did what he did best.

He walked away.

Turning my face into the upholstered seat, facing away from the window, I softly wept. I didn't want comfort and I didn't need anyone to tell me it would be okay. I just needed to feel everything I was feeling in that moment.

I was the child of a thief. Forever fatherless.

It was a lifelong dream laid to rest. Fantasies of a child's heart shattered. I knew I wasn't that little girl anymore and I knew I didn't need that man out there, but I mourned for her anyway because she had to learn hard truths the hard way.

Some people were simply undeserving of my kind heart. I wouldn't soon forget this heartache. I didn't want to. I needed to feel it now—in all of its horrible fullness—so the pain could protect me later. This lesson would serve as a reminder that my love was meant for those who truly appreciated me and deserved my kindness.

The door clicked and we pulled away in silence.

It was such a numbing release. Perhaps part of my disappointment delivered relief. Now, I knew.

I would never have to suffer that longing again. No more hollow moments of wishing my dad was there. No more questioning what was wrong with me or why he'd abandoned me. The weight of all that blame was gone. Now, I knew it was my choice to let him go. I didn't want him.

Once we were on the road heading back to New York, Martell asked, "Is there anything I can do for you, Rayne?"

I was the first time he used my name and as I met his concerned stare in the mirror I smiled. This man, who barely knew me, would protect me. Somehow I knew that loyalty went deeper than a paycheck.

But there was nothing anyone could do, so I sniffled and wiped my eyes then said the one thing I needed to hear in that moment, "I'm fine."

Despite my broken heart and the overwhelming disappointment hollowing my stomach, that was true. This, too, would pass and in the end everything would be fine. I just had to get past the hurt.

"Perhaps you should call Mr. Davenport."

I stared out the window as tears silently fell. The world looked foreign on the other side of the glass. A strange haze separated me from reality, and I needed that buffer right now, so I didn't respond.

Yes, I needed to tell Hale all of this. But for my own sanity I needed time to process first.

This wasn't a few weeks gone wrong. This was thirty years' worth of ideals dashed right before one of the most important moments of my life.

He didn't have to meet me, but he did. He dangled that carrot and I gobbled it up whole. I always loved the idea of my dad, but meeting him made him real and I fell in love with him that day we met. He stole my heart and I handed it over with the trust only a daughter could muster when looking into the affirming eyes of a father.

I blew out a breath.

I'll be fine…

I'll be fine.

But for me to be fine I needed to share this at my own pace. Somehow, I knew, saying it out loud would destroy me. I needed time to process, time away from all the wedding stuff to put my emotional needs first.

Then I would tell Hale everything and we'd figure it out together.

Hale would never judge me, but his acceptance couldn't curb my humiliation. I knew this was not my fault. But it hurt. My dad, a man I hero worshipped from afar all my life, used me. And then he abandoned me all over again.

The truth would come out, but right now I was drained. I lacked the strength to explain, to say the words out loud.

My dad doesn't love me.

Yeah, it was going to take me a minute or two to get there.

When I got back to the hotel I slept. I slept for hours upon hours, and then I slept some more. My phone continuously woke me up with texts from Quinn and Devyn and Josette and countless calls from Hale. So I shut it off.

I was hiding from the crushing weight of reality I didn't have the strength to bear.

Sometime after the sun had set, Percy nudged me awake. "Madam?" He stood with a cordless phone on a small silver tray. "Mr. Davenport's on the line for you."

I sighed and put the phone to my ear. "Hale?"

"What the fuck is going on, Rayne? You leave

without telling me and then you don't answer your phone for hours. I've been worried sick."

"I'm sorry," I said with little emotion.

"What is this? What are you doing?"

"I just…needed to get here."

"Why?"

"I…" The words stuck in my throat as more tears rushed to my eyes. I wanted to tell him. I wanted him to know how much that man had hurt because I knew Hale would be the best person to console me, but I just couldn't get the words past my lips. The pain seemed to physically block my throat. "I can't talk about it."

"That's not good enough, Rayne. You don't just take off without notice and shut off your phone for the entire day. We were supposed to fly out together. The three of us and Andrew. There was a plan."

"I'm sorry." It was the only thing I could think to say.

"Are you having second thoughts?"

"What?" I struggled to sit up. "Hale, no. Everything's fine."

"Then why did you leave like that?"

I tried again, but I couldn't command my voice to vocally say that my father was a complete loser who was only using me to steal from my future husband.

"Please don't be mad at me, Hale. I'm just…" I was still too fragile and on the verge of breaking and he was too far away. I wanted him here. "I never should have left without you."

"Then why did you?"

"Because I was trying to handle things myself."

"What things? What's going on?"

"Everything's f—fine." I almost got the statement out without my voice breaking. Almost.

"Rayne…" he rasped, hearing the pain I couldn't articulate. "Whatever's going on, just talk to me. I won't be mad."

My chin trembled. No, he wouldn't be mad. But it still hurt too much to explain. I couldn't think of anything to say.

"Rayne, baby, whatever it is, just talk to me."

I wanted to. I wanted to give him exactly what he asked, but I couldn't. "Just get here and everything will be perfect. I promise. Everything is going to be fine."

If I kept telling myself everything would be fine it would eventually happen, right?

"You're not telling me something. You said there was bride drama. What happened? Did you and Elle have another fight?"

I didn't want to lie. "No. It was stupid. One of my…accessories turned out to be broken. I handled it."

"An accessory? You're sure that's all that's going on."

"Yes. Everything's…fine." And in the big picture, it was. I had Hale. I was safe. Elara was safe. My dad was not going to overshadow those blessings. "I love you and I can't wait to see you."

He sighed and I could tell he wanted me to give him more. "What was it—the accessory that broke? I'm sure we can replace it if it has you this upset."

He was so good to me. "No one will even realize it's missing. Besides, it didn't fit anyway. I'm over it."

"You don't sound like you're over it. I can tell you're upset. If it's something you want, Rayne, let's replace it."

Too numb and empty to think up more excuses, I said, "Please drop it, Hale." Even talking proved too strenuous. "I'm exhausted and I haven't eaten all day. I just want to go to bed and start over. I don't want to think about it anymore."

"You're sure?"

"Very."

He sighed. "Fine. Get some sleep, baby. I'll be there tomorrow morning and we can talk more then."

"Okay."

"And answer your phone."

As soon as we ended the call I turned my phone back on and collapsed into bed, drawing the pillow over my face.

I'd eventually tell Hale the truth but tomorrow seemed too soon. Ideally, I'd like to push all this family drama under the rug until after the wedding, but knowing Hale that wouldn't happen.

He liked to attack problems head on. He was extremely solution oriented. There was no solution here. Just a deadbeat dad and a disappointed daughter. Some things just needed time and space to process.

On Your Marks...

I'D FALLEN BACK into a restless sleep, which I awoke from several times, hungry and looking for food, but whenever I checked the cabinets and fridge my appetite disappeared.

The following morning, when my phone vibrated on the nightstand, I croaked out a hello and awoke to Seraphina's exuberant voice.

"I have a surprise for you and Hale as soon as you get here!" She assumed I was still in Florida with Hale. "I've scheduled the two of you for an all-day spa treatment!"

"Oh, Phina, you didn't have to do that." I really wished she hadn't.

While most women liked being massaged and rubbed down with oil, I did not. I was awkward and very particular about who touched my body. Basically, Hale was the only person I could tolerate touching me without going stiff and goofy, so massages were usually excruciatingly embarrassing, but of course Hale's sister wouldn't know that.

"You'll love it! Your couples massage starts at one. It includes a ninety minute lymphatic massage to relieve any pre-wedding swelling. Plus, a hot stone treatment and a mint scalp massage. You can thank me later."

If I had a shell, I'd climb into it and hide.

I coughed. "Thanks."

"Uh-oh, are you getting a cold?"

I cleared the tickle from my throat. Was my nose running? Crap. I could not be sick for my wedding.

I was prepared for a breakout, stomach issues, and even a cake crash, but I hadn't considered actual illness as a possibility. I would just will myself into perfect health.

"I'm not sick," I croaked. "I'm just not fully awake yet." My throat was probably swollen and sore from the lump that was in it all day yesterday.

"You should pick up some cough drops and vitamin C, just in case."

"Cough drops are a gateway drug." The minute I tasted eucalyptus my brain would be convinced I had the plague. A hot, steamy shower was all I needed. "I'll be fine."

That seemed to be my mantra now.

"I hope so. Also, I've sent your clothes to the hotel. Everything's been pressed and steamed, but it should be uncovered and hung right away. Have the butler see to it."

I couldn't ask Percy to do that, so I banked on twenty minutes of organizing my wardrobe myself.

"Okay." I pinched my nose, convinced my sinuses felt off from crying.

"I spoke to Devyn this morning and everything's all set for tonight. The bar has your signature cocktail ready to go and shuttles will transport guests from the hotel to the restaurant at six thirty."

It was finally happening. Everything we planned was starting to unravel and take shape. There was no going back now and I couldn't tell if the tingle in my stomach was anxiety or excitement. "Okay. Thanks—for everything, Phina."

"That's what sisters are for."

Her words filled me with calm and warmth. I doubted she realized how much I truly appreciated her presence in my life these last few months. "Will you sit next to me and Hale tonight?"

"Aw! Of course. I'd love that, but… Shouldn't Elle and Barrett sit with you?"

It wasn't Barrett I was worried about. But the thought of sitting near Elle and, of course Paul, put a damper on the entire night. I didn't want that energy, and somewhere in the last twenty-four hours I'd made the decision that I was only going to surround myself with people who filled my cup.

"It's not the ceremony and I'm the bride. I get to sit by whoever I want. I'd really love it if you were by my side."

"Gosh, Rayne…" She was quiet for a moment. "Thank you. That means a lot." She chuckled and I could sense her smiling. "I'd love to sit with you and Hale."

It was Seraphina who deserved all the thanks. Hale was truly blessed when it came to having wonderful siblings.

"You and Hale should get to the restaurant

early, so your guests don't see you before your grand entrance."

I didn't understand why we couldn't ride over with everyone else, but I'd come to simply accept these things that added to the overall production. Broadway should seriously option us for their next show.

"In that case I'll ask Tyler to keep an eye on my mom." She would be the first person to arrive at the wrong restaurant and I couldn't have any more issues with my parents this week.

"Perfect. I'm about to run into the salon for a blowout. Let me know if you need any help with your dress tonight. I'll be at the hotel early."

I'd been dressing myself solo for three decades so I didn't understand why people suddenly assumed I needed help, but then I saw Percy wheeling in the cart with all the clothes. That was a lot of fucking clothes.

"Yeah, maybe keep your phone on. Thanks." I hung up and blinked at the rack. "That can't be all mine?"

"I'm afraid so."

"But it's Hale's too, right?"

"No, madam. Mr. Davenport's wardrobe has been pressed and hung in the guest closet. And Lady Elara's dresses are in the au pair's suite."

"Well shit." This was going to take much longer than twenty minutes.

It took an hour to unbox and hang everything. Our wardrobe for the wedding was the equivalent of a down payment on a house. In some states, it might have been the entire loan.

Such affluence was sometimes hard to process.

No wonder so many people assumed the wealthy had money to burn, but it was still their wealth. Theirs to spend and theirs to withhold. It was not there for the taking by morally bankrupt, degenerate, deadbeat dads.

I'd clearly moved onto the angry stage of grief and had some rage to work through.

I sneezed and reached for another tissue. If these allergies didn't clear up I was going to look like Rudolf the red nosed reindeer coming down the aisle—alone.

"You're not sick. It's obviously the dust from the clothes."

"Pardon?" Percy appeared, never more than a few feet away even when he was out of sight.

"Sorry. Just talking to myself."

The butler nodded and disappeared.

I returned to the closet to organize my shoes and bags.

As I organized, my thoughts returned to my father and my jaw tightened. The worst part was that my dad's deceit touched Hale. That was where I drew the line. These were my Davenports. They were more of a family to me than my father could ever be. I would never let anyone take advantage of them or hurt them.

The doorbell rang and I looked down at my disheveled appearance. I still hadn't showered and I was already getting visitors?

Percy reappeared. "Your mother has arrived." I could hear her voice before he finished his announcement.

"Oh, Mylanta, will you look at this place," my mother's squawky voice ricocheted off the porcelain tile as she entered the penthouse. "Have you ever seen anything like it?"

Who was she talking to?

"Gorgeous," said a male voice in an approving tone.

My head perked up. "Tyler?"

"Ray? Where are you, girl?"

I scrambled off the floor where I'd been trying to sort out which shoes went with which outfit and sprinted to greet them.

As soon as I hit the landing, he held open his hands and yelled, "Calamity Bride!"

I squealed and raced down the stairs not stopping until I flung myself into his arms.

He grunted at my not so soft landing. "I see you still have the grace of an inebriated gazelle."

"They tried charm school. It didn't take."

He laughed and stepped back, holding me by the shoulders as he looked me up and down. "Wow, I like the high lights."

"And the lashes?" I fluttered my extensions.

"You clean up pretty nice. Where's Elle?"

Of course, that would be his first question. For most of our lives we were a trifecta. "She's getting in later today."

I wondered if he'd notice differences in her through their long distance communication. I decided not to influence him by sharing my Elle drama and simply see what conclusions he drew on his own. If Tyler felt the need to say something he would.

He frowned. "Shouldn't she be here early? She's your maid of honor."

I found it easiest to minimize my feelings and

act like things didn't bother me when, in reality, it really, *really* bothered me that Elle wasn't arriving until the very last minute—with Paul.

So I smiled. "I'm not worried. I've got you here now, my ultimate bride-kick."

He laughed. "Clever."

"That's me." I glanced at my mother who was trying to lift a painting off the wall to see if anything was printed on the back. "Hi, Mom."

"Oh." She abandoned the art and turned. "On *Antiques Road Show* they teach you how to appraise things like this. You never know if something's a work of art."

I kissed her cheek. "I'm glad you're here."

She hardly acknowledged my hug as she continued her inspection of everything that wasn't nailed down. "Is that lamp real crystal?" She crossed the room and nudged the heavy accent piece. " It is! *Actual* crystal. Imagine that."

"That's great, Mom. How was your flight?"

"Oh!" She drew in a long breath. "You should have seen the way they took care of us in first class. They gave us heated washcloths and blindfolds. I even had a cocktail before ten a.m. I might still be drunk!"

I glanced at Tyler and he shook his head and muttered behind his hand, "It was a cranberry juice with a splash of Malibu." He looked around the room. "Where's Hale?"

"He and Elara should be here around lunch time. I need to get dressed and fed."

"You're a bride, not a horse."

"I *am* the bride, so you're not supposed to lecture me. I'm feeling peckish. We should go downstairs before they switch from breakfast to afternoon tea. Did you guys eat?"

"I had a coffee before our flight."

"So?"

Tyler did one of those adorable glances at his trim stomach and sighed. "I'm starving."

"Perfect. The food here's delicious."

"How did I know you were going to ruin my wedding diet?"

"Um, because you know me and you also know diets are dumb. But you know what's not dumb? Chocolate croissants. The ones they serve downstairs are to die for." I was glad my appetite had returned. "Give me five minutes and I'll be ready."

As I washed up in the bathroom, Tyler lingered by the door. "I got an email from someone named Quinn. I have to get my tux at two."

"That's fine. Hale and I have a couple's massage this afternoon." I edged my way past him to peruse the closet.

I didn't have a daytime outfit for today, so I just threw on jeans and a lightweight sweater. It was much nicer in New York now that the weather had broken and the snow had melted. But evenings were still chilly.

"I just have to pull up my hair." I flipped my head and twisted my waves into a stable knot that looked more intentionally messy than incompetent.

When we got to breakfast I peppered Tyler with one question after another, needing a full run down on hometown gossip.

"They tore down the White Lotus Café."

"No," I said with a great sense of loss. The hundred-year-old hangout was a social landmark in Portland. It had been closed for years, but I thought it should have stayed as a sort of monument.

"Yup. Demolished. They'll probably build a storage facility there or some other tacky structure."

"They should build another café."

"Yeah, that's just what Oregon needs."

"This is real silver." My mom remarked, lifting the cutlery and informally weighing it by balancing it between her fingers.

She was on sensory overload. Every time we passed a chandelier or a plant or a person wearing any sort of fashionable attire, she stopped and asked random strangers questions.

"Oh, where did you get that hat?"

"Do you know if the sconces are original from when the hotel was built?"

"What kind of plant is this? Is it poisonous to cats? Rayne, cut off a small leaf so I can take it home and propagate it."

When I refused to hack into the hotel greenery she pouted. It was like walking with a toddler through a no-touch museum.

"Do you think this is tap water?"

"Mom, eat." One more question and my head was going to explode.

"I think I'll wash my hands." She excused herself to visit the restroom and I watched her stop a bellman on the way. What on earth could she be asking him?

"You're cranky," Tyler commented.

"She acts like she's never been in public before."

"Yeah, I know. Her daughter acts the same way sometimes."

I winced. "You're right. I don't know why I'm being so snippy with her." It was as if my father's behavior had made me overly self-conscious of my mother's, which wasn't fair to my mom.

He squeezed my hand. "It's probably just jitters. Moms are easy targets."

When we got back to the penthouse Hale and Elara had arrived. The welcome was awkward and tense, so I took Elara and carried her around like a shield. I also tried my best to get Tyler to stay, but he eventually had to go back to his room to unpack.

Hale watched me suspiciously, but I mirrored him like a flipped magnet, never letting him come within a few feet of me. While I was making emotional progress, I still felt overly fragile. Too much focus could break me in ways I really wanted to avoid.

"Andrew's setting up Elara's crib and changing table. Soon as he's done she can go down for a nap. Then we need to talk."

I didn't want to talk. The wedding stuff was starting. Guests were arriving. We spent so much time and money arranging everything and, now, wedding week was finally here. I didn't want my deadbeat father and his crappy behavior to touch any part of the precious moments Hale and I had spent so much time planning.

I realized then that my sadness had transformed into anger. I was furious with my dad but also irritated with myself for ever trying to involve him. More stuff to work through. But the last thing

I wanted to do was talk about the man at the root of my aggravation.

Yesterday was over. It was time to move on. Time for fun, happy wedding stuff.

Pretending I didn't hear him, I went about changing Elara's diaper.

"I just did that, Rayne."

"Well, she smells like she made a tinkie." She didn't smell. I was totally avoiding him. "I'm going to take her upstairs and clean her up."

I didn't have to see his face to know he watched me. My goal remained. I would avoid any and all confrontations that could wait until after the wedding.

Unfortunately, Hale wasn't easily sidetracked and he followed us into the master bedroom. "Hard to change a diaper without a diaper bag."

"I was just going to grab it."

"Rayne." He caught my arm as I tried to brush past him. "Are we okay?"

"Of course. We're fine."

He frowned and I felt horrible for making him question us when he'd done absolutely nothing wrong, but I couldn't have this conversation right now with guests coming and going and everyone asking a million things of me at once.

He studied me. "Before everyone gets here, I want to—"

"Hello?"

Relief washed over me as he cocked his head. "Is that my mother?"

"Hale?" she called in a tone that commanded a response.

I'd never been so grateful for my future

mother-in-law. "You better go," I rushed him toward the door. "I'll be down in a minute."

As it turned out, Naomi, Hale's mother, was able to get an earlier flight. The woman loved her son and I loved how much she was going to monopolize him while I dodged his questions and suspicious looks.

He watched me like a hawk as his mother doted on Elara and asked about the plans for the next few days. The second we were alone he'd corner me. I suddenly wanted to be around all the people.

When Andrew arrived to announce the nursery was ready, I insisted on going with him to inspect it. Unfortunately, when I came back to the penthouse Hale and I were, once again, all alone.

"Are you finished avoiding me, now?"

"I'm not avoiding you, Hale."

He just looked at me, not even dignifying my lie with a response. "Come on, Rayne."

That was the tone he used to broach big discussions, so I blurted, "Phina made us an appointment for a couple's massage. We have to get moving or we're going to be late."

"Huh?"

"A couple's massage, Hale." I grabbed my purse and handed him his phone. "It's for our lymph nodes."

"When did this happen? No one told me."

"It was a gift. A surprise. Let's go."

I typically didn't like wellness salons, because they felt like stuffy libraries with too much nakedness. But today the spa suited me just right.

In the common areas, signs requesting silence

hung on various walls and a sense of safety co-cooned me. A serene flute harmonized with soft bells and the air smelled of fresh lemongrass. The ambiance demanded quiet, so when Hale tried to speak, I pressed my finger to my lips and whispered, "Shh, no talking."

As soon as we checked in, Hale and I were escorted to private dressing rooms where we stripped out of our clothes and changed into robes. I waited in the dressing room as long as possible before returning to the lounge.

"Right this way, miss. Your fiancé's waiting," one of the spa attendants whispered.

I entered a room upholstered in soft, creams and delicate pinks. Hale sat in a crisp robe holding a flute of champagne. I smiled nervously.

"Your champagne." The attendant lowered a tray and I accepted the glass.

"Thank you."

As soon as she left I sipped thirstily, emptying the glass. The lounge quickly transformed into a padded cell.

Hale appeared more at ease with the schedule shift. "This was nice of Phina."

"Very," I agreed, tapping my foot nervously. "We should get her a gift for everything she's done to help. Something extra."

We already had special favors for the wedding party that Quinn helped me put together. The girls were getting personalized Christian Dior totes, Chanel perfume, and Tiffany & Co. compacts, plus a few other more personal items I threw in. Hale was gifting the guys with Hermes overnight bags.

His finger traced over my knee and I stilled.

"Nervous?"

I was always a little nervous when Hale touched me, but today I felt especially jittery. "Just eager to get my rub down."

He frowned just as my face blanched. We both knew I hated being touched by strangers. I needed to stop acting more than my usual level of weird and chill the hell out.

Keeping his hand on my thigh, he leaned back and sighed contently. "I can't believe we're finally here."

"It's crazy," I agreed.

"Sometimes it felt like this week would never come."

It was interesting how differently we saw situations. For Hale, he acted like it took a lifetime for us to reach this moment. For me, it felt like we just met yesterday. In reality, we hadn't even known each other a year and any sane person would think we were rushing to the altar at breakneck speeds.

I looked around. "Did they leave a bottle for refills?"

"Here." He poured his champagne in my glass.

"I'm disappointed," he whispered and I turned, panic tightening in my chest.

"Why?"

"I wanted some time alone with you today."

"We are alone."

"No. I mean *alone*, alone." His finger dragged slowly up my thigh, parting my robe.

"Hale." I caught his wrist. "They probably have cameras in here."

"So?"

"So…" My face burned. "You can't do that."

"I think I can." He pressed his hand deeper and stilled when he met an unexpected layer of cotton. "Are you wearing underwear?"

"Don't laugh at me. You know I'm uncomfortable being naked in front of people."

He withdrew his hand and smirked. "I'll admit, I'm a little pleased."

I looked down at his lap. "Are you wearing—"

He flashed his cock.

"Jesus, Hale!"

He laughed. "What are they going to do, Rayne?"

"You can't just expose yourself like that in public places."

"We're not in public."

"What about the cameras? You're suddenly an exhibitionist? Flashing people with that semi-hard Gonzo nose. Let's see the tabloids publish that?"

"I think they'll need bigger pages."

I scoffed and rolled my eyes. "God has some sense of humor."

"What does that mean?"

"Just that the assembly lines up there aren't all functioning at the same efficiency when they're deciding which humans get what parts." I shook my head, refusing to look at him and the small tent he'd pitched between his legs. "You're already too pretty, but then they gave you that thing. I swear, you could make a horse jealous."

He chuckled. "This is the first I've heard you complain. Would you rather I had a smaller one?"

"I'd rather you not expose my toys without my permission. Look, I bet that shell decoration on that shelf has a camera pointed at you right now."

"It's a spa. They're used to seeing the human body in its natural form. Do you know how many naked asses have probably sat on this sofa?"

"Then I'm glad I opted for underwear," I mumbled.

There was a soft knock on the door. "Welcome, Mr. & Mrs. Davenport. I'm Arina," the woman wore a white lab coat to finish off her sterile appearance. "Your masseurs are waiting this way. Follow me please."

"Mrs. Davenport?" I raised a brow, glancing over my shoulder at Hale.

He cupped my ass. "Has a nice ring to it, don't you think?"

I swatted his hand away. "I do."

As we walked after Arina, he tugged the belt of my robe loose and I caught the lapels just in time.

He laughed and I hissed, "Stop it." Glancing back at the bulge in his robe, I rolled my eyes. "I hope they make you lay on your stomach first."

"I hope to fuck you in the sauna when we're done." He pinched my ass and I squeaked, jogging after Arina.

The massage was more enjoyable than I expected. The champagne had relaxed me and being that it was ninety-minutes I had plenty of time to adjust. I'd say the last ten minutes were my favorite part. By then they were mostly working on my scalp, which I could handle.

Afterwards, Hale and I took a steam, which felt like a self-induced asthma attack. I left before the timer went off and before Hale could fulfill his fantasy of a hot-coal-fuck. He stayed to enjoy the heat a while longer while I took a cold shower.

By the time we returned to the penthouse we needed to get ready for dinner. Hale's college friend, Noah, and his wife Avery, were joining us. This would be the first time I met them. It really bothered me that Elle wasn't there yet. The rest of the wedding party had called at some point during the day to check in. But not the maid of honor.

Tonight's dinner wasn't an official part of the wedding, but it felt special, like a moment with the people who mattered most. Remington should have also checked in by now.

"Why are you frowning?"

"Huh?" My gaze met Hale's reflection in the mirror. "Am I?"

"Yes. What's wrong?"

"I was just thinking it's a shame your dad's not here yet?"

"Why? Your dad's not here yet either."

I blanched and dropped my gaze. That was true. My dad wouldn't be there for any of it.

"Rayne, what's going on with you?"

"N-nothing." I reached for my jewelry but clumsily knocked over my water bottle.

"Hey." He caught my hand. "Stop. Talk to me."

"Not now." I was out of shields and we were out of time. I couldn't risk spoiling my makeup with tears.

Crouching before me, he looked into my eyes and frowned. Whatever he wanted to say to me, he seemed to let it go for the sake of my sanity. Kissing the top of my head, he looked into the mirror once more. This time, when he smiled, it didn't reach his eyes. "I'll get your coat."

The comment about my dad's imminent arrival made me believe he didn't suspect anything. I wanted to ask if he knew about the charges on the credit card bill, but that would open the door to more questions.

I received a text from Miles on the drive to the restaurant, alerting me that the big guy had landed.

"What's got you smiling?" Hale whispered in my ear.

"Your dad arrived."

He nodded, but didn't share my reaction.

If only he knew how lucky he was. Yes, Remington could be a massive pain in the ass with narcissistic tendencies. And he definitely criticized his children's choices too much, but he loved his family and he would never do anything to purposefully harm them.

Jasmine was a fluke and while Remington's actions had wounded Hale's ego, Hale never thought of her as more than a casual companion. In the end, Remington had married her to protect his son, because he would stop at nothing to keep his children safe. I couldn't say the same about my father.

Per the production plan, all guests should have been seated before we arrived. Most were.

"There's Noah," Hale said, pointing out his other groomsman as the maître d led us to the table.

Noah's wife, Avery, sat across from him, looking absolutely stunning in a shimmering gold dress that matched her glowing skin. "Wow. Was she a model?"

"Sugar baby."

I did a quick double take to see if Hale was joking. "Seriously?"

He smirked. "I'll fill you in later."

When we reached the table, everyone stood and welcomed us with hugs. I thought it might be overwhelming, hosting so many different personalities at once, but it was actually rather comforting to be surrounded by so many people I loved.

Once we greeted everyone, we joined them at the table. Since Hale rarely saw Noah, I insisted they sit together. I took the seat between Avery and Seraphina.

The conversation flowed naturally. Noah and Hale chatted like old friends and it made me happy to see him laughing with someone so openly. I understood why he'd chosen Noah now that I saw them together.

At first, Avery intimidated me, but she had a comforting disposition that put me instantly at ease.

"It's overwhelming, isn't it?" she observed, leaning close so only I could hear.

I lifted my brows as I downed a guzzling sip of my cosmopolitan. "Hmm?"

Avery tipped her angular jaw toward Hale and Noah. "Them. Look at them. If only they knew."

I shared her view of Noah and Hale and immediately understood what she saw. Power. Sex appeal. Authority. Confidence. Bone structure that looked airbrushed. "God, I could so easily hate them."

She laughed. "I know, right? Noah puts one little dab of product in his hair and achieves all that. Meanwhile, I spent three hours getting ready tonight."

"Well, you look gorgeous."

"Thank you. So do you."

The men turned in unison and caught us staring.

Hale held my gaze from across the table and smiled. "What?" He silently mouthed.

I flashed my teeth and pointed to my mouth. "You have something in your teeth."

"Your tie's crooked," Avery said at the same time to Noah, and we both laughed as each man made a quick adjustment then returned to their conversation.

I snickered. "It's best to remind them they still have flaws."

"I completely agree."

The mothers chatted about baby memories while Barrett got to know Tyler. Remington, always one to make a fuss, insisted on making a champagne toast. For Hale's sake, I hoped he kept it short and sweet.

The crystal chimed as he stood. "I just want to say it's good to see my son so happy. Hale, I'd say you picked a good one, but I picked her first. You're welcome."

"Remington," I warned and laughed.

My boss and future father-in-law chuckled. "Meyers, it's good to see you dolled up for a change." He held my stare for a moment, his weathered eyes creasing affectionately at the corners. "Who knows what twist of fate blew you into harbor that day you first set foot on my yacht? Under-qualified, underdressed, and shockingly under-prepared. I thought, there had to be a reason you, of all people, were sitting at my table. And so there was. Here you are. Exactly where you belong." He lifted his glass. "To fate. Cheers."

"Cheers!" the guests echoed back in chorus.

As everyone returned to their conversations, Remington walked to my side of the table, bending to my cheek. "Kill anyone today?" he whispered.

I smiled up at him as if he told me I looked beautiful. "Not yet."

He chuckled, squeezing my shoulder affectionately. "Then I'd say things are going well." His nearness put me instantly at ease.

"It would seem."

He glanced down at me in question, always a little more perceptive than most.

Before he could dig any deeper I said, "That was a nice toast."

He smiled, his assessing eyes accepting that I didn't want to delve below the surface while so many other people were nearby. He patted my shoulder. "It's going to be a good week, Meyers. You tell me if there's anything I can do."

"I will. Thanks, Remington."

The waiter returned to review the chef's intentions for the night. Hale had arranged to have a private menu prepared for the occasion and this was the big reveal.

Tyler, seated on the other side of Avery, leaned closer and whispered, "Where's Elle?"

I couldn't do Elle math right now so I shrugged. "I guess she's late."

We delayed as long as we could, but by the time Elle and Paul arrived, the first course had been served and cleared. They took their seats without even a *sorry we're late*.

"Maybe I should switch seats," Phina said. "As your maid of honor, Elle should be closer to you."

Should be, but she wasn't. I placed a stilling hand on Phina's arm before she could rise. "Everyone's exactly where they should be. Please stay." Lifting an untouched champagne flute, I placed it in front of her. "Let's drink to sisterhood and stop worrying about etiquette."

"I always worry about etiquette."

"I know." I tapped my glass to hers. "Drink."

Phina grinned but did as she was told.

Noah owned a company that did something with extreme sports which lead to several threats to take Hale and I skydiving. I would literally shit myself if I had to jump out of a plane, so there was no way that was happening. And I was not letting Hale try it either. People didn't spend their lives searching for a husband only to chuck him out of a plane at ten thousand feet.

At least not the good ones.

Dinner was wonderful. The chef did an outstanding job, and I had the added delight of taking home the leftovers.

By the time we got back to the hotel, I was exhausted. Being around so many people massively tired me out. Barrett, Noah, and Hale stayed downstairs to have a drink at the bar, while I took Elara upstairs for some cuddles before bed. By the time Hale got in, I was sound asleep.

I awoke to a clatter of coins and keys as he emptied his pockets on the dresser. Peeking through my lashes, I acknowledged that I'd successfully avoided him all day—just like I'd wanted to do. So why did I feel like an utter failure?

He climbed into bed, pressing a bourbon-scented kiss on my lips. "Goodnight, baby." He settled onto his side of the bed and was asleep within minutes.

I knew then I needed to find the courage to tell him. While I didn't want to taint the perfection of our wedding week, I also didn't want this distance between us to fester into something more.

I missed our closeness. Lying next to him wasn't enough. There was intimacy in truth and I wanted that more than anything with Hale. I just didn't know how to explain everything to him without ripping myself to shreds in the process.

Hopefully, a solution would come to me soon.

Come Rayne or Come Hale

"April showers are here in the Northeast," the cheery meteorologist declared, as torrential downpours pummeled the windows of The Plaza.

New York was a disaster when it stormed, and this was apparently the storm of the century. Our beautiful view had been obliterated by an ominous, grey sheet of rain and everything in the tri-state area was a soggy mess.

"Hale?" I called, as I stared at the television in horror while blowing my nose. "Hale, this is bad."

"Stop watching the news," he yelled back from upstairs.

I looked toward the master bedroom, then turned my gaze to the monsoon spilling over Central Park. "Can I look out the windows?"

"You're supposed to be resting." Hale knew I couldn't turn down a nap, so he convinced me to rest as much as possible during our downtime.

My sore throat had turned into a bit of a head

cold but I wasn't sick. It was obviously allergies. They were putting too much pepper in the food.

Everyone kept trying to give me medicine, but if I took something it would be admitting defeat.

"Rayne, you're not even lying down."

Who could sleep at a time like this? They were predicting massive flooding. "Did you know that a few years ago, New York was completely underwater? What if this ends up like that?"

"That's not—"

"Shh!" I held up a hand as the meteorologist appeared on the television.

"Expect travel delays," the man reported. Then he went on to say that not only could there be flight delays but there could also be issues with all three Metro-north train lines.

We were at the epicenter of it all and if the rain didn't stop soon, New York was going to be underwater for my wedding. The television went off and I turned to find Hale holding the remote control.

"Hey, I was watching that!"

"You need to get dressed. We're meeting my mom for lunch."

"No, we're not. I have a full day scheduled with the girls. We're christening the bridal suite. We have to make sure everyone's accessories arrived and then we're doing something with a champagne bucket, followed by paraffin dips, and IV therapy." When he crinkled his brow, I said, "Don't look at me like that. These aren't my traditions. I don't even know why we're doing half that stuff. I just follow my handlers' directions."

He sighed. "Fine. I'll go to lunch with my mother alone."

"You and Naomi will have fun."

As it turned out, I should have gone to lunch with my future husband and mother-in-law. Getting everyone's attire situated turned the beautiful suite into a madhouse. Seraphina and Quinn had every detail mapped out.

They even had a nifty label system in play so every item of clothing was tagged with a specific day or event—a system Phina recommended when I'd apparently paired a day shoe with evening attire.

"You're lucky I didn't wear my slippers," I told her.

My entire week had been choreographed by wardrobe changes, photo shoots, meet and greets, and pitstops for beauty or booze. I was exhausted by noon.

"Devyn will be here to keep you on track," Quinn said, texting with her left hand as she held an iPad in her right.

"Where will you be?"

"I'll be overseeing the main events and the guests."

"Shouldn't I be at the main events?" I was the bride after all.

"You will be. But only after you make your debut."

"Isn't tonight's welcome dinner my debut?"

It seemed every night included another welcome dinner and another debut. At what point did the people just accept that we were there?

"Every moment is an opportunity to reinvent

and reintroduce yourself," Quinn explained. "By the end of the week, you're going to be New York's darling. Everyone and their mother is going to want a peek at the wedding of the century, so we need to capture plenty of moments."

But I didn't want staged moments. I wanted real ones.

"Shoot. Phina, what was the name of the driver transporting the ice sculptures?" Quinn left me holding two samples of champagne. I downed them both.

"His name's David. Why, is there a problem?"

I stared down at the walkways where puddles glistened and umbrellas moved about. Cars splashed through the streets as a spattering mist turned the world a murky grey.

But when the photographer—yes, there was already a photographer on set, and I say set because things were starting to feel very artificial— when the photographer snapped a picture and then flashed me the image, everything appeared pristine and flawless. The reality was much different.

"Has anyone seen the blue folder?" Josette yelled.

"People would not be walking around in that water if they knew what was in there," Tyler muttered into his mimosa, as he came to stand beside me and stare down at the rain soaked world below. "Don't they realize what's washing up?"

"Sir, are you supposed to be in here?" a woman dressed in a service tuxedo asked as if her position gave her such authority.

Tyler scowled. "Yes, I'm supposed to be in

here. I'm the bride-kick." He rolled his eyes at me. "Ray, get your servants in order."

"He's fine," I told the woman while mouthing a silent *sorry* for his rudeness.

Tyler glanced down at his phone. "Uh-oh."

"What?" The rain created a constant rumble against the exterior windows, muffling everything spoken slightly out of earshot .

"Nothing." He looked at his phone again, but angled the screen so I couldn't see.

"What is it? Tell me or I'll call back the staff police to harass you some more."

He pocketed his phone and finished his mimosa. "There's an issue with her dress."

"Her?" I asked, but I already knew he was talking about Elle, the one female currently missing from the room where all important wedding party people possessing boobs were supposed to be. "What now?"

"I'll take care of it. Quinn, I need some club soda and a cotton rag."

I caught his sleeve before he could abandon me. "Now? She has to deal with this right now?"

"She's your maid of honor, Ray. Her dress can't have a stain."

More like maid of horror. "Why can't someone else fix it? Why do you have to leave?"

"Look, I'll take her the club soda and I'll be right back. Relax." He looked into my eyes and frowned. "Are you feeling okay? You look a little run down."

"Gee, thanks."

He sighed. "Let me run her something for the stain and then I'll be right back. But don't think she's making whatever this is." He waved his hand about in reference to the room's current festivities.

"We're christening the bridal suite!" Didn't anyone read the itinerary?

Devyn appeared. "Rayne, we need to get started. The photographer wants some pictures of you at the champagne fountain."

"Good, I could use a swim," I mumbled following Devyn to my mark.

I was handed another champagne flute that had been adorned with strawberries, they instructed me to stand beside the three-gallon, gold-trimmed champagne fountain in my robe, which was not my robe, but a robe I'd been given for this very-staged particular moment of my life.

"Seraphina, Avery, come stand next to the bride. Where's the maid of honor?" the photographer asked. "We're missing one, right?"

"She's not coming," I grumbled, nudging the fruit along the rim of my champagne flute so I could take a sip.

"Oh, Rayne, don't drink that until we get the shot."

My soul started to seethe.

"Here," Avery said, sliding me a small shot of something clear. "It's vodka."

I gratefully tossed it back. "Thanks."

"I've got a flask holstered to my thigh if you need more."

I grinned, deciding I really liked Noah's wife. "Do you have any food on you? I'm starving."

"You can eat after the shoot," the photographer said, even though I hadn't been talking to her.

"Aren't they getting pictures of us enjoying the food?" Avery asked through a posed smile as the camera flashed.

"Apparently we're only supposed to pretend to eat."

We were instructed to use straws so our makeup didn't get mussed. I wasn't allowed to touch my hair and I was positioned in uncomfortable poses no woman would naturally occupy. All for the *end result.*

I thought the end result was marrying Hale but that was just a conspiracy to get me to agree to all this. The real goal, apparently, was every stranger's enjoyment of my wedding over mine.

An hour later I was finally allowed to drink what I wanted to drink and eat the food that had been laid out, but my mouth hurt from smiling for so many photos so I had a hard time chewing.

"Now what?" I asked Seraphina and Quinn as the photographer switched cameras.

"Now, you enjoy. They're going to take candid shots while we pamper ourselves. Just act normal and pretend they're not there."

None of this was normal.

Tyler finally returned, but not with Elle.

"Where is she?"

"She needed to run out to get something for her hair."

"What does she need? I'm sure we have whatever she's looking for at the hotel." I reached into the toiletry basket and held up a tube of cream. "Here, do you need some of this? Or maybe this." I lifted three different shades of pantyhose. "We have everything."

He frowned. "Why is there hemorrhoid cream in there?"

I tossed it back into the basket. "Apparently it helps with puffiness under the eyes. But not a selfish maid of honor."

"Whoa, Ray, take a breath." He stood in front of me, providing the slightest bit of privacy between me and the cameras and countless other people witnessing my meltdown. "You okay?"

I blinked rapidly. "I'm fine."

"Uh, well, that's a lie. What's going on?"

I pressed my lips tight. I'd promised I wasn't going to let Elle spoil this. "Why is a hair product more important than me?"

Tyler's face softened. "Oh, honey, it's not."

"Then why isn't she here?"

Sighing, he said, "I wish I had an answer for you." He hugged me and then looked directly into my eyes. "You're getting married. Think about that for a moment. Forget anyone who doesn't see how monumental that is."

I laughed, coming out of my spiral to share his shock. "Pretty crazy, huh?"

"Not as crazy as you think. Hale's a good guy. He goes after what he wants. Anyone who sees the way he looks at you can see exactly how you got here."

"But you like him?"

"I like seeing you happy and I think he makes you very, very happy."

Now it was my turn to hug him. "I'm so glad you're here, Ty."

"I wouldn't have missed it for the world. Come on. Let's go find some chocolate."

We ate, drank, laughed, and enjoyed all the pampering treats that had been arranged. The paraffin dip was lovely. Our hands were scrubbed with sugar and then dipped into warm wax and wrapped in giant mittens to make our skin extra soft. Everything was going great until they plugged an IV in my arm for some vitamin therapy.

"What is this again?" I had no idea that when I signed up to be a bride I would be drugged, and I was helpless to stop it as my hands had been swaddled in big oven mitts.

"This is micronutrient therapy. You're getting a high dose of vitamins and minerals directly into your bloodstream, which your body will absorb rapidly."

"You'll love it, Rayne," Seraphina commented. "Plus, it should boost your immune system and get rid of that head cold."

"I'm not sick."

"Of course not." She looked completely at ease on the settee in her paraffin mittens as vitamins streamed directly into her vein, somehow managing to make even an IV look like a fashionable accessory.

I, on the other hand, looked like a patient at a psych ward doing some Mickey Mouse cosplay.

When I got back to our personal suite I crawled into bed with a groan. The penthouse was empty and silent, and I prayed it would stay that way for at least a—

The door opened and voices carried. Hale and his mother laughed and chatted softly. It was only day two and I was ready to quit.

"Let me see if she's upstairs," Hale said and I

made no effort to move out of my face-plant pose as his steps carried closer. "Rayne?"

"No more," I groaned into the pillows. I smelled like lemongrass and self-doubt.

Hale quietly went downstairs and said something to his mom. Then the penthouse was silent again. I thought they both left, until the mattress dipped and his hand dragged softly down my back.

"How did your afternoon go?"

"I don't want to talk about it," I groaned, face still plastered to the pillows.

"Keep in mind, this is supposed to be fun."

I dragged my pillow away from my face to look at him. "They stuck a needle in my arm and wanted me to submerge my face in a bucket of ice."

He frowned. "Who did?"

"The army of helpers."

"That's your army. They work for *you*. Tell them to fuck off."

It didn't feel like they worked for me. It felt like I lost all autonomy and had absolutely no control over my life. "Why didn't we elope?"

The creases in his brows disappeared as his face went slack. Real concern reflected in his eyes. Then his jaw hardened and he stood, pulling out his phone. "Rest. I'll handle this."

He left the room and spoke softly. I wasn't sure what he said or who he called, but I could tell immediately that he'd intervened.

The next day, no one directed me. They asked. No one ordered. They requested. While we continued to respect the itinerary, I was now permitted to experience the little moments organically. The photographer was told to only gather candids and the chronic staging and posing stopped.

While it didn't correct the fact that our wedding would be a three hundred guest circus, Hale's interception did ensure that I got to be one of those guests and actually experience my wedding first hand. I got to be present and that mattered to me.

"Thank you," I told him as we sat in a back room of Gotham Hall waiting for our guests to arrive at yet another welcome dinner.

He took my hand. "For what?"

"Toning down the performance stuff."

"You let me know if it happens again. This is our wedding. It's for us. I plan to make damn sure you enjoy it."

Hale's love overwhelmed me on a daily basis, but when he rescued me from situations like he had today, he truly shined as my hero. "I love you."

He closed the distance and kissed me. Left in a daze of lust, the world seemed softer when he pulled away. He glanced down at my lace top where only white floral appliqués covered my breasts. "You look incredibly beautiful tonight."

A knock interrupted and Devyn appeared. "They're ready for you."

"Give us a minute," Hale said with absolute influence.

"Of course. Whenever you're ready, sir."

Devyn bowed out politely and I smiled up at him. "You're so hot when you throw your authority around."

"You have just as much authority as me, Rayne. Never forget that." His thumb dragged slowly across my plump lower lip and he grinned. "Four more sleeps until you're mine."

If only he understood, I was his since the first moment he clapped eyes on me.

The welcome dinners were like a tournament of scrimmage weddings. Sort of *Hunger Game*-ish, but with less bloodshed, sabotage, and, unfortunately, less Jennifer Lawrence—my ultimate girl crush.

Tonight's mock wedding included our family and wedding party and whatever guests arrived early for the festivities. Sprays of white flowers and twinkling lights created the perfect ambiance for people to socialize and sip cocktails while the chefs put on a show.

Elle and Paul arrived before the first course this time but after our introduction. I had been talking with Barrett the moment they sat down and his expression completely changed mid-sip.

"Barrett?" I followed his gaze to Elle, looking as beautiful as ever. And there was bloated Paul by her side. Were his arms actually getting bigger?

When I looked back at Barrett, his mouth was a flat line. He set down his glass. "Excuse me."

I thought to alert Hale, but he was currently occupied with other guests. I cursed under my breath, dropping my napkin onto my seat and rising to go after him.

He disappeared through a private door marked for the restaurant staff and I found him in a long narrow hall. "Barrett, wait."

"Go back to the party, Meyers."

"Not without you."

He stopped and let out a frustrated huff. We

were in some sort of employee portal. Servers kept passing with trays of champagne and clatter spilled from the kitchen whenever the service door swung open.

"You can't let her get to you." He was clearly upset that he lost control of his emotions.

"She's allowed to fuck whoever—"

"I know she can sleep with whoever she wants. You've said it enough. But that doesn't make it hurt less to see her moving on."

He looked up at the ceiling, his eyes closing in frustration. "Why that guy?"

I laughed. "What, you don't like Paul?"

"What does she see in him?"

"I have no idea." I smirked, understanding his confusion. "I don't think it'll last." I hoped it wouldn't. Not that I wanted Elle to have her heart broken, but the guy was a total tool bag.

"Tell me I'm better than that guy."

"There's no competition, Barrett." I held his arms and looked him right in the eye. "You're an incredible guy. You're fun. Sensitive. Caring. And hot. Almost every woman out there has fantasized about sleeping with you. The men out there want to be you. You could literally have your pick of almost anyone in this entire building. Plus, Paul's a putz."

He laughed then glanced over my shoulder. "Not every woman."

I sighed. "She's not over you. She's trying, but you're not an easy person to forget."

His smile was sweet. "Thanks." He looped his arm around me and pulled me into a hug.

It was nice hiding in the shelter of his arms,

away from all the strangers on the other side of the door. For a moment, I fantasized that I didn't have to go back to the party. But then the hug ended and reality beckoned.

"We should get back." We both turned and stilled. Hale stood at the end of the narrow corridor, his expression blank and his eyes cold.

"Uh-oh."

Speak Now

OR FOREVER HOLD YOUR PEACE

"Are you going to talk to me?"

"I have nothing to say." Hale removed his tie and tossed it onto the accumulating pile of accessories.

"You haven't spoken to me since dinner."

"It's late, Rayne. Tomorrow's another big day. I just want to shower and get some sleep." Without fully undressing, he closed himself into the bathroom and started the shower.

This was an unfamiliar side of Hale. He didn't avoid confrontation. That was my schtick.

Hale found confrontation constructive and believed in resolving challenges the moment they arose, so I didn't have a clue why now, of all times, he was choosing to avoid me.

He was obviously bothered by finding Barrett and I hidden away in a private corridor—hugging. I'd explained the situation. His brother was upset. A perfectly normal response to watching Elle with Paul. But Hale didn't see it that way.

"People were looking for you," he'd said accusingly, and I knew that wasn't true.

"Who?" He and I both knew I wasn't important enough to provoke a search party after five minutes.

"Tyler."

Okay, maybe Tyler was wondering where I'd disappeared to, but other than him and Hale, no one else would have noticed that I left.

I'd tried to reason with him. "Hale, if you would have seen how upset Barrett got you would have followed him too."

"No, I would have remembered that my brother's a grown man perfectly capable of taking care of himself."

When it was clear he was going to be a total bitch about it, I gave up and returned to the party. There were too many people around for us to continue bickering, so we let it drop. Mostly.

All night, whenever I asked him if he was okay, he just said, "I'm fine."

Did he think I was born yesterday? I knew more than anyone what a crock of bullshit that line was. No one was ever fine when they said they were fine.

He took so long in the shower, I passed out before he made it to bed, which was probably a good thing. Sometimes the best solution was a little space to cool off—especially when one person was dead set on being a total drama queen about absolutely nothing.

The next morning I had a full schedule. I needed to get my wedding spray tan so it had time to set and the stink could wear off. Then I had to visit the florist with Quinn to preview the flowers —not really sure what I would add to that, but it was nice to be included.

Then I was having lunch with my mom and future mother-in-law at *Le Crocodile* at the Whythe Hotel over in Brooklyn. And after that we had the rehearsal dinner, which meant I needed to have the conversation I'd been putting off.

By the time I showered and put on a robe, Hale was already fully dressed to conquer the world and reading a freshly printed copy of the *New York Times*.

As soon as I sat, Percy brought me my usual— a macchiato and fresh croissant from the patisserie I loved over in Greenwich Village.

"Thanks, Percy."

Hale barely looked up from his paper.

My desperation to explain myself was over-shadowed by annoyance. It was bad enough that I had to go to bed last night with him upset with me, but was he seriously carrying his mood over into a new day?

"Good morning," I said pointedly.

"Morning." He turned the page of his paper, but still didn't look up.

I gaped at him—not that he noticed. "You have your meeting with Clayton today?"

"Correct. I'm leaving shortly and I should be back no later than three."

I frowned at his cool tone. He still hadn't kissed me or even made eye contact for that matter. I forced a smile and tried again. "It's our rehearsal dinner tonight."

"I'm aware of the schedule." His eyes scanned

the columns of dense text. "Maybe you could attend the entire dinner this time."

"That's it." I yanked the paper out of his hands. "Your brother was upset. I was making sure he was okay—"

"Barrett's a grown boy, Rayne. He doesn't need you coddling him."

I scoffed. "I wasn't *coddling* him. I was being a friend."

"He has plenty of other friends to help him. You're the bride. People notice when you disappear."

"Is that what this is about? You're afraid people might see me disappear with your brother and think something's going on between us? Do you know how ridiculous you sound, Hale? I'm marrying *you.*"

He glanced at Elara's shoes and folded outfit laid out on the settee to his right. "It's not that ridiculous to be territorial when it comes to those I love."

Once again, this was about Jasmine and his father. "Well, thanks a lot. I'm so glad we're getting married in two days and you still don't trust me." I grabbed the baby clothes and headed toward the door.

"I trust you."

"If you trusted me you wouldn't be acting this way."

"I do trust you, Rayne. But you have to understand how your behavior looks to others."

I slowly turned. He was not doing this to me. Hale was the guy who finally made me believe that I didn't need to change to suit the world. "Don't."

"Don't what?"

"Ask me to perform for them."

"Decorum is not a tall order."

"Decorum? *Gah!* You sound like a total snob. He's your brother, Hale. He's your brother and he's hurting. I won't apologize for comforting him, no matter how weird or scandalous high society thinks that is. The problem is with your perception of the situation, not my actions. You're making this into something it's not and now you're pissing me off."

"Rayne—"

"No. I get it. Fragile Hale needs to prove his virility."

"That's not true."

"Then what is this? Why don't you just piss a circle around me so the world knows I'm taken." I showed him my engagement ring as if flipping him off with the wrong finger. "This isn't an ear tag, Hale. I'm your partner, not your property. I can talk to whoever I want. And do you honestly think your brother would ever betray you like that?"

"No, I don't," he snapped. "But I never believed my father could either."

"Jesus." I pinched the bridge of my nose. "How many more times are we going to come back to this?"

"As many times as it takes." He looked away and I understood that these insecurities were as frustrating for him as they were for me.

I reminded myself that we all came with baggage, and I had plenty. We could deal with this— whatever it was.

I never knew what to call it. It wasn't irrational

behavior. Jealousy, yes, but I could sympathize with how he got here. Hale was territorial for a reason. The man had severe PTSD from his father's betrayal. While he trusted me a lot more than he trusted anyone else, I seemed the exception to the rule. This wasn't really about trust, though.

It was about saving face. All of it.

No one outside of Hale, his father, Jasmine, and myself knew the reality. Yet he constantly acted like he had something to prove. But the world wasn't getting it, because they didn't know the score.

Hale feared having their shameful history exposed. He liked control, and that entire traumatic experience had stolen his control in ways he was still trying to process. Still, that didn't excuse him to go around pounding his chest and making insulting accusations at the people who loved him.

While he tolerated my endless idiosyncrasies, I simply didn't have the energy to jump back on the merry-go-round of his daddy issues today. Not when I was exhausted from mentally contending with my own.

"I'm going to check on Elara. Then I have a full day. I just wanted to tell you, my dad's not coming."

His entire disposition changed and his bullshit took a back seat as he looked at me with a mixture of concern and shock. "What happened?"

There was my answer. If he knew about the credit card charges, he hadn't linked it to my father.

I shrugged, not wanting to insert any of that

ugliness into our special week. The man had already spoiled enough special moments in my life.

"Change of heart."

"Oh, Rayne." Hale crossed the room and hugged me. "I'm so sorry, baby. Is there any way we can change his mind?"

I shook my head. "It's fine." That phrase was the biggest lie in the English language. "Anyway, we'll have to let Quinn know so she can rework the ceremony."

"Will you ask your mom to walk you down the aisle?"

I shrugged. "I don't know. I'll figure something out by tonight."

His brow pinched and he studied me for a long moment. "Are you okay?"

I forced a smile and repeated my bullshit mantra, "I'm fine."

I left before he could say anything else.

The day moved quickly yet somehow still felt a hundred years long. My life had become a series of holding patterns. I dressed for an event, was transported to said event, and placed in the next isolation booth as I waited for the event to get underway.

I was grateful that tonight's rehearsal dinner would be the last so-called welcome dinner of the week. Once I had my makeup, dress, and shoes on, my work was basically done, so I waited in the master bedroom of the penthouse until it was time to leave.

I could have easily waited downstairs with the bridesmaids, but...I was hiding. These moments of quiet were few and far between and I needed them to build up my strength.

Hale was checking in with his groomsmen down the hall. As soon as he returned, we would be on our way.

When someone knocked at the door, I tensed. "Who is it?"

"Remington."

That was unexpected. I crossed the room, my rehearsal dress whispering softly with each step as I opened the door. "What's wrong?"

"Nothing's wrong. I wanted to speak to you in private."

He entered the master bedroom and took a seat on the gilded chair by the window, then on second thought moved to the settee at the foot of the bed. The rain had aggravated his bad leg and his steps were stiffer than usual.

"Where's your cane, Remington?"

"In my closet at home where it belongs. Sit down." He patted the seat next to him.

I lowered to the settee. "What's up?"

"I was talking to Hale."

"Oh, boy."

"Relax. It was just a talk. I'm not going to argue with him during the week of his wedding."

If the man was capable of biting his tongue for one week he could do us all a favor and aim for other occasions as well. But I was grateful for what I could get.

"Thank you for taking it easy on him."

"Anyway…" He patted a weathered hand on my knee and sighed. "Hale told me about your dad."

His words hung in the silent room for a moment, both of us recognizing the weight they carried. Remington wasn't much for touchy-feely sentiment, but that didn't mean he was incapable of compassion.

"My father's a, um, complicated man."

"Your father's an idiot."

I laughed. Not hard, but a small chuckle slipped out. I had to agree with him.

"You know, when I met you, Meyers, I thought you were an absolute basket case. But there was something special about you. Something impossible to ignore. Hale saw it too. It's hard not to fall in love with you on the spot. You're like a helpless kitten, going the wrong way on a busy highway. Big men can't resist that sort of temptation."

"Thanks," I said dryly, not exactly loving the scenario where I was the helpless idiot or victim.

"I mean that in the best possible way. There's an innocence about you. Not naiveté, but innocence. Sweetness. You're a good girl. A good man appreciates that and wants to protect it. Too many hardships can harden a girl, but you've somehow managed to stay the perfect measure of wholesome and hardy. You're soft when it matters, but resilient where it counts."

That was much better than being compared to a lost kitten with zero survival skills. "Thanks."

"You know I care about you."

I gave him a shoulder bump. "Don't make me cry, Remington. I have six pounds of makeup on my eyes and no desire to put it there again."

He glanced at my done-up face and nodded his understanding. "Sometimes, parents miss what's right in front of them. We don't always see our children the way the world sees them. It's our loss." He took a moment to process his own words and I knew he was thinking about Hale, Barrett, and Seraphina. "I'm sorry your father couldn't appreciate the gift he was given when you came into his life."

My chest and throat instantly tightened and my eyes started to prickle. "Remington…"

"Just let me get this out." He cleared his throat and grimaced. "I, uh, guess what I'm trying to say, is… I…" He cleared his throat again. "I love you, Meyers. I don't like seeing you hurt."

Remington avoided sentimental words like the plague so his confession stunned me. "What are you doing to me?"

He held up a hand, playing down his admission. "I think of you a lot like the way I think of my other children. I worry about you when you're sick. I want to do what I can to make the difficult stuff easier on you, but I also want to see you overcome the challenges life throws your way. You're innocent, Meyers, but you're also tough. That's the one thing you can thank your dad for. He's made you resilient. Growing up without him taught you independence. You don't need him. Not today, or on your wedding day, or any other day."

A tear fell past my lashes, but I didn't care. My heart lodged in my throat and I couldn't speak, but that was for the best. I heard everything he was saying, and I treasured his words.

"I want to say something to you, but I want to make it clear that I have absolutely no expectations. I didn't come here with a motive. I only came here because Hale told me what happened and I wanted to make sure you were all right. But, Meyers, if you want someone to walk you down that aisle on Saturday, it would be my honor to escort you."

My hand covered my mouth as my composure crumbled. "Oh, Remington."

"Now, see, you're going to spoil your makeup." He pulled the pocket square from his jacket and stuffed it in my hand.

I dabbed my eyes and tried to level my breathing, but I was a mess. "Oh, God…" I blubbered and he looked away uncomfortably. "Did Hale put you up to this?"

He scowled. "Hale doesn't even know I'm here."

"But he told you."

"Yes." He looked at me with those perceptive silver eyes, so similar to Hale's but glassier and flecked by time. "He knows I'd do anything for you, Meyers. If that was him manipulating me, this is one case when I'm okay with it."

I shut my eyes and breathed a deep sigh. That wasn't just Hale playing his dad. That was Hale putting his own feelings about the man aside in order to do something nice for me. No matter how much they butted heads, or how frustrating Hale found our relationship, he knew Remington was the closest thing I had to a father. And if my dad couldn't give me away, Hale was going to do whatever he could to find the next best solution.

"Thank you, Remington."

He patted my knee and stood. "You think about it. We don't have to decide tonight."

"But it's the rehearsal."

"So? I've lived my whole life without rehearsing. I prefer it that way. Keeps things interesting."

The wedding planners wouldn't like that, but having Remington's blessing to take my time meant no one would dare rush me to make up my mind.

I stood. "Thank you. I'll let you know."

He placed his hand on the doorknob and looked down, presenting me with his back. "You look gorgeous, by the way."

I smiled. "Thanks."

"Fix your face before you go out there."

He slipped out the door and I laughed.

Remington was the only one who didn't care about impressing others. But he did care about me.

Everyone Just Calm Down!

THE REHEARSAL WAS FUN. More fun than anything else so far. We got to see the rooftop where the ceremony would be and, once we had everyone standing in their designated spots, I could finally envision our big day.

The turf on the roof was still soggy from the rain, but Quinn assured me it was nothing but blue skies until Saturday and everything would be dry in time for the ceremony.

After rehearsing we went to dinner and enjoyed another incredible meal. Elle seemed to finally start filling her role as maid of honor. She stayed by my side, listened to the advice of the planners, and was very helpful. I should have appreciated her efforts, but it all seemed too little too late, as if she was only stepping up because others were watching. I knew then, we were officially broken.

I also knew I didn't want to process everything that meant until after the wedding, so I accepted it and put it away for another day. Smiling, I took her hand and squeezed. "Thank you."

She paused as if taken off guard. "For?"

"Three decades of good memories." It was more than most people got and I decided to be grateful for the good times we shared.

Her expression eased. "We did have fun, didn't we?"

I laughed, thinking back to the keggers, breakouts, breakups, bad dates, sleepovers, dances, and all the other special memories. "A lot of fun."

Maybe Elle was only meant to be a part of my earlier life. I wasn't even mad about the things she said anymore. I was sad that that chapter of my life was coming to an end, sure, but not devastated. I had a new chapter to look forward to, now, and I couldn't wait for the next adventure to begin.

I scanned the table, my gaze falling on Hale as he had a lively discussion with Noah about sports. There was my real best friend. And he was in his glory, surrounded by those he loved.

"Rayne, taste this." My mom nudged her way between Elle and I and Elle took the interruption as a chance to return to Paul. "It's made from passion fruit. I couldn't even tell you what a passion fruit looks like." She was tipsy, but no longer hosting regular inquisitions with strangers.

I tasted her drink, my face pursing tightly. "Wow, Mom, that's really tart."

"You think it's too sweet? I like it." She hiccupped. "This is my second one. That's the most passion I've had in one night in probably… Well…" As she started counting on her fingers I moved on.

Barrett seemed to be handling the Paul situation better. He'd been flirting with the waitress as a distraction. Elara was behaving, and Remington had made what was probably one of the sweetest gestures of my lifetime.

In short, I was happy.

Odette was in attendance, which I thought might be weird since Hale's mom was also there, but Naomi had a special relationship with her ex-husband no other woman could touch. As Remington's first love, Naomi was the only person alive who could get away with calling him Remy. It was as if Remington was perpetually a young man in her eyes. Odette was happy to give them their memories and claim the seasoned version of the man he was now.

As I looked around the table at our family and closest friends, excitement swirled in my stomach. No cramps. No nerves. Just excitement.

Hale had spent the day with Clayton and that seemed to be enough to cool off his temper from the night before. That, and I think he realized that I was dealing with a lot on account of my father. And he didn't even know the worst of it.

Learning that my dad wasn't going to show up for our wedding, brought out Hale's compassionate side, which was probably why he didn't open the manilla folder he had in hand when he returned from Clayton's office earlier that afternoon.

I knew what it was.

When Hale was in the shower I unwound the fastened string and peeked at the cover page. I'd seen our names printed like that before and I knew perfectly well what those red SIGN HERE tabs implied.

We were going to sign the prenup after all. That was fine. I knew he wouldn't be able to get out of it. I'd already come to terms with the fact that these things came with obscenely wealthy spouses. The sting would wear off eventually.

Strangely, the impending ick wasn't associated with Hale. I connected those unsavory feelings of marital business deals to his father, a man who admittedly loved me, but would always love his assets a little more.

I didn't want Hale's money so I didn't care if he or his father protected it. I just wanted him. A piece of paper wasn't going to change that. And my love wasn't enough to change how the Davenports conducted their affairs.

Remington did love me. But he wasn't the person that should give me away.

I looked to my mother. Should I ask her? She'd been the one to raise me after all. I just couldn't shake the feeling that assigning her such a duty might stress her out more than flatter her. She'd been having such a good time all week I didn't want to ruin it.

As I looked across the table, I watched my mother laugh and pat Hale's cheek with such affection. Hale teased her, sort of the way he teased me. It was such a sweet picture, I took a mental snapshot, wanting to keep it in my heart always.

A glass clanked and voices quieted.

"Can I have your attention, please?" Barrett stood, something amber filling the rocks glass in his hand, strong enough to cause his words to come out slightly slurred. He leaned heavily into the chair at his left. "When my brother told me he was going to ask Rayne to be his wife, my first thought was it's too soon. But then I considered Hale and I got to know Rayne, and it somehow made complete sense."

He looked at his brother and shook his head then chuckled to himself. "Hale, you've always *relentlessly* gone after whatever you want. It's easy to see why you'd want Rayne. She's beautiful, clever, quick with a comeback, and able to laugh at herself in the best way." He glanced at me and the room collectively held its breath. "All-in-all..." He smiled, our stares holding. "You're the whole package, Meyers." He cleared his throat and looked back at his brother. "When you told me you wanted to marry her, I knew it was a sure thing."

The weight of Hale's arm rested protectively over my shoulders. I looked up at him, but his stare was locked on his brother—his expression unreadable.

Barrett's gaze returned to mine. "No one's ever made my brother smile the way you do. You've given him more..." He hiccupped. "...for the rest of us to envy."

The air thinned and tension tightened around us. I smiled nervously. Where was he going with this?

"Wrap it up, Barrett," Hale said under his breath.

The ice clanked in Barrett's glass as he lifted it high overhead. "Meyers, you have a way of making imperfection sexy as hell." He grinned and winked at me. "Never change." Tossing back the rest of his drink, he swallowed the last gulp. "To both of you."

"Kiss!" someone yelled as silverware tapped crystal and there was an eruption of chimes and cheers.

Hale, with his hand on my back, bent down and kissed me sweetly. Then he shook his brother's hand and lifted his own glass in salute.

"Rayne and I would like to thank all of you for traveling here to be a part of our special day. We did our best to plan an extraordinary week, and I hope you're as happy as we are to finally be here. Tonight, I feel like a king—on top of the world." He glanced at me and smiled. "And I've finally found my queen."

"Here, here!"

Hale's lips pressed to mine and my stomach cartwheeled. I might never get over the thrill of having the complete attention of such a potent man. As he pulled away, I caught a glimpse of Barrett staggering toward the bar.

The final courses were served and cleared, but liquor continued to pour and Barrett didn't miss a drop. He finally slowed down when Elle and Paul left just before the coffee and desserts were served.

I thought I was done wondering what I had or hadn't done to deserve her indifference. There wouldn't be a redo on this milestone and Elle missed all of it. Physically she was here, but mentally and emotionally she abandoned me.

I wanted to be stronger. I didn't want to chase people who didn't want to love me. I had so much in front of me to celebrate, and that should be enough. But something still hurt when I thought about Elle. Maybe it always would.

So I sulked, ruining a perfectly fine slice of tiramisu.

"You okay?" Barrett slid into the vacant seat to my left.

"I'm fine."

"When a woman says she's fine she's full of crap. You're mutilating that cake."

I set the fork down and pushed the plate away. "She hasn't even congratulated me."

"Are we talking about Elle and Bozo the Beefcake?"

"Yes. She's showing up for the bare minimum and acting like a hero. But behind the scenes there's this sense of animosity I can't shake and no one seems to feel or see it but me."

"Do you think she's jealous?"

"Of me?" I laughed. "No. We've never been competitive with each other."

"*You're* not competitive, but that doesn't mean she can claim the same. Maybe she always felt like she had her life more together and she can't handle that things look different now. Things changed, Meyers. Look around."

My brow pinched. "But I'm still me. This isn't what my day-to-day life looks like." Usually, it's a dumpster fire racing downhill on wheels.

I sighed. It wasn't even all Elle. It was Elle and my dad, the two of them teaching me a life lesson I didn't want to learn right now.

Barrett bumped my shoulder. "Your life's never going to go back to what it was. It won't always be a wedding, but it will be other things. Hale's a high-profile guy. You're his person. Sorry to break it to you, but the fanfare doesn't go away." He sipped his drink. "It's also annoying how easy Hale makes perfection seem."

"Your brother's far from perfect."

"I know that, but the world doesn't. After a while, even our closest friends fall for the charade and start to covet what's ours."

I thought of the droves of women who hit on Hale, especially since the wedding coverage. Females wanted what they couldn't have, and they could not have Hale. He was mine.

Barrett was right. I reached for more champagne and confessed, "I hear what they say—in the lady's room—when they don't realize I'm listening."

"There are women out there who would stop at nothing to steal him from you, but Hale's one of the most loyal men I know. You don't have to worry about trusting him. But never trust them, Rayne. Once you're officially a Davenport—"

"I'll still be me."

"Maybe. But to the outside world, you'll be one of us. Then you'll see."

I took his glass out of his hand and set it aside. "I'm sorry she stopped seeing you for you. It's her loss, Barrett. *Hers.*"

He retrieved his glass. "Don't let them change you, Meyers. You're going to attend all those things. You know how this world works. Mark your territory now. On the surface, it's going to look like an endless cycle of galas, gowns, and glamour, but your life will be surrounded by sharks. Don't let anyone get close enough to hurt you. Protect yourself and what's yours."

"I get it."

"Do you? You can't be Rayne Myers the cotton-clad townie anymore if you want to be Rayne Davenport wife of Hale Davenport. Aristocracy is a part. It's the role we play. The moment we show any vulnerability the vultures come to eat us alive."

"I thought they were sharks."

He tipped back his glass, sucking down the last drop. "Sharks, vultures, snakes, they're all a bunch of blind fucks who can't see past our wealth. You're lucky Hale's loyal. Don't expect the rest of them to be."

"You're drunk and you sound bitter."

"I am drunk, but I'm giving you pearls."

"Yeah, well, the vultures have already pecked the meat off the bone where I'm concerned."

Just that morning I read another tabloid smear about a poll that let people vote on ten other women better suited for Hale. According to the media's views, he was supposed to be marrying some perfume heiress from Finland. It still stung to read such hateful drivel, but I was learning not to let their words affect me as deeply as they once had.

"Hale likes me the way I am and that's how I intend to stay."

Barrett picked up my hand, which had been dipped and polished and manicured to glove model quality. The diamond of my ring flashed under the candlelight.

"Sorry, kid. It's already happening."

I frowned at my fingers, no longer covered in

ink smudges or pen. My once bitten-down nails, now artificial and long.

Diamonds glinted in the candlelight as I turned my ring. These superficial things didn't change who I was, but I understood what he was saying.

"Inside, you're still you, but outside the world sees the affluence. In their eyes, this is what you've become." He tapped the enormous stone of my engagement ring. "I wish I could say our friends are immune to the impact of privilege, but they're not. When they say money changes people, they're not just talking about the people who have it. They're mostly talking about the people on the sidelines looking in."

"Elle and I have never been rivals."

"Because it wasn't a competition—back then. That's what I'm saying. Things change. Perspective changes. Look at the view, Rayne. You're on top of the world."

He was right, but understanding the why didn't make it any easier to process. "Why can't she just be happy for me?"

"Because she's too unhappy with herself."

I looked at him, the profoundness of his words cutting right to my heart. "I did everything I could for her."

He nodded. "And now it's time to stop worrying if she's okay and start focusing on yourself again."

I tried, but it wasn't that simple. I didn't know how to just turn off my concern for someone I loved longer than my memories.

He nudged my shoulder. "Good advice for both of us." Looping his arm around me, he defused the conversation by minimizing the loss. "Fuck her. Or, better yet, maybe I'll fuck the waitress."

I rolled my eyes. The way the restaurant staff fawned over him he could form a harem. "Which one, the blonde or the redhead?"

"Maybe both."

I elbowed him and his arm tightened, yanking me into a jerky side hug. "You're such a pig—"

"Why is it every time I turn around your hands are plastered on my fiancée?" I froze at Hale's sharp, disapproving tone.

"Hale," I admonished, appalled that he would make such an accusation, but he remained unfazed.

Voices quieted and guests glanced at us. He was making a scene.

Barrett frowned and lifted his arm off my shoulder. "What's wrong with you?"

Hale towered over us, scowling with dark disapproval. "Why are you always touching her?"

"We were just talking."

"Talking like you were talking the other night?"

"Whoa." Barrett stood and I followed. "Is there something you want to say to me?"

"Hey," I whispered, trying to defuse the situation.

"Yeah, stop touching my fucking fiancée."

I grabbed his arm, stunned he would speak that way to his brother, especially in front of guests. Keeping my voice low, I tried to pull him away from the table. "You're not doing this right now—"

"This isn't about me." He pulled his arm out of my grip. "It's about the two of you, always whispering, always acting secretive. Sneaking away."

"Yo, why don't you ease up?" Barrett snapped. "You're making an ass out of yourself."

Hale scoffed. "Right. You put your hands all over my fiancée, I call you out, and somehow I'm the asshole."

"We were sitting at the damn table!"

Seraphina approached and whispered through a fake smile, "I don't know what you two are arguing about, but you're making a spectacle."

Everyone had stopped talking. Our mothers, Andrew, Tyler, Noah, and Avery, even Remington stared at the three of us wondering what they missed. A scorching heat washed over my face. I could only be grateful that this was a private dinner.

Hale looked around, his composure sliding back into place, but not before Barrett opened his mouth again. "Yeah, why don't you take a walk and cool off."

Hale's glare snapped to his brother. "Because the minute I turn my back you'll be all over her again."

"Hale!" I could not believe him.

"Boys," Remington growled.

"Stay out of it!" Hale barked.

"You're out of line," Barrett snapped, storming off and purposefully knocking into his brother's shoulder.

I glared up at Hale. "Nice. You just insulted me and your brother. Apologize to your guests." I turned to leave, needing a minute to cool off, and Hale caught my arm.

"Don't you dare go after him."

I shook off his hold and scoffed. "I wasn't, you big jerk. I was getting away from you." Mortification burned through me as everyone stared.

"Pardon me," the server appeared at absolutely the worst moment and Hale snapped.

"What?"

"Sir, there seems to be an issue with the bill."

I could feel the earth shifting beneath me.

"Your credit card has been declined."

My stomach plummeted.

"That's impossible," Hale snapped and I took a step back as the room grew further and further away. "Run it again."

"I did. Several times, sir. There seems to be a hold on the account. Perhaps you'd like to try a different card or make a call?"

Remington approached. "What's going on?"

"Nothing that concerns you. I have everything under control." But things were spiraling. This was it. He'd already pulled his phone out of his pocket and started to dial the number on the back of the card. It was going to happen here, in front of everyone.

Remington turned to the server. "Where's the manager? Do you know who we are?"

"Stay out of it," Hale growled.

"Here. Use my card."

"Do I look like I need your help?"

"Yes!"

The two broke into a pissing match that only drew more attention to the situation, the volume of their voices climbing until everyone knew something was wrong. When Naomi approached, I backed away.

This wasn't how this night was supposed to go.

Hale was acting like a possessive jackass.

Barrett had run off.

Elle was gone.

My mother was drunk.

Remington was yelling.

And now Elara was crying.

Someone spilled a glass of wine and chaos broke out among the guests who noticeably tried to eavesdrop. The bill wasn't paid and my dad was to blame.

Hale spoke into the phone and frowned. Time slowed down. I couldn't breathe. I needed to get out of there.

This was it. This was the moment of humiliation I'd been dreading. My secret would be revealed, not just to Hale, but to everyone. Come morning, they'd all know I had a father who didn't love me.

A cheat and a thief.

And I, somehow, wasn't good enough for him, so how on earth would I be good enough for Hale?

I couldn't bear their glances or their pity.

I'd be laid bare, in front of the people I wanted to impress most. They'd have questions, but I had no answers.

I didn't know why the first man meant to love me found the job so impossible. What if the second man discovered the same?

I stepped back, again and again until I bumped into the wall.

It was coming. The truth was coming and I couldn't bear the shame so I left, twisting to push through the door into a hall where I ran as fast as I could manage in my towering shoes.

I didn't stop until I was outside of the restaurant looking for Marty. He wasn't there. The street was narrow and cars bottlenecked at the end of the block where some scaffolding and cones had the shoulder blocked off.

At the corner, I spotted Barrett hailing a cab. He might as well have been waving a white flag and holding a life raft. "Barrett, wait!"

He turned and I rushed toward him. "I'm coming with you."

"Meyers, I don't think that's a good—"

I slid past him into the cab.

"Where's Hale?" Barrett scooted onto the back seat and the cabby turned.

"Where to?"

"Away from here."

Barrett frowned. "Rayne, what's going on?"

"I just need to get out of here." On the verge of tears, I snapped, "Drive!"

The cab jerked into traffic and Barrett studied me under the shadows. A tear rolled down my cheek, the dam that had been holding back my emotions started to crumble. One more crack and everything would fall.

"Hey, I'm sorry for whatever I said up there. I'm drunk and I'm an idiot."

"It's not you."

"Don't be mad at Hale. He's a jealous ass, but he loves you. He didn't mean any of it. He and I will be fine. Like water under the bridge. Shit, please don't cry, Meyers."

I swiped away my tears but more fell in their place. "It's not that."

"Then what? Did something else happen?"

"Everything's falling apart! Hale wants a perfect wedding but he's fighting with you and your dad and now the restaurant manager."

"Folks, you gotta give me a destination," the cabby chimed in.

"Just keep driving," Barrett commanded then looked back at me. "What the hell happened after I left?"

I wiped both my eyes and a black smudge smeared across my fingers. "There's a situation. A big situation." My stomach twisted painfully. "Oh, God." I started to hyperventilate.

"Shit. Are you okay?" Barrett pressed a hand to my back, bending me forward. "Breathe. You have to calm down and tell me what the hell is going on."

Sharp, shallow breaths pumped into my lungs but I couldn't seem to exhale or hold enough air in. The dam was breaking and the verbal diarrhea was building. I couldn't hold it in anymore so I let it spill.

"I just...He...I tried...I can't...My dad... Hale..." I wheezed and sobbed shrill snippets of hysterical gibberish.

Every wasted breath left me dizzy and motion sick, but I needed to keep going. I couldn't keep it in any longer.

"He's going to know what he did and wonder why I kept this from him. Fuck! I'm not a liar, Barrett. He's *the liar!* Why? Why wasn't I enough for him to just be my dad? And now… Oh, God. What if he calls it off?"

"Hey, hey, hey. You have to chill out, Rayne. You're not making any sense."

I sat up and swayed, the car turning and my stomach lurching. "I don't want his fucking money!"

"No one thinks you're like that. Did something happen?"

I nodded and sniffled, the scent of pine and cigarette smoke making matters worse. My entire face was soaked with tears and I needed to get out of this cab.

"Can we go somewhere? I can't go back to the hotel right now. I don't want to run into anyone we know. But if I don't get out of this car I'm going to be sick."

"Sure. We'll go somewhere we can hide out for a while." He knocked on the divider. "Head for the Queensboro Bridge."

"You got it."

Barrett pulled the pocket square out of his jacket. "Here. Mop yourself up. You're leaking everywhere."

"Thanks." I blew my nose. "I'm sorry Hale talked to you like that. You didn't do anything wrong."

"I know."

"Hale's just…complicated. He's been through a lot."

"I'm not an idiot. I can put two and two together."

I frowned at him. "What do you mean?"

"Come on, Rayne. My dad. Jasmine. Their marriage isn't a secret."

No, but it was something no one openly discussed. Did Barrett know that it started before Elara was born? And if so, how much did he assume about his niece? "What are you saying?"

"I'm saying she dated Hale first. My dad could have had any woman he wanted. But he poached from his own son."

That didn't clarify how much Barrett actually knew. Did he know they slept together when Hale was still dating her—when Remington's wife, Rachel, was still alive? Did he realize that Hale wasn't Elara's biological father?

"My point is," he continued. "I get why my brother has trust issues. But I'm not his rival. He was out of line tonight."

"He was," I agreed.

"If he wasn't getting married, I would have punched him in the mouth. I'd never betray him like that. I think you're great, Meyers, but you're Hale's. That he could even accuse me of crossing that line infuriates me, but I get how he got that way. The fact that he can somehow stand in the same room with our father shows how strong he is. But he's still human. He's allowed to have a human moment every now and then."

"Hale loves you, Barrett. This jealous side of his, it isn't something he's proud of. I think the closer the wedding gets, the more terrified he is that something's going to ruin it."

He studied me for a long moment. "Are you having second thoughts?"

"No, but there's other stuff going on." We still

had to deal with the prenuptial agreement and then there were all the problems my dad had caused. "Tomorrow's going to be stressful."

"Tomorrow's the bachelor and bachelorette dinner. Maybe that's what he needs, a few drinks to loosen him up."

I wasn't worried about the parties. I was worried about the hours beforehand.

Eventually, Hale would ask me to sign that contract and then I'd have to tell him about my dad. Compiling the stress of a prenup—a document that essentially stated money and trust do not go hand in hand—with the additional taxing proof that deceit and immoral behavior was a direct part of my family tree, well, it was enough to make me run away and hide, which seemed to explain my current situation.

I looked out the window as we traveled under an overhang for the trains rushing above. The buildings had shrunk from skyscrapers to two-story storefronts. Most of the windows were covered with metal cages for the night.

"Where are we?"

"Queens."

The commercial district was clogged with small delicatessens, nail salons, and check cashing stores. The buildings were underwhelmingly brick and concrete, and every free-standing street sign had a bicycle locked to it. We had definitely left the posh luxury of 5th Avenue and Manhattan's Upper East Side.

"Pull over up here." Barrett reached into his pocket and pulled out a wad of cash.

"Do you know where we are?"

"I told you, we're in Queens."

I followed him out of the cab. "What now?"

"You said you wanted to disappear. Now we disappear."

We walked into a small corner bar. The air was thick with cigarette smoke and the patrons didn't look up when we entered. Our attire was an extreme contrast to the casual dress of the other patrons.

"Two beers," he ordered, sliding onto the stool directly in front of the taps.

I climbed onto the seat beside him. "Have you been here before?"

"No."

The bartender dropped two napkins in front of us then covered them with two beers. I looked around at the patrons piled in the booths. A television screen displayed a bright blue background with a music note and a man did something on a laptop to the left. A microphone stood like a lone flagpole at his side.

My gaze moved to the special's board. "They're setting up Karaoke."

Barrett followed my stare. "You want to sing?"

"God, no." But also…kind of yes. "I mean… No. Never mind."

"Chicken."

I scoffed. "Would you sing?"

He shrugged. "Sure."

I glanced back at the man with the laptop. He had a pretty thick binder of song options. Maybe belting out my frustrations was exactly what I needed. That and perhaps something stronger to drink.

"I'd need more than beer to get up there."

He pulled out his black card. "Are we going to Russia or Mexico?"

"Huh?"

"Tequila or vodka? Pick your poison."

The logical voice in my head reminded me that I had a fiancé to worry about and responsibilities in the morning. A sensible bride would get back in a cab and return to Manhattan to face the music. But karaoke dude had music right here and that somehow felt safer than the music waiting at home.

"Let's run for the border."

Barrett whistled at the bartender and held up two fingers. "Two shots of your finest tequila."

There was no Casa Dragones Blanco here, but that was fine. The bartender delivered the shots with a shaker of salt and two questionable lemon slices. I debated briefly if I was going to regret this.

"Let's go, Meyers." Barrett grabbed my hand and slathered it with lemon, then sprinkled the wet mark with salt. "Bottoms up."

I licked, drank, winced, and bit. All while making unpleasant grunts for each increasingly tart step of the way. We slammed down our empty glasses and gasped.

Barrett coughed. "Every time you and I hang out I wake up with rot gut."

I washed the citrus taste down with a swig of beer. "I guess that's our thing."

He laughed and clanked his mug to mine. "The drunken duo."

Forty minutes and several shots later, we were at the microphone belting out the lyrics and yodeling to the Cranberries' *Zombie.* No one clapped when we finished. Nor did anyone ask for an encore. Luckily, we were feeling generous so they didn't have to.

Barrett told Darnell—the guy running the karaoke—to play another one.

As soon as I recognized the beat I cheered, "Ohhhh shit!" My hands were over my head as I swayed to the background *shoops* and shut my eyes, channeling my inner Salt-N-Pepa. No lyrics were needed for this one.

I looked up at Barrett and asked, *"How you doing, baby?"*

He frowned, not knowing *Shoop* as well as I obviously did. "Huh?"

"No, not you." I pushed him out of the way and grabbed the guy at the bar. *"The bow-legged one."*

The man grinned the moment I started dancing in his space.

"What's your name?" I sang, knowing the lyrics by heart.

"Brian," he shouted.

This wasn't about Brian. This was about shooping. I'd gone to the place of no return and there was nothing to do but sing the song to its entirety, so off I went. *"Damn, baby, that sounds sexy."*

"Uh, Rayne." Barrett tried to pull me away, but I was too far gone. "Sorry, man, she's had a long night."

I spun and shouted into the mic just as the beat picked up. *"Here I go!"*

Salt-N-Pepa's timeless lyrics belted from my long-term memory with precision borne of alcohol and accuracy no one sober would trust.

But to my ears, I sounded Grammy-fucking-tastic.

As I danced around the bar, sticking the microphone in the face of any woman over thirty, they jumped in. Our rap skills were magically delicious. My moves were on fire. My voice was a derailed locomotive grinding down the tracks with the melodic grace of an asthmatic smoker. But everyone loved it. Or at least I loved it enough not to care if others were enjoying the show.

After that, I annihilated *Rappers Delight*. Then Barrett performed an earth-shattering rendition of *Benny and the Jets* while I danced backup.

We kicked an entire bottle of Cuervo and dominated the mic, jumping from hip-hop to rock, segueing into some old-school gangster rap then dropping in a Barbara Streisand and Neil Diamond duet to show off our range. It was thirsty work, but we literally sang until the bar closed.

"Where do we pick up our royalty check for tonight's show?" I snorted at my own joke, stumbling into Barrett.

He steadied me, but he was also having a hard time standing. "We should at least get a free drink."

I reached for the microphone only it wasn't there. Darnell was packing up the last of his equipment and our audience was long gone.

"Huh." I looked around. "I think it's time to boot-scoot-and-boogie on out of here. Where's my purse?"

Barrett searched the shadows of the stools. "What did it look like?"

"White. Small." I searched my pockets for my

phone only to remember I was wearing a dress. "Uh-oh."

"What-oh?"

"I think I left my stuff in the cab."

"Fuck." Barrett paid the bartender, but his counting was sloppy and I was pretty sure he tipped more than two hundred percent.

We wandered outside and I shivered. "D'ju have a coat?"

Barrett paused then frowned.

I patted my body. It had gotten a lot colder outside, but hey, it wasn't raining and that was a win.

"We're never going to get a cab this late."

I had nothing on me to call an Uber or even Martel to come get us. "Maybe I left my stuff at dinner." I couldn't remember.

"Goodnight, guys!" Darnell called as he carried his equipment out to an emerald-green Monte Carlo.

"Whoa." I stepped off the curb and my foot landed in a puddle, drenching my shoe. "Oh, man. My pretty shoes."

"Careful." Barrett caught my arm to steady me. "We need to find a taxi."

I searched the empty street. "Maybe a Lyft?"

"Right." He patted his pockets then frowned. "Shit."

"What shit?"

"My phone." When he pulled the door to the bar, it was locked. "No!" He pounded his fist on the darkened window. "Hey, my phone's in there!"

But the place was locked and all the lights were out. The bartender must have gone out the back.

"Barrett?" I shivered, wrapping my arms around my chest as I began to really regret how much I drank. "Please tell me we have a way to get home."

He looked back at me and I knew by the regret in his eyes that we were fucked.

The Snozzberries Taste like Snozzberries

"Fuck, fuck, fuck, fuck, fuck!" I stamped my wet foot. "Barrett, we need a phone!"

"I'm trying." He pounded on the window, but no one answered the door. "Damn it!" He snapped, dragging his hands through his hair as he paced the cracked pavement.

A sharp whistle snagged our attention and Darnell pointed to his car. "If you guys want, I can give you a ride home. I just have to make a few stops along the way."

Barrett and I exchanged glances and he nodded. "Thanks. We really appreciate it."

"Not a problem, my man. Hop in."

I rounded the car with one wet foot and Barrett waved me toward the front passenger door. "No way," I hissed, pushing him to the front seat as I angled for the back.

Every single exposed inch of the interior was upholstered in red velvet. Blue accent lights illuminated the space and gold ruching trimmed the seats. The steering wheel was a silver chain and the car reeked of skunk.

Darnell got behind the wheel. "Can I interest you guys in some Mary-J-Weedies?" He held out a thickly packed blunt the size of a baby's arm. Was he planning on smoking that while he drove?

"No thanks," Barrett said.

"Suit yourself." Darnell lit the reefer and pulled out of the parking spot. "So, where ya'll from?"

"California."

"Oregon." I cocked my head at Barrett. "You're from California?"

"Originally."

"Don't you two know each other?"

It occurred to me there was a lot about Barrett's life I still didn't know. "I'm marrying his brother."

"*Mozel tov*!" A plume of smoke blew from Darrell's lips and hung beneath the red velvet ceiling of the car.

I coughed and tried to find a button for the window, but there wasn't one. "Does this window work?"

"Nah. Old cars."

The longer he smoked the more I was certain I was getting a contact high. When he pulled over, I was grateful for the chance to open my door.

"I should only be five minutes." Darnell grabbed a bag from under the seat and left the car, taking the keys with him.

"I need air," I gasped, pushing open the door and hanging my head out to breathe. Once the smoke left my lungs, I looked at the houses, but didn't see Darnell. "Where did he go?"

"Inside that one." Barrett pointed to a row home with a two-flight stoop.

The lights were on but the curtains were drawn. The longer we waited the more the car cooled.

"Shut the door, Meyers, you're letting all the heat out."

I closed the door and we waited some more. "It's been longer than five minutes, don't you think?"

"At least fifteen."

"What time do you think it is?"

"Probably close to three."

Hale was going to kill me. I started to feel sick with guilt. He must have called my phone twenty times by now.

"Do you think we should see what's taking so long?"

Barrett's frown reflected in the glass as he watched the front door of the house. "I don't know. Let's just wait a little longer."

"I feel like we've been abducted by Snoop Dogg."

"We weren't abducted. We were rescued."

"Oh, come on, Barrett. We're in a red velvet lowrider waiting outside of what I can only assume is a drug deal."

"Here he comes."

I flung myself back in my seat and folded my hands on my lap. "Act casual."

The door opened and Darnell slid behind the wheel. "One down, six to go."

Six? Did he say six?

The next five stops were very much the same. Darnell grabbed something from under his seat and told us to wait in the car, promising to be back in five minutes which was always closer to thirty minutes.

I was exhausted, freezing, and whatever buzz I had was long gone. As we waited outside of what was hopefully the last spot, I was bouncing in my seat.

"What's wrong with you?" Barrett asked, looking over his shoulder.

"I have to pee."

He glanced at the dark, empty road. "No one's around. You can squat—"

"No."

We looked at the row of houses. "There's only one other option."

"You have to come with me."

"Did you think I'd let you go into a strange house alone?" He opened the door and I rushed up the walkway, praying I could hold it long enough to make it to a toilet.

Barrett knocked and the door flung open. A small woman with alabaster skin and a sharp widow's peak stared at us, pursing her dark red lips. "Who are you?"

Music spilled from the door on a cloud of smoke.

"Oh, they're with me." Darnell appeared, pulling the door open. "You guys want a drink?"

"She has to use the bathroom," Barrett said, with a protective arm around my shoulder as I bounced in place and squeezed my thighs together.

"Come in then." The woman turned, forgoing any sense of welcome. "It's this way."

I followed her long swishing ponytail through the house. Every piece of furniture had a person lounging on it, sometimes more than one. No one paid us any mind as they all seemed pretty relaxed and happy just to lie around and chill.

She knocked on the door to the bathroom and it creaked open. "In there."

I rushed inside. When I came out, the girl was gone and Barrett waited.

"We should try to get an Uber," he said. "Darnell seems to be in no rush."

"What time is it?" Bars had closed hours ago and I needed to get home before the sun came up or Hale was going to lose his mind.

"I haven't seen a clock. Let's find someone with a phone."

"Good idea."

We returned to the living room and the music was louder. Darnell was making out with widow's peak.

I looked up at Barrett. "I think we need the jaws of life to break them apart."

He scanned the rest of the room. We seemed to be at the epicenter of a Roman orgy. "Let's just go back to the car."

"I'm not going back outside. Look at him. He's never going to leave. Maybe if he sees us waiting he'll get the point." I was tired and hungry and I just wanted to go home.

"Fine." Barrett motioned toward a battered love seat that was empty.

We sat and I tried to ignore the pornographic

sounds disrupting the music. My stomach growled and Barrett looked at my belly.

"Did you eat a wookie?"

"Shut up. I'm starving. I barely ate at dinner and that was hours ago."

"Here." He handed me a bowl of fruit snacks sitting on the table.

"I'm not going to just eat random candy sitting in a stranger's house. That's like the setup of every after school special."

"Fine." He set the bowl between us on the love seat.

Five minutes later, someone crescendoed into a near climax and I lost my patience. "Give me the damn fruit snacks." I poked through the selection and picked out a yellow one, sniffing it suspiciously. It smelled like pineapple.

"Hmm. These are actually pretty good. Try one."

He gave his selection way less thought and popped one into his mouth. "They are good." He took another one.

"Ooh, the pinks are strawberry."

Barrett tried a pink. "I like the orange ones better. They taste like marmalade."

We sat back and passed the time eating fruit snacks and waiting for Darnell and widow's peak to finish. A guy with a long ponytail asked if we wanted a drink but I couldn't drink anymore.

"No thanks."

"You sure? We have tea."

Tea actually sounded great. Since losing my coat I couldn't shake the chill in my bones. "I'll take a hot tea."

"How about you?" he asked Barrett.

"How about a phone?"

The man laughed and Barrett mimicked the sound with a cranky lilt. When the guy walked away I nudged him. "Be nice or they'll kick us out."

"Oh no, whatever will we do then?"

"I'm not going back to the cold car."

When the guy with the ponytail returned with two hot teas, I gratefully accepted mine. It was warm and my stomach needed something to silence the stress grumbles.

"*Bleck!*" Barrett grimaced. "This tea's bitter as shit."

"Really? I think it's sort of earthy and calming. I mean, I've had better, but it's not terrible. At least it's warm." I stared for a long time at the nap of the carpet as I sipped from the mug. "Do you think this is shag?" I dragged my foot over the brown fur.

"Shag?" Barrett repeated, cocking his head. He looked ready to fall asleep as he leaned into my side. "Shaaaaaaaaag." He laughed. "Shhhhhhhh-hhh-ag." He laughed harder.

"What's so funny?"

"Shagagagagagagag. I don't know." He slid his foot out from the loveseat and dragged it next to mine. "I'm thirsty. My tea's gone."

I became very aware of my tongue. "Mine too. Here. Have another fruit snack." We continued to contemplate the carpet as time lost all meaning.

"Yo." Darnell stood over us, the single syllable of his speech coming out like the slow note of a Whitney Houston song.

"Sup, dog?" I said, doing my best Randy Jackson. Randy had something to do with Whitney, right? Or was that Mariah? "I fucking love Christmas."

"Did you guys eat that whole bowl of gummies?" His voice faded like a dream.

Suddenly everyone was there but far away. I was trapped in some sort of soundproof barrier safe enough to make Nixon jealous. No matter what I said, no one could hear me. "It's like super-Watergate. We're invisible."

Darnell spoke, but I couldn't hear him. I laughed and looked at Barrett, but he was staring really hard at his fingernails. I snorted and pushed him, then he looked at me and gasped.

"Meyers? When did you get here?"

"Oh, fuck," Darnell said his voice coming closer again. "We've got a green out, people!"

"Darnell," Barrett laughed. "Where's your… thing?"

"My what?"

"Your…" Barrett mimed something long and slender, then patted his lips. "You know. The stick. With the noise."

I squinted one eye as my lip lifted like Elvis. "Spear? Yodel? Javelin! Spoon." I tried to guess at whatever game he was playing. "Animal or mineral?"

"No, you can't eat it," Barrett said itching his ear. He suddenly flinched when he noticed the lamp to his right. "When did that get here?"

Widow's peak came over. "Why are your friends laying on my floor?"

"Hey, we *are* on the floor." I laughed, shoving

Barrett who was talking to a lampshade. "You're in love with that light."

"The shade's so fringy. D'you get this at Bergdorf?"

He was speaking cursive. Nothing made sense yet it all made perfect sense. "I feel good."

"They ate an entire bowl of gummies." Darnell said, looking down at us. "They're high as fuck."

"Microphone!" I yelled.

"Yes!" Barrett grabbed me and shook my entire body. "That's it!"

"Darnell has a microphone!" I snorted, unable to stop laughing.

A bunch of people gathered over us, staring down as they formed a circle.

I suddenly stopped laughing. "Whoa. Am I dead? Am I looking up from the grave?"

Next thing I knew I was sitting on a bench outside of a twenty-four-seven quickie mart eating an ice cream cone. "I love ice cream."

Barrett sat next to me, turning his own cone to lick around the edge. "I like when there's a little chocolate surprise at the end."

I snorted and doubled over in laughter. When I caught my breath, I looked around. "How did we get here?"

He paused and cocked his head. "I don't know."

I shrugged and continued licking my ice cream. "Do you think there was something in that tea?"

"Like what?" He gasped. "Aw, man, I hit the chocolate prize. Yes!"

The lights inside the quickie mart were really bright. Every few seconds they flickered and hummed. "Do you hear that?" I swatted the air around my ear.

"I hear everything," Barrett said, covering and uncovering his ears. "I hear Taylor Swift right now."

"I always hear Taylor Swift."

"Let's go find her."

We were up and moving. Then we were standing in front of the clerk at the counter. "Is Taylor here?" Barrett asked.

The man at the counter frowned. "You're back."

"We're looking for T-Swift. Tell her Davenport and Fickledump are here."

"What the? Am I Fickledump? What does that even mean?" But Barrett had moved on to the chip aisle and left me standing over there. "Hey, I thought we were a team, man! You don't leave a bear out in the woods with no coverage, you got me? There are spies everywhere!"

"Quiet." He struggled to open a bag of cheese puffs.

I snatched it out of his hands. "You have to pay for that first or we'll go to jail!"

"Hey, I'm workin' ova' here!" He looked around. "Whoa, it's daytime in here." Then he gasped. "I hear Taylor Swift. Come on!"

I followed him to the front of the store and smiled at the cashier, slowly pushing the cheese puffs toward the register. "Hi."

The clerk rolled his eyes and sighed.

"Is this Tay-Tay?" Barrett asked, looking around for a speaker.

The clerk pointed to the radio by the cash register. "This is The Red Hot Chili Peppers."

"Oh, man. I was way off."

I shook my head with the sobriety of an Olympic judge who just witnessed an epic fall. "Way off."

"Are you guys going to pay for the chips?"

I looked up at Barrett expectantly. "I have no dollars."

"I have dollars," he gasped with excitement, as if just realizing his power.

I clapped for him. "Will you buy me something with your dollars?"

"Yes."

We stood there.

"Guys?" The clerk snapped his fingers. "Hello?"

"Huh?"

"You've been standing there for ten minutes. You either have to buy something or leave."

Next thing I knew, we were leaving the store. "I feel like this was a sound purchase." I tugged my new T-shirt over my dress. It had the cutest little rainbow unicorn on the front and said *I'm fucking fabulous!* "You should give me your wig."

Barrett adjusted the long fuchsia wig on his head. "No way, Jose. I look hot."

We started walking down the empty sidewalk. "But my shirt has a unicorn. Mine matches the wig."

"Nope. It's my wig." He said all of this while eating a hot dog.

I should have got a hotdog. "You either have to give me that wig or give me the rest of your hotdog."

"Why?"

"Because those are the rules."

He stopped walking and sighed. "Fine." He took off the wig and handed it over.

"Your shirt's a Harry Potter shirt anyway. You need more sophisticated accessories, like a scarf or a wand or glasses."

"How do you know it's Harry Potter?"

"It says *Word To Your Muggle.* What did you think that meant?"

"I thought it was coffee humor or something about mugs."

I snorted. "No! We're muggles." A large neon light flashed behind him and I gasped, shoving him aside. "We're here!"

The sign said BEER & 24 HOUR TATS.

"What is this magical place?"

"Dude, your face is covered in cheese puff dust." I tugged open the door. "It's like they knew we were coming."

"Did I get it?" Barrett asked, delicately wiping the corners of his mouth.

I looked back at his orange face. "Sure. Come on!"

The bell over the door rang. Barrett followed me inside and a man appeared from a beaded curtain in the back, next to the long wall of beer freezers.

"Can I help you?" A man with a porn-stache appeared and I smiled at his warm welcome.

"*Helloo!*" I said with a Mrs. Doubtfire accent. "We would like some beers and tats."

Barrett stood by the cash register eating his hot dog without a care in the world. I wasn't sure he remembered where he was or that I was there.

The man pointed to the wall. "Beer's there. Tattoo options are over here."

I grabbed a six-pack out of the fridge. "Barrett, pay for this."

He perked up. "Hmm? Oh." He dug out his wallet and finished the rest of his dog so he could use both hands to pay. "Are you a fireman?"

"Huh?" The man took his money.

"I thought you had to be, like, a fireman or a detective to have a mustache like that."

"Or a pornstar," I mumbled, as I cracked open a beer.

"Yeah! Or that! I thought you looked familiar."

I snorted. "How hard are you looking at the men in your porn, Barrett?"

"What? I like to compare."

The man's mouth formed a flat line that disappeared under his push-broom mustache. "I wasn't in a porn."

"Oh. Well, you look like you could be. That stache definitely makes you qualified to swing an ax."

"Or star in a paper towel commercial," I added.

"Are you guys getting ink, or what?"

I looked at Barrett. "You totally should."

"I don't think I should."

I sipped my beer and handed one to him.

"Why not? The sign says anything on the wall is only forty dollars. That's a steal."

He laughed and took the beer. "True. But what would I get."

I tried to think of everything I knew about Barrett. He liked pretty women, boats, taking off his clothes, tequila, karaoke, and he was a total Swifty. I looked at the beer man. "Can you do Taylor Swift?"

"I can only do what's on that wall."

The three of us went to the wall and stared. I pointed to a portrait of Britney. "This is close."

"On behalf of all swifties everywhere, I'm going to argue that it absolutely is not."

"Oh, come on, Barrett. This would be hilarious. Tell him," I said to porn-stache guy.

He shrugged. "It could be pretty funny."

"I don't know." Barrett bobbed from side to side, his hands buried in his pockets. "Needles are ouchie."

"Come on, you're a big tough guy! You can handle it!"

"I can knock twenty bucks off the price."

"Deal!"

Before we left the tattoo parlor, we grabbed another six-pack of beer. The bottles clanked and clattered with every step. I forgot where we were going, but that didn't matter. Something in my gut told me we were almost there. I'd always had excellent instincts.

"Turn here," Barrett said, leading us down a side street.

"My feet are starting to hurt."

He paused and scanned our surroundings. "How much further?"

"I don't know. I was following you."

We both looked at the unfamiliar buildings. The fact that the sun was coming up confused me. "What day is it?"

Cars were starting to drive on the road. I glanced down at my white satin heels, which were now black and covered in grime. "Aw, man."

"I'm gettin' kinda tired."

"Me too." I yawned. "How much money do you have left?"

"Why?"

"Because we need to figure out how to get home." I was broke and completely at his mercy. "I could sell my blood."

"What are you talking about?"

"Ways to make money. I have blood."

"Where do you think we are, the underbelly of a vampire apocalypse?"

I shrugged. "Where are we?"

"No clue."

Then I saw it.

Angels sang and trumpets blared as the sun crested the buildings and shined down on a lone payphone in the middle of a vacant parking lot.

"Oh my God, oh my God, oh my God!" I raced across the lot toward that stunning relic of technology. "Give me a quarter!"

He ran after me and shook his head. "That's not going to work."

"Ew!" I retracted my hand the second it touched something sticky. I gagged and used the material of my unicorn shirt to lift the receiver. "Ha! Dial tone!"

"Who the hell are you going to call?"

It occurred to me that I didn't know Hale's phone number. "What's your brother's number?"

"I have no idea."

"Your dad's?"

He shook his head.

"Damn it, we have to call someone to get us!"

"What about Elle?"

"Yes!" I nearly cried. "We can call Elle! I need a quarter."

He searched his pockets. "I have cash, credit cards, a condom, and three beer caps."

"A condom? Seriously?"

"What? It's wedding week."

I rolled my eyes. "What about collect?"

"Does that still work?"

I wasn't sure. We were literally in a technology Armageddon and lost without our cell phones. Did phone operators even exist anymore? And, if they did, were they trapped in a tiny closet somewhere with a switchboard and wearing saddle shoes?

"Hey." A car pulled over and a man yelled from the window. "Hey, are you guys okay?"

We were in trouble. I stood very still like a statue so the man wouldn't see me. Barrett did the same.

"Miss?"

Shit. He definitely saw me. "We're fine," I yelled then looked at Barrett and hissed, "Say something."

Barrett stumbled forward when I shoved him. "We're cool."

"Did you need air?"

I smiled nervously at the stranger in the car, speaking quietly at Barrett through my teeth. "What is he talking about?"

Barrett shrugged, then yelled back at the man, "Do *you* need air?"

The man got out of his car, mumbling something about morons as he approached us. I had a feeling we were the morons.

The man took the phone out of my hand and hung it up. "This is an air pump. For a car."

I looked at the pump then I looked around for the payphone, which wasn't there. Something wasn't right. Barrett scratched his head.

"You know," I said, taking in our surroundings and finding nothing familiar. "I think… I think we're high."

"That would make a lot of sense."

The man looked at us and hesitated. "Do you guys have someone you can call?"

"Do you have a phone?"

The man nodded. "Yeah. Hold on."

He went to his car and came back a second later with a phone in hand. I plugged in Elle's number, which was the only number, aside from my mom's, that I knew by heart. It rang several times and went to voice mail.

"Let me try again." I hit redial and then her beautiful, groggy voice picked up. "Elle! Oh, thank God you answered! I'm in a parking lot and I lost my phone and my purse and my Hale."

"Rayne? Slow down. Where are you?"

I looked at the man. "Do you know where we are?"

"Brooklyn."

"We're in—Wow. Really? Brooklyn?" Barrett waved a hand for me to keep talking and I remembered I was on the phone. "Yes, we're in Brooklyn."

"It's six-thirty in the morning, Ray. What the hell are you doing there?"

"I have no idea. But I'm with Barrett and we need someone to bring us a phone so we can get a ride home."

"I have your phone."

"What? How do you have my phone?"

"Hale gave it to me."

I frowned. "Why would he do that?"

"He said you two had a fight and you left it at the restaurant. He went out looking for you and told me to keep it charged in case you called. Are you okay?"

This wasn't good. I should call Hale, and I would, as soon as I learned his phone number. "Elle, I need you to bring me my phone."

"Where are you? I need an address."

I looked around and saw a hotel in the distance. I told her to bring my phone there. When I hung up, I thanked the man who helped us. He wished us luck.

"You know, you could have just asked her to come pick us up. If Elle's coming here to drop off the phone anyway—"

"That would never work."

"Why?"

"Because, Barrett. Trust me. I know things."

"True."

It was back to us versus Brooklyn. Thank god we had beer to stay hydrated.

"Holy crap, I'm tired," I said, after trekking several blocks and not seeming to get any closer to the hotel where Elle was delivering my phone. She was probably already there and waiting. "It didn't seem this far away when we called her."

"Do your blinks have a sound?" Barrett contorted his face, winking obnoxiously.

"I need food."

"You're a bottomless pit."

"I didn't have a hotdog like some people."

"My back hurts." He rubbed a hand over his ass and winced. "I think something bit me."

"I'm pretty sure my toes are bleeding." I had literally walked from Queens to Brooklyn in four inch heels.

"Let's sit for a while."

"Okay."

We sat on the curb in between parked cars, I leaned forward and waited but nothing happened. What were we waiting for? My mind started to wander.

"Do you ever think about math?"

Barrett lounged back on the sidewalk. "You mean, like, adding and subtracting and stuff?"

"Yeah. It's so…poetic. And dependable."

I took a moment to really let my newfound respect for arithmetic process. I was nearly moved to tears until I remembered that math doesn't lie. That got me thinking about numbers which made me think about money, which inevitably reminded me of my dad.

"Do you think Hale will blame me?"

"For what?"

"My dad. He's not my friend anymore."

"My dad's never been my friend."

I gasped in shock. "Remington loves you, Barrett."

"Yeah, okay."

I shoved him. "He does!"

He shook his head. "My dad doesn't love anyone but himself. He thinks of all of us as assets, little extensions of his empire—"

"That's not true!" I pulled on my earlobes, because it made my jaw feel really good. "An artist doesn't have to paint masterpieces to love painting. Your dad might never master parenting, but he still loves you in his own Remington way."

"That's deep."

"I know. I'm like a modern day Socrates." I leaned back to lay by his side. "Not my dad, though. My dad definitely doesn't love me."

Barrett twisted awkwardly and looked down at me. "I love you."

"You do?"

"Yeah. Screw your dad. You've got us for family."

"I'm not going to cry over him anymore. I've made up my mind and I'm done."

"Good." We stared up at the morning sky. "I haven't cried in years. Did you ever see that Budweiser commercial with the cowboy and the dog? That was the last time I cried."

A wheezy laugh crackled from my chest and I couldn't stop. "A beer commercial?"

"That horse and dog loved each other!"

I turned my head, my hair clinging to the pavement. "You're a lot deeper than people realize."

"People think I'm shallow because I'm beautiful."

"Must be tough."

"Like you don't know. You're pretty as hell."

"Yeah right. I'm awkward and clumsy and most days my clothes don't match."

"That doesn't matter. You've got eyes and legs and all the right pieces."

"Ears."

"Exactly." A flock of pigeons cooed from the soffit of the buildings. I hummed, completely relaxed. "It's so peaceful here."

"It really is." He dragged a hand over his forehead. "What is that?"

"What?"

He sat up and touched his head. "Something's in my hair."

I groaned and sat up. "Looks like fluff. Did you have fluff?"

"What the fuck is fluff?"

Remembering that there was a lot of junk food the Davenports had never heard of because they grew up with private chefs, I quickly explained. "Oh, it's gooey marshmallow stuff you put on bread with peanut butter. It's so freaking good." I sniffed the clump of goop in his hair. "But this is bird shit, not fluff."

"Aw, man."

"Don't worry. We'll get it out."

Sometime later we were standing inside of a bank. A woman in a snappy business suit looked up at us from her desk. "I'm afraid you have to leave."

"Can we use your bathroom? He has bird poop in his hair."

The woman glanced at my unicorn shirt and dirty shoes. "No. You have to leave."

I looked up at Barrett, who wasn't handling this well. "What do you mean, no? Don't you have a soul? A *bird* pooped on my hair!" He'd wrapped his tie around his head like Rambo. "What? It's to stem the bleeding."

"You're not bleeding."

The woman cleared her throat. "If you don't leave I'm calling the police."

I huffed. "Fine." Then I snatched the scissors out of her pencil holder and shouted, "Run!"

Back out on the street, about a block away from the bank, I clutched my knees and caught my breath. "I can't believe I just robbed a bank for you."

Barrett skipped after me. "That was fun."

"Where did you get a lollipop?"

"Dunno, but it's root beer. Want some?"

I took a lick. "I love root beer. Bend down so I can fix your hair."

He tipped forward like one of those bird desk ornaments.

"There." I handed him his hair. "Crisis averted."

"*Pheww,* that was close." He looked up and grabbed me by the shirt. "Look."

My gaze lifted as I stared up at the hotel we'd been trying to reach. "Fucking. Bingo."

We jumped and screamed with relief. "We

made it!" It was the achievement of a lifetime and I wished Hale was there to share it.

"We'll take our trophy now!" Barrett yelled, peacocking about like he'd just scored a touchdown.

"Come on." I tugged him toward the hotel doors and he stumbled after me. "Hi." I plastered my upper body to the reception counter. "Did a woman drop off a phone here for Rayne Meyers?"

"No."

My heart sank. "Are you sure?"

"A man did. Big guy. Dark hair."

"What man?" My eyes narrowed. "Did he leave a phone for Rayne Meyers?"

"He left this." The hotel clerk reached under the counter and revealed my clutch from the rehearsal dinner. Relief shot through me as I snatched it to my chest.

"Thank you, thank you, thank you!" Pulling out my phone, I winced at the multiple missed calls from Hale and my euphoria quickly faded. "This is bad."

I scrolled through his texts, which didn't start until the middle of the night. The fact that he hadn't started to worry until after three, showed one of two things. Either the damage to his card was that bad and needed that much attention, or he was that pissed at me for leaving.

I wondered how to respond. After the tenth, *where are you* he started demanding I answer him. That was several hours ago.

"Here." Barrett handed me an uncapped beer.

I couldn't think and my mouth was dryer than a sock, so I drank. "I don't know what to text him." When he started to walk, I rushed after him. "Where are you going?"

"I got a room and a pizza from room service."

"But what about Hale?"

"What about him?"

"He's mad—"

"Hale's always mad when he doesn't have complete control over a situation. Text him that you're safe and tell him you'll call him after we get some sleep."

My brain was working really hard yet I couldn't decide what to do. There were definitely still drugs in my system.

"How do you spell safe? My keyboard doesn't have an F."

"I'm going this way. Are you coming or not?"

I panicked and hit send. "Wait up."

My Life is an Endless Screech

I CAN'T RECALL the day I was born. I have no memories of the labor or my body contorting through my mother's in order to enter a new world. I don't remember the shock or the struggle to breathe.

Was there fear? Probably. Confusion? Absolutely. I imagine there were screams and pain and a great deal of pressure.

I've also never had a baby, so I can't speak on such experiences from a maternal point of view. But I can say, with 99.9 percent certainty, that neither birth nor labor would have been one-fifth as traumatic as what I awoke to that next day.

The first moments were a blur of blinding pain, confusion, bodily dysfunction, more confusion, throbbing pain, and disorientation. And confusion.

Did I mention confusion?

Barrett—not Hale—bolted upright, scaring the shit out of me. Nothing was right. He was in my bed, missing hair, and naked! From there everything spiraled into mayhem.

There was so much screaming.

"What the fuck did you do?" Barrett yelled.

My throbbing head shook. His hair, the tattoo, the weird clothes, the ungodly fucking stench of it all. I had no explanation for any of it. But Hale was on his way and my heart was pounding out of my chest as I panicked and tried to think of a way to explain this.

"I didn't—"

"*Where's my fucking hair, Rayne?*" He ransacked the suite.

"Maybe this is a new look for you—" I shut my mouth when he stormed toward me, detached sad, little man-bun swinging from his fist.

"You. Cut. My. Fucking. Hair."

I held up my hands in a gesture of peace. "Memories are a little sketchy, but I'm pretty sure you were on board with it."

"I'm going to fucking murder you!"

"Barrett—"

We silenced as there was a knock on the door and Hale's voice cut through the chaos, "Rayne?"

My heart plummeted fast and hard enough to leave me woozy with fear. I covered my mouth, wondering if I was about to get sick right there on the carpet. It was too late. This wasn't happening. What was I going to do?

I'd never been so physically unhinged by my reality. "That's Hale. You have to hide."

"No."

"Barrett, please. If he finds you here—"

"Let him."

"I know you want to punish me right now, but in my defense, I don't remember anything from last night. Your brother gets really jealous, and everything's supposed to be perfect for the wedding. Please don't mess this up any more than it already is. If not for me, for Hale."

"Rayne?" Hale knocked again and bile rose in my stomach as a rank sweat broke over my skin.

My chin quivered. "Please. I'll do anything. A permanent favor for the rest of your life."

"Fine." Barrett stormed into the bathroom. "I'll hide in the shower. You have thirty seconds to get out of here."

Hale knocked again as I dressed quickly. "Rayne?"

"One sec! Ah, ah, ah..." My feet were too swollen and battered to squeeze into my ruined shoes.

"Rayne, open the door." Damn his persistence.

"If you find any of my stuff, bring it back to The Plaza. Don't make a sound until we're gone," I hissed, pulling the bathroom door shut.

Panic built like a tsunami as I turned the knob and took a galvanizing breath, then I smiled. "Hale. What took you so long?"

I didn't make it out the door before red flags blew up around me and his grin faltered.

His hand shot out, catching the door before it locked. "Hold on."

"Um, I'm really hungry—"

Not listening to me, he pushed into the hotel room and scowled at the disaster. Bottles littered the floor and a pizza box hung open on the dresser, nothing but a cemetery of half-gnawed crust and bottle caps scattered inside. He bent down to retrieve one very large male shoe. "And this belongs to…?"

My insides locked. "Please don't be mad."

"Why would I be mad, Rayne? I find my fiancée in a hotel room on the other end of New York, a bed that stinks of God knows what, sheets a mess, your hair looking as though you've been fucked hard, and a *dead man's* shoe on the floor."

"It's not what you think."

"No? Then explain it to me."

My head pounded as a sweat broke across my skin. "I… Let's just get out of here and get some coffee. Once I have food in my stomach—"

"Whose shoe is this, Rayne?"

Before I could answer, something clattered to the shower floor. Hale's gunmetal eyes snapped to the bathroom door and he dropped the shoe, his hands balling into fists as he barreled forward.

"Hale wait!"

He shoved open the bathroom door and flung back the shower curtain.

Barrett froze like a deer in the headlights.

I shoved my body between them before any more regrettable mistakes happened, but all of Hale's anger shifted to shock and then hurt. "Barrett?"

"It's not what it looks like, Hale."

His scowl dropped, his disappointment cleaving through me with physical force.

"Hale…" I repeated his name, but his shock cocooned him in emotional armor that reason couldn't penetrate.

"I need to get out of here." He was out of the

room and moving faster than I could manage on my scraped feet.

"Hale, wait! I'll come with you—"

"Not this time, Rayne."

The world and my legs screeched to a stop with an earsplitting whistle and my ears filled with thunder. My heart took the brunt of his rejection, but my entire body absorbed the pain as I staggered back, the wind knocked clean out of my lungs as my heart cracked in two. There seemed a literal split in time and reality and I might have actually died.

"This time, I think distance is best."

"But…" My body swayed from the impact.

He couldn't shut me out. I would fight. Do whatever he wanted. I'd plead. Literally beg. I just needed him to give me the chance to make this right.

"Hale," my voice cracked.

"I need time to cool off. *Alone.*"

Hale… His name was a hollow breath, an ache too great to make a sound, a silent plea overshadowed by the ping of the elevator as he left me there.

Alone.

Unwanted.

Ashamed.

I staggered into the wall, tears welling in my eyes as I covered my mouth to hold back a sob.

"Hey," Barrett appeared at the door, eyes apologetic.

When he reached out to comfort me, I held up a hand. If he touched me I'd shatter and then who would put me together again?

"He left." My shock betrayed my composure as I physically crumbled.

Ignoring my request for space, Barrett caught me. "It's okay," he whispered, pulling me to his chest.

Nothing was okay. I was speechless. Breathless. Abandoned by the man I trusted most in this world to never leave me.

I pushed him too far and he couldn't forgive me. He left me here. He just left. Walked away and turned his back on me.

How had I let things come to this?

Glancing down at my battered feet and filthy clothes, I smudged the tears from my eyes. Gasping for breath, I tried to find the answers I needed so I could fix this. "What happened last night?"

"We drank too much."

I shook my head. This wasn't just alcohol. "The last thing I remember is being in a red car. Was that real?"

He nodded. "The karaoke guy gave us a ride and we got stranded at a house party. Then…" He frowned. "This is where things get fuzzy. I think we accidentally took some drugs and got ditched or lost or… I honestly don't know."

My head throbbed as I tried to piece together the tattered scraps of what used to be my beautiful life. The drugs might have been an accident, but I'd been the one to run off when I didn't want to face the mess my father made. Part of this nightmare was my fault.

We still needed to address the situation with my dad. And then there was the prenup—if that even mattered anymore. What if Hale couldn't forgive this? Would he call off the wedding? Were we over?

The unknown taunted and terrified me. I had no control, no memories, and no fiancé. "I need to go after Hale."

"I think you should give him some time to cool off—"

"No! I don't want to give him time! I want to fix this! He has to know that I would never cheat on him! I love him! He's my world! I can't breathe without him!"

"Hey, hey, hey." Barrett caught my shoulders. "Take a breath. He's not an idiot. He knows you love him and you'd never betray him."

A jagged sob shook my chest as I wiped away more tears. "This hurts."

"It's never fun to disappoint those we love."

"I have to catch him!"

He caught my arm. "Stop." Forcing me to pause, he wrapped me in his strong arms and held me tight. "Listen to me, Rayne. You have to give him time to cool off. Trust that when his anger calms down he'll see things rationally. It's Hale. I know how he is. He loves you. Give him time and he'll come around."

I sniffled against his chest, terrified that the longer I stood there the more I was losing him.

What if he didn't come around? What if he finally realized I was too much of a hot mess for his tidy, perfect world and things would be easier with someone who was less of a calamity?

"I have to go."

This time he didn't stop me.

Hale was long gone by the time I made it outside. My walk of shame brought no answers. The pain in my feet concerned me and I was grateful for how quickly I found a cab. I needed a shower and something for my head so I could get past this awful throbbing and think.

But I wasn't sure anything could fix the ache in my heart or fix me and Hale.

My life was officially in crisis mode. I read over all of Hale's texts on the cab ride back to Manhattan. His worry and panic broke me.

How could I have been so irresponsible and selfish? What was wrong with me that I couldn't talk to him? I should have told him about my father and trusted him to handle it the moment it happened. But I didn't.

All this overthinking about prenuptial agreements and trust had diluted my common sense and awakened my insecurities. My dad didn't help matters either, since he was the root of my abandonment fears.

For months, I scrutinized Hale, constantly wondering if he was keeping secrets or if his trust issues were starting to impact us. When, in reality, I had just as many trust issues and secrets as him.

I hated that my insecurities could sometimes cripple me. I knew better than to let toxic self-doubt in. Usually we helped each other with that. But we couldn't help each other if we shut each other out.

Hale… He was just a private guy who was still learning to share. I, on the other hand, clammed up whenever I got scared.

My trust issues came from a fear of abandonment that my dad had planted in me when I was little girl. Hale's came from a fear of betrayal his father created when he was a grown man. Understanding where our demons came from didn't make them any easier to manage. They were still demons we both battled every day. Some days we beat them and some days they won.

The trick was in giving ourselves grace, accepting that we deserved love on our good days and our bad. We needed to trust each other for our relationship to work, but we were both scared. Paradoxically, the love we shared made us brave. But it was hard to be open and vulnerable when life left us fragile.

It had been wrong to keep something that hurt me so deeply from Hale. I should have trusted him to be patient as I forced the truth out. But, instead, I ran. And this was where my avoidance had landed me.

Once I reached the Plaza, the true abasement began. My excruciating walk through the lobby punctured the last of my confidence like heavy lashings. I had no choice but to accept my penance and keep my head down as strangers stared and whispered while I made my walk of shame.

I kept my gaze on the polished floor. I just needed to get to the elevators, then I needed to get to the penthouse, then I needed to face Hale, and then I could fall apart and cry.

Just get me there so this horrible sense of judgment would end…

"Ma'am, can I help you?"

Head down, I tried to ignore the bedecked bellman as I limped past the front desk.

"Ma'am, is there a guest I can call for you?"

Another staff member appeared, casually blocking my way to the elevators. I clutched my shoes to my chest, holding the ruined soles like a shield. I could only imagine what they thought.

"Ma'am, perhaps you want to step over here so we can help you."

"I—I don't need h—help." I hated how my voice shook but I was holding on to my tattered composure by a thread. "I'm a guest here."

Both hotel employees looked at me suspiciously and then traded glances. "Do you mind telling us what room?"

"I'm in the penthouse."

Both men frowned.

I smelled of things I couldn't name. Terrible, dirty things. The longer they detained me, the more people slowed and stared as they walked through the floral scented atrium.

"Please come this way."

Not wanting to make more of a scene, I followed the men to the reception desk. "I'm with the Davenports," I whispered, sliding my driver's license out of my clutch. "I have a key."

"Wait here, please." He took my license, so I couldn't leave.

I awkwardly waited by the counter as the men whispered.

More people flooded from the elevators, trafficking through the lobby. Terrified one of the many passers-by might be a wedding guest, I hid behind the messy curtain of my hair. The longer I waited the hotter my face singed with a scorching burn.

"I just want to go to my room. I've been

staying here, on and off, for three months. I don't understand why you can't just let me pass."

The man at the counter lifted the phone. "Just a quick call to Mr. Davenport to verify you are who you say you are."

"No. No Mr. Davenport." I gripped the counter, my voice a mere hiss as I aggressively tried to compel him not to make this worse than it already was. "Hang up the phone. Just leave him out—"

"Hello, Mr. Davenport," the man said into the phone, his dispassionate eyes never fully leaving me. "I apologize for disturbing you, but there is a woman here claiming to be your—Yes. Yes, of course. No, sir, we didn't. I—" He gently hung up the phone. "He'll be right down."

My jaw locked. There was no need to involve Hale. I had my key. They just needed to let me go.

As my humiliation multiplied like a wet Mogwai I fought the urge to cry. I closed my eyes, pretending I was invisible, while they detained me and stole the last of my dignity.

The steadfast cadence of Hale's leather-soled footsteps approached the reception desk. I kept my head down and flinched, inwardly cringing at how bad this was when he caught my arm.

"Mr. Davenport," the man at the reception desk greeted. "Thank yo—"

"Let me make this perfectly clear," Hale cut him off, his icy tone leaving no room for argument. "If you ever detain or prevent my wife from entering this hotel again, it will be the last time you see a Davenport here and the absolute last time you work in the state of New York. Do you understand me?"

"Y—yes, sir," both men stammered.

"Apologize to her."

"We're sorry, ma'am."

"Our apologies."

Hale snatched my license off the counter, retaining a firm hold of my arm. "Let's go."

Directing me toward the elevators, steering me by the arm like a parent might hold an unruly child, he kept his gaze forward and made no attempt to speak to me.

The elevator ride took three hundred years. My gaze never left the floor.

The penthouse was silent when we entered. "I imagine you'll want to shower." He tossed the room key onto the polished table.

"Hale…"

He stilled at the end of the foyer, his shoulders bunching with tension as he presented me with his back, refusing to turn.

"I'm sorry—"

"So am I. Go shower, Rayne." With that he walked away.

The amount of dirt that washed off my body was alarming, as were the cuts on my feet. My brain continuously retraced my steps from last night, but there were major gaps in the space-time continuum. The rehearsal dinner was a distant memory and, beyond the ache in my legs and back, an incredible pain in my heart had taken up residence.

Combing back my damp hair, I dressed in a robe and went to the sitting room to find Hale.

The knot in my hollow, sour stomach tightened as he watched me approach. His expression held no warmth and I truly feared this level of damage was unfixable.

I lowered to the edge of the settee, folding my hands and lowering my gaze. "I'm sorr—"

"Did you sleep with him?"

His question stole my breath and I drew back. I reflexively prepared to say no, but my mind went back to this morning. Barrett had been naked and I had been missing some of my clothes, neither of us could remember anything beyond getting in a car with the karaoke guy.

"Hale—"

"Answer the question, Rayne."

Ice formed around my heart. "There's a lot I can't remember, but I have to believe that neither I nor Barrett would ever do that to you."

My vision blurred as I waited for him to say he agreed, that he knew I wouldn't betray him like that. That he trusted me.

"Hale…" His silence gutted me. The lump in my throat moved higher and a tear fell past my lashes. "Don't you trust me?"

"Are you attracted to him?"

"What?" I dashed away another tear. "Hale, he's your brother—"

"I'm perfectly aware of who he is. That doesn't answer my question. Are. You. Attracted to him?"

I sniffled and shook my head. "No."

He exhaled and looked away. "Why did you go after him last night, when I specifically told you not to?"

"I didn't. Not purposefully. I left and ran into him by accident."

"What were you running from?"

Never in my life had I wanted someone to hold me so badly, but I knew he wouldn't touch me until he understood the full situation. There was so much to unpack.

"Last night…" I stalled, not knowing where to start. "Everything was fine until…"

He cleared his throat and frowned. "I was out of line. The thought of anything or anyone taking you from me…" His hand tightened into a fist. "I can't fucking lose you, Rayne. I hate how terrified the mere thought of it makes me, but there you have it."

"I love you, Hale. Only you."

"I know that. But I also know how women see Barrett. He's always been the fun one. The easy-going one. I realize how difficult I can be. I know I'm not easy and I like things a certain way, but…"

It was like reaching into the cage of a starved lion. I moved slowly, desperately needing to touch him. The moment I placed my hand on his back he sighed and his shoulders rounded. He pressed his fist to his lips and his face pinched tight. That was when I realized how hard he was trying not to cry.

"Hale, I'm so sorry. For everything. You're not difficult. To me, you're perfect. I'm the one who messed up."

"Stop." He shook his head, rejecting my words. "Last night, when I couldn't find you, I was certain I'd gone too far. My temper… My jealousy…" His gaze swept back to me and he glared. "But then I find the two of you in a hotel room together and I don't know what to think."

"Hale." I closed the distance and dropped to my knees, laying my head in his lap. "There is nothing between me and Barrett. I swear to you. Please trust that my heart belongs to you and only you."

I'd beg. I'd do whatever needed to happen to erase the last twelve hours. He didn't touch me and his indifference destroyed me.

"You just left me there, Rayne. You didn't say anything. You forgot your purse, your phone. It was our rehearsal dinner. It was supposed to be perfect."

"I'm never going to be able to deliver perfect, Hale."

"Fuck perfect. I just need you. I was worried sick when I realized you were gone. I couldn't reach you. I had no clue where you went or when you were coming back. I thought…" He sucked in a hard breath. "I thought I lost you."

His love and concern broke through all we'd ruined like the light of a new day and I clung to that tiny wisp of hope. "You didn't lose me. You have me. I was scared. I acted terribly. Sometimes, I do things without thinking and—"

"And then to find you all the way in Brooklyn," he said in a cold accusatory tone that stomped out my flicker of hope.

"I'm sorry." I wiped my eyes. "I shouldn't have run away like that. I panicked."

"If you're having second thoughts about getting married tell me now. I deserve to know."

"I'm not, Hale. I want to marry you. It's all

I've wanted through this entire process. Please, believe me. I'll do anything. There's no one else. I swear. What can I do to prove how much I love you?"

He studied me. Still not touching me. Time became an excruciating torture.

My breath caught and I choked on a sob. "Tell me what to do."

He pulled me from the floor so I was once again sitting eye level with him. "I need time."

That wasn't the answer I wanted. My insides locked as I forced back my objections. If I gave him time, would we eventually return to normal again?

"I do trust you, Rayne, but the last twelve hours have been a nightmare. I haven't slept and, by the looks of things, neither have you. I'm calling off the parties tonight. You're going to go upstairs to bed and I'm going to find a doctor. Your feet have cuts all over them and I don't want them to get infected."

"But what about us? What about the wedding?"

He shook his head and stood. "There will be no more surprises, Rayne. The wedding's on. Do you understand? You're going to sleep this off and stay put until I come back."

This cold, unfeeling dictator was not my Hale.

I worried he was only going through with the wedding at this point to save face. Why wouldn't he touch me? Why couldn't we talk this through? I didn't want to sleep. I needed to fix us.

"But—"

"You will do this without arguing with me, Rayne. You owe me that much."

He was right. I was the one who needed his forgiveness and I would do whatever it took to fix us. "Do you hate me?"

He stared at me as if my question were completely ungrounded. "How you could even ask that? I'm doing this *because* I love you. We're going to get married, as expected, and put this entire event behind us."

He moved toward the front door and picked up his leather briefcase. I spotted the familiar envelope of the prenup peeking from the back pocket.

"Hale—"

"Go to bed, Rayne."

But there were still things I needed to explain. We were so far from fixed. I couldn't go on like this. I didn't want to say our vows with all of this ugliness still between us.

I flinched when his phone rang and he glanced at the screen with a sigh. "This is the police. I have to take it. Do as I said. I'll be back in a few hours."

Why were the police calling him? Was it about my dad? Or did he have them scouring all of Manhattan for his missing maniac of a fiancée?

"Hale, wait…"

Ignoring me, he turned and answered the call. "Davenport."

He left without even a goodbye.

Put a Freaking Bell on His Neck

"RAYNE." The distant echo of my name barely penetrated my deep sleep. But then something whacked me on the head. "Rayne, wake up."

I gasped, my brain coming awake with a start as I stared up at Tyler. Rubbing my head, I frowned. "Ty?" I hadn't heard him come in.

"You've got a problem." He dropped several tabloids onto the bed. Each one featuring a shot of Hale.

I sat up and squinted, unsure what I was looking at. "Huh?"

"You need to look at this."

Tucking my socked feet under my knees, I rubbed the sleep from my eyes. "How did you get in here?"

"The butler let me in."

Percy had shown up with a doctor sometime after Hale left. After giving me a tube of ointment for my feet and something for my head, the doctor instructed me to cover my feet with socks and stay off them for a solid day if I hoped to walk down the aisle without limping. Since no one was going to be holding my arm for that long walk, I figured that was sound advice.

"Is Hale back?"

"I haven't seen him."

I had a feeling he was sleeping things off in Elara's suite.

Lifting one of the magazines, I frowned at the glossy cover. "Who's this woman touching Hale?"

"Which one?" Tyler shoved the tabloids closer and sat on the bed. "Ray, are you prepared for this? I'm not sure what happened last night, but I think someone needs to check in with you to make sure you fully understand what it is you're signing onto."

Why were these women touching my fiancé? "What do you mean?"

"Look at the dates, sweetie. Every time this guy has gone out in the last few months the paparazzi has found him. So have all the single women."

I stared at the shot of Hale walking swiftly. Yes, there was a woman at his side, but she wasn't actually holding his arm. It looked more like she was reaching for him. He appeared disinterested.

"This doesn't mean anything. The Davenports have always been followed by the press."

"He's not the only person they're following." He tossed another tabloid onto the bed. "Page nine."

I flipped open the book and my stomach lurched. "No."

"That's you and his brother, right?"

That was definitely me and Barrett. But unlike

the women chasing after a disinterested Hale, I was laughing and plastered all over Barrett. It looked like we were at a bar. It looked bad.

I frowned at my outfit. "This is from weeks ago." Words jumped off the page. *Brother. Fiancée. Scandal. Warning Signs.* "Those vultures!"

Tyler pulled the magazine from my hands. "You know you can tell me anything, Ray. I'm on your side. Always."

My brows pinched. "There's nothing to tell."

"You're sure?"

"Tyler, yes. I'm with Hale. Just Hale. There's absolutely nothing going on between me and his brother."

"Does Barrett feel the same way?"

"Yes! The only reason we started hanging out was because he's been so banged up about Elle."

"Are you sure? I mean, maybe there's more to it and that's why Elle's been so distant."

"No—" I covered my mouth. "Oh, my God. No. No! She doesn't think that. She can't." Then a worse thought occurred. Could Hale? "Oh, my God, everyone probably saw these!"

"Okay, relax. I didn't bring this up to stress you out. I just wanted to see if you needed to talk about this. Obviously, this is just a case of shitty pop culture and toxic media coverage." He blew out a breath. "Who knew you'd one day qualify for celebrity status news?"

I covered my face and groaned, falling forward on the bed. "This is not my life."

"It doesn't mean anything." Tyler rubbed my back. "We all know everything in the media's staged. And these magazines are trash. They thrive on rumors. This is just a gross misrepresentation of the truth.”

“But it’s hurting real people, Ty.” I fisted the glossy pages and shook them violently. “They’re dangerous!” This explained so much. “Hale probably saw this when it was published and that probably planted a seed of doubt. He’s been so weird about me spending any time with Barrett and now I get it.”

“Rayne, are you interested in Barrett romantically?”

“Not even a little bit!”

“Do you love Hale?”

“With all of my heart.”

“And you still want to marry him?”

“Yes!”

“And you’ve told him this?”

“Yes!”

He shoved the magazines on the floor. “Then none of this matters. Your words have to mean more than theirs. If they don’t, you two don’t stand a chance, because this is the world we live in and you’re not marrying into a low-profile family.” He reached for my hand. “You have to stop doubting yourself, Ray.”

My gaze dropped. “It’s hard not to.”

“I know. But that man loves you. Last night, after you disappeared, he lost his mind trying to find you. Nothing else mattered to him other than making sure that you were safe.”

“I fucked up, Tyler.”

“It happens.”

“I don’t know if we can put things back the way they were.”

"Who says you have to? Ray, life is about moving forward. You're getting married tomorrow. It's a whole new chapter. You can't bring everyone with you. Maybe that means it's time to let go of some people and stop crucifying yourself over the past."

I met his stare. "You mean Elle, don't you?"

He smiled sadly. "I never thought you two would grow apart."

"Me neither." I sighed, actual acceptance finally creeping in. "Somehow, no matter how much I tried not to, I just…lost her."

"I think Elle lost herself. Sometimes people we love change and it has nothing to do with us. We can only be grateful for the time we had and treasure the memories we get to take into the next stage."

I sniffled and wiped my nose. "When did you get so wise?"

"You bitches left me. I've had nothing to occupy my time but self-help books for the last six months."

I laughed. "Have they helped?"

"Not really, but I sound smarter." He handed me a tissue. "You have a booger."

I blew my nose and tossed the tissue aside. "If I haven't already told you a million times, I'm really glad you're here."

"Me too. And not just because I love a good wedding."

"That's if Hale still wants to marry me."

He shoved my shoulder. "Of course he does. You're great."

"*This* is not great." I fanned my hands down

my body, encompassing my disheveled appearance. "And I still have to talk to Hale about something that I'm pretty sure is only going to make matters worse."

Tyler frowned. "What is it?"

I drew in a breath and let out a long sigh. "I know who hacked his credit card."

"You do? *Who?*"

This was good practice. If I could say it to Tyler, then maybe I could say it to Hale. "My dear old dad."

He stilled then rasped, "Oh, Rayne."

I wasn't going to cry. "I know." I helplessly tossed my hands in the air as my voice broke despite my effort to keep it together. "I should have expected…"

"Hey, hey, hey… No. It is not your job to anticipate other people's shitty behavior, do you hear me? You are not going to feel guilty for giving people the benefit of the doubt."

"But if it wasn't for me, he never would have gotten close enough—"

"He's your father, Rayne. You waited your whole damn life to meet him. Whatever financial damage he did, that's on him. Even if there was a way to know that might have happened, Hale would have still told you to go through with meeting him."

"No, he wouldn't."

"Yes, Rayne, he would. That man… He *loves* you. He's going to take care of you and be there for you the way a real partner should. He sees it as his duty to keep you physically and emotionally whole. And while this credit card shit isn't what anyone would ask for, it's not like it's something Hale can't handle. He had it straightened out in a matter of minutes last night."

"Really?"

"Yes. I was there. His *only* concern was finding you and making sure you were okay."

"But he doesn't know it was my dad."

"And when you tell him, or when the police do, his only concern is going to be you."

With a soft creak, the bedroom door whispered open and Hale stood in the opening. Startled, I sprang back and wiped my eyes. "Hale."

His brow pinched with tension. He glanced at Tyler. "Can we have a minute?"

Tyler sprung off the bed. "Yup." He quickly gathered up the magazines but several slipped out of his arms and landed on the bed. He looked at me apologetically. "Sorry. I'll just… see myself out."

Hale waited for him to leave and then shut the bedroom door. How much had he heard?

He turned, the manila folder in his hand, and a pen in the other one. "We need to talk."

Let's John Hancock this Pitch

AND CALL IT A DAY

My stomach rebelled as Hale closed the distance. He stopped at the edge of the bed, looking down at the sea of tabloid pictures strewn across the blankets. Tossing the manila folder in front of me, he swept up the magazines and carried them to the bathroom, where he dropped them in the trash.

"Trash goes in the garbage, Rayne. I told you not to read that rubbish."

"Tyler brought them." I scooted back, folding my feet below my knees as he sat down.

He studied me for a long moment then said, "Tell him not to do that anymore."

"Okay." I agreed, no good came from looking at that trash.

He gently rubbed my foot through my sock. "How are your feet?"

That little touch helped me breathe a little easier. Small talk was good. "Better. The stuff the doctor brought helped. So did the aspirin."

"Good." He pushed the manila envelope to the center of the bed and fully faced me. "Rayne, you could have told me about your dad."

I dropped my gaze. "I guess you heard."

His hand moved to my knee. "Why wouldn't you come to me?"

"I was ashamed. He's my dad." Then I realized how that sounded so I looked up and blurted, "I wasn't trying to protect him. I only wanted to protect you. I'm so sorry he did what he did, Hale. It was my fault. I left the card out when I went to the bathroom during one of our lunches. You trusted me and I should have been more responsible. If I had the money to fix the damage, I'd pay it back—"

"Enough. That man is not your responsibility." He lifted my chin, forcing me to meet his stare. "But you're mine. Baby, I can only imagine what this did to you." He took my hand and squeezed. "That's a lot to handle, especially right before a wedding. And I know how much you were looking forward to him walking you down the aisle."

I scoffed. "Not anymore. I never want to see or hear from him again."

Hale sighed. "I wish I would have had the chance to be there for you when you needed someone. All week I sensed something bothering you. You should have told me."

"I was scared."

"Hey, you don't ever have to be scared about coming to me. We're a partnership. We're going to be husband and wife. Forever. Whatever comes, good or bad, rich or poor, sickness or health, we face it together. Understand?"

I nodded. "I'm sorry I worried you."

"I'm sorry I wasn't there for you. I just chalked it up to jitters. I should have known something was up the moment you started avoiding me."

I was done avoiding things. I glanced at the ominous envelope. He followed my gaze and unwound the seal. My heart beat wildly.

"I thought this might cheer you up."

I frowned, a boulder rolling in the pit of my stomach. "Why would that cheer me up?"

"I just want to say one thing about parents before I give it to you." He gripped the envelope. "After I learned how my dad betrayed me and discovered Jasmine was pregnant, nothing was the same. My whole world shifted. We assume parents are these infallible beings, but they're just human. This is their first time living as much as it's ours. Realizing that a day will likely come when I do something to disappoint Elara has helped me work toward forgiving my own father."

"You would never purposely hurt her, Hale."

"No. Never purposefully." He smiled sadly. "And I'm not sure my dad would either. It was one thoughtless action that changed all of our lives forever."

He never talked about that day, so I sat quietly, giving him plenty of space to get out what he wanted to say.

"I'm sure it wasn't easy for you to confront your father, Rayne. When I confronted my dad it was one of the ugliest fights of my life. Then he had a heart attack and took a spill down a flight of stairs and I felt responsible. I realized the worst part about hating him was that I didn't know how to stop loving him." He looked at me with glassy eyes. "No one will blame you for forgiving your father, baby. You have a good heart. Don't let him change that."

I looked away, losing the battle against my own tears. "Maybe one day, but I'm not there yet. I may never be."

"And that's fine too. Just know that Tyler was right. I'd never stand in your way if that was something you needed to do."

"Thank you."

He sighed and looked down at the thick envelope in his hands.

What was he waiting for? "Did you want me to sign that?"

"Very much so."

Ouch. That wasn't necessarily the response I'd expected, but I suppose he was being honest. Time to get this over with. "Give me your pen."

"Before you do, I want you to really think about what it is you're agreeing to, Rayne. There's no going back after this. I'm asking you for forever and this is an ironclad contract."

"I'm sure."

He withdrew the prenup and handed it to me with the pen.

I wasn't going to read it.

Marrying Hale had never been about getting his money. It was about spending the rest of my life with the man I loved. I flipped up the cover page and frowned.

"What is this?" Why was Elara's name added to our prenup?

"It's the adoption papers. Isn't that what you were expecting?"

I looked at him in shock. "What?" My eyes scanned the page until they blurred. "Adoption papers?"

"Yeah. She and I are sort of a package deal. I thought you knew that."

"I'm such an idiot."

"Why?"

"Hale, I thought this was the prenuptial agreement."

"No!" He laughed. "I told you I wasn't going through with that."

"But… What about your trusts?"

"The only trust I need is the trust between you and me."

His words brought so much relief I nearly fell over. "You really want me to adopt peanut?"

"She already thinks of you as her mom. This would just make it official."

He'd truly surprised me. "I really thought I was signing something to protect your assets."

"Rayne, I love you. I know it's never been about my money for you."

"You do?"

"Yeah. I mean, no offense, but you're pretty much the cheapest person I've ever met."

"It's called being thrifty."

"Whatever you call it, I know you aren't marrying me for my fortune."

"Of course, I'm not!" I lunged forward, knocking him back as I kissed him. Smiling against his mouth, I mumbled, "If anything, it's for your dick."

"Brat."

I shoved off of him and eagerly grabbed the papers and the pen. I couldn't sign fast enough. "I can't believe this. I'm going to be a mommy! Elara's going to officially be *my* peanut!"

Navigating the multiple SIGN HERE tabs, I scribbled my consent on every black line and grinned. "Done!"

"Congratulations, Future Mrs. Davenport. It's a girl."

Warmth spread through my body as an incredible sense of rightness blanketed me. I could never pick a nail color or an ice cream flavor or even a lane, but when it came to Hale and Elara it was a no-brainer. I'd pick them every single time.

The Last Mile

THEY SAY the last mile is the longest and the hardest, but for me it was the easiest part of my journey. No Stephen King green tones here. This final mile was coming up pure unicorn dust.

"Ready, Rayne?"

I looked at Quinn and smiled. "Does my dress look okay?"

"You look perfect."

"Then let's do this."

She smiled. "Tyler, you and Mom are up first. Then Noah, Seraphina, and Elara. Then Elle. Places everyone."

Tyler pressed a quick kiss on my cheek. "Remember what I said, Ray. No looking back. Nothing but blue skies and green lights from here on out."

"Tyler, you're up!"

The doors cracked open, only enough for Tyler and my mom to slip out. I caught a quick glimpse of a few guests and my heart cartwheeled. Dabbing the gloss on my lips, I fidgeted with my bouquet as I took a deep breath.

Quinn, peeked out the door and turned. "Seraphina, Noah, you three are next."

I waved and blew raspberries at peanut as she passed in her bedecked vintage carriage. She laughed and waved back.

"Are you nervous?"

I looked at Elle, wondering if she asked out of concern or because that just seemed like an appropriate question for the moment. I could count on one hand the conversations we had this week. In the end, it seemed like a blessing that she hadn't inquired about my dad or asked any follow up questions about the night of the rehearsal dinner.

"Not at all," I told her honestly. "This is exactly where I was always meant to be."

"Elle, you're up," Quinn called, and then I was on my own.

I stepped forward and the wedding planner smiled as Josette fluffed my hair. "Ready to become Mrs. Hale Davenport?"

I nodded and a rush of butterflies took flight in my stomach.

Quinn reached for the door as the first piano note played in the tune of Florence + the Machine's *Never Let Me Go*. My spine tingled as the cymbals punched through the air, carrying over the New York skyline, and the choir hummed.

Just as the female vocalist belted out the chorus about being carried away in the arms of the ocean, the doors opened, bathing us in sunlight, and my breath hitched. The moment I crossed the threshold he was there, waiting at the altar.

And so our journey began.

When I stepped, he stepped.

It was perfect.

It was Hale and me.

I didn't tremble or hesitate. As long as I kept my eyes on him my balance didn't falter. Steady and sure, he remained my anchor through any storm.

When we met in the middle, he smiled into my eyes. "You made it."

"*We* made it," I corrected.

His gaze dropped to my dress. "You're stunning."

I blushed and touched his lapel. "Garage sale?"

"You know it." He pressed his forehead to mine and grinned. "Ready, gorgeous?"

I slipped my arm into his. "Don't let go."

"Never."

The angelic voices of the choir echoed his promise to *never let me go* as we stepped closer toward our future. Sunlight spilled over the guests and greenery, casting the world in pinks and gold. It was, indeed, the most surreal moment of my life.

I'd never forget how my mother looked when she smiled at me. Or how Remington nodded his consent and blinked back the tears clouding his sharp silver eyes. Or how Phina clutched her hands to her heart or how Barrett lovingly gripped his brother's shoulder and winked at me when we reached the altar. Tyler bounced Elara on his hip and whispered in her ear, pointing and drawing her attention to us. She squealed happily and chattered our names.

Everyone I needed to be there was there.

As the minister stepped forward, chills danced over my arms. I wish I could recall what he said, but I couldn't hear anything over the rapid beating of my heart in my ears.

When he told me to repeat something I did. And when he asked for the rings they magically appeared. Everything was so flawlessly orchestrated.

All I needed to do was hold onto Hale and say I do.

And boy, did I.

When the minister proclaimed, "By the power vested in me by the state of New York, I now pronounce you husband and wife!" I threw my arms around my husband and kissed him like there was no tomorrow.

The crowd cheered, their applause spilling over us loud enough to reach the civilians below.

"You're finally mine, Mrs. Davenport."

"Silly man, I've been yours since the first moment you looked at me." I glanced at the diamond band circling my finger. "But this was definitely worth the ring."

Entwining his fingers in mine, Hale lifted our hands overhead and the guests went wild. Elara filled my arms, and the photographer snapped pictures as we each kissed her pudgy cheeks.

Together, as a family, we took our first steps toward the rest of our lives.

The End—

Just kidding! It would be terrible if I ended the story there! Come on, now. How much of a letdown would that be if you came all this way and missed the actual circus? *I mean wedding!*

No one heard that.

Champagne erupted the moment we said our I dos. And then it was off to the reception in a horse-drawn carriage where more guests waited while white-gloved servers saw to their every wish.

My jaw hit the floor the moment we were announced. It was so much more than an inspirational pillow. The space looked nothing like it once had. Every detail from the vision boards had come to life. Ceilings were draped in lace and candles cast every ivory inch of silk in amber and gold.

The centerpieces were the size of yoga balls. Crystal chandeliers dripped from the rafters. While trees—real trees—bloomed overhead. It was an absolute fairytale come to life, and I was the princess.

Hale made a toast about his dreams coming true. My mom blubbered into Tyler's shoulder, leaving smears of makeup in her wake.

Barrett's best man toast was full of old stories that had everyone laughing and cheering for the amazing groom. Elle didn't make a speech, but I didn't need her to. My needs were met.

Music played and we danced right out of our shoes, which was fine because I had pre-arranged with Quinn to have flip-flops handed out as soon as the final dinner courses were cleared. No one cared about my shoes anymore, because everyone's feet now looked the same.

And the cakes! Oh, the cakes! We had five different styles since I never made up my mind which one was best. And then there was one massive five tiered cake to cut when it came time to do the whole first slice ritual thing. I got to shove frosting all over Hale's face, and he got back at me by giving me one of the sloppiest kisses of my life, but it tasted delicious.

"Will Remington Davenport please report to the dance floor?" the DJ announced as we cleaned up from the cake.

I looked over at Seraphina, who smiled and nodded her approval. I didn't want to do anything that might take away from her, but I also wanted to do something that acknowledged how much I loved and appreciated this other man in my life.

Hale smiled and released my hand as I turned to his scowling father.

"What is this, Meyers? I was just about to have my dessert."

"Dessert can wait." I slipped my manicured hand into his cool, wrinkled one just as the first notes of Van Morrison's *Someone Like You* started to play. "I need five minutes."

The lights dimmed and the guests cleared the floor as we took the spotlight. Remington, always a class act under all the gruff intolerance and grouchy grumbles, fell into formation and started to lead. I smiled and rested my cheek on his sturdy shoulder.

"What you said to me the other day…" I thought long and hard about what I needed to say, but it took work to get the words out. "It was more than I ever imagined hearing from a father figure, Remington, because it was genuine."

His hand pressed at the center of my back in a sort of hug as we turned. "Well, I meant it."

"I know. And, Remington…" My throat tightened. "I look at you like a father. And I know you'll always watch out for me and love me, even on my worse days."

A gruff chuckle left his throat. "Have I been around for one of your good days?"

"Shut up." I laughed. "Thank you."

"You don't have to thank me, Meyers."

"I know I don't. But I want to. Without you, I wouldn't be standing here. You changed my entire world. In a way, I think you saved me. But more than that, I think you saved Hale."

He cleared his throat. "I don't know about that."

"I do." I sniffled. "Healing takes time. It's a process. You two will get there. Just give him time."

"If that's true, Rayne, then I'd say you're the one who saved me."

I sucked in a breath. It was one of the few times he called me Rayne, not Meyers. "Oh, hell." I wiped my eyes. "Don't make me cry on my wedding day."

"Don't dish it out if you can't take it."

I drew back and looked into his weathered eyes, a shield of tears blurring the grey. We both laughed, finding emotions incredibly tedious and intrusive. Then my smile mirrored his. "I love you."

"I love you too, kiddo."

The nickname caught me off guard and I stilled, then my smile widened. It was perfect. Remington had earned the right to call me that. He earned my love by showing me kindness and support when I needed it most. So I hugged him.

His arms tightened around me in a hug. I'd chosen this song especially for him, because I'd waited my whole life for someone like him. Someone I could go to for advice, someone I could count on in a crisis. Someone I could count on.

In a husky whisper, he sang the closing line of the song and promised, "The best is yet to come."

Everything was, just as Hale said it would be, perfect.

When I left Remington, I found Hale holding Elara on his hip as he fed her small bites of frosting. I kissed her little sugary lips then hugged my husband.

"Thank you for convincing me to dance with him."

"It went well?"

"It was perfect."

"Good." He kissed my forehead and looked at Elara. "Sometimes fate helps daughters find the father they need, rather than the one they were given."

I wondered if the universe had given Elara to Hale so that Remington would have room for me. "I think you're right."

"I know I am. You make him a better father to all of us, Rayne. We're your family. That's how it was always meant to be."

I hugged them both as we danced slowly in the shadows, a plate of cake between us and love all around. Elara babbled and Hale and I laughed, taking a mental picture of this moment so I never forgot it.

This was where I was meant to be.

He loved me, through all the chaos and wild, unrefined calamities. And I loved him, through all of his anal-retentive, control-freak peccadillos.

He melted for me on the days he caught me in mismatched clothes as much as he melted for me in luxury gowns. And I melted every time he looked at me in that hungry way he was doing right now as he crossed the dance floor.

I bopped about to Icona Pop's *I Love It*, and the sea of guests parted as he closed in on me. As always, the universe seemed to be operating on his schedule. The fast song faded and the DJ slowed the mood down with *Time After Time*.

Hale caught my bedazzled hand and pulled me to his chest. "May I have this dance, Mrs. Davenport?"

"Why, yes, you may. But I should tell you, my friends call me Fickledump."

Sparse memories had started to come back from the night that shall never be repeated. Barrett and I both agreed not to judge or think too hard about the things we did that evening.

Hale had apologized to his brother for questioning his loyalty. In the end, he actually thanked him for watching out for me.

I wasn't sure if "watching out" was the right way to put it when Barrett had been the one eye fucking a lamp, hallucinating Taylor Swift, and rolling around in bird shit most of the night. But I thought it was a nice sentiment, so I let it slide.

We were glad no one, besides us, had been there to witness our behavior at the peak of our dysfunction. Those secrets would stay in the vault, a place where only Barrett and I knew the truth. Oh, and Britney, because she had been there too.

"You're looking very pleased and introspective." Hale dipped me at precisely the right moment, supporting me so I not only didn't fall, but I also looked semi-graceful.

"Of course, I'm feeling introspective. It's Cyndi Lauper. She's as deep as it gets." Everything outside of us and that moment no longer existed. Only me and Hale.

"What are you thinking about?"

"How much I love you." I smiled up at him, cheekily.

He twirled me slowly. "How much?"

"New York's not big enough to hold it."

"No?"

I shook my head. "My love's basically infinite."

"Is that so?"

"It's a big, fat love. The biggest there is, actually."

My love for Hale crossed state lines and oceans. It delved into the deepest parts of the sea and soared far beyond the clouds. I loved this man more than I ever imagined possible.

And he loved me the same. He didn't need me to be smaller, prettier, or quieter. He only needed me to be myself. Because he loved every imperfect part of me.

And that was pretty freaking special.

Gasps broke out as the guests rushed to the windows, staring over the panoramic views. "What's going on?"

"Come on." He took my hand and we cut through the crowd. Fireworks burst over Central Park in a spectacular display.

"Did you do this?"

"I did. Do you like it?"

I smiled, staring through our reflection in the glass. "It's perfect."

"Everything about today has been perfect. I knew it would be." His fingers tightened around mine.

"There's only one thing left, Mr. Davenport."

"What's that, Mrs. Davenport?"

"The honeymoon."

He chuckled and glanced down at me, nothing but promise swirling in the darkening depths of his gunmetal eyes. "You're going to be a sore pup, Mrs. Davenport."

"I'm counting on it, Mr. Davenport."

THE END
Or is it?
Surprise! Book 4 is Available Now!
But first…
Read the Wedding Night Bonus Epilogue HERE!

And find out what Calamity got Hale for a wedding gift.
And don't miss book 4, Calamity Rayne Over The Moon, which is AVAILABLE NOW!

Visit www.LydiaMichaelsBooks.com for more series details!

Calamity Rayne Gets a Life
Calamity Rayne Back Again
Calamity Rayne Gets Hitched
BONUS: Calamity Rayne Veiled & Railed
Calamity Rayne Over the Moon

THE SURRENDER TRILOGY
Falling In
BreakingOut
Coming Home

Ruthless Billionaires
One Billion Secrets
Two Billion Enemies

MASTERMIND
Blind
Untied

NEW CASTLE
First Comes Love
If I Fall
Shattered Vows

ADDICTED TO YOU
Crush

Bang

Throb

THE ORDER OF VAMPIRES

Original Sin

Dark Exodus

Prodigal Son

Immortal Bastard

Primal Kill

STAND ALONES

La Vie en Rose

Simple Man

Sugar

Breaking Perfect

Hurt

Protege

About the Author

To receive Lydia's Newsletter and receive a FREE Book, Visit www.LydiaMichaelsBooks.com or subscribe HERE !

Lydia Michaels is the bestselling and award-winning author of more than forty novels. She writes heart-clenching, unpredictable romance with dark elements and high heat. Her work is character-driven and bursting with broken heroes and badass females. With a sweet spot for overbearing, territorial types, her deeply emotional books are spicy, emotionally satisfying, and guaranteed to leave readers with many book hangovers.

Lydia is the consecutive winner of the *2018 & 2019 Author of the Year Award* from *Happenings Media* and the recipient of the *2014 Best Author Award* from the Courier Times. She has been featured by *USA Today*, *Romantic Times Magazine*, the *Women in Publishing Summit*, and more.

Michaels started her author career in 2007, becoming a recognized presence and advocate within the publishing industry. She is the CEO of LMC Consulting, a certified author coach specializing in character and plot development, and the founder of the *East Coast Author Convention*, the *Be-

hind the Keys Author Retreat, and <u>www.LydiaMichaels-Books.com</u>.

She is happily married to her childhood sweetheart. Her favorite things include cooking Italian cuisine, hosting extravagant dinner parties, sipping espresso martinis, listening to her husband play piano, and escaping to her coastal home on the Jersey Shore. She's an LGBTQ ally, a BLM supporter, a firm believer that the patriarchy must end (women's rights are human rights), and an advocate for pediatric cancer research.

LYDIA

Follow Lydia Michaels on social media!
Facebook | Instagram | TikTok

Thank you for your review!

Reviews help authors so much! If you left a review for this book, I greatly appreciate it!
Thank you,
Lydia

Click **HERE** to return to Amazon.

9 781957 573649